The Chronic Warrior Chronicles

Complete Season One

Episodes 1-5

Angie Thompson

Quiet Waters Press
Lynchburg, Virginia

First published as an online serial and in ebook form 2022-2024
This publication May 2024

Cover design by Angie Thompson
Photo elements by Arte de Catrin, Elen Bushe, and Svetlana Kleine, licensed through DesignBundles.net and jirawat, licensed through DepositPhotos
Sheep logo adapted from original at PublicDomainPictures.net

ISBN: 978-1-951001-38-4 (pbk)
ISBN: 978-1-951001-37-7 (ePub)

Publisher's Cataloging-in-Publication data

Names: Thompson, Angie, author.
Title: The chronic warrior chronicles. Complete season one, episodes 1-5 / by Angie Thompson.
Description: Lynchburg, Virginia : Quiet Waters Press, 2024. | Summary: Four young adults suffering from various chronic conditions seek out an experimental treatment and end up forming an unconventional team of superheroes. Contains five stories: On the Brink, Uncommon Sense, Team Up, Car Alarm, Savior Complex.
Identifiers: ISBN 9781951001384 (softcover) | ISBN 9781951001377 (epub)
Subjects: LCSH: Superheroes—Fiction. | Superheroes with disabilities—Fiction. | Chronic pain—Fiction. | BISAC: YOUNG ADULT FICTION / Superheroes.
Classification: LCC PS3620.H649 C476 2024

TABLE OF CONTENTS

The Chronic Warrior Chronicles

Episode 1

On the Brink

Angie Thompson

Quiet Waters Press
Lynchburg, Virginia

For my fellow chronic illness warriors

God has plans for you beyond what you could ever dream!

Huge thanks to everyone who encouraged and supported me in every part of this venture! I know without your enthusiasm, I would have decided this strange idea should never see the light of day. ;P

TABLE OF CONTENTS

Prologue

Dear Eden,

Yes, I'm awake at this hour and staring at a screen. Yes, I know it means a migraine tomorrow. No, I'm not *trying* to give myself one…exactly. I just can't sleep. And I'm…not really scared. It's more like…maybe excited? Nervous? Okay, yeah. Scared.

It's not because the treatments aren't working. Although yes, that does terrify me somewhere deep in my core. If the most committed doctors in the world with all their crazy-experimental tech can't beat this, then what's left? Watching you turn your back on life to take care of me like Mom did? Like you've done for the last three years? I can't do it, Eden. I know everything you'd tell me if I said that to your face, and I know you mean it, but I can't. You and Josh are so perfect for each other, and you know God wants you both on the mission field. No, I know you didn't mean for me to hear that conversation, but I did.

You can't ignore His call to take care of me instead, Eden. You can't. If nothing else, how long do you think I'd last in a fish's belly? Way less than in some African hut, I can tell you that. And I'm sure—like ninety…six…percent—that God wants me in this treatment program. I don't exactly see why, if nothing's working, but maybe tomorrow…

You should have seen the stack of forms I had to sign today. I'm pretty sure there are encyclopedias with fewer pages. Forget the screen and the late night—if trying to read and decipher that doesn't put me down for the count tomorrow, I don't know what would. Come to think of it, it's probably better you *didn't* see. Really good thing I'm not a minor anymore too. I guess this last idea they have is…on the experimental side of experimental. Yes, I know you're freaking out right now, but—I have to try. I just have to.

I love you, Eden, and I don't know how I can even start to pay you back for everything you've done for me all these years. I know it's not easy being my sister, even though you don't care. I'm praying this…thing…tomorrow—man, I hope it's tomorrow. They can't do it unless I'm actually having an attack, so…no, I'm not *exactly* trying to trigger one, but—you know…I wouldn't complain too much? Anyway, I'm really hoping it's part of God's plan to get us both where He wants us. If not…yeah, I'll cross that bridge when I come to it. I'm praying hard I don't have to.

Of course I'm not sending this. But if anything…happens…well, you can find it then. I'm okay, Edie; you know that. Josh and missions and all the kids you want to have someday—let them be my gift to you. God has a plan for me too, even if none of us has a clue what it is yet. And this treatment figures into it somehow. I can't really see to write anymore, so I guess we'll find out tomorrow.

Love you, big sis,

Brady

CHAPTER ONE

"How long before he comes out of it?"

The words filtered softly—gently—through Brady's returning consciousness.

Eden?

No, not Eden. The accent was wrong for one thing, and besides, Eden was back home in Georgia. And the vinyl-covered mattress and pancake-flat pillow said he was definitely still in Dr. Mattox's lab, tucked away on the basement level of the medical research center, somewhere on the outskirts of downtown Detroit.

"Do you really think it'll work this time?"

Was she talking to him? Pretty silly if she was. How was he supposed to know? That was the doctors' job—except he'd learned years ago that they rarely did, at least when it came to *his* body.

"I always think it'll work."

That was Dr. Mattox herself, with her small rainforest's worth of papers and sixty-dollar medical jargon that could've sparked a headache in even a normal person. Weird how he knew her voice right away when he'd only met her yesterday. Had she answered the earlier question too, and he'd just missed it? And was he imagining the edge of annoyance in her tone as she went on?

"Don't talk as though it's completely untested. You know we've had great success with cell cultures and animal studies."

"I know you told us to have a room ready."

The quiet challenge in the softer voice was slightly unsettling. Who was she? Not one of his regular nurses, he was sure. And what kind of room was she getting ready? A critical care unit? A padded cell? A morgue slab?

Now that was just creepy. Whoever she was, she and the doctor could probably use a lesson in not talking so…candidly…in front of their patient, even if they thought he was still out of it.

"Merely a precaution."

Yeah, the sooner he ended this, the better. Blowing out a fortifying breath, Brady cracked his eyes open. The low light in the room didn't stab knives into his skull the way it had—how long had he been out? Minutes? Hours? Surely not days.

He rolled his head just a fraction of an inch to the side, but before he could fully register the lack of pain, the utter emptiness of the room struck him like a lightning bolt. Nothing in sight but gray walls and blinking equipment. They'd unhooked him from the various tubes and instruments except for the wireless patch monitor he'd worn for weeks—it should probably be a good sign that they knew he'd wake up.

But the voices had been right in his ear just before he opened his eyes. Could they really have moved that quickly? Or had the sedative totally warped his sense of time?

A soft sigh that seemed to come from just above his shoulder sat Brady bolt upright with his heart pounding like a jackhammer. By some miracle, the room didn't spin around him, giving him a second to catch his breath.

"So how desperate is he?"

Man, were these walls that paper thin? They had to be standing just outside, but he could have sworn they were sitting right next to him and talking directly in his ear. Or was it the remnants of the migraine amplifying the sound? But then where were the waves of pain that should have been vibrating through his skull? Living life with earmuffs wasn't the worst idea in the world, but this would definitely take some getting used to. Eden and Josh would need a warning about that for sure—even remembering to close the door to the porch might not save the next conversation they didn't want overheard.

The doctor was talking again. Going over his case history.

Twenty years old. Severe migraines starting at age thirteen. Quickly progressed to chronic.

Brady slid from the bed and took the two quick steps to the door, noting almost as an afterthought the lack of the usual heavy fog and lingering pain that always followed one of his worst attacks. Hopefully he'd be able to fully appreciate the extent of whatever relief this injection had given him once the disorienting sensation of hearing himself discussed by invisible voices was past.

He pulled the door open and leaned into the hall, then had to hold onto the frame to keep from pitching onto his face.

The litany of his history continued unabated in his ears.

Unable to work due to severity. No relief from any treatment so far.

The hallway was completely empty.

No doctors.

No nurses.

Not so much as an off-duty orderly lounging against the walls.

Brady jerked his head toward the ceiling, searching for cameras—speakers—even an open pipe that might funnel the sound.

Lost mother to cancer two years ago.

Down the hall. His steps propelled him away from the door and in the direction of the voices without conscious thought. His vision blurred and narrowed, and he could suddenly see Dr. Mattox standing next to a girl with dark curls, serious eyes the color of melted chocolate, and a pink blouse and long skirt that didn't look like any kind of nurse's uniform.

Sister quit school to look after him. New boyfriend seems to be the main catalyst.

Brady's breathing started to seize as he pushed past a set of double doors and paused at a junction. Left. He broke into a run. What was happening? Something was seriously wrong. No way should he have been able to hear them from this far away. So why had he? Why could he still?

Talk of taking some job overseas.

Another corner, and his vision blurred again and then snapped back to normal. There were the doctor and the girl, standing in front of a desk, just the way he'd seen them. In real time. Through a door and around two corners.

Brady saw the girl's eyes go wide over the doctor's shoulder only an instant before he slammed to a stop and all but fell against the wall. He couldn't catch a full breath, and his heart pounded in his ears. Then suddenly another rhythm joined it—the unmistakable beep of a heart monitor on the floor above. A second monitor. Then a third.

Brady squeezed his eyes shut and clapped his hands to his ears, but the sounds only grew and sharpened. A nurse's tablet dinged with a notification. A desk phone rang. Garbled words came over an intercom. A man coughed. A woman groaned. A little kid cried. Cars rushed past on the street. A low, pounding beat came from someone's truck stereo. A bird sang from somewhere far, far away.

Then the light faded, the sounds muffled into an indistinct roar, and Brady felt himself falling before the world snapped to nothing.

Chapter Two

"Brady?"

Something cold touched his head, clammy and clinging like a wad of wet paper, and Brady flinched away. A gentle hand gripped his shoulder, and the same quiet, sweet voice that he could almost have mistaken for Eden's caught and cradled his fractured attention.

"Brady, it's all right. Just breathe—nice and slowly. That's it. You're going to be okay."

Brady pried his heavy eyes open to find the chocolate brown ones of the lab assistant—or whatever she was—bent over him where he lay on the floor, a few tiny wisps of her dark curls tickling his cheek. He instinctively reached up to brush away the sensation, and the girl sat back, pulling the curls into a loose bunch with one hand as her other fumbled in the pocket of her skirt.

"Sorry. Do you think you can sit up? Take it slowly. Don't try to move too fast."

Brady put a hand on the floor and pushed himself up, shuddering at the grit that dug into his fingers. He quickly brushed it off and turned to survey the floor, but the whitish tiles looked as clean as ever. What on earth was happening to him? Where was the doctor?

A quick glance down the hallway showed no trace of her, but as he turned back toward the assistant, his vision suddenly blurred and narrowed again. The wall in front of him seemed to dissolve, and he could see Dr. Mattox bent over a whole bank of screens and monitors, apparently taking furious notes. The scratch of her pen and clack of her keyboard rang in his ears.

Brady drew a quick, sobbing breath, and suddenly the whole cacophony of sounds rushed over him again. Tapping footsteps. Beeping monitors. Groans. Coughs. The whimpering breaths of a child who'd cried itself quiet. Covering his ears didn't help, but he tried it anyway, burying his head in his knees as a moan escaped him.

"Brady." The soft words were truly right in his ear now. He could feel the girl's breath on his cheek and her hand on his arm. "Breathe. Just breathe. It won't last. I promise it won't. I want to help. Can you tell me what's happening?"

Her voice was like a lifeline, and he clung to it hard. Somehow just the effort of concentrating on it helped to muffle the rest of the cascade that pounded in his ears. But what kind of ridiculous question was that?

"Shouldn't you—be telling—me?" The words gasped out around breaths he still had to force himself to take.

"Oh, believe me, I would if I could." The girl gave a little, choked sound somewhere between a laugh and a groan. "I'm going to tell you everything I know just as soon as I can, but I need to know how to help you right now. Can you tell me what you're feeling? Is it your head?"

"It—no. Yes. I don't even know." Brady caught a deep breath for the first time in what felt like hours and lifted his head just enough to see over his knees. "It's not—not a migraine. Not like any I've—ever had. It doesn't even—really hurt. It's just—too much."

"What is?" She leaned down to meet his eyes, and he forced himself to blink back the moisture that was starting to gather there.

"I can see—through walls. Feel dirt that's—not even there. Hear—everything." Just the words brought the torrent rushing back, and he gripped his head hard.

"Brady. Brady!" Her hands were over top of his, lifting his face to look at her. "Stay with me. Breathe. Try to focus. Concentrate on me and block the rest out. Can you do that?

"Maybe." He barely gritted out the word, but the girl nodded encouragement.

"Do your best. Focus on me. Breathe." She modeled a long, slow breath, then sat back against the wall and continued to talk in the same low voice. "I'm Rachelle, by the way. Rachelle Rivera. It's probably not fair that I know so much more about you than you do about me, but I'm happy to fix that. I'm twenty-two years old, born and raised in Detroit. I'm here for help with Ehlers Danlos syndrome and fibromyalgia, which I've been fighting for half my life now. My only living family is a little sister who I would give anything for. And almost a year and a half ago, I signed on to try Dr. Mattox's newest treatment."

Brady had let the words flow past like the quiet trickle of a creek, allowing them to block out the rest of the clamor that pressed in from every side, but not paying special attention to their meaning. But the last sentence sat him bolt upright, focused on the girl—Rachelle, had she said?—like a laser, as all the other thoughts and sensations melted away.

"You—you've done this? Felt—this?" He gestured helplessly, and Rachelle offered an apologetic shrug.

"Not exactly what you're feeling, no. Dr. Mattox's compound—it's made to target the pieces that don't function right. In her other studies, it works delayed-release and long-term, a lot more like the cure she's trying for. But—I don't know if it's because we're so intractable or because the human body is just so incredibly complex—but in all her human trials so far, the compound seems to go into action all at once, improving whatever's wrong with us to an absurd degree for just a short burst of time before it quits and leaves us right where we were before."

"I have no idea what you just said." Brady crossed an arm over his knees and pillowed his cheek against it, knowing he looked like a tired little kid but too drained to care. If this was going to devolve into medical jargon, he might pass out again just to get away from it.

"This is what I mean." Rachelle held out a hand with one finger bent at an unnatural angle, then quickly slipped it into place again.

She reached over and began gently rubbing his shoulders. "My problem is in my joints, my muscles, and basically all my connective tissue. If I'm not careful, I can dislocate something just by moving the wrong way, and some days I ache so badly that I can't get out of bed. But when I get an injection, I can lift a car without breaking a sweat."

It took a few seconds before the meaning of her words sank in, and then Brady's jaw would have dropped if he'd had the energy to let it. Lift a car? The girl couldn't be taller than five two and looked like she couldn't carry a gallon of milk without stopping for a rest.

"You can't be serious."

Rachelle gave a little snort.

"You're the one who just said he can see through walls, and *I* can't be serious?" She sat in silence for a moment, still rubbing his shoulders, then leaned down to meet his eyes again. "You have any foods you need to avoid?"

She was going to drop something like that on him and then ask about his diet? He should probably fight her on it, but he was too worn out to try, so he surrendered the answer he barely had to think about.

"Just bananas. Don't ask me why. And nothing too spicy—but that's more the scent than anything. Nothing else really helps or hurts, no matter how much they tell me it should."

"Oh, believe me, I've been there." From her sigh, he really thought she had. "Just stay here for a minute. Try to breathe and only focus on one thing at a time, okay? I know Dr. Mattox said you hadn't eaten yet today. I'm going to grab you something from the kitchen, and then we can talk."

CHAPTER THREE

Okay, so maybe the whimpering little kid upstairs hadn't been the best pick for something to focus on. But it was such a hard sound to ignore, especially when it fit so well with the deep-down ache in his soul.

God, I was so sure this was Your plan. Did I totally miss it? What on earth are You doing here?

"Brady?"

Rachelle again. Somehow he'd zoned in on the kid's misery so hard that he'd missed the footsteps right beside him. This was beyond freaky.

Brady rubbed his eyes against his arm the best he could without being obvious as he turned back toward her, hoping that she wouldn't notice whatever traces of tears he'd missed. She held out a cup full of a thick, purplish substance that looked like some kind of milkshake-slushie hybrid had sat down in a bucket of blue--berries.

"What's that supposed to be?" He eyed the concoction warily, but Rachelle only smiled.

"DeAndre's finest. He's our nutritionist and about the best in the world at making what's good for you taste like something you actually want to eat. Drink up."

She held the cup out and waited until he had a firm hold before letting it go, then loosed her curls from the messy knot that she must have thrown them into sometime after he'd first woken up.

Brady lifted the straw to his lips and took a cautious sip, then nearly inhaled the thick liquid as a barrage of flavors flooded his mouth. Rachelle gently rubbed his back as he coughed and choked.

"How—" Brady tried hard to keep tears of frustration from his voice as he finally got his throat clear. "How can I taste every single ingredient in that shake, even though I can't name half of them?"

"Try again." Rachelle offered the cup she'd somehow rescued when he dropped it. "See if you can't back off from all the different flavors a little. Get more of the bigger picture."

"You have any clue how I'm supposed to do that?"

"The same way you're looking at me and not through me right now. The same way you're not drowning out my voice with everything else around us."

And how was he doing that exactly? It wasn't entirely on purpose. Something about her presence just seemed to anchor him in reality, or at least what used to be his reality. Could he somehow bring that same control to whatever bizarre side effect had set fire to his tastebuds?

"Try it, please, Brady." Rachelle was still holding out the cup, her chocolate eyes warm and pleading. "You've had a rough day already, and it's not even half over. This will help, truly."

Brady let out a shaky breath as he surveyed the flavor-saturated slush.

"If I drink it, will you please explain what's happening in words that don't need a medical dictionary?"

"I'll do my best." Rachelle smiled as she handed the drink back and waited for him to take another sip.

Brady closed his eyes and forced himself to concentrate, to make the scattered sensations blend together. After a few tries, they finally melded into a sweet, cold, creamy puree, much more bearable than the exploding kaleidoscope of tastes from his first encounter.

"Better?" Rachelle asked, and Brady grimaced a little as he swallowed the mouthful.

"More normal. Still not the biggest fan of blueberry."

"Mmm, fight DeAndre on that. They're his favorite superfood." Rachelle motioned for him to keep drinking, then settled back against the wall. "Dr. Mattox will have a full draft of an academic paper in a day or two, but here's what I think happened. Your migraines are neurological, right? Some sort of misfiring between your brain and your nerves?"

"Something like that, I guess." The doctors had never been explicit, but Eden had done tons of research online, although it all still got scrambled in his mind.

"So if the compound's acting the same way it has before, then it went to work on those pathways, but instead of stopping at normal, it's gone incredibly aggressive and bumped all your senses up to an extreme level. You said it's your hearing, your taste, your sight, your touch. Probably smell too, if you stopped to think about it."

"Oh, please, I'd rather not." Brady took a long sip of the shake, praying hard that her suggestion wouldn't open that specific floodgate.

"I don't blame you. Concentrate on this, right here, right now. You're doing an amazing job of controlling it."

"Controlling it." Brady blew out a shaky breath and shook his head. "Since when were my senses something I had to control? Or could control at all? If I ever wanted something like that, it was to turn them down, not up."

"I totally understand." Rachelle gave his arm a gentle squeeze. "This wasn't exactly what any of us would have chosen, and it's certainly not what Dr. Mattox meant to happen. She's still convinced she's going to find the key someday. Maybe she will. I don't know."

"And she couldn't slap on a warning label in the meantime?"

"Oh, she did." Rachelle huffed a brittle little laugh. "Somewhere buried in all those releases you had to sign is a warning that the possible side effects include 'superoptimal biophysical capacities.'"

"Super-what?" Brady buried his head in his knees with a groan. "How am I supposed to get anything out of that? Can't she speak plain English? I was prepared for weird side effects, but not—"

The unfinished thought hung in the air between them for a long second before Rachelle finished it quietly.

"Superpowers?"

"Did you have to say that?"

"It's the closest I can get in plain English."

"Eden is so going to kill me." Brady clutched his legs tighter as his body began to tremble, and Rachelle reached over to rub his shoulders for what felt like the tenth time that day.

"Eden is your sister?"

Brady nodded.

"Was it her idea for you to come here?"

"No. She hated it. She'd take me back in a second if I went home, but I can't do that to her."

"Because of her boyfriend?"

"No." Brady shook his head with a groan. "I know the doctor doesn't get it, but it's not Josh. He's a great guy. It's—they're both called to missions, and they know it, but they're stuck on me. I can't be what keeps them back. I can't. Not if I have any other choice."

"Are you a Christian, Brady?" The question was a whisper, but every word rang crystal clear in his head.

"Yes. And I was sure God was leading me here, but—" His words choked off. Let her mock his faith if she had to, but there was no use laying out his own questions as ammunition.

"Maybe He is."

Brady slowly lifted his head to meet Rachelle's eyes and found a spark there that he hadn't seen before. Something like recognition? Reverence? Hope? But before he could fully process it, she nodded to the half-full cup at his side.

"Finish that up. Then I want to show you the den."

CHAPTER FOUR

True to her word, Rachelle waited until he had finished the last swallow of his shake before she stood and offered him a hand. Remembering what she had said about her joints, Brady ignored it and pushed to his feet with the help of the wall. Rachelle gave him a little smile as she motioned him in the opposite direction from the way he'd first come.

"Down this way. The den is our own mostly private space. Dr. Mattox keeps her quarters there, and we can get a nurse if we need one. But we're pretty isolated from the rest of the center, and I think everyone prefers it."

"Who is 'we' and 'everyone'?" Whatever was in the drink had taken the edge off his shakiness, but his brain still hovered on the brink of overload. Every time his focus slipped from her, the world around him threatened to crash in—noises of lab animals, smells of food pellets and bedding, glimpses of cages and charts through walls that shouldn't have been transparent.

"Myself and my sister to start. And a couple of others like us—like you and me, I mean, not Grace. She's perfectly healthy, thank the Lord."

"When you say 'like us,' you mean—"

"I mean roughly the same combination of debilitating chronic conditions, willingness to try a totally untested treatment, and the resulting weird, for lack of a better term, superpowers." She turned down another hallway and paused at a door with a keypad lock, where she entered a four-number combination.

Brady couldn't help noticing that she didn't try to shield it in any way and wasn't sure if that indicated some level of trust or just surrender to the fact that he could have gotten the numbers if he wanted to, no matter how she tried to hide them. Not that he would have done that—at least, not on purpose—but it wasn't like she knew him yet, no matter how much of his background the doctor had given her.

"I'll take you to meet them later, but I'm not going to dump that on you right now. Just keep quiet and come with me."

She led him down a short hall and turned opposite a doorway leading to what looked like a large, open room. The hallway facing it had much more the appearance of a regular hospital corridor, with three doors evenly spaced on each side and an exit at the far end. Rachelle pointed him to the last room on the left and sat down on the end of the bed, motioning for him to join her.

"You don't have to make a choice right now. But this is your room if you want it. I know it's small and a little bare, but you wouldn't have to keep it that way. Bare, I mean—there's not much you could do about the size. There's a connected bathroom, so you'd have total privacy in that regard. Although we take care of each other as much as possible, so we tend to have pretty free access. But if you wanted your room off limits, we'd definitely respect that."

"Rachelle." Brady rubbed his forehead and pinched the bridge of his nose. "Thanks for—all this, but—I still don't understand. So the treatment gives me—us—superpowers, but—you said it doesn't last?"

"Right." Rachelle slipped her shoes off and crossed her feet beneath her. "If you hadn't gotten the treatment—if today was one of your normal migraines—what would tomorrow look like?"

"Just like today." That was much too easy to answer. "Two days is the minimum for a bad one. Sometimes three. I can't stand light, noise, or smells, and I can't keep anything down until it's past. After that, there's a day where I can barely drag myself out of bed, and then I might get a few days of close to normal or regular headaches or lower-level migraines before a bad one hits again."

"Well, if it works for you like it does the rest of us, you can expect that pattern to continue. We usually get one day symptom free—and with our…enhancements—before we snap back to our baseline. The good news is that the treatment, and any exertion from the days we have it, doesn't seem to make us any worse. We basically get to skip a day out of our worst episodes."

"But only with superpowers."

"Yes, that's the catch." Rachelle sighed. "There are ways we—keep ourselves busy—on those days, but it would be totally up to you what you wanted to do with yours."

"Please don't talk in riddles." Brady hated the way the quiver in his voice made him sound like a lost little kid, but he was way beyond the point where he could even pretend to understand her.

"I'm sorry." Rachelle put a hand on his knee, and the regret in her voice said she really was. "I feel like a bad comic book, but I'll try. We can't be—what you'd think of as normal crimefighters. I guess we really can't be 'normal' anything. It's too inconsistent. Too unpredictable. Too short-lived for anyone to depend on. But we—well, I—can't help but think God must have a purpose for it, so—we try to do what good we can when we can."

"So you're telling me I'm—some kind of discount, knockoff, temporary version of a superhero?" Brady closed his eyes and lifted his face to the ceiling in a silent, desperate prayer. He'd been ready for the possibility that things might go horribly wrong, but nothing had prepared him for this.

"That's not what I'm saying, Brady." The pressure of her hand tightened on his knee, and his sharpened senses traced the slight tremor of her fingers and the unnatural slipping of her knuckles. "I'm saying that there's a place for you here if you want it. And maybe work that God can do through you. This is the last available treatment, for all of us, so I can't offer much hope on that score, although maybe they'll have more ideas in a year, or two, or five. Or you can go back to your sister and the life you know. You have that choice. Most of us don't."

She let the silence stretch between them for a long moment before gently tugging his chin down to meet his eyes again.

"Don't try to decide right now. You're exhausted, and for good reason. Try to rest for a while. See if you can't catch a nap. You'll feel a lot better afterward. I'll check in on you in a bit, and you can meet the others then, if you're up to it. Or if you can't rest at all, come find us in the common, just across the hall. But give it a chance first, okay?"

Brady managed a nod, and Rachelle squeezed his shoulder, then slipped off the bed and back into her shoes before leaving the room and closing the door behind her. Brady curled up on the bed and buried his head in the pillow, letting a quiet moan escape him.

God, how can this be Your plan? I don't understand. Please show me what You want from me.

With nothing left to do but wait, Brady closed his eyes and worked to surrender the control he had fought so hard to gain. His heightened senses sharpened, swirled, and faded. And an answer came on the gentle wings of sleep.

CHAPTER FIVE

Brady had no idea how much time had passed before his senses began to stir again. They came in as a trickle at first—the intricate texture of the blanket beneath him, the whisper of footsteps on the floor above, the faint smell of broccoli seeping through the cracks around the door. Then as he stirred and opened his eyes, they crashed over him like a flood—pitiful wails from somewhere upstairs, the musty scent of car exhaust, Rachelle in the hall, unmistakable in her pink blouse and skirt. Brady buried his head in his arms and drew a deep breath, pulling his attention with difficulty back to the four walls of his room.

He had just succeeded in gathering up the last of the scattered threads when the latch clicked softly. Brady raised his head just as Rachelle slipped hers noiselessly through the crack. When she saw him awake, she pushed the door open and knelt next to the bed with a smile.

"Hey, Brady. You got a few good hours of sleep in. A lot more than I was hoping for. How are you feeling?"

"Okay, I think." Brady raised himself a little on one elbow and let out the breath he'd held. "Sorry. I didn't sleep well last night."

"That's completely understandable." Rachelle's smile softened, and she held a hand out. "You missed lunch, but DeAndre put it aside for you. Want to come try it?"

As much as he would have liked to bury himself under the covers and never come out, that wasn't really an option. And it wouldn't be fair to the girl who had gotten him through the worst of his world being turned upside down. He might as well give in to the inevitable.

"Is that the broccoli I smelled?" Brady swung his legs over the side of the bed, and Rachelle moved aside to give him room to get up.

"That's part of it. Is broccoli on the same level as blueberries?"

"Nah, I don't have any gripe with broccoli. Carrots on the other hand..." Brady gave an exaggerated shudder as he stood, and Rachelle chuckled.

"You might have to fight Grace on both counts. Come on, your plate's in the common."

Brady followed her down the hall and through the open doorway leading to the large room he'd only glanced at before. A round, family-style table sat at one end, facing a corner filled with shelves and cube organizers on the shorter side of the door. The rest of the room was lined with long couches, footstools, and recliners and looked like it had been designed for relaxation and nothing else.

The room's only occupant was a young man in a wheelchair, who sat with his eyes closed, apparently listening to something on his tablet. He looked up when they entered, but he didn't say a word while Brady took a seat at the table and Rachelle laid a tempting medley of lightly seasoned broccoli and rice in front of him. Brady was in the middle of a quick, silent blessing when a suddenly cleared throat made him jump, and a raspy voice asked, "So, what's your name, what's your shtick, what's your problem?"

"I—I'm sorry?" Brady opened his eyes to see the guy in the wheelchair now sitting across the table and surveying him with a challenging stare.

"Obviously, but do I get an answer?"

Rachelle sighed as she slipped into the chair next to Brady.

"Dash, be gentle."

"Ehh, that's your job." The guy's face twisted in what might have been a smirk, although it was hard to tell for sure. "And I'm not prying. We'll all find out sooner than later. Saves time and trouble this way. You got a name, or you want one assigned?"

Unfortunately, Brady had absentmindedly taken a bite while listening to the exchange, and when the question turned back on him, he couldn't answer for a few seconds as he tried to swallow.

"Take your time," Rachelle instructed as the young man she'd called Dash scoffed.

"Aww, come on, let's not start this." The rasp deepened into a growl, and he gripped the wheel of his chair and started to turn away before rounding on Brady again with the abrupt command, "Your name, recruit!"

"Brady Ray Owen!" The words snapped out as a reflex, and Brady wanted to kick himself, although he wasn't sure if it was more because he'd let himself be jerked by the collar or because he'd defaulted to his full name for no good reason. The guy's mouth twisted into the same almost-smirk again.

"Do they call you Brady Ray back home in Mississippi?" The hoarse rasp in his voice didn't lessen, but there was no mistaking the fake southern drawl that was clearly meant to mock Brady's own.

"Georgia." Brady gritted his teeth as his face burned—almost literally, thanks to the ridiculous sensitivity of his skin. "And no, they don't, and don't you start."

It might not have been the absolute truth, but there were only two people in the world who had ever called him Brady Ray, and he wasn't going to let those tender memories be tarnished by this brash young man he'd barely met. Unfortunately, the spark that leapt in the guy's eyes said he knew he'd hit a sore spot and probably wouldn't hesitate to take advantage of it. He opened his mouth, but before a word could escape, Rachelle's quiet voice cut in.

"Dash, I wouldn't."

There was nothing special in the three soft words beyond the vague warning in her tone, but Dash swiveled to face her, and their gazes locked for a moment.

"*You* wouldn't." The defiance in his voice shriveled a little at the end, and Rachelle continued to watch him with a partially raised eyebrow until he lifted both hands in surrender. "All right, all right!

Names off limits." He crossed his arms and turned back to Brady with a scowl. "It's Dash. Just Dash, and nothing else, comprende?"

"Okay?" What on earth was he getting himself into? "Is that…short for something?"

"Short for the fact that I can run five blocks faster than you can say it." He huffed as Brady's eyes widened. "On the injection, *obviously*. I'd suggest staying on my good side because if I attempt payback, you'll never see me, let alone touch me. Get it?"

"Sure…" What he was getting more than anything was the feeling that this guy could be very difficult to live with. Rachelle squeezed his elbow gently under the table, but when he looked back at her, she didn't appear especially annoyed. In fact, he could have sworn he saw a little smile playing around her mouth when she answered.

"Don't you think you should find out what Brady can do before you get too much on *his* bad side?"

"If you recall, that was one of the questions I asked." Dash leaned back in his chair, keeping his arms crossed. "Go ahead. Impress me—or try to."

Man, he wasn't even used to having these abilities yet, let alone showing them off. But he'd been on his back foot with the guy ever since he walked into the room. Maybe it was time to quit hiding behind Rachelle's skirts and start sticking up for himself. But what was he supposed to do? Curling up in a ball with his hands over his ears might have been enough to convince Rachelle, but he doubted it would have the same effect on Dash, or whatever his real name was. And how could he prove these weird sensations were more than an easy guess at best or pure imagination at worst?

Brady closed his eyes and drew a long, deep breath, letting the odors of the room, the center, and the world outside swell until they threatened to suffocate him. Then a faint, tart scent closer than the rest caught and held his focus, and Brady felt a tiny grin begin to blossom.

CHAPTER SIX

"Apricots." Brady opened his eyes and glanced around the table.

Dash's brow wrinkled, and Rachelle's eyebrows lifted, waiting. Okay, so maybe that hadn't been the clearest way to make his point.

"It's—yeah, okay. Explaining. Someone—I don't know who—was eating apricots at this table. I can't tell you when. All I know is I can smell it. Something with apricots."

Rachelle and Dash exchanged a questioning look, but then Dash's head started to shake.

"I don't know what you're trying to prove, but you're completely off your rocker. We haven't eaten anything with apricots in I don't know how long. Mangoes or pineapple, maybe, but—"

A wave of doubt that was almost panic threatened to swallow Brady for an instant, but another deep breath steadied him.

"No, it's apricots. I'm positive. Someone's been doing something with them, right—" His hand brushed a sticky spot on the edge of the table, and he leaned just a little closer. "There. See that spot?"

"Where?" Rachelle leaned closer and touched the area carefully with a finger. "This? My word, that's barely tacky! And I don't get any smell from it at all."

"I'm telling you—" Brady started, but Rachelle suddenly cut him off with a gasp.

"Dash! Saturday!"

"Is 'Saturday' supposed to tell me something more than 'apricots'?" Dash growled the words, but Rachelle didn't seem to care as she crossed her arms on the table and leaned toward him.

"Saturday Grace was complaining that she was *so bored* of both strawberry and grape jelly, remember? So I passed it along to DeAndre, and he sent her…"

"Oh, of all the—" Dash closed his eyes and let his head fall.

"Go on. Tell him." Rachelle shot a grin at Brady, but he had the feeling that she wasn't actually talking to him. "A sandwich made with what?"

"Apricot preserves." Dash barely mumbled the words, but Rachelle appeared satisfied.

"Which she hated even more than strawberry or grape, by the way." Her smile flashed brighter for just a second as she turned her attention fully back to Brady. "And you're right, this is the chair she would have sat in. I still don't know how you could smell it from such a tiny spot, and having a plate full of broccoli right here."

"It's, um—a gift, I guess?" Brady gave a self-conscious shrug, and Dash lifted his head and pierced him with a glare.

"So you've got what? The nose capacity to smell four-day-old preserves? What kind of ridiculous power is that, and what good's it supposed to do? Super gas leak sniffing?"

"That's not such a useless job." Rachelle's encouraging smile warmed Brady's heart. "But it's not all he can do either."

To be fair, he still wasn't sure exactly what kind of good these powers were to anybody, least of all him. But he couldn't let Rachelle down—not with that proud, confident look in her eye. Brady turned his attention to the wall and let his vision blur. Wow, it was weird to do this on purpose! And would Dash take his word for having seen Dr. Mattox cross the hall from one of the labs to her command center? It wasn't likely.

He turned his gaze slowly toward the end of the room and froze. Now there was something unusual—and maybe provable. Did the building have any kind of security feed? Well, he'd find out if he was challenged. He'd better take the chance now if he wanted it.

"Okay, so I've never been on this level before, right?"

"Couldn't have been." Rachelle's answer came quickly. "You need a security code."

"And which way did you bring me in here?"

"The east door, straight from the data center."

"Then how do I know that the therapy pool is that way and to the left?" Brady pointed toward where the far wall connected with the ceiling. "Beyond that, how can I see a girl in a bright blue warm-up suit who's just left the stairs and—" Oh, wow, this was better than he'd hoped! "—is going to hit the door at the other end of the hall in five, four, three, two…" He waited while the girl worked the keypad with the same code Rachelle had used. "One."

From the shocked look on Dash's face when he pulled his focus back to the room, it wasn't just his accelerated hearing that had caught the heavy click of the door.

"Well?" Rachelle laughed. "Satisfied?"

"That—is beyond freaky!" Dash rolled back a pace and surveyed him with eyes that seemed to be stuck somewhere between wide and narrowed. "What…exactly are we dealing with? Does Mattox know?"

"Ohh, he's awake!" The girl in blue bounced into the room and plopped herself into the chair next to Dash and across from Brady. "Hi! I'm Harper. I go invisible; how about you?"

Brady's attention was caught by the fact that what he had assumed was a hood was actually the girl's very blue hair, and it took a second for her words to register.

"You—what?"

"He somehow saw you coming from the stairs." The scowl on Dash's face deepened, but Harper giggled.

"I'm kind of hard to miss. Ohh, wait, you mean he saw me from here? Like x-ray vision? That's so cool!"

"Something…like that, I guess." Brady shrugged. "It's like—all my senses are cranked up to twenty. Pretty overwhelming, honestly."

"Pretty creepy is what it is!" Dash slapped the arm of his wheelchair. "You'd better sleep on your right side is all I have to say.

Better yet—" His face paled suddenly, and he shook his head. "No, you know what? Just sleep on your right side."

"What are you talking about?"

"Dash's room is next to yours." Rachelle's soft smile and the pressure of her hand on his arm were a lifeline in this world where everything seemed to be shifting beneath him at a moment's notice, and Brady closed his eyes and let it anchor him for a second before turning back to Dash.

"Look, man, I have no intention of becoming some nasty super-powered peeping Tom, all right? I sure didn't ask for any of this, and I'm not—"

"Hey, we get it." Harper shook her head and scooted her chair a little closer to the table. "I can do the same kind of thing—see stuff I didn't mean to or wasn't supposed to—I just have to go in the room on purpose. You'll figure out how to work it, just like the rest of us."

"You—said you turn invisible?" Brady focused his attention on her again, relieved to be able to shift the question, if only for a little while. "How is that even possible?"

"How is any of this possible, really?" Harper shrugged philosophically. "I have a skin condition, secondary to a blood disorder. Polycythemia and erythromelalgia, if you want to look it up. Basically, too many red blood cells, which causes extreme redness and burning, especially in my face, hands, and feet. The injections clear up the redness—and all the other colors with it. Just wait till you see me—or don't." She giggled again. "On my invisible days, I go by Shadow. We'll have to figure out a name for you too. Super senses…hmm…"

"So what kind of weird disorder would make the injections kick your senses up like that? What are you on normal days, some kind of vegetable?"

"Dash."

It was the first time Brady had heard sharpness in Rachelle's tone, but he couldn't let her fight this battle for him. This was his cross to carry—had been since he was thirteen—and the sooner he got it out in the open, the faster he'd know where he stood in this group of misfits, or if he had a place with them at all.

CHAPTER SEVEN

"Migraines." Brady crossed his arms and leaned forward on the table. Rachelle touched his arm, but at the slight shake of his head, she sat back again, and he locked eyes with Dash. "And when I say migraine, I don't mean an irritating headache. I mean a crippling neurological condition that puts me flat on my back for days at a time at a moment's notice. I mean feeling incredibly blessed if I can get through a whole week functioning at a semi-normal level. I mean trying every medication and alternative therapy and coping strategy on the market and having random people on the street still think they know what I'm feeling and how to fix it."

No, that wasn't right. It was all true, but that last part especially had been too harsh—too bitter. He'd worked so hard to forgive the people who didn't get it—years ago in a group and as individuals every new time it happened. It was baggage he shouldn't have been carrying at all, let alone airing to a group of near-strangers. Brady dropped his head into his hands.

"I'm sorry, I—"

"Don't!" The word came harsh and fierce in Dash's rasping voice, but the next one almost quivered. "Don't. You think we haven't been through it? Well, we have. You threw me for a loop is all—and for the record, I still think your power is extremely creepy. But you don't jump into a treatment like Mattox's for nothing, so I'll make you a deal. You don't tell me I'm too young for Parkinson's, or that I'd get better if I just put my mind to it, or that every time I drop, spill, or trip on something, I'm acting out for attention, and I won't pretend you're a wimp who can't handle a lousy headache. Take it or leave it."

Brady raised his head and met Dash's eyes for only an instant before the young man jerked his wheelchair around and left the room without another word. Rachelle shifted in her chair like she wasn't sure whether to follow him, and Brady laid a hand on her arm.

"It's okay. We're good."

Rachelle sat back with a little breath of relief, and Harper leaned her head on one fist as she looked up at him.

"Don't let Dash bug you. He's a serious grump, but he's really pretty fun when you get to know him."

Brady opened his mouth, then shut it again. He might have doubts that both could be equally true, but there was no use stirring up the water when it was finally starting to settle.

"Did I forget your name already or just forget to ask?" Harper yawned, and Brady chuckled.

"I guess I forgot to give it. It's Brady. Brady Owen."

"That…is an extremely cool name." Harper sighed. "And…I can't wait to find out more, but…" She yawned again and pushed slowly to her feet. "Guess it's my turn for a nap." She flopped onto the nearest couch and stretched out with one arm under her head. "Sorry. Don't go away, huh? I still…want to…talk…" Her voice trailed off, and her eyes closed.

"She okay?" Brady whispered, glancing over at Rachelle, who smiled softly.

"As okay as she can be. The fatigue is her baseline, especially after exercise. Mostly because of her blood issues. Although—" She waved a hand around at the other couches. "She's not the only one who needs to lie down randomly. Just the one who falls asleep fastest."

"I feel that." Brady glanced down at the food lying forgotten on the table, and Rachelle shook her head.

"You want me to warm that up for you?"

"Nah, I'm good." He scooped up a bite, and Rachelle grimaced.

"Brady…"

"Seriously, it's fine." Brady mumbled the words around a mouthful of rice and broccoli, feeling just the tiniest pang at the thought of how Eden would have scolded.

"Cold rice?" Rachelle stuck her hands on her hips, and Brady couldn't help a grin.

"More like—slightly lukewarm."

"Give me that." Rachelle scooped the plate up and took it to a microwave, then leaned her shoulder against the shelf as she waited for it to heat. "Thanks for not killing Dash. I know he didn't make it easy."

"Not really the violent type." Brady shrugged, and Rachelle ducked her head.

"No, I know. I didn't mean it that way."

"Yeah, I know." Brady waited for her to look up again and offered a small smile. "He's been hurt pretty bad, huh?"

"Very." Rachelle swallowed hard. "I'd like to tell you, but—"

"No, it's private. I understand. Let him decide what he wants me to know. Besides, I have to agree with him. I'd be creeped out by someone like me too."

"You'll find your way, Brady." Rachelle removed his plate from the microwave and brought it back to the table. "And your purpose. God brought you here for some reason. I know it's not easy to see, but He'll show you when He's ready."

"Are you a Christian, Rachelle?" He thought he could guess the answer, but somehow he needed to know for sure.

"Yes." She gave him the same smile she had when he'd answered the question for himself—the one that he now recognized as an acknowledgement of kinship—and motioned toward his plate.

"Are they?" Brady obediently picked up his fork, and Rachelle waited until he'd taken a bite before she answered.

"Harper isn't. You wouldn't guess it from watching her, but she's taken a lot of hard knocks in her life. Dash…I don't know. He grew up in the church, but…he's been hurt."

"I get that." Brady scooped up another forkful of broccoli but paused before it reached his mouth. "Is it just the three of you, or are there more I'm supposed to meet?"

"No, it's just us. And Grace. Speaking of which—" She twisted in her chair to glance at the clock, then jumped to her feet, but in the next instant, she fell back into her seat with a pained cry.

"Rachelle?" Brady shot out of his chair and hovered over her helplessly, trying to fight the sudden panic that engulfed him.

"It's okay." The strain in the terse words told him it definitely wasn't. "Just—dislocated my kneecap."

"That—sounds painful."

"It is." Rachelle attempted a laugh. "But it happens."

"What can I do?"

She let out a long breath between pursed lips—a move Brady knew all too well—then turned an apologetic gaze on him.

"Can you—help me to the recliner?"

"Just show me how." Brady slipped an arm around her back and held her upright as well as he could as she limped to the chair. He bit his lip as Rachelle raised her footrest and sank back into the cushions with her eyes closed. "What can I get you?"

"A couple pillows? And the pill box from my nightstand—first room on the left."

Brady quickly obeyed and waited while Rachelle took the pain medicine and settled her leg carefully on the pillows. She threw another glance at the clock and winced.

"I hate to ask this, but with Harper asleep—"

"Name it."

"Would you knock on Dash's door—the one between us—and see if he can meet Grace? I wanted to introduce you to Shavonne—her carpool—but that can wait."

"You relax. We'll take care of it." Brady gave her hand a gentle squeeze, then squared his shoulders and walked back down the hall, hesitating only an instant before giving a light tap to the second door on the left. After a few seconds of silence, the latch clicked open, and Dash fixed him with a glare that held less hostility than it might have.

"You want something?"

"Rachelle wants to know if you can meet Grace for her."

"She all right?" Dash's face barely changed, but there was no mistaking the protective spark that leapt into his eyes.

"Dislocated her kneecap. She's resting it, but Harper's asleep, so..."

"Yeah. Tell her I've got it. You know what, no. She knows that. If you're joining this freak show, you might as well make yourself useful. Come on, and I'll introduce you to the carpool."

CHAPTER EIGHT

Brady worked hard to keep his senses functioning at a semi-normal level as he followed Dash down a corridor, up an elevator, and into the main lobby of the medical center. The sounds and smells that had pressed in on him so hard in the isolated lab took on even more strength here, particularly the child's cries, which were currently alternating between pitiful moans and outright shrieks.

Father God, let them find some way to help him, please.

The brightness of the sun caught Brady off guard when he stepped out the door onto the small circular drive, and he had to shield his eyes for a moment before he could see again. Had he seriously forgotten to grab his sunglasses before stepping outside? Where were they, anyway? Probably still in his old room—but was he really calling it that now? Had he accepted the place that this group was offering him, or had he just let himself be carried along without thought? What was he supposed to do here, and more importantly, how was he supposed to find out?

When the worst of the glare faded, he hurried over to join Dash, who sat watching impatiently from beside a nondescript blue minivan. Brady's adjusting vision immediately cut through it to reveal half a dozen kids of varying ages, sizes, and skin tones—all apparently stuck on maximum volume, which he was pretty sure wasn't an effect of his enhanced hearing. He blinked the door back into focus and offered an apologetic smile to the dark-skinned woman in the driver's seat.

"Sorry. Brady Owen. Nice to meet you."

"Got it. I'll try to remember." The woman threw a half-curious, half-distracted glance at him before jerking her eyes up to the rearview mirror. "Y'all quiet down! Rowan, help Grace find her shoe! Matt, please give Lonnie the elephant. Alonzo, no hitting!" She turned back to the window with a sigh. "I'm sorry. Shavonne Jackson. Been a crazy day."

"Same here." She had *no* idea. "Sounds like you've got your hands full. Anything I can help with?"

"No, we're good. Watch the door."

As she spoke, the side door popped open, and a little girl of five or six in navy plaid with hair just a shade lighter and a touch curlier than Rachelle's hopped out—purple lunch box nearly falling out of an unzipped yellow backpack, one scuffed black tennis shoe on her foot and the other in her hand, and some kind of berry lip gloss smeared from much too high on her lips to halfway across her cheek.

Dash barked a laugh, and Shavonne gave a little sigh as the girl came to an abrupt stop in front of Brady.

"She's here in one piece. Give me extra stretch arms and we'll talk about more. Tonya, close the door and buckle up. Two more stops before tee ball, and we're late already."

Brady briefly considered offering to help again, but with Grace still standing in front of him, staring up at his five ten height like it was the Eiffel Tower, the move would have been awkward at best. Tonya—or someone—must have gotten it done without him because the door slammed shut and the minivan lurched away, leaving the three of them alone on the pavement.

"Hi." Brady bent down to put himself closer to the little girl's level, and she backed up a step and tried to lift her thumb to her mouth, only to be thwarted by the shoe she still held. She dropped it on the ground and wriggled her foot into it, jamming her thumb into her cheek so hard that Brady winced.

"Monster, if your looks today don't send him packing, I don't know what will." Dash rolled his chair up next to Brady, and Grace cut her eyes in his direction but didn't move the thumb from her mouth.

"Where's Ellie?"

"In the den. Tweaked her knee is all. She's fine."

"Ohhh." Grace's stiff little body wilted in relief. She took a shuffling step forward and all but collapsed against Dash's leg.

"Hey." He raised a hand to awkwardly pat her shoulder. "What's the problem? I've picked you up plenty of times. There's no need to be scared."

"Who's that?" Grace cut her eyes back to Brady, but before he could figure out how to explain, Dash was speaking.

"Who do you think?"

Grace studied him for a few seconds, then suddenly her face lit up.

"Ohhh! Do you got—" She stopped and glanced around as if to protect a carefully guarded secret, then whispered, "Superpowers?"

Well, that was direct enough, and at least she hadn't asked what he planned to do about it. Brady nodded, and Grace clapped her hands and bounced on her toes, her thumb forgotten in her excitement.

"Can you tell me a story?"

"Um…" Brady glanced helplessly at Dash, who offered a slight change of expression probably meant for an eye roll.

"She's a sucker for superhero stories. Go figure. He hasn't actually done anything with it yet, munchkin. Besides"—he lowered his voice to a rasping whisper—"we can't talk about it here, remember?"

Grace clapped both hands over her mouth, spun around, and took two running steps toward the door before tripping on her untied shoelace and pitching forward onto her hands and knees.

"Grace…" Dash nearly growled the word, but before he could say anything else, Brady was next to her, ignoring the mess spilling from her backpack as he scooped her up in his arms.

"Hey, shh. It's all right." With an instinct born of some long ago memory, he laid her head against his shoulder and gently patted her back, and the little girl melted into his neck, her sobs quieting as her arms tightened around him. "That's it, Gracie-girl. Shhh. You're okay." He gave her a few seconds before trying to move, but his first attempt to shift her for a better look at the damage brought renewed moans and a grip so tight it could almost have torn his shirt. "Grace, shhh. You're all right. I just want to see your knees, okay?"

"Don't put me down," Grace whimpered, and Brady threw a helpless glance at Dash, who lifted his hands with the same almost-smirk he'd worn before.

"Don't look at me. You're the kid whisperer, apparently."

"Thanks a lot." Brady sighed and turned back to the clinging bundle in his arms. "What if I let you sit on my knee while I pick up your papers and look at your scrapes? Then I'll carry you till we get back to the—what do you call it?"

"The den?" The words came in a whisper, but her desperate hold relaxed a little, and Brady smiled.

"Right. I'll carry you back to the den. I promise." He waited a second before trying again to move her, and this time she let her arms be pried away and only scooted closer to his chest when he crouched down to perch her on his knee. Brady let out a breath of relief as he examined her scrapes and found only a few faint lines of blood beginning to bubble. "That's not bad. A couple bandaids'll fix you right up. Oh, and I'm Brady. I think I forgot to tell you that. But since I already know who you are, tell me about the den. Who named it that? Do you know?"

"Ellie." Grace leaned her head against his chest as he started gathering up the papers, crayons, and other school supplies scattered across the ground.

Dash snorted.

"Who'd you think? 'Lair' and 'base' weren't *homelike* enough, apparently."

"Hard to disagree with that."

"Yeah, you wouldn't." Dash huffed, and Brady glanced over at him but decided whatever he meant wasn't worth fighting over.

"So how long have you all been here?" He nudged Grace enough to slip her backpack from her shoulders and began refilling it, trying not to make it more of a mess than it already was.

"Rachelle and Grace, coming up on a year and a half. Me, just over a year. Harper, almost seven months."

"Doesn't that give Rachelle some kind of founder's rights, then, at least as far as what you call the place?"

"Oh, dry up," Dash muttered, and Brady hid a grin as he zipped up the backpack and slid it over his own shoulder.

"All right, Gracie-girl, let's go." He slipped his arm around her and lifted her onto his hip, and Grace wrapped her arms around his neck and rested her head against his shoulder as they followed Dash back toward the medical center.

Chapter Nine

"Grace! What happened?" Rachelle sat up straight and scooted forward in her chair, but before Brady could open his mouth, Dash's growl was ahead of him.

"Don't even think about it, Midge." He parked his chair next to her recliner, effectively caging her in place, and Rachelle fell back with a sigh.

"Relax. She's okay. Just scraped up her knees a little." Brady patted Grace's back as her hold tightened. "Where do you want her?"

"Here, please." Rachelle scooted to the side of her chair and held out her arms, and Dash gave her a last warning look before moving aside so that Brady could set the little girl next to her. "Come here, baby."

Brady gently pulled Grace's arms away from his neck and waited until she cuddled into her sister's side with her thumb in her mouth before he touched Rachelle's arm.

"Got a first aid kit?"

"Third shelf down, on the right." Rachelle gave him a grateful glance as she pointed to one of the bookcases, wrapping her other arm around Grace's shoulders. "What happened?"

"I wasn't being careful." Grace's voice was a murmur, but it still carried clearly to Brady's ears as he dug through the indicated box for bandaids, antibiotic ointment, and antiseptic wipes.

"I'm afraid I wasn't either," Rachelle whispered, and Brady turned around in time to see Grace frowning up at her for all the world like a disapproving older sister. "I know." Rachelle gave a little sigh. "Do our penalties cancel, or do we both get one?"

Grace paused and seemed to think for a moment before she replied.

"Both get one."

"Okay." Rachelle smiled down at her, then over at Brady as he knelt by her side and tore open a wipe. "What's my penalty?"

"Hold on, Gracie-girl. This'll sting for just a minute." Brady tried to ignore the burning of the alcohol against his overly sensitive fingers as Grace stiffened and buried her head in Rachelle's shoulder. He cleaned her scrapes as quickly as he could but couldn't keep back a hiss as he finally dropped the wipe and shook his hand out.

"Brady…" Rachelle started, but he shook his head and nodded at Grace as he smeared the antibiotic ointment on her knees and covered it with the bandaids.

"There you go. Good as new." He patted her leg, and Grace shifted one eye out of Rachelle's pink blouse to peer cautiously at the result.

"What do you say?" Rachelle squeezed her shoulder, and Grace snuggled in next to her as she turned to face Brady.

"Thank you," she whispered, and Brady offered her a smile.

"Welcome, Grace. So, why do you have to give Rachelle a penalty?"

"'Cause we have to remember to be careful, or somebody gets hurt." Grace lifted her gaze to Rachelle, who gave a little rueful laugh.

"Case in point." She motioned from Grace's knees to her own, then settled back against the chair again, lightly stroking her sister's hair. "What's my penalty today, baby?"

Grace rested her chin in her hand as though thinking hard for a moment before she answered.

"Two bedtime stories."

"Okay. But short ones. You still have school tomorrow."

"Okay." Grace sighed, and Rachelle ruffled her hair a little.

"And for you…no tablet until your homework's done."

Grace stuck her lip out in a pout but nodded slowly.

"Speaking of which, where's your backpack? We might as well work on it while we're both sitting here."

"I'll get it." Brady gathered up the remnants of the first-aid project and deposited them in the trash before grabbing up Grace's backpack from where he'd dropped it next to the bookcase and setting it gently on her lap, still rubbing the last of the alcohol sting off on his jeans.

"Wash your hand," Rachelle whispered as Grace unzipped the backpack, and Brady chuckled.

"Okay, *Mom*." The teasing name slipped out just like it would have with Eden, and he froze for a half-second before Rachelle's answering smile and Dash's cheeky "there it is!" snapped him back to normal. Man, it was weird how comfortable he had started to feel with them in such a short time. Did that mean something, or was it just a distraction?

He went to the sink and washed his hands, unable to contain a breath of relief as the cool water soothed away the remaining burn. Then he turned back to the table and picked up the mostly full plate still lying there with a rueful grin.

"Mind if I just throw this away before something else happens?"

Rachelle gave a little sigh.

"I guess we're coming up on dinner anyway. Sorry you never got to finish."

"More than I would have eaten today. I'll live." Brady tossed the cold rice and broccoli and glanced around the room, a bit lost for what came next, when Grace's whispered words again caught his ear.

"Can Brady get my desk?"

"Why don't you ask him, baby?" Rachelle whispered back, and Grace turned suddenly shy brown eyes up to him.

Brady barely caught himself before nodding in answer to the question she hadn't actually asked yet. Yeah, he should probably tell the little girl about his hearing at some point, at least if he planned on staying at all.

"Can you get my desk?" The whisper was barely louder than the one he hadn't been meant to hear, but at least it was directed at him this time, and he followed Rachelle's nod to the little colorful lap desk in the corner and waited for her to lift the jumble of worksheets and coloring pages before setting it carefully over Grace's legs.

"What—" Rachelle started, but before she could finish the question, Grace had wrapped her arms around Brady's neck and was hugging him hard.

"I love you, Brady," she murmured, but before he could process the declaration, let alone figure out how to answer her, she let go and sank back next to Rachelle, looking up at him with hopeful eyes. "Can you carry me to carpool tomorrow?"

The words stole his breath like an ice-cold shower. Of course she didn't understand how rare this was—how little he had to offer on his best days, let alone his worst. How could he have let her even start to get attached like that, when he was only going to let her down too many times to count?

"Oh, Grace, baby." Rachelle's voice caught a little. Was she realizing the same thing? Questioning her willingness to add one more member to their circle who could only bring more disappointment and pain? "Brady's going to be very sick tomorrow." She raised her head to meet Brady's gaze, but instead of the remorse or regret he'd expected, her chocolate brown eyes shone warm with compassion. "We'll have to be very, very quiet, so we don't make his head hurt worse, okay?"

"Oh." Grace dropped her eyes, and Brady's heart tore in two. He couldn't promise her tomorrow, or even the day after, but he certainly couldn't leave things like this.

"Can I give you a rain check, Grace?"

"What's a rain check?" Curiosity started to chase away the disappointment on her face, and Brady felt a hint of a smile struggling to break through.

"It's like—a promise that maybe I can't do something now, but I'll do it later." Even if he didn't stay, surely he could offer her that much. The puzzled frown didn't leave her face, and Brady shook his head. "You know what? Work on your homework, and I'll show you in a minute."

Ignoring Rachelle's quizzical look, he returned to the cubby nearest where Grace's desk had been and confirmed that the bin with paper poking out of the top contained a child's art supplies. Taking it back to the table, he pulled out a clean piece of scrap paper and a mostly full set of crayons and set to work at the vague idea his imagination had pictured.

Chapter Ten

Brady wasn't sure how long he'd been at work when Harper shuffled over to the table and slid into the chair next to him. When had she woken up? Not that it actually mattered. She rested her chin on her fists and leaned over so she could see his face.

"Okay, I *have* to know what you're working on." Her blue eyes blinked at him with a combination of curiosity and sleepiness, and she offered a playful, coaxing smile.

Brady hesitated, then moved his arm so she could see the drawing, and Harper gave a little gasp and clapped her hands to her heart.

"Oh, it's *so* cute! I love it so much! Dash, come look at this! Isn't it adorable?"

Brady tried not to wince as Dash came up on his other side and inspected the drawing, then shot a look across at Harper.

"Seriously, isn't it?" She gave him a puppy dog face, and Dash offered a slight eye roll.

"If by adorable you mean *serious* overkill, then sure. It's absolutely *that*."

"You know what?" Brady squared his shoulders as he picked up the crayon and made a few last strokes, then scooted his chair back from the table. "My rain check, my design."

Without waiting for their reaction, he took the one quick step to Rachelle's recliner and dropped on his knee to offer the paper to Grace, who tipped her head curiously at it, then up at her sister.

"What's it say?" she whispered, and Rachelle covered her mouth with trembling fingers for a second before she answered.

"It says 'Rain Check. To: Grace. From: Brady. For: One day of carrying you up to carpool, as soon as I'm feeling better.'" Her voice caught on the last words, and Brady looked up, suddenly afraid that in his attempt to make things right he'd somehow gone too far. Rachelle's eyes were full of tears, but the corners of her lips fluttered upward, and she mouthed "thank you" before resting her head against her sister's curls.

"Oh!" Grace lifted her gaze from the picture suddenly, her whole face alight. "It's like rainy days and we can't go to the park, but we can go later when it's sunny! Except the rain"—she pointed to the crying raincloud filling the top left corner—"is sad when you're sick, and the sun"—waving at the smiling sun opposite—"is happy when you're better!"

"You're right, Gracie-girl; it's exactly like that." Brady had to swallow hard against a lump in his throat. "So as soon as the rain in my head stops, I'll carry you up one day. Okay?"

"Does it rain in your head for real?" Grace's eyes flew wide, and Brady choked on a laugh as Rachelle gave a little watery chuckle. Harper didn't even try to hide her giggle, and Dash huffed.

"Walked yourself right into that one. She's *nothing* if not literal."

"No, it doesn't." Brady sat back but kept his focus on Grace. "Although that probably wouldn't be the weirdest thing you've seen around here, would it? My head just hurts really, really bad, and that's what makes me sick. Kind of feels like a thunderstorm in there sometimes."

As if on cue, a deafening clatter shook the room, sounding like a whole mess of marbles, silverware, and broken glass had been thrown on a tile floor. Brady clapped his hands to his ears, shaking in agony as the sound tore through his eardrums and clawed at his brain.

"Brady. Brady! It's okay. Shh." Rachelle's voice struggled through the noise, trying to reach him, but it was someone else's hand that awkwardly patted his shoulder. "Dash—no, Harper, can you get him some water? Brady, breathe. You're okay. Just breathe."

The hand pulled away, and a deeper shudder ran through Brady at the loss of even that weak crumb of comfort. After a few seconds, an even more hesitant hand barely rested against his back, the tremor that ran through it evident even in that lightest of touches.

"Here." Warm fingers pried his arm away from his knees and pressed a cold glass into his hand, then helped him lift it to his mouth. Brady managed a sip, and the seizing pressure lessened its grip on his head. He gulped in a ragged breath and looked up to find Harper kneeling at his side, watching him worriedly, while Rachelle leaned over the arm of the recliner as though she had attempted to reach him even through her current imprisonment. When his eyes met hers, she let out a relieved breath and sank back, and Grace burrowed into her side, her thumb in her mouth again.

"What on earth, dude?" Dash's voice stayed low, but it held a hint of worry, even as his hand jerked away from Brady's back.

"What—was that?" Brady sucked in another breath through lungs that ached as he slowly straightened.

"What was what?" Dash still sounded entirely mystified, but Rachelle shook her head sympathetically.

"Trash bag dropping on the floor upstairs. We've all gotten used to it, but none of us has to deal with your hearing. That had to be excruciating."

"Are you serious?" Brady took another drink of the water before resting his head in his hand with a sigh. "That's all? I could have sworn it was at least two full cabinets worth of metal and glass that fell."

"Wow. No wonder it got to you." Harper offered something between a smile and a wince. "Guess you've found your occupational hazard, huh? Mine's getting accidentally bumped into or stepped on, mostly. Dash's is not paying attention to what's around him before he reacts to something."

"Meaning…" Brady's brain was still struggling to catch up, but the conversation was definitely helping to ground him again.

"Meaning if you startle me into running into a wall, you *will* regret it. Capiche?"

"Got it." Brady huffed out a breath of a laugh. "What's yours, Rachelle?"

"If you knew how many things around here we've had to replace—or that now have permanent dents in them—you wouldn't ask." Rachelle's smile deepened. "It's way too easy to forget my own strength when I have it."

Grace mumbled something incomprehensible behind her thumb, and Rachelle bent down to hear better.

"What was that, baby?"

"You throw things into the ceiling sometimes," the little girl murmured, and Rachelle chuckled.

"Yes. Yes, I do. And listen, you don't have to worry about Brady, okay? He hears sounds a lot louder than they are. That's all that happened. He can also smell things and see things and feel things and taste things a lot better than everybody else too."

"Can he hear me now?" Grace whispered at a volume he could probably have heard without any help, and Brady grinned.

"Sure can, Gracie-girl." He chuckled as her eyes rounded. "I don't know how it's supposed to help anything yet, but yeah, that's what I can do." Brady finished the last of the water and let out a long breath. "Man. I almost—" He shook his head and swallowed hard. "No. That's not true. I don't—honestly think I'd rather have a migraine today. It's just—really hard to get used to."

"You are *so* not alone in that." Harper took the empty glass and set it back on the table, then slipped into her chair again. "Don't get me wrong; I love the invisible thing. But it was incredibly freaky the first couple of times. Give yourself a chance to get used to it. Don't expect to fully love it overnight."

"Yeah, same." Dash's gravelly voice was quieter than Brady had ever heard it. "It's the best thing that's happened to me in a long time, but I'd still give just about anything for an actual normal day sometimes."

"I think you all know how I feel." Rachelle's soft, gentle words soaked into his heart like a soothing balm. "This was never what I wanted, but it's what I've been given, and I do my best to be content. I'll never tell anyone it's not hard. But we're here for you. Every one of us. As much as we can be for as long as we can be." She gently stroked Grace's hair as the little girl relaxed against her. "I still can't help but think we've been brought here for a reason. And we'll find it. All of us. Together."

Chapter Eleven

"Brady?"

"Hmm?" Brady pulled his eyes open and shook himself fully awake. He shot a look at Grace, curled up against the arm of the couch beside him, but she was completely engrossed in the fourth or fifth episode of her rescue dog show and didn't seem to notice that he'd almost dozed off. Rachelle smiled over at him from the chair where she was still banished, although she'd let the footrest down after dinner.

"Don't worry; she's fine. You've got infinitely more patience for kids' shows than some people she's tried to rope into watching with her."

Brady couldn't help darting a glance across the room at Dash, and Rachelle chuckled.

"No, actually. He just puts something else on his earbuds and ignores it. Harper's the one who complains."

"Seriously?" A grin twitched at Brady's lips as he looked over at the blue-haired girl, who currently lay with her bare feet propped on the back of a couch, a book in one hand, and the other arm curled around a shiny pillow stamped with a colorful illusion of a vortex that looked like it could swallow her at any minute.

"She can stand about an episode at a time, if it has any semblance of a plot. Her tolerance for pure slapstick is pretty low."

"Make it stop..." Harper mumbled under her breath, and Brady barely stifled a snort.

"So." Rachelle gently pulled his attention back. "Not to make you think too much about tomorrow, but when it hits, is there anything that helps, even a little bit? I don't want you to go without—or to have to explain in the thick of it."

"There's really nothing." Brady swallowed hard. "Noise down. Lights off. No strong smells. And no food—please don't even ask. If you leave some water on the table, I'll try to sip it, even if I can't keep it down."

"Any thoughts on electrolytes?"

"I don't…think?" Brady wrinkled his forehead, trying to sort through the litany of things Mom and Eden had tried. "Just for hydrating, you mean? If you've got something that doesn't taste like week-old, watered down Kool-Aid, I'm willing to give it a shot. Otherwise…" He shuddered.

"Got it." Rachelle's smile softened. "What else?"

Brady dropped his gaze and pretended to focus on Grace's tablet, biting his lips together as a familiar pain burned in his chest.

"Brady?" Rachelle waited a moment for him to answer, then tried again. "Talk to me."

"I wish I had something to give you." The words came slowly, with an effort. "Something to give anyone that I could honestly say helped anything, so they wouldn't sit around feeling bad that there's nothing they can do."

"Brady, no, that's not what I'm asking." The shift in Rachelle's tone forced his eyes up to meet hers again. "I know that feeling. Believe me, I know. This isn't about needing to feel useful. If the best we can do is stock you with water and shut the door, then that's what we'll do. It's not—not really the migraine I'm asking about. But *you*. What makes things more bearable, when you can get it? Someone sitting with you? Complete isolation? Touch? No touch? An extra blanket? A favorite set of sheets?"

"Sheets, really?" A half-chuckle caught on the lump in his throat, and he blinked hard.

"Don't. Laugh." Dash's voice rumbled the words in an ominous growl, and Brady clamped his lips shut to prevent even a smile from escaping.

"Let me ask it a different way." Rachelle's soft voice deftly sidestepped whatever land mine he'd just walked into. "If you were home tomorrow, what would Eden do that you've missed since you've been here? What have you wished she would do but never got the courage to ask? What do you tolerate for her sake but really just want her to stop? And what does she know better than to even try?"

It wasn't like it was the first time he'd thought about Eden today. Or even the most vulnerable he'd been when it happened. But Rachelle's persistent questions reminded him so much of Eden's stubborn mantra—"I can't make it better, Brady Ray, but I won't let you fight it alone"— that tears suddenly flooded his eyes. He slammed them shut and drew a shaky breath, and the next instant, he felt the slight shift of the couch cushion as Grace turned toward him.

"Do I need to stop 'cause your head hurts?"

The lump in his throat had grown to the size of a boulder, and Brady didn't dare speak. He shook his head instead, trying desperately to gain enough control to reassure her without making a fool of himself in front of everyone. He heard Rachelle's barely mouthed "it's okay, baby," but even his enhanced senses gave him only a second of warning before Grace launched herself from her corner and into his side, wrapping her arms around him and holding on like a little octopus.

Somehow that artless hug managed to pull him back from the brink, and he patted her back gently for a moment before whispering, "Thanks, Gracie-girl. I'm okay. Finish your show."

Grace let go but snuggled closer as she turned back to her tablet, and Brady kept his eyes closed for a moment, trying to make sure the tears were in full retreat before he met anyone's gaze again.

"You know you don't—"

"Baseline understanding that you're not asking and no one's obligated." Rachelle's tone somehow blocked any further argument without losing a fraction of its gentleness, and the last of his resistance melted away.

"Eden would sit with me—not talk, but stay close—not all day, just when she could. She'd rub my back when things got really bad—but if you ever try it, you have to stop when I say. Sometimes it's okay; sometimes I just can't take it."

"Understood." There was nothing either flippant or condemning in the answer, and Brady pressed his eyes closed for a last second before raising them to meet hers again.

"Whatever you do, please don't touch my head. My hair, anything. It helps for regular headaches sometimes. Not for migraines. At least not mine. And a cold washcloth? I know most people swear by it, but I guarantee it makes me worse. Can't explain it. Might give in and try again if you push, but I *will* regret it."

"Got it." Rachelle nodded, and Brady lifted his gaze to the ceiling, pulled it back when it started to penetrate the floor above, then shook his head slowly.

"That's—pretty much it. All I can think of anyway."

"And the beds here aren't a problem? You don't have a special pillow you need, or any issues with the blankets?"

"I mean, I did bring a pillow. I don't know that I actually need it—I'm sure the ones here are fine, but—" Honesty was one thing, but there was no way he was ready to confess just how threadbare the tag on that one particular pillow had become from his habit of rubbing it when the worst of the pain made him desperate for the smallest distraction.

"It's upstairs?" Rachelle sat up straight, looking nearly ready to spring from her chair, and Brady raised an eyebrow.

"Unless they put my stuff in storage when they brought me down this morning, I guess. Where do you think you're going?"

Her face scrunched in frustration, then she bent forward to see around him.

"We never got Brady's stuff moved down here before my knee interrupted. Who's available?"

"He's a big boy, Midge. Pretty sure he can handle it," Dash muttered, and Brady's cheeks flamed, but before he could answer, Rachelle was speaking again.

"Like you and Harper did?"

"You gotta admit he's not nearly as conspicuous wandering the halls with a suitcase as Harper would have been."

"I don't need—" Brady started, but a little snort from Harper cut him off.

"Oh, you're months too late for that." She stretched hard and sat up, slipping her feet into a pair of flip-flops. "We're all sucked into Rachelle's 'all for one, one for all, nobody stands alone' thing, like it or not. Dash is coming too; he just has to grumble about it first."

"Seriously, I can—"

"Shut it, Owen," Dash growled. "I'd rather face Harper's bad cliches than Rachelle's pitiful puppy eyes, that's all. You coming, or you trust us not to swipe your stuff?"

"I—" Brady was halfway to his feet before the catch in the question hit him, leaving his mind scrambling for a response.

"Ignore him." Rachelle gave a resigned sigh, and Harper laughed.

"Do better. Stick him with the heaviest bags. You're part of the team now, so payback's fair play. Let's go."

Brady could only shake his head as he threw a last glance back at Rachelle and Grace, then followed Harper and Dash out the door.

CHAPTER TWELVE

"So how much stuff are we looking at?" Dash asked as they exited the elevator, and Brady sighed.

"Not that much. I don't really need—"

"Quit." Harper elbowed him in the side. "It's a Rachelle 'you're family' thing, not some primitive challenge to your manhood. Don't be a drama queen."

"Wait, *you're*—" Brady swallowed the remaining words with an effort, and Dash choked on a snort and burst into a coughing fit. Harper turned and surveyed them with folded arms.

"If that's an implication that *I'm* a drama queen, then *I* can go back to Rachelle and leave you two Neanderthals to club each other over the head or something." She started to walk away with the requisite lofty tilt of her chin, then paused without looking back. "Where…am I going again?"

Brady chuckled and nodded in the direction of one of the side hallways as he passed her, and Dash cleared his throat with a last cough.

"'Not that much' says next to nothing, you know. Are we talking Harper showing up on a bus with a backpack? Or a pampered heiress with only one cart of luggage for the weekend?"

"Please." Brady rolled his eyes. "We're talking two suitcases and a duffle bag. That's all. And half of it my sister insisted on. I haven't even taken…most of it…" Without warning, the combined sounds and smells of the center suddenly crashed over him like a waterfall, and he had to grab the handrail along the wall to keep himself from crumpling, gasping for breath as he tried to pull his focus back.

"Brady?" Harper's hand was on his arm, grounding him in the here and now, even if her voice didn't hold quite the comforting steadiness of Rachelle's. He blinked hard and tried to focus on her, to let the clicking shoes and beeping monitors and swirling scents of antiseptic and sickness fade to the background. Just her, the rail, the wall—

"How far to your room, Owen?" Somehow the terse question managed to shake his focus without making his senses spiral again, and the hallway sharpened in front of him.

"Two doors. Right."

"Think you can get there? Harper, grab his arm."

Somehow he was able to stumble the few steps down the hallway, his heightened senses still pressing uncomfortably close, and drop onto the bed, where he buried his face in his hands.

"Harper, door. Now you want to explain what's going on?"

"No—idea." Concentrating hard on one sense at a time, Brady was able to pull his awareness back from the worn threads of the hospital blanket, to narrow his vision to Dash sitting in front of him. "It hasn't—felt like this since—morning."

"Felt like what?" Dash pressed as Brady struggled for breath against the suffocating medley of smells.

"Should I call Rachelle?" Harper's voice was barely audible in the cacophony, but Brady managed a shake of his head.

"No. Call Mattox," Dash commanded without waiting for permission. "She created this mess; she needs to figure out what's going on with it."

Any response from Harper was drowned out by a child's screams, and Brady gripped the bed hard and willed himself not to pass out as he tried to swallow the lingering taste of bile and vanilla yogurt. The sensations faded slowly, leaving only his hearing on overload, but when he tried to pull it back, the screaming only intensified. Harper's low, urgent words from the corner became an indecipherable murmur, punctuated by the deep, sharp snap of whatever Dash was trying to say as the overwhelming cries claimed more and more of Brady's attention.

He'd been able to focus on their words before. He'd always been able to focus on Rachelle's. The same child's cries had pressed on him at different times throughout the day—sometimes faint and whimpering, sometimes loud and anguished. They'd intensified when he let them, but never when he'd consciously tried to block them.

Lord, please! What's it doing? Why isn't it working?

The best he could do was hold onto the bed and try to force himself to breathe. The tenor of the buzz that was his actual surroundings shifted, but before he could try to identify the source, something changed in the scream that was holding him fast. Something high-pitched—breathless—struggling—

"No!" Brady sat up straight with a gasp as the sound began to retreat and the room around him snapped into focus again. Dr. Mattox jerked back just in time to keep his head from hitting her chin where she must have been bent over, trying to talk to him.

"Mr. Owen, can you please explain—"

"No!" Brady gulped air, trying to fight the creeping panic. "There has to be something! You have to help him!"

"Help who?" Dr. Mattox stared at him with intense eyes, as though she could somehow bore into his brain and figure out exactly what was happening there. Brady cast a desperate glance around the room, and his vision blurred and narrowed, just like when he'd pinpointed the doctor and Rachelle in the hall. The little boy was straining, gasping on the bed, his cries growing thinner and thinner. How was he supposed to—

A chart on the wall caught Brady's attention, and he gritted his teeth and willed the words to focus.

"Lawson White. Room 1157. Please, do something! He can't breathe! He's—"

The doctor whirled on her heel so fast that her lab coat fanned him with its breeze, and the next instant the door slammed behind her, the echo fading into the choking squeaks of the little boy as they crashed in again.

God, please! Please help him! Why is this happening? What can I do?

Slowly, one at a time, other sounds began to penetrate. Beeping monitors. Hurrying footsteps. A strident voice barking out orders. Sounds from Lawson's room, he realized dimly, and somehow the recognition that it was Dr. Mattox directing operations brought a bit of the breath back to his aching lungs. After a long, agonizing minute, something snapped in the tight, high-pitched whine, replaced with desperate but productive gasps for air, and Brady suddenly collapsed on the bed as his focus dissolved and slowly re-formed in his own room.

"You back with us?" Dash's voice rasped as hard as ever, but there was no bite to it, and Brady allowed himself a few deep breaths before he answered.

"I—I think so." He pushed himself up on the bed but had to grip the side again as the world spun around him.

"Whoa, take it slow. Really slow." The bed shifted a little as Harper slid next to him. "That—whatever that was—did not look fun."

"Yeah. It wasn't." Brady blinked hard and glanced around cautiously, half expecting his vision or his hearing to blur and crash in again. "It was like—almost like I felt when my senses turned on this morning, except—I couldn't focus them. They almost—focused themselves."

"On some kid in another room who couldn't breathe." Dash's face was inscrutable, but Brady nodded.

"Yeah. Wouldn't pull back when I tried. I guess I need more practice controlling it. Or something. Do yours get—weird at night like that?"

"Not really." Harper shook her head slowly. "Taper off, maybe, but it's early for that. I guess that's assuming yours work exactly like the rest of ours, though. Who knows?"

"Oh, I am *definitely* getting answers from Mattox on this." Dash crossed his arms, and his eyes narrowed. "There's no way you're going out in public if *that* could happen again. Even if you don't get yourself killed, how are you supposed to explain that kind of reaction?"

"Easy." Brady managed a weak laugh. "Bad headache. Not even a lie, either. I sure felt like it was about to explode for a minute there."

"Yeah, well, we're still getting answers." The stubborn glint in Dash's eye was oddly reassuring. "You ready to move back to the den, or you need to stay put for a while?"

"I haven't even…" Brady waved a shaky hand at the room, and Harper hopped off the bed with a shrug.

"We got it. Just grabbed everything that didn't look standard mostly, but you can sort that out later. Feel up to walking?"

"Think so." Brady slid off the bed but had to hold onto it when his legs trembled under him.

"Starting again?" Dash nudged his wheelchair closer, and Brady shook his head with an effort.

"Not—not again, just—drained."

"Totally get that." Harper laid a hand on his arm. "This was rough. Need to use my shoulder?"

"Better idea." Dash motioned her to the side and quickly maneuvered next to Brady. "Harper, take the suitcases and hand me the bag. You lean on the chair and try to at least *look* like you're pushing it. Maybe we can get out of here before anything else happens."

And between his utter exhaustion and the inexplicable desire to get back to the bed he'd only ever slept in once, Brady didn't even try to argue.

Chapter Thirteen

Brady's exhausted senses picked up the slow tap of shoes and what sounded like the squeak of a wheel in the hall, but his lack of energy far outweighed any hint of curiosity, and he didn't even bother turning onto his other side. The door whispered open, and the sounds came closer, then a soft hand was on his arm, squeezing it with a tight but tremulous grip. How was it possible to have missed someone so deeply when you'd known them less than a day?

"You're not supposed to be up." He hadn't meant it to be a whisper. Clearing his throat, Brady pried his eyes open and finally managed to turn his head far enough to see over his shoulder.

"I'm being careful." Rachelle motioned to the rolling walker she was currently sitting on as her thumb gently stroked his arm. Brady was pretty sure walking all the way down the hall when her room was so much closer didn't exactly fit the definition, but he didn't feel like arguing the point, and after a minute, Rachelle continued talking softly. "Dr. Mattox came down, but I didn't guess you felt up to her brand of explanations yet."

"She had some?" The idea of answers felt like it deserved sitting up at least, but the best he could do was to roll the few inches onto his back so he didn't have to keep straining his neck.

"Not many." Rachelle sighed. "Mostly guesses. Theories. You were right; the little boy was in bad shape. They'd tried a new medicine, and he's apparently allergic, but he'd been crying all day, and the nurses had pretty much tuned it out. Didn't notice the difference."

"He's all right?"

"Yes, they caught it in time. Well, *you* caught it. They know not to try that treatment again."

"Not like I deserve credit. I wasn't even controlling it."

"I know." The pressure of Rachelle's hand tightened again. "Dr. Mattox's going hypothesis is that your senses picked up on some miniscule change in the atmosphere, like the way some animals can sniff out cancer and things, and then they zeroed in hard on the source."

It was a plausible theory, as far as he could tell—at least if you started from the premise that any of this actually worked in the first place. But something in her tone made his brow furrow just a little.

"You have a better idea?"

"Not one you could write up in a lab report." Rachelle gave a quick little shake of her head. "I just..." She trailed off and raised her eyes to the ceiling for a moment before she looked back down at him. "I can't help thinking there's more to it, Brady. God put you here for a reason. And maybe...maybe this is part of it."

"That's—" Brady paused and swallowed hard. "That's a lot to think about."

"I know. And you're tired tonight—no wonder. Don't worry about it. If there's something more to all this—well, it's obvious you don't have to look for it. He knows where to find you."

"Guess so." Brady closed his eyes, pulled in a deep breath, and let it out slowly before he met her gaze again. "How bad did I freak everyone out?"

"They're fine." Rachelle smiled softly. "And they get it. Dash is only a bulldog because he worries—not that he'd admit it. How are you doing? You've probably got a truckload of adrenaline working out of your system, huh?"

"Didn't know it was possible to be so spent and still so keyed up at the same time." He tried to return the smile, but the corners of his lips quivered, and Rachelle's eyes clouded with sympathy.

"I should've come sooner. I hoped you were sleeping."

"Don't. You didn't have to come at all. It's not—"

"Shhh." Rachelle reached to brush a stray piece of hair from his forehead with a feather-light touch. "I won't feel bad that I wasn't here before if you don't feel bad that I'm here now. Fair?"

"I can live with that," Brady mumbled. Somehow just having her close was draining the tension and pulling his eyelids down. They were nearly shut when someone tapped at the door and he realized with a little start that this time he hadn't heard footsteps in the hall. What scientific explanation would the doctor have for the fact that Rachelle seemed to focus his senses better than he could do it consciously? On second thought, maybe he didn't want to know.

Rachelle offered a quiet "come in" but thankfully didn't try to stand, and the brighter light from the hallway gave a glow to Harper's blue hair as she cautiously poked her head in.

"Dash and I offered to do the story and toothbrush bit, but she wants to say goodnight to Brady."

Brady managed a tiny nod, and Harper pushed the door wide enough to admit Dash's wheelchair, including Grace, perched on his lap with her thumb in her mouth.

"Come here, baby." Rachelle nodded toward the bed. "Brady's okay—just tired."

Fighting against the ridiculous weakness, Brady scooted himself up just a tiny bit on the pillows and stretched out an arm, and Grace scrambled from her seat and onto the bed, wrapping her arms around him and burying her face in his neck.

"Hey, Gracie-girl." He patted her back gently, searching for something he could say to reassure her. He was okay? Rachelle had covered that. This was normal? Even a little kid would see through the lie. He'd be better in the morning? Not if everyone else's pattern held.

"Want a hero story tonight, baby?" Rachelle's question rescued his floundering mind, and Grace wriggled her head around to face her.

"Can Brady hear too?"

"Absolutely Brady can hear." Rachelle leaned back against the walker, and Brady noted from the corners of his eyes that neither Harper nor Dash moved to leave the room. Grace nestled into the crook of his arm with her gaze fixed on her sister, and Rachelle's voice took on a soft, proud note as she began.

"Once upon a time, there was a little boy who was very, very sick. His family wanted to make him better, but nothing they tried helped. So they took him to doctors—lots of them—better and better ones, only none of the doctors could help him either. But they kept trying and kept trying, and one day they heard of a medical center where a doctor was trying new things that no one had done before."

"Like here," Grace whispered.

"Yes, exactly like here. So they came to the center, and the doctors tried more things, but the little boy was still sick—so sick that he cried and cried and cried. And everyone wanted to make him better, but they didn't know how, so they kept trying more and more, but what they didn't know was that one of the medicines they thought might help actually made him sicker."

"Oh, no!" Grace gave a little gasp, and Brady's heart warmed as her arms tightened around him.

"Oh, yes." Rachelle nodded solemnly. "But God was watching out for the little boy, and He'd put a hero right there in the center—a hero who could hear when the little boy's crying got sicker and sicker, even when the nurses couldn't. And because the hero knew what it felt like to be sick and sad and wanted the little boy to get better, he told the doctor what was wrong, and the doctor got a new medicine to take the old one away and make him better again."

"Is he all better now?" Grace asked, and Rachelle's answering smile was tinged with sadness.

"He's better than he was before he started the medicine, for sure. He's not all better yet, but the doctors are still trying, and now they know what not to give him that will make him worse. Thanks to God and the hero He put here today."

"I knew it was here." Grace hummed happily as she turned and nestled her head against Brady's neck again, then leaned up to whisper in his ear. "I'm glad you're a hero, Brady."

"How did you—" The lump in his throat choked his words, and Grace giggled.

"Cause we live in a place with lots of doctors, and you can hear everything!" She pushed herself up on the bed to survey him thoughtfully. "Does being a hero make you tired?"

"I guess so. Kind of funny, huh?" Brady offered her a wobbly smile, and Grace nodded solemnly.

"Then you need to go to sleep. And I'm gonna make you a hero picture for when you get better!"

"You need to go to bed too, Grace," Rachelle warned softly, and Grace sighed.

"I know. I'm gonna draw it tomorrow. I draw lots of hero pictures at school. My teacher thinks it's funny, cause I don't tell her they're real." The little girl flashed Brady a mischievous grin and then scooted off the bed and back onto Dash's lap with a yawn. "Night, Brady."

"Night, Gracie-girl." The words wavered, and Rachelle reached over to squeeze his hand.

"Can you let Dash and Harper get you ready tonight, baby? I'll be there in a few minutes."

"After Brady's asleep?" Grace asked the question as if it were the most natural thing in the world, and Rachelle nodded.

"Probably. Or close to it. Even heroes need taking care of sometimes."

"Uh huh. Lots of times."

Brady couldn't help thinking her experience of superheroes was a bit skewed, but he couldn't argue with her perspective. And yet with all his limits, she and Rachelle and even Harper and Dash saw something of value—something to be cared for—something worth the effort they'd put forth to bring him into the team.

Dear Eden... The message began to compose itself in his mind as he let his eyes drift closed. *I'm still not sure what exactly God's planned for me here, but I'm going to stick around a while and find out. Oh, and I'm starting to make friends. I think you'd like them…*

The Chronic Warrior Chronicles

Episode 2

Uncommon Sense

Angie Thompson

Quiet Waters Press
Lynchburg, Virginia

To everyone struggling to see God's plan in their circumstances

He is still working, even when things seem darkest!

Thank you to everyone who followed along with me while writing, and to God for being faithful to give me the ability to write each chapter when it was needed, even if it wasn't on my own timeline!

TABLE OF CONTENTS

CHAPTER ONE

"Should be a guy in a ball cap and red hoodie heading west from Freeland, just south of Puritan. If you cut across Grand River and come up Greenfield, you should be able to cut him off." Harper lay on her stomach on the floor with her bare feet in the air, blue hair falling in a curtain around her face as her eyes roamed the laminated map beneath her.

"On it."

The words were painfully loud in Brady's head, deep and resonant in spite of the couch pillow he'd laid on top of the earpiece. Of course he could have just turned it off, but there was no guarantee that getting rid of the noise would improve his headache in the slightest, and he was pretty sure the strain of trying to follow the situation from the girls' sparse comments wouldn't be any better.

A long, angry honk blared from the earpiece, and Harper clapped her hands to her head.

"Dash, be careful!" Rachelle sat forward in her chair, voice sharp and face tight with worry.

"Wasn't me. Car on the crossing street ran a red. Coming up on Puritan now. Any word?"

"Radio patrol lost him after Freeland." Harper stared at the map as though her intense gaze could somehow make the suspect's location appear. "Police are five minutes out, but if you—"

"Got him!" Dash's voice was triumphant, if a little breathless. "Call it in, Midge! West on Puritan, just past Greenfield and the market."

"You're sure?" Rachelle rubbed the knuckle of her thumb against her lower lip as she fingered the button of the radio on the seat next to her. "We can't be wrong on this."

"Right. Could be an innocent guy out for an afternoon run with his favorite catalytic converter." Dash snorted. "Call it in! I'll try to slow him down."

"Bethune C.B. Patrol, this is Mighty Midge." If his headache wasn't so bad and the situation wasn't so urgent, Brady could almost have laughed at Rachelle's deadpan delivery of the ridiculous code name. "We have eyes on your car stripper. Heading west on Puritan past Greenfield. Update the police. We'll stick with him as long as we can."

"Good to have you with us, neighbor!" The enthusiasm that crackled through the weak radio signal was the one thing that kept the whole situation from tipping over into some bizarre game of make believe. They were helping people—people who were grateful for what they could give, even if they had no idea what was truly happening behind the scenes.

It was better that way, everyone agreed. Let the wrong person in on their secret and who knew what could happen? Realistically, what reporter in their right mind wouldn't want to get their hands on honest-to-goodness superheroes if even a whiff of the truth leaked out? And from there…well, maybe clandestine government labs and military research projects were the stuff of comic books, but it wasn't much of a leap to too many other potential consequences. Being turned into test subjects by a battery of scientists more interested in studying their powers than curing the conditions underlying them wasn't a future any of them were keen to sign up for. Neither was the idea of Dr. Mattox's funding being channeled away from the patients upstairs—some of whom she was truly helping—if her donors got wind of the flashier potential of superhuman creation.

But beyond the overarching issues, Brady suspected that each of them had their own reasons for maintaining secrecy. He hadn't missed the way Rachelle's eyes tracked Grace whenever the subject came up, and it wasn't hard to imagine that CPS might have an opinion or two on the matter. Dash's hands balled into fists at the mere whisper of publicity, and Harper seemed to curl in on herself at the idea of being moved to another lab. As for him—well, beyond the fact that Eden would freak, any spotlight on him would mean the end of a normal life for her, completely wrecking his reason for being here in the first place.

"Dash, status!" Rachelle's hand went to her earpiece, and Brady zoned back in to the sound of Dash's increasingly ragged breathing.

"Don't bug me, Midge. Not much to—work with here. Hold it." A rush of air whined through the tiny speaker—Brady had no idea how he managed to keep the thing in at the speeds Harper and Rachelle swore he was capable of—before his voice came back, panting. "Strong breeze—keeping him on course—best I can do."

"Can't you trip him up?" Harper's fingers drummed nervously against the map, the tap of her nails grating in Brady's ears.

"Make him drop evidence—before the cops come?"

"No, forget it." Rachelle shook her head as though he could see her. "Don't engage. Just keep eyes on him. You don't want to spook him."

"Little late."

The ominous words froze Brady's breath, and he raised his head from the couch, fighting the dizziness that threatened to swamp him as the pounding in his skull intensified.

"Get out of there." Rachelle's knuckles went white on the arm of the recliner. "Dash, it's too risky. Abort now."

There was no answer from the earpiece except Dash's harsh breaths, and Brady tried to swallow the sick feeling in his throat. How would they even know if something went wrong?

"C'mon, Dash, you're scaring people." Harper tucked her hair behind her ear and tilted her head at the ceiling, her relaxed posture and scolding tone a stark contrast to the crackling tension in the room. "If you don't give us a word pretty soon to prove you're not hurt or trapped, we might have to call in the cavalry."

A huff that might have been a laugh or a nasty trick of the static was the only answer for a few seconds, then Dash's voice came back.

"Like we—have one." A siren blared somewhere in the background, and the next huff sounded like relief. "Cops almost here. Fifteen seconds."

Rachelle bit her lips together hard and closed her eyes, pressing her knuckle to her mouth, and Harper rocked back on her hands, staring at the ceiling.

"What—" Brady barely formed the word before Harper shook her head sharply, putting a finger to her lips to keep him quiet.

The stillness stretched for interminable seconds that felt like minutes, against a backdrop of indistinct shouts and scuffling that only pulled the knot in Brady's stomach tighter. But finally, just as the strain was becoming unbearable, Dash's voice came back.

"Over. Safe." His breathing was still harsh and labored, but Rachelle slumped back in her chair, and Harper's shoulders relaxed. "Breathe—worrywarts."

"You said fifteen. That was closer to twenty." Rachelle's voice held just the faintest trace of reproach, and Dash gave a little snort.

"So sue me."

"Cops got him?" Harper asked.

"Not hard when he, uh—inexplicably trips—right in front of them."

"That's right on the edge of too close, Dash." Rachelle closed her eyes and let out a slow breath. "Where are you now?"

"Up a tree on—St. Mary's. No one's looking."

"Good. Stay there and breathe for at least five minutes, got it?"

"You're seriously—putting me on a timer?"

"Would you rather I pulled your vitals?"

"Fine. Five minutes."

The ache in Brady's head doubled as the last of the tension drained away, and he lowered it carefully back onto the pillow, trying to regulate his own breathing as the waves of pain crashed in.

"Harper, make sure he stays put." Rachelle's voice suddenly shifted into the soft tone that almost didn't hurt his ears, and the next thing Brady knew, her hand was on his shoulder. "Getting bad, huh?"

A nod would have been too painful, but Brady managed a non-committal hum.

"Thought so. Come on, let's get you to bed. If it doesn't help, at least you'll be there if it gets worse."

He wasn't crazy about the idea of moving, but she did have a point, and he didn't really feel up to arguing at the moment. Steeling himself hard, Brady managed to push to his feet and somehow not fall on top of her as she wrapped an arm around his back to steady him.

"Easy." Her whisper was low and soothing, pitched toward his chest instead of on a direct line with his ear. "It's okay. I've got you."

Brady let his eyes stay closed and concentrated on putting one foot in front of the other, trusting her to steer him in the right direction. In less time than he would have expected, she had him back in his room and was gently smoothing the covers over him.

"Think it's going to be a bad one?" Rachelle's hand stroked his arm in comforting circles, careful not to touch his pounding head, and Brady swallowed hard.

"Might sleep it off. Might not. Hard to tell."

"Don't stress over it. You rest, okay? Call if you need anything." She tapped the button on his nightstand, as if to remind him where it was, and he managed a tiny nod.

"Everything out there—all right?"

"Don't worry about Dash. That's an order. He's going to give me gray hairs one of these days, but with as many close calls as he's sailed through, he's got to be at least nine-tenths cat. As soon as he catches his breath, he'll be hassling me about trying to call him off. I'd offer to send him in when he gets back, but he's all about milking these days for every last second of freedom, so it won't be till late. Try to be asleep by then, okay? If he hits anything more serious than his nine-hundredth life, I promise I'll wake you up, and if not, he'll stretch the stories out for days, so you won't miss anything."

It wasn't like he could do much if things went wrong anyway, but somehow knowing that Rachelle understood helped calm the churning restlessness.

"Thanks," Brady murmured, and she stroked his arm one last time, then closed the door softly and left him to sleep.

CHAPTER TWO

Even before he opened his eyes the next morning, Brady knew he was in for it. The nausea swirling in his gut was a dead giveaway, even without the hot knives stabbing into his skull. He moaned as he curled into a tighter ball, burying his face in the blanket as though it could somehow shield him from the misery.

It had been almost two weeks since he'd finally been able to drag himself out of bed after the remnants of the migraine that Dr. Mattox's injection had temporarily interrupted. The headaches had continued, of course, but not in their worst form, and after he'd actually backed down from the beginnings of a full-blown attack a few days ago, he'd started to harbor a tiny seed of hope that maybe he'd actually be allowed to skip this round. Yeah…he really should have known better.

He had no idea what time it was. Had his internal clock woken him up, or just the intensity of the pain? He'd always been an early riser, much to Eden's disgust, but all bets were off in the throes of a migraine, except that it tended to fall on the side of less sleep, not more. The temptation to glance at a clock was strong, but his stomach was already in his throat, and even the dimmest light possible would probably be enough to tip it over the edge.

Not that the time mattered all that much anyway. It wasn't like he was at home, where he could calculate what time Eden would be out of bed, and how quickly she would realize that he wasn't. The den, as Rachelle had christened it, had its own rhythm of sorts, but Brady was still working out what was within everyone's normal range and what was cause for concern.

Rachelle was by far the easiest. Grace's carpool pickup was scheduled for seven thirty, so Rachelle was up by six thirty at the latest, and it was a sign of a bad pain day if the headquarters for school prep was Rachelle's room rather than the common.

Dash's appearance was semi-consistent in the range of ten o'clock, give or take a half-hour on each side that seemed to correlate roughly with the severity of his tremors on a given day, although Brady had no idea when he actually woke up, or how much of that time he spent in preparation. Yesterday had been a notable exception; Brady had reached the common at six to be greeted by a sleepy-eyed Rachelle, curled up in the recliner with a radio, an earpiece, and the news that Dash was already on patrol.

Harper was a puzzle he hadn't even come close to solving. Some days she dragged herself into the common just before lunchtime, still wearing pajamas and trailing her blanket; other days she was fully alert and watching TV on the couch when Brady came in, although he couldn't help but suspect that she hadn't gone to her room at all the night before. One evening when her skin condition had flared—Brady hadn't known that color red was *possible* in the real world—it had taken commands that were nearly threats from Rachelle to get her to leave the common and go to bed, but other days she stayed tucked away contentedly in her room until dinnertime with no more explanation than the plot of the book she was reading.

If anyone was going to notice his absence, it would almost certainly be Rachelle, but the question was whether she'd been able to pick up enough of his own patterns to sense if they were off. In the weeks he'd been with them, he'd had a couple of late mornings after restless nights and a day when he'd kept entirely to his room to stave off an attack that the smallest trigger would have escalated, so it was possible no one would notice he was missing for a while.

The call button on his nightstand taunted him with its nearness, but realistically, what good would it do? It wasn't like anyone could actually help at the moment—nothing would lessen the pain, and the water bottle Rachelle had filled the night before would last him most of the day. Was he seriously going to risk waking her up at what might be an unearthly hour just so someone else in the world would know he was suffering? He hoped he wasn't quite that pathetic.

Time inched past in what he might have called a fog except for the searing, white-hot agony that shredded it. At some point, he finally lost the battle with his stomach and managed to use the seconds before his stinging eyes closed again to glance at the clock. Just after six. Lovely. He wasn't even really late yet, let alone enough to trigger alarm bells.

Blindly, cautiously, mindful of the slightest jar to his head, Brady managed to find the fraying tag on the corner of his pillow and began rubbing it between his fingers, the repetitive motion managing to ground him somehow even if it couldn't touch the ache. He forced himself to concentrate on one breath at a time. Not counting—that would have driven him mad—but silently willing himself through one breath more. Then one more. Just one more.

Whether he had only zoned out or actually dozed off, Brady wasn't sure, but when a gentle hand on his back returned him to full consciousness, he wasn't sure how much time had passed.

"Please tell me you haven't been like this all night." The words were barely a whisper, and Brady swallowed hard, trying to frame his answer in as few words as possible.

"Just today."

"Why didn't you call?"

"Couldn't help."

"Brady, I know that. I'm not—" Rachelle broke off, apparently with an effort, then breathed a long sigh. "Sorry. This can wait. What about today? Do you want an injection?"

How was it that in all his thoughts that morning concerning the den, its occupants, and even their activities, the idea that he could elect to pause the pain had somehow never crossed his mind?

"Forgot."

"Easy to do when you've never had a choice before." She didn't sound nearly as bothered by that fact as she had about not being woken up. "I'm not trying to pressure you. The injections are always voluntary. But the earlier you take it, the more benefit you get. Do you want me to leave for a little while so you can think?"

Admittedly, his mind wasn't in the best space for lucid thought right now, but it wasn't like he had to counterbalance an unhealthy habit of trying to avoid pain. Even before the migraines, his tendency had always been to grit his teeth and deal with it, forgetting that such a thing as medicine existed in the world until Mom or Eden reminded him. Realistically though, if he wasn't going to use what Dr. Mattox could offer, incomplete and ridiculous as it was, then what was he staying for? Was it fair to lean on his new friends' acceptance and care while rejecting what had brought them together in the first place? And if Rachelle was right and this was somehow all part of God's purpose, then shouldn't he be willing to step out of his comfort zone, just like Eden and Josh were planning?

Brady barely caught back a snort that would have murdered his head as the last idea trailed away. Was he seriously comparing his sister committing her life to an African mission to him running around town, trying to use the bizarre side effects of his treatment to trip up petty criminals?

God, I wish I could— The silent prayer tore from his heart, but before it had even finished, something quiet and gentle stopped it in its tracks. A conviction—an assurance—maybe a peace? But whatever it was, it was enough like the confidence he had felt in coming to Detroit to make the choice one of faith and not obligation.

"You're blooming right where you're planted, Brady Ray." He could almost hear Mom's sweet Georgia drawl as she stroked his hair while he lay on the couch the first time his head had kept him home from youth camp. He'd cried at first—tried not to show it—but later in the afternoon she'd walked in on him whispering scripture to himself and joined in softly in what had become one of their most special memories. And when his words had begun to slur as his exhausted body took over, she'd kissed his throbbing forehead and whispered, "God'll get you where He wants you. You just do your best while you're there, okay?"

"I'll come back in a little bit." It was Rachelle's voice this time, not a memory, and Brady drew a deep breath and caught her hand before she could leave.

"No. Tell the doctor—I'm ready."

Chapter Three

"Soon, baby." The quiet words drew him gently out of slumber, not as though they were trying to wake him but as though he'd slept long enough and it was time to rejoin the rhythms of life. "You know Dr. Mattox needs to make him sleep before she gives him the shot."

"Why do you have to sleep to get your superpowers?" The second voice was smaller, shriller, and somehow a little bit muffled in comparison to the first. Grace. Waiting for him to wake up from the sedative the doctor had insisted on?

"Because it might not be fun to be awake when your body is changing so much all at once." The first voice again. Rachelle. With an excellent point, as usual. Forget the thought of skipping the sedative. Someone else could guinea pig that idea.

"But what if I have to go to school before he wakes up?"

Brady blinked his eyes open and turned his head, expecting to see messy curls peeking through a half-open door, but instead it was closed and latched tightly, just as Rachelle had left it. Memories of his first injection washed over him, and Brady forced a deep breath as he sat up, burying his face in his knees as the recalled panic threatened to consume him.

It was different this time. It *was*. He knew what was happening now—mostly. And he'd learned to control it—sort of. Plus, he'd chosen it for himself this time, so he was just going to have to learn to deal. Concentrate on here, now, the things that were right in front of him. Or the things that somehow—maybe God?—pressed on his senses from farther away. Like Grace.

Pushing out of bed, Brady gave himself just a second to appreciate the absence of pain before pulling the door open to find Rachelle and Grace standing just across the hall. At least he hadn't picked up conversation from two hallways over this time. That was improvement, right?

Grace didn't utter a word as she flung herself across the short distance, and Brady barely had time to lean down and catch her before she would have—he wasn't entirely sure what. Probably wrapped herself around his legs or something, considering her velocity and their respective heights. He scooped her up in his arms instead, and she hugged him tight, fisting her hands in his shirt. Brady gritted his teeth as his skin protested the irrationally painful bunches.

"Careful, baby," Rachelle murmured, and Grace relaxed her grip a little and looked up at him.

"Does hugging make you hurt?"

"Not most times. It's just—remember I can feel things most people can't? That's all over my skin, I guess, and I'm not used to it yet."

"But you can get used to it today!" Grace wriggled in his arms, and Brady set her carefully back on the floor. "Can you be a hero again? Can you stop bad guys? Can you take me up to carpool?"

"Um…maybe, no idea, and sure, I think?"

Rachelle hid a smile, but Grace just blinked at him blankly, and Brady gave a tiny chuckle.

"Carpool. Let's start with carpool, okay? What time is it, and do I have time to change first?" He motioned to the sweat-damp t-shirt and shorts he'd slept in, and Rachelle nodded.

"We've still got a quarter hour or so. Go ahead. Grace can be patient." The hint of emphasis on the last word was obviously not meant for him, and Grace sighed in response.

"Okay. But please don't go very slow."

"Deal." Brady offered a grin before retreating into his room, where he quickly readied himself for the day. When he came out again, Grace was sitting against the door of the empty room across the hall, slumped with her chin in her hands, but she jumped up immediately, grabbed his hand, and tugged him over to where Rachelle waited in the common.

"Hurry! We'll make Mrs. Jackson late!" Grace reached one hand out to Rachelle but kept hold of Brady's with the other as she bounced on her toes, and they exchanged amused looks over her head.

"Mrs. Jackson won't be late for another few minutes, baby. And how do you ask?"

"Can we go up now, *please*?" The little girl started to sag to her knees, letting her weight dangle from their arms, and Rachelle caught her breath sharply.

"Grace, don't pull!"

As soon as the words left her lips, Brady was reaching for Grace's other hand, but she was back on her feet in the same instant, dropping Rachelle's hand like it burned and jamming her thumb into her mouth. Rachelle gave a little moan, and Brady hesitated, not sure which to try to help, but Rachelle dropped to her knees and wrapped both arms around her sister.

"It's okay. It's okay, baby. I'm okay. I promise. You didn't hurt me. You remembered in time. It was an accident. I know that."

Grace mumbled something around her thumb that might have been "I forgot," and Brady swallowed a lump in his throat as Rachelle's next breath shuddered.

"I know you did. Just like I forget sometimes. Just like we all do. I'm not mad at you, baby. I got scared for a second, and there wasn't time to say, 'Grace, please remember not to pull on my arms like that because my bones like to pop out of their places and I'm not super strong today.' That's the only reason I yelled. I'm sorry."

"Me too," Grace whispered, and a little wet hand finally edged around Rachelle's back in a tentative hug. Brady shot a glance at the clock but waited another few seconds before crouching beside them.

"Want a ride up today, Gracie-girl?"

Grace immediately wrapped her arms around his neck and held on hard, and Brady lifted her onto his hip as he stood. Rachelle rose from her place on the floor and took a step back, seemingly very interested in the toes of her shoes. Quickly checking to make sure Grace's head was turned away, Brady brushed her sister gently with an elbow.

"Hey." Watery chocolate eyes raised to meet his, and he mouthed the next words as quietly as possible. "You okay?"

She nodded quickly, but her smile stayed at only half-strength, and Brady considered offering to take Grace up himself but hesitated, unsure if it would make things better or worse.

"Are you coming, Ellie?" Grace's right hand loosened on his neck, like it was in danger of reaching for her mouth, and Rachelle lifted her chin and took a quick, shaky breath.

"Yeah, baby. I'm coming. We'd better hurry for Mrs. Jackson, huh?"

Grace nodded emphatically, and her sticky fingers attached themselves to Brady's neck again as Rachelle followed him out of the den and to the nearest elevator.

Ears tuned as they were to catch the slightest noise of distress from Rachelle, Brady was in no way prepared for the cacophony that greeted him when they emerged onto the main level of the medical center. Dozens of voices, each somehow distinct amid the combined babble. Groans, sighs, and coughs. Whirring machines, hissing tubes, and beeping monitors. A low but grating clatter and squeak of trays, spoons, and cups that almost curled his toes.

Brady closed his eyes and clutched Grace tighter for an instant, his entire attention focused on not dropping her as the sounds swirled and began to mix with an nauseating array of smells. Then Rachelle's hand was on his back, grounding him as always, helping him pull his awareness back to the hallway where they stood.

"Breathe. You're okay, just breathe. Do you need to put her down?"

Brady forced a deep breath, then another, and the overwhelming clatter retreated into a muffled roar. He shook his head and concentrated hard on the hallway ahead, and his senses finally adjusted and began to settle back to a normal level as they approached the main door. A new cascade of sounds and smells engulfed him when they stepped outside, but they dissolved more quickly, and Brady gave a thankful sigh as he set Grace on the ground again.

"Yay! Mrs. Jackson's the late one today!" Grace plopped down on the edge of the drive with no thought to her presumably clean school uniform, and Rachelle winced.

"Grace, that's not polite. She'll be here in a minute."

"But she says it all the time! Somebody's always the late one. Sometimes it's her, and sometimes it's me, and sometimes it's Deedra. I don't know if it's Matt sometimes. And sometimes it's Rowan that's the late one that makes her late, and sometimes it's Lonnie, and sometimes it's Tonya. And whoever's the late one makes us all late, and if we ever get to school early when we're all in the car, then she thinks she might be dead and gone to heaven."

The transformation of Rachelle's face during Grace's rambling explanation had been a study to behold. From embarrassed consternation at the outset, it had progressed first to thoughtful analysis, then to reluctant amusement, and by the time the little girl finished, her sister had clapped a hand over her mouth to hide the silent laughter that only she and Brady could hear.

"I—I believe she says that, Grace. Just don't—don't tell other grownups they're the late ones, okay? Mrs. Jackson is a special case."

"Okay!" Grace agreed without hesitation, and the next second a familiar blue minivan pulled into the circular drive. "Bye, Brady!" She turned and hugged his legs tightly, adding, "Have a good hero day!" in her too loud whisper, then took Rachelle's hand and skipped to the van.

Chapter Four

The minivan door popped open as Grace exchanged a last-minute hug with her sister, then clambered around legs and over backpacks to the empty booster seat in the far corner.

"Seatbelt quick-quick-quick, Grace!" Shavonne Jackson's voice carried clearly over a chorus of children's complaints, even after Rachelle shut the door. "Rowan, give the hat back. Matt, put it in your bag, honey. Grace, just shove the crackers on the floor. We still have to get Deedra, and I'm the super late one today."

"Ellie says that's cause you're a special case," Grace answered as the van pulled away, and Brady gasped half a laugh but dropped it suddenly as Rachelle's shoulders slumped. It only took an instant's reflection to realize that she likely hadn't heard her sister's last comment, and his earlier worry surfaced again.

"Sure you're okay?" He touched her shoulder gently, and she turned to look up at him, blinking fast to dispel the traces of moisture in her eyes.

"I'm fine." The words on their own were less than convincing, and the hard swallow at the end only strengthened the impression. Brady crossed his arms, and Rachelle sighed. "Brady, I promise. I'm not hurt. I just—" She broke off and looked away, but he waited her out, and after a moment, she spoke again. "It's so unfair to her. She's lost so much—her parents, her home, everything she knew. She was only four. And I can't even let her swing from my arms like a normal little kid."

Brady winced. He didn't have an answer to her pain. How often had he lamented the limitations that his own illness had placed on Eden? And he was only a baby brother, not an older sister and guardian to boot. But as he played her words back in his mind, he realized she'd left out an important piece of the equation.

"She still has you, Rachelle. I know it's not what you would choose, but you mean a lot to her. You know that, don't you?"

Rachelle pressed her lips together and nodded slowly, but it was obvious that his clumsy attempt hadn't touched the root of her trouble. Regardless, she took a deep breath and straightened her shoulders, then smiled up at him.

"Come on. You need to get breakfast if you're doing this today. Car'll be here in a few minutes."

"Rachelle…"

"Brady, I mean it. We can talk later. There's plenty of time. And I'm letting it go, okay? I don't like it, but I can't fix it, and I have to trust God to give her the things I can't. Like you carrying her. She loves that, and I love that she loves it. But you have to eat. These skills are exhausting. DeAndre said he'd work up something that'll help your energy and be easy on your stomach tomorrow, and you're going to finish it before you step foot outside again. Got it?"

The same command coming from Eden would probably have brought on a sigh or an eye roll, but Brady found a grin tugging at the corners of his mouth instead. Her protective streak was just part of her, whether that meant trying to give Grace a normal childhood or making sure he was eating. The least he could do was not fight her, especially when she was right.

"It's going to involve blueberries, isn't it?" He matched his stride to hers, trying to breathe deeply as they stepped inside and the concentrated sensations of the center hit him like a freight train again.

"Probably." Rachelle's smile deepened until it touched her eyes, and she put a hand on his elbow to steer him, freeing the rest of his focus to rein in his scattered senses. The smells grew stronger—less like sickness and more like food—as they turned into a back corridor and paused at a staff-only door that opened to Rachelle's code.

Two more turns brought them to the back wall of the kitchen and a sliding window that looked way too much like a takeout counter to belong in a medical setting, even though Brady knew its purpose was to keep unauthorized visitors from contaminating the food. Rachelle pushed it open and poked her head in, and a burly black man in a hairnet and apron, who Brady was still convinced looked more like a security guard than a nutritionist, set a cup with an unmistakable purple hue on the narrow counter. Brady tried to stifle a groan but must not have been entirely successful, judging by the man's raised eyebrow.

"You complaining?"

"Just a little?" Brady gave a tiny grimace, and DeAndre rolled his eyes.

"You want high energy, easy on the gut, no bananas, and doesn't taste like tree bark? You can stand a couple of blueberries. Just the antioxidant properties alone are worth—"

"DeAndre." Rachelle cut him off with an apologetic smile. "Can we get the nutrition homework later? Car's on the way, and Brady *won't* eat if he's distracted."

DeAndre shook his head but paused the lecture as he thumped a thermos mug next to the cup.

"Eat whatever you feel like for lunch, as long as you drink this with it. Don't do it and pass out, don't blame me. And you, sweetheart—" He slapped a cup similar to the first but with a butterscotch tone to the slush inside in front of Rachelle. "Don't tell me he's the only one who skips eating when he's focused. Two days in a row? You'll have to be sharp."

"Thanks." Rachelle lifted the cup and took a long sip, and Brady scowled.

"Seriously? Why does she get a pass? Aren't they as good for her as they are for me?"

The look the nutritionist shot him reminded Brady of his second-grade teacher, although maybe he deserved that. Was he actually whining about a meal, and to the person who'd made it, no less? He'd let bad habits creep in around Eden's attitude toward her own cooking. Mom would've had his hide.

"She's got more restrictions than you do, and it's half banana. Still want to swap?"

Brady winced and took his own cup, but in spite of the better judgment that was starting to take hold, he couldn't help asking, "So, what would you do if I was allergic?"

"Get a raise," was DeAndre's dry answer, and Brady couldn't keep a grin from breaking through. He took a sip and then tried not to choke as the one sense he hadn't attempted to calibrate that morning flooded his mouth with disparate flavors and textures.

Rachelle's hand found his arm and rubbed it gently, anchoring him as he worked to pull back his awareness to a single, unified taste. When he finally accomplished it and managed to swallow, he sucked in a deep breath, then opened his eyes to find DeAndre still watching from the window. What must that have looked like in light of his earlier complaining?

"I'm sorry. I wasn't—" Brady felt his face flush with shame, but before he could find the words to explain, DeAndre was shaking his head.

"If I had to taste every single thing I put in a dish, I think I'd become a fruit bat. Cut down as much as I could, but I'll keep looking for ways to simplify. Lean on nuts and whole grains today if you can—good for energy and not too many flavors at once. Or send word that you're coming back here, and I'll have something ready."

"Thanks."

The gratitude was genuine. While Dr. Mattox's special experiments were an open secret among the staff at the medical center, DeAndre was one of a very few who actually knew the full truth. Ostensibly, they couldn't have kept it from him because their bodies' demands were so wildly different on the days they took the injection. But from what Brady had gathered during his short time in the den, it seemed the nutritionist had slipped into the role of a sounding board and de facto mentor on all topics, no matter how far removed from food. Rachelle especially seemed to view him as an adopted uncle of sorts, and Brady was thankful that she had someone she could rely on for the kind of help and encouragement that Dr. Mattox seemed to entirely ignore.

"Keep drinking." Rachelle nudged his elbow gently and smiled over at DeAndre. "I need to go make sure Harper's awake and knows we're leaving."

"You're going with?" DeAndre raised an eyebrow, and Rachelle lifted her chin.

"First day, and we don't know how this works outside the walls of the building? You really think I'm not?"

"Just take care of yourself out there. Watch your limits, and don't forget you're *not* amped up today. Got vests for both of you?"

"Grabbing them as soon as I talk to Harper."

"All right." DeAndre studied them both for a long second before nodding. "Use your heads and be safe out there, yeah?"

Brady couldn't help the feeling that none of this really qualified as safe, but he nodded and watched as DeAndre turned back to his work before taking the thermos mug and following Rachelle back through the halls and down the stairs to the den.

Chapter Five

"Sure you've got it?" Rachelle hovered near the couch, remarkably reluctant to leave for someone who'd insisted on coming along in the first place. Brady wondered if he'd be starting to get impatient if he'd actually been looking forward to—whatever it was they expected him to do.

Harper rolled her half-lidded eyes and waved a floppy hand in the general direction of the portion of the room she occupied.

"Map. Radio. Earpiece. I'm set." She yawned. "Let's see what you can do, new kid."

Brady barely resisted a snort. By her own admission, Harper was half a year younger—not even twenty yet—and this morning she looked even more like a high schooler, with the messy blue bedhead that she hadn't even tried to tame and the silky purple short set that was probably still her pajamas.

"And Dash?" Rachelle shot a glance toward the hallway, and Harper smirked.

"He hates letting me help, but he also hates being left out of the action. My money's on he gives in eventually, but whether he gets me or a nurse is anyone's guess. If I'm wrong, I'll bug him every couple hours and make sure it's just stubbornness that's killing him and not anything worse."

For some odd reason, that promise didn't seem to comfort Rachelle, and Brady shook his head.

"You know you don't have to come. I'm sure I can handle—whatever. If he's going to need you—"

"No." Rachelle's shoulders slumped a little. "There's not much I can do anyway. If he doesn't get up, he won't want me sitting with him. As much as he hates these days, he absolutely loathes anything that feels even the slightest bit like pity."

"What are 'these days' for him?" Maybe the question was prying, but a hint of real concern tugged at Brady's chest. Dash hadn't seemed any worse than usual on the evening before he'd gotten his injection, and from a couple comments he'd dropped, it almost seemed like he'd scheduled the day in advance, so the idea of side effects coming directly from the drug and not from an existing flare was worrying to say the least.

"Higher 'on,' lower 'off' is the best Dr. Mattox can figure." Rachelle gave a little shrug that felt far too familiar to someone who'd spent hours in doctors' offices with nothing but best guesses to show for it. "Dash is different in a lot of ways. Parkinson's is progressive—it doesn't flare as much as slowly go downhill. His regular better and worse days aren't really that far apart. Not like ours. So he can have the injections basically whenever, but his system reacts pretty hard the day after. Since we have no idea what they'd do closer together, he's limited to one every two weeks. That seems pretty safe for the rest of us, and it's not accelerating the decline as far as we can tell. He'd take them more often if he could, and chance the consequences, but even Dr. Mattox isn't willing to try it."

There was a low murmur from somewhere, and Brady jumped and glanced around, almost expecting to see Dash glaring at them from the door, but Harper grinned and tapped her earpiece.

"Get going, Rachelle. Car's waiting. I can do the no-pity thing better than you can, and maybe it's my day to prove it. Or—ooh, if Dash sticks to his room, then I have the whole place to myself! Maybe I'll redecorate."

"Oh, please no!" Brady winced at the rudeness of the words as they left his mouth, but if Harper's taste for bright colors and loud patterns took over more than her outfits and the occasional throw pillow, there was no way his head would survive.

"Are you trying to convince me to leave or stay?" Rachelle raised a skeptical eyebrow at her, and Harper giggled.

"Leave! Find a mission that needs backup so I can keep busy without painting the walls."

"I'm pretty sure that's a threat." Brady turned to Rachelle, who gave a resigned sigh.

"We're leaving. We're leaving! Watch the radio, and put that devious mind to work figuring out how Brady can help, will you?"

"Oh, and you still need a hero name!" Harper propped herself up on an elbow, looking really alert for the first time that morning. "Any ideas? I mean, Brady is cool, but not nearly enough for a superhero."

"I thought you wanted us to go." Rachelle stuck her hands on her hips, and Harper waved an arm dismissively.

"Yes, get moving. We'll brainstorm from a distance. I'll ask Dash for ideas when he wakes up too. Car's got to be incredibly bored up there. Go!"

"Wait…" Brady was still trying to process her last words, but Rachelle scooped a pile of dark blue fabric out of a bin and tugged his arm.

"Come on, before she thinks of something else. This could go on all day. Harper, call if you need something, okay?"

"You got it, Mama Midge!"

Brady tried to smother a snort as he followed Rachelle down the hall but didn't completely succeed, and Rachelle shook her head.

"I should warn you, if you care at all about what you're called, you'd better think of something yourself. 'I don't need a superhero name' is apparently not an option to those two, and you *will* be stuck with whatever they settle on."

"I take it 'Mighty Midge' wasn't your idea?" Brady grinned at her as they stepped into the elevator, and she shot him an unamused look.

"Dash's. And Grace thought it was funny, so I didn't react beyond an eye roll. I figured it'd fade in a month or two, but as you can see…"

The elevator door opening prevented an answer, and Brady concentrated on keeping his senses centered while hopefully not drawing too much attention. He had no idea how well he'd done on the last part, but at least the first was a little easier than it had been before.

"You're doing great," Rachelle whispered, and Brady managed to shake his head without scattering his focus.

"I feel like it shouldn't keep hitting so hard. I need to get better at this."

"Given that it's only your second day, and this floor's so crowded, and you haven't passed out once, I'd say you're getting much better. I always end up throwing something across the room first thing in the morning. It takes time to calibrate."

"If you say so."

"Trust me." Rachelle's smile was impossible to resist, even if it didn't cure his own doubts about how well he was adjusting. Instead of heading for the front entrance, she led him through staff doors and along side hallways until they stepped out into a back parking lot, where the smell from two massive dumpsters hit him with the force of a firehose.

Brady couldn't help a gasp, which was exactly the wrong move, as both his mouth and nose were now flooded with the foul air. Rachelle's voice was saying something, but he couldn't process it—couldn't focus on anything but trying not to gag. He was dimly aware of movement—some of it his own—and finally the choking smell began to fade, leaving him panting for breath and slumped weakly against the seat of a car that Rachelle had somehow gotten him to. A car that was apparently moving—yeah, that wasn't disorienting at all—and had already left the medical center behind.

"You back with us?" Rachelle asked softly, and he met her eyes, hoping that would be answer enough until he got more of his breath back. "Brady, I am so, so sorry. I didn't even think. Car always meets us there because—well, it's quieter, and I was nervous, and

Harper would draw attention opening a door. Not you, though. Not ever again. Especially not in the mornings, when you've barely had time to adjust. I don't know why I didn't remember—"

"Rachelle." The word came out raspy, and he had to cough to clear his throat, but he managed to reach over and lay a hand on the one that gripped his arm. "Not your fault. Normal people don't have to pay attention to how much trash they walk past, or how bad it would smell kicked up by about a thousand. I've got to learn to deal."

"With normal trash, maybe. Not with that awful stuff hitting you right in the face. You don't have to adjust to everything. We can change things too."

"Noted. Front door pickup for super senses." The new voice came from the front seat, and Brady jerked his head up to note the driver for the first time—a young woman with warm chestnut skin, long thick braids, and eyes so dark they almost blended into her pupils. "Quite an introduction, new guy." She grinned at him in the mirror even as she deftly changed lanes to pass a turning car. "I'm guessing from Shadow's commentary that you don't have a code name yet, so I won't ask. I'm Carmel Manigault. Your personal driver and general, all-around sidekick. And don't worry about my rates; the doc pays for these days, so I'm totally at your service."

"You're—what?" Brady blinked, and Carmel's mouth quirked up at the corner.

"Reliable, discreet, and available is what I am, on top of being an excellent driver. And DeAndre's cousin, so I know how to keep my mouth shut."

"There's no good way to get around in Detroit without driving," Rachelle put in, and Brady's eyes jumped back to her face. "I got my license by the skin of my teeth, but it's murder on my joints, and I don't want to know what would happen if I tried it on the injection. Try to hit the brake fast or tweak the wheel a little too hard—" She grimaced, and Brady shivered at the thought. "Add in the accidents you'd get with an invisible Harper behind the wheel, even if she had her license, and what would happen if your senses suddenly kicked in on the road, and yeah. Car's the obvious solution."

"I'll take obvious." Carmel winked back at her from where she'd stopped at a red light. "It's way more fun than carting random strangers around, or dropping off groceries and takeout. Mr. McSpeedy's the only exception, and I'm still planning to get a look at his face one of these days."

"You know he can't hear you, right?" Harper's distant voice suddenly broke in on the conversation from two directions, and Rachelle quickly fitted her earpiece while Carmel stole a glance at her phone.

"Oh, I know it. Doesn't mean I give him a break."

"Even though he's legitimately faster without you?"

"Never said he had to use me. But the hiding out so I can't even catch a look at him is getting pretty silly, don't you think?"

"She and Dash have a bit of a feud going." Rachelle smiled as she held out a second earpiece. "I've got this on the lowest setting. See if it doesn't blast your eardrums and still lets you concentrate. Car, can we swing by a drugstore? I need to pick up a couple things before we get started."

Brady's attention was distracted for a minute by Harper's cheerful "testing" monologue in his ear, but when the words belatedly registered, he gave Rachelle a bewildered look. Then suddenly the pieces came together, and he shot one disbelieving stare at Carmel, then buried his face in his hands.

"Rachelle." The word came out as almost a moan. "For the love of everything right and proper in the world, please tell me you do not call your *driver* 'Car.'"

Chapter Six

"You got a problem with my name, Ginger?" When Brady looked up, Carmel was raising an eyebrow at him in the mirror, although a hint of a saucy smile lingered on her lips.

"Ohhh…" Somewhere amid the stereo sound of Carmel's phone and his earpiece, Harper was devolving into moans of laughter. "That is too perfect. We've got to make that part of your hero name."

"Over my dead body!" Brady could feel his cheeks flushing almost as red as his hair. Not that he actually cared what ridiculous code name they slapped on him, but being stuck with "ginger" forever was a bridge much too far.

"Harper, be serious." Rachelle looked like she was fighting a smile, but she somehow managed to keep her voice even. "That's a Car-level nickname, not nearly cool enough for a superhero."

"Wow, thaaanks." Carmel drawled the word out sarcastically, but Harper gave a little sigh and subsided, and Brady shot a grateful glance at Rachelle.

"And as for Car, I swear we're not the only ones." Rachelle gave a helpless shrug, her tone almost apologetic. "She's been called that since—"

"Since I was knee high to a toad and grabbing my brothers' Hot Wheels." Carmel's grin was back in full force. "You call a boy Jet, you're setting him up for a pilot. Call a girl Car, you're just asking her to drive. So get over yourself and don't try to fight it, or I'll scrape up a couple hundred more ginger jokes and spring them on you one at a time until you're begging for mercy."

"All right! I give. I'm begging!" Brady held up his hands with a groan. "Call yourself whatever you want. Just—" He broke off helplessly, and Carmel smirked.

"You'll fall to the dark side before you know it. In the meantime, I also accept 'Her Royal Highness, Miss Manigault, Empress of the Universe.' That's all one title; don't split it up."

"Wouldn't dream of it." Brady rolled his eyes as he let himself relax against the seat, just in time for Car to pull the—he was so not doing this!—to pull her vehicle into the parking lot of a small drugstore.

"You want to come with or stay here?" Rachelle's tone offered no judgment for either option, and Brady hesitated just a second, glancing between her and Carmel, then at the store.

"Come with. No time like the present, right?"

"No problem taking it slow either. But you're welcome to come. Car, we'll be right back."

"I'll be here, Captain." Car gave a sloppy little two-fingered salute as they climbed out of the sedan. Brady noted for the first time that the model was at least a few years old with a handful of scuffs and scratches in the gold paint job—not a beater or a show-piece, but a good, solid working car.

"So, does *it* have a name?" He cast a last look over his shoulder at the vehicle as he fell into step next to Rachelle, and her brow creased.

"Does what?"

"The actual car. Or do you legitimately ask Car to bring *the* car?"

"Well, they're usually together for all practical purposes, so it's not really necessary." Rachelle's face creased in a smile again. "But yes, she calls the car Tanner. I don't ever think to call it that, but she'd be tickled pink if you did."

"Can you guarantee me she didn't name it after its color?"

"How badly do you want me to lie to you?"

"Never mind." Brady shook his head, and Rachelle chuckled.

"She's extremely good at pointing out the obvious, in case you didn't notice. You'll get used to it before too long. Ready?" She reached for the door handle, and Brady drew a deep breath and nodded.

A wave of sound rushed over him as they stepped inside the store, over and above the too loud bell in his ear. Pills rattled and bags crackled in a back room; shoes squeaked and scuffed in the aisles; a harsh, barking cough broke from a child's throat, followed by a weak moan. Brady turned toward the sound without conscious thought, and his gaze focused in on a young mother three aisles down, lugging an infant car seat on one arm and holding a clearly sick and clingy toddler with the other as she scanned the shelves of cough syrup. But as though just the sight of the familiar boxes had opened the floodgate, a cascade of smells rushed in—fake cherry and bubble gum, menthol and cheap perfume, too many variants of soap, shampoo, and lotion. Brady gritted his teeth to keep his mouth shut this time and reached for a shelf to steady himself against the dizzying rush, but the buildup of gritty dust and oily fingerprints and vaguely sticky residue that met his fingers nearly sent his stomach over the edge.

"Deep breaths," Rachelle murmured, and for once he shook his head, afraid that another inhale would finish him. "Then any breaths at all. You have to breathe, Brady. I know it's a lot. Find something to focus on."

Her voice was already helping to quiet the noise, although sound was the least of his worries right now. Brady drew a shallow breath that still swam with scents, although maybe not quite as badly since he was braced for it, and worked to concentrate on the wall.

"That's it. Good. Maybe see if you can find one smell and isolate it. Wait here, okay? I'm going to grab a couple of things, and I'll be right back."

Brady managed a nod and tried to center his focus on the overflowing bulletin board next to the door, in hope that the flood of words would engage his mind enough to dull his senses. Rachelle's advice was rarely wrong, but most of the smells he could identify well enough to isolate at the moment were not the kind he wanted to dwell on. Instead, he attempted to keep his breaths steady and shallow as he cataloged the disparate items. A tear-off for a kid's lawn-care business. An introductory deal for a new hair salon. Business cards for a dog breeder, dog groomer, and dog kennel, all at the same address. A laminated newspaper clipping for a local youth soccer team. A too dark copy of a handmade missing poster, showing two pictures of a teenage girl—one most likely a school yearbook photo, and the other an off-center cell phone shot of the same girl with her arm around a preteen boy, whose face was scrunched in disgust.

The little boy looked nothing like him. The girl looked nothing like Eden. But the pose was one he'd seen in too many Christmas-card outtakes, and a lump formed in Brady's throat as the scent of cherry-blossom shampoo disentangled itself from the swirling mass and brought a hint of moisture to his eyes.

Bet you'd give anything for one of those hugs now. Brady blinked hard against the threatening tears, unable to pull his gaze away as a prayer for the family rose in his heart. He wasn't sure exactly how long he'd stood there, but after a while, the barest hint of lavender mixed with the cherry blossoms, and Rachelle laid a gentle hand on his arm.

"You okay?" she asked gently, and Brady gave a faint nod.

"Yeah, I—" He had to stop and clear his throat for a second before continuing. "I'm fine."

Rachelle followed his line of sight and gave a little hum of sympathy.

"It happens too often. God, take these people off our streets for good."

Brady knew instinctively that her prayer wasn't directed at the missing girl but at whoever was responsible for her disappearance. He added a whispered "amen" before Rachelle pointed him out of the store and back to the waiting sedan.

"How'd it go?" Car started the engine and turned to look over her shoulder as she backed out, and Brady sighed.

"Not good. What use is this if it takes me five minutes to adjust every time I walk into a building?"

"Yeah, you sounded pretty rough for a while there." Harper's voice from his ear startled him almost as badly as the reminder that she'd been there all along. For all her playfulness and teasing, at least it seemed like she knew how to keep her mouth shut when necessary.

"We'll figure it out." Rachelle put a gentle hand on his arm. "We don't know exactly how it works yet. It's still early, and there were a lot of chemicals and fragrances in there. New ones, that you hadn't had to adjust to before. Am I wrong, or are you more comfortable outside?"

"Maybe." Now that she mentioned it, he didn't really have to concentrate as hard outdoors to keep his senses from flying everywhere. "How does that make sense? You'd think there's way more going on outside the walls than in them. And it's not like walls matter to this—thing—anyway."

"There's more going on outside, sure, but there's more space for it to dissipate. The walls probably reflect and hold things in. Car, drive us around a little bit. Show Brady some of the tourist places. We're going to experiment."

"Lab Lady with the plan." Carmel saluted in the mirror, and Brady squinted at her.

"Lab Lady? Is that supposed to be Rachelle?"

"It's her mild-mannered alter ego. When she's not Mighty Midge, cleaning up neighborhoods and striking fear in the hearts of criminals, she's Lab Lady, aspiring scientist and part-time research assistant. Could have been one of the greatest scientific minds of our generation if her body and her sister hadn't—"

"Carmel Esmee!" There was real distress mixed with the embarrassment in Rachelle's tone, and the other girl subsided. Rachelle closed her eyes for a second before turning back to Brady. "It's not like she makes it sound. I was working on a biology degree, but super slowly. Lab days were murder on my joints. It's something I'm interested in, but not something I can actually do for that long. Dr. Mattox lets me work for her part-time to pay for Grace's school, but it's just entering data, transcribing reports, that kind of thing. And she's super flexible, which I need for obvious reasons."

Brady hadn't missed the hours Rachelle spent on her laptop, but he hadn't put it together with Dr. Mattox, or where she was getting the money to care for Grace. His heart hurt for how much it must cost her, adaptive aids or not, but that didn't explain the pleading, almost frightened look in her eyes as she waited for his answer.

"And?" he prompted gently, and Rachelle blinked at him in confusion.

"And what?"

"Why wouldn't you want me to know that? I never got a chance to even think about college, but I love that you tried for it. And the way you take care of Grace? I think it's incredible—let alone figuring out how any of this works. Why would I think less of you for that?"

"I just—it isn't—" Rachelle stumbled for words, and Brady felt a prick of fear invade his heart. "I do—work for Dr. Mattox, but—the den—it's different. I'm not—a researcher. Not an assistant. It's not a job—there."

Understanding hit Brady like a wave. Their situation was beyond unorthodox—the injections, secrecy, and permanent monitors a stark reminder of the bizarre experiment that was their lives. Rachelle was the one constant they could almost always count on—willing to push past all but the worst of her pain at the slightest hint of a need from anyone. And if she was acting as the doctor's assistant—watching and taking notes on them like rats in a lab—then any illusion of normalcy, of home life, of anything approaching friendship was completely and irreparably shattered.

Chapter Seven

"Rachelle…"

She closed her eyes and stiffened, as if preparing for a blow, and Brady sighed. After a second, he reached over and touched her hand, and she raised startled, misty eyes to his face.

"You really think you're that good of an actor?" A slight smile touched his lips, and Rachelle's forehead creased. "That you could what—watch us? Write us up? Spy on us, day in and day out, and never show the tiniest hint of guilt that anyone could pick up on? Because I can guarantee you, you'd make a terrible agent."

Rachelle gave a little, startled laugh that was almost half a sob and rubbed hurriedly at her eyes, and a soft snort came over the earpiece.

"Plus, if everything she does around here is on Mattox's payroll, either she owes me a really fancy shopping trip or the doc needs reporting to the labor commission."

"Come on, Chelle." Car's voice from the front was softer than Brady had heard yet. "I don't even live there, and I still know better than that. It's your *good* alter ego—saving the world one piece of knowledge gained at a time. Eyes right, Spy Boy; that's Little Caesars Arena. You into basketball? Hockey? Concerts?"

"Yeah…" Brady drawled the word out with the deepest ironic tone he could muster. "You've never had a migraine, have you?"

"Sorry. Crowds get to you?"

"Not the crowds so much. Noise. Lights. Especially reverberating off the walls." Even the portable speakers of a visiting gospel quartet had laid him out for days; the thought of a full-blown concert made him dizzy in spite of the injection. Maybe Rachelle had a point about confined spaces.

"Not a sports fan, then?" Carmel's hand seemed to hover over her turn signal for an instant, and Brady shrugged.

"Open air might be better, but it's too much to plan and too much to pay for a ticket I might not be able to use. I track baseball mostly, but on TV or radio."

"Perfect. Look left, then. That's St. John's Episcopal—" Brady barely had time to wonder how the massive old stone church was supposed to be any better than the arena for acoustic purposes before Carmel finished triumphantly. "—and *that's* Comerica Park."

Brady shook his head and bit back a grin as he looked. It was a nice-looking stadium, as those things went, but there had been way too much pride in her words.

"You know, that's a thought. Maybe I will try to catch a game up here. What do the tickets sell for—three bucks?"

"Oh, please! What are you, a Cleveland fan?" Car's indignant tone confirmed he'd hit exactly the spot he was aiming for, and Brady quit trying to hide his smile.

"Hardly. Braves family for generations. Of course, we've actually been *good* some of those years."

"Oh, no, you did *not*!" To Carmel's credit, she didn't take her hands from the wheel or her eyes from the road, although the way she glanced at the lot in front of the stadium made him wonder if she was actually considering pulling over. "Four back to back divisions!"

"In the AL Central…" The words drawled out to the accompaniment of slow claps. "Wow…"

"And a pennant!"

"How many years ago?" Brady coughed it into his fist, trying hard not to dissolve into laughter. He hadn't had anyone to talk sports with since he'd left Josh behind with Eden, and even then the debates had been harder to come by, since his brother-in-law-to-be (he hoped) held almost all the correct team loyalties.

"Within my lifetime!"

"That's not bad. If you were six."

"So we're rebuilding." Car shot him a scowl in the mirror as she waited for the light, and Brady shook his head solemnly.

"Y'all don't need a builder, but you'd better sign a jeweler, 'cause that's the only way you're ever getting your hands on a ring."

"Oh, it is *so* on, Super Snout." She slapped the steering wheel just as the light turned green but somehow didn't miss a beat with the pedal. "What do you want to bet we take the series this year?"

"The Series?" That was upping the ante if he'd ever heard it, but Car huffed a disgusted breath.

"Not the Series series, Tomahawk Boy. Our series with you. If we come out at least one up, what'll you give me?"

"My mama taught me better than to gamble." Brady narrowed his eyes half-playfully, and Car rolled hers.

"Forget money. If we take you, you wear a Tigers cap your next day out."

"Think I'll plan on being sick that day," Brady whispered in a pretend aside, catching Rachelle's smile from where she sat watching them. "And what's your end? *When* we beat you?"

"You're telling me you didn't pack a single ball cap?"

"I'm telling you a Braves cap would be a trade *up*. I'll buy you a Guardians cap or something."

"You got a mean streak a mile wide, you know that?"

"Worth it?" Brady smirked, and Car growled.

"I'll think about it. Left. Ford Field. Say whatever about the Lions. I don't really care."

"Me neither. Never got into football."

"Figures." Car shook her head, and Brady leaned back in his seat, grinning harder than he had in months.

"Did you get…any of that?" Harper's voice in his ear was utterly baffled, and Brady muffled a snort as Rachelle replied.

"No, but I think they're bonding."

"I'll *bond* him to something," Car muttered, but the corner of her mouth twitched up. "Better yet, if the cops pick him up, I *won't* be bonding him anywhere."

"Aww, did the poor little tiger get her tail tweaked?" Brady teased, and he caught the beginning of the hiss in her throat just in time to block her playful claw swipe with a chop of his own.

"We need cameras on this! I don't know what I'm missing," Harper moaned. "Help me out, Midge. Are they going to kill each other or marry each other?"

Rachelle choked on a squeak, and Brady's jaw dropped as his face flamed, but Car broke into real, full-throated laughter.

"Oh, Shadow, I need you in my life, girl! And don't worry, Scarlett O'Hara. Your awful baseball tastes aside, a boyfriend's the last thing I've got time for right now."

"Good!" That had probably come off ruder than he meant it. Brady dropped his head into his hand, only to realize it was the one still covered in microscopic dust and residue from the pharmacy shelf. He shuddered as he tried to brush off the sensation with his other hand, and Rachelle passed him a baby wipe that had miraculously sprung from somewhere.

Brady breathed a sigh of relief as the invisible dirt melted away, but his mind continued to race. What would have made Harper say that? Had he come across as flirting? Had he *been* flirting? He certainly hadn't meant to, but he'd barely known any girls besides Eden since he'd started high school. Sure, he'd meant to be teasing, but not *that* kind of teasing. And even if Car thankfully wasn't interested, what was to stop him from giving some other random girl the completely wrong impression?

"Hey. Mr. Sensitive." Something shifted in Carmel's tone, and Brady lifted his eyes hesitantly to the mirror. "You should know, Shadow's alter-ego is some variety of dreamy romance enthusiast. Haven't decided if she ends up a screenwriter or a novelist or something boring with a secret passion for sappy love stories. But either way, she sees it everywhere. Baseball talk tells me I'm right where I'm supposed to be—just another one of the guys. Ever want to tell a girl more than that, you'll have to do *way* better."

Her mouth resumed its mischievous quirk, and Brady ducked his head, but he felt his own smile returning as his face began to cool.

"Aww, did I embarrass him? That's so cute!" Harper giggled, and Rachelle shook her head.

"I'll show you cute when I turn you off," Brady threatened, and Car chuckled.

"Come on, Shadow, you're my only company today. Be good. Bet you'll have at least a dozen spied-on love stories to make up when Eagle Eyes here gets his act together."

"Speaking of which." Rachelle cut in with a little sigh. "Car, can you find us a place to park for a while? Somewhere we won't be conspicuous. It's time to get some answers."

Chapter Eight

"What do you mean, they don't have a record of it?" A blonde woman in a stylish but conservative skirt suit paced the length of her office back and forth in sets of three quick strides. An incomprehensible murmur came from the phone in her hand, and the woman's scowl deepened further. "They'd better get it done fast! I've got a docket in half an hour, and I will absolutely throw you under the bus if I have to face the judge without it."

"What's going on?" Harper whispered in Brady's ear, and he hissed a quick "shh" as the woman in the other building broke in on the voice from the phone again.

"No you don't, Martin! Who ate the last muffin from the box *with my name on it*? If I have to face Judge Bryant on an empty stomach, that's a hundred percent on you. Now fix it!" She dropped her phone back onto her desk as she continued to pace, and Brady couldn't help a chuckle.

"What?" Harper begged, and Brady let his concentration lapse as he returned to her voice and the sounds of the parking garage.

"Nothing. Breakfast crisis."

"In the prosecutor's office?"

"What, you think lawyers don't eat?"

"I think you've got to have seen something more interesting in there than a breakfast discussion," Harper mumbled, and Brady's mouth quirked in a grin.

"Not sure I can tell you any more. Don't attorneys have some kind of privilege?"

"Very funny, Ear Trumpet," Car scoffed. "Pretty sure there's no way they can guard against a super spy in the next building, and either way, it's not *your* privilege."

"Yeah, well, there's nothing exciting to report. I guess Jacob Ayers has agreed to plead to count three in exchange for dropping the other two, which you'll see for yourself if you watch court tomorrow. The rest was bits and pieces—sounds like they're working with a victim who doesn't want to testify and checking up on evidence for an OWI. Believe me, the muffin discussion was the most interesting one yet."

Harper gave a little huff, and Brady leaned against the wall as he worked to focus his hearing on the building across the street again. Something touched his arm, and suddenly all his senses were entirely present in the parking garage.

"Hey. Take a break for a minute." Rachelle held out one of the packets of trail mix she'd bought at the pharmacy, and Brady took it and slid down next to the wall, feeling fatigue wash over him. He wasn't sure how she'd picked up on that before he'd even noticed himself, but he offered a grateful smile and a silent prayer of thanks as he poured out a handful of nuts and dried fruit and closed his eyes to concentrate on the flavors.

"So what have we learned so far?" Car asked quietly, and Brady heard the soft swish of Rachelle's skirt hitting the window as she must have leaned against it.

"Sight is good for at least a city block unobstructed. Works through two exterior walls and several interior, but the range is more limited, and it won't break through a third. Same issue with metal doors and large concentrations of plumbing. Not nearly as much work outside, or from inside the building he's trying to watch. And it has to be on a line with his eyes—they can go through corners, not around them."

Brady listened with an almost dispassionate interest as he took another helping of trail mix, as though she was describing the abilities of a character in a comic book and not what she'd observed in him that very morning. He had to admit she was good; he'd been too busy pushing his senses to the limit to register exactly what those limits were.

"Hearing seems to have about the same range, although it's not blocked quite as much by obstructions. Might work through that last metal door, but not too much farther. Smell's a lot more limited—one exterior wall at most, and only with hard concentration. Much easier to pick up inside a building. Guessing normal range is about a floor in either direction, but that's a hard one to test for sure. Touch needs direct contact, obviously. Same with taste for the most part."

"The most part?" Harper yawned, and Brady clenched his jaw to keep from following her example. "What is he, a snake?"

"Strong smells can manifest as taste in anybody." Rachelle gave a little sigh. "Not really a perk unless you're standing in a bakery."

Brady unconsciously took a deeper breath, then opened his eyes with a moan to meet Rachelle's concerned gaze on him.

"Do you have any idea how disappointing it is to think 'bakery' and get a lungful of tire rubber and car exhaust instead?"

Her worried look melted into a smile as she nodded at the half-full packet of trail mix.

"Finish your nuts, Brady. I know this isn't the easiest place to stay for so long. Maybe we'll make the next stop a bakery to help you reset."

"You promise?" Brady gave her his best sad puppy eyes, and Rachelle shook her head with a laugh.

"Don't start that! You're worse than Grace."

Brady attempted a smile, but a sudden crash and cry spun his head back in the direction of the office building across the street, searching for the source before the reaction even registered.

"Brady?" Rachelle asked softly, but her voice was muffled amid the hum of everyday conversation as his eyes sped down corridors, opened walls, and cut through corners, seeking the source of the sound. They finally narrowed in on a young secretary in the break room, shaking out her hand and breathing hard as she pulled gingerly at a dark brown stain on her blouse that matched the puddle on the floor. "Everything all right?"

"Yeah." Brady blew out a breath and let his eyes shut for an instant. "Mostly. Coffee spill. Pretty hot, looks like, but it's not like I can help."

"Where in the building?" Car asked, and Brady focused in and then slowly backed out again as a young man hurried into the room and knelt down next to the girl with a handful of paper towels.

"Um—off to the right—near the back somewhere—I think?"

"And you weren't 'in there' already when you heard it?"

Brady shook his head, forgetting that she couldn't see him, and Rachelle ran a gentle hand over his shoulder.

"Some sounds are meant to stand out. You hear a yell or a cry or a brake screech even if you're not listening to conversations or whatever else is going on. Just like a smoke smell or a red signal. So it makes sense that he'd pick up on danger signs quicker than anything, even from farther away."

"Sounds like it could come in handy for figuring out where to help." Car's words didn't seem to hold any irony, and Brady mentally filed the point as something to think about later. "Oh, and you guys might want to at least look like you're moving. Someone's headed your way from the elevators."

"On our way back to you. I think we're done here."

Rachelle motioned Brady off the floor and headed them back in Car's direction, nodding for him to finish the packet of trail mix. A businessman passed them in a hurry, listening intently to his cell phone, and Brady did his best to look like any other person randomly walking through a parking garage, and definitely not like someone who'd been using it as a convenient spot to test out his super senses by spying on the building next door. Whatever happened, he was certainly not spending his day doing *this* every time he had an attack.

"Okay, so I can see plenty of use keeping eyes on known fugitives, if there's a radio patrol already on it." Car hesitated a moment, and Brady wondered if he could actually hear her fingers drumming the steering wheel through her phone and his earpiece. "But what do you see him doing with the rest of these danger signals after he picks them up? No offense, Spyglass, but you don't exactly have the skills to *stop* anything, and you can't just start showing up to court every week and still stay safe on the streets—assuming not a single defense attorney has the brains to ask just where you were standing when you saw something."

A cold knot formed in Brady's stomach, and he swallowed hard. He'd given plenty of thought to the general uselessness of super senses to help much, but not to the awful situation of seeing someone hurt and not being able to do anything about it.

"I know." Rachelle sighed. "I haven't fully figured that out. We'll have to find a way of giving just the right pieces of information to someone who's capable of acting on it. Anonymous tips, maybe, if they don't get lost in the noise."

"That stinks." Harper's voice was muffled, and an unnatural discouragement laced her words. "What good's a superpower if you can't use it for anything good? Trust me, spying on random people for fun gets old *really* fast."

Brady's heart gave a silent but emphatic agreement—not that he'd ever considered spying on someone for fun, but to go around watching people without even as much purpose as he'd been able to claim this morning was *not* his idea of making a difference, or of what God's purpose for these abilities might possibly be.

"Harper, take a nap." Rachelle's tone was infinitely gentle. "There'll be a way when we need it, but you need to have your mind alert to help us find it."

Harper sighed, but Brady could hear her squirming into a more comfortable position on the couch.

"Earpiece out; I still hear your breathing," Rachelle coaxed, and Harper groaned.

"Who's going to be your backup? Dash still hasn't woken up."

"We'll take it easy for a while. Brady could use a rest, and when we need you, we'll need you sharp."

Harper gave a noncommittal grunt, and a hint of a smile touched the corner of Brady's mouth.

"Get some sleep, Harper. I kind of wish I could trade places with you right now."

"And that settles it." They had reached Car's spot, and Rachelle climbed in and shut her door with a snap of decision. "Car, find us a park. We're all taking a break."

CHAPTER NINE

Despite his purported envy of Harper, Brady hadn't actually meant to fall asleep. But as the sensations around him faded in slowly—the rough fabric of the blanket from Car's trunk beneath him, the sharp scent of freshly cut grass surrounding him, the soft rustle of leaves and twitter of birds in the trees overhead—he knew that he had.

Lovely. A couple hours of using his senses at full capacity and he was tired enough to actually fall asleep, despite the nuts that were supposed to replenish his energy. Couldn't he get anything approaching a normal day even on the injection, without having to be watched and coddled and sent off for a nap like an invalid? Granted, an invalid was pretty much exactly what he was, but what good were the injections if they didn't help with that?

He heaved a sigh and opened his eyes to see Rachelle leaning against the tree next to him, watching him with a soft smile.

"Sleep well?"

"Unfortunately." Brady groaned as he pushed himself to his elbows, and Rachelle's forehead creased.

"You'd rather what? Sleep badly?"

"How about not fall asleep in the middle of the morning on the one day I can actually do something useful?"

"Brady…" The shade of sorrow in her eyes matched her voice, and she shook her head slowly. "Why do you hold yourself to a standard you wouldn't put on anyone else?"

"What?" He squinted at her, not comprehending, and she motioned toward her earpiece.

"Do you think less of Harper for falling asleep before you did, or staying asleep longer?"

"That's different."

"How?"

"It's not her day out."

"Then Dash is a wimp for giving in when I made him rest yesterday?"

"Of course not."

Rachelle raised an eyebrow and crossed her arms, and Brady groaned.

"Rachelle, be serious. How is what I've been doing for the last couple of hours remotely comparable to the kind of insane workout he gets?"

"You really think the human body was made to take in and process as much information as you are, from as far away as you're getting it? That's got to take an incredible amount of brain power, not to mention eye strain. Hey." She touched his arm as he started to look away. "Don't do this. It's a different skill set, and maybe more mental than physical, but that doesn't mean your body doesn't feel it. And it's only your second day. Give it time to adjust, and stop acting like you have to prove yourself. We're still testing all of this out, and I'm going to make you go slow until we're sure of your limits. Blame me in your head if you want. I won't mind."

Brady only managed a huff at the ridiculous suggestion before a sudden cry brought him instantly alert.

"Stop! Please stop!" The voice was a child's, and Brady felt a thrill of fear shoot through him as he spun his head in the direction it had come from. His gaze shot past the handful of women talking in a picnic pavilion and centered on the little cluster of children's play equipment. Two boys were standing on either side of a small merry-go-round, spinning it faster and faster as a smaller boy lay on top, quivering and clutching the middle pole for dear life.

"Brady?" Rachelle's voice was muffled as he scrambled to his feet. The child's terrified cries were slipping into nearly inaudible sobs, and Brady took off at a run without waiting to explain.

Dash's super speed would have come in handy about now, but when he reached the tiny playground, the situation was the same as when he'd first spotted it—only the merry-go-round was spinning faster and the little boy was shaking harder. The others entirely ignored his presence until he gripped one of the handles, slowing the equipment without slamming it to a stop that would have jarred the kid even more. The other boys set up a cry of protest, and Brady stuck one hand on his hip as he reached for the next handle to slow the spin further.

"Hey, yourselves. When someone tells you to stop, you have to stop. You wouldn't like it if someone wouldn't let you off when you wanted it."

One of the boys dropped his eyes to his shoes, but the other glowered, and from the contemptuous look he shot at the little one, Brady couldn't help wondering if there had been more to the situation than mostly innocent fun. The merry-go-round creaked to a stop, and the shorter boy slid off and fell to his knees, his face drained of all color.

"You okay?" Brady crouched next to him, and the little boy drew a shaky breath.

"Excuse me!" The words hit his ears like a bullhorn, and Brady jumped and tried not to wince as he jerked his head up to where an angry woman stood towering over him with her hands on her hips. He instinctively straightened, but the extra inches didn't deter the woman from continuing to invade what even the narrowest of definitions would have counted as his personal space. "What do you think you're doing, accosting children in the park?"

"I was—" The two words were the only ones that reached his lips before the woman jabbed a very sharp finger at his chest.

"You have nothing to say! You're lucky I'm not calling the police. How dare you come over here and bully these children right under their mothers' noses?"

"Ma'am—" Brady tried again, but the boy who so far hadn't quit scowling at him suddenly burst into tears and threw himself at the woman's side, wailing at an ear-piercing frequency as more women arrived from the picnic table.

One of the newcomers scooped up the littlest boy, who was shaking harder than before and promptly threw up all down her back. She retreated in a flurry of mingled shrieks and attempts at comfort, leaving the angry woman now flanked by two others. One of them grabbed the third boy, while the other stepped between Brady and a pair of children playing on the swing set that he hadn't even noticed.

"You should be ashamed of yourself!" The woman jabbed her finger into his chest again, and Brady nearly gasped at the sharp stab. "Terrorizing little children on their own playground! I ought to report you for harassment!"

"They were—" Brady made one last attempt, but the woman's face darkened with fury, and a quick rush of air was his only warning before a hand caught him full on the cheek, snapping his head to the side so hard that his vision blurred.

"Leave him alone! What do you think you're doing?" The indignant voice rang in his ears as a jumble of sounds from the park, the street, and every building within a block's radius blared and faded in and out like someone was cranking a radio dial. His cheek was ablaze with pain—burning, aching, and tingling all at once—and it was all he could do to keep his feet.

"Don't you dare blame these innocent children for your own twisted motives! If you had even an ounce of self-respect, you'd be out holding down a decent job, not stalking babies in a park! And I'd suggest *you* keep your creep of a boyfriend away from here in the future if you don't want to see him arrested."

"This is a public park, and we have just as much right to it as you do." Rachelle didn't raise her voice, but her tone spat fire as she wrapped an arm around Brady's back to anchor him. "And you have no idea what you're talking about. You want to call the cops? Who do you think they'd arrest for assault?"

Brady managed to blink his eyes back into focus in time to see the woman flash a last venomous glare before grabbing the arm of the boy whose crocodile tears didn't entirely mask his enjoyment of the scene and stomping back to the pavilion to retrieve her purse, while her companions took their own children and scattered to their vehicles. Rachelle held her post like a statue—except for the way her hand quivered on his back—until they all disappeared from view, then she turned and gently cupped Brady's chin in her hand, carefully drawing it to face her.

"Are you all right?" The words were a whisper, but Brady wasn't sure how to answer her. His head was beginning to clear, although pain still crackled along the acutely sensitive skin of his cheek, but the unexpected encounter had thrown a lot more than his body out of equilibrium.

"What on earth happened here?" Car suddenly came up beside them, breathing hard from her jog—or possibly the run it had morphed into when she heard the commotion. "I swear, I leave you out like a log and under the best guard we've got, and you somehow manage to get yourself surrounded by angry mama-bears without calling in backup? You got an awfully convincing baby face for a cold-blooded kidnapper, new kid."

Brady loosed a breath that should have been at least an attempt at a chuckle, but it came out as a shudder instead. Rachelle's gentle pressure on his back got him moving almost without conscious thought, and she steered him over to a picnic table a little way from the playground—thankfully not the one where the mama-bears, as Car termed them, had congregated. Brady sank down onto a bench and buried his head in his hands.

"What happened?" Rachelle's tone held more compassion than curiosity as her hand began rubbing his back, and Brady sucked in a shaky breath.

"Kids were pushing another one too fast. Wouldn't let up when he begged them to stop. I guess I should've figured their moms would be nearby, but—"

"But they weren't stopping it. So you stepped in, drew their notice, and got blasted for it."

"Pretty much." Brady rubbed at his cheek, hoping to draw away some of the sting, but the motion only served to intensify the ache. He closed his eyes against the threatening moisture and tried to swallow the lump forming in his throat. "Harper was right. What good is any of this if I can't even break up a kids' bullying match without causing trouble?"

He braced himself for Rachelle's argument—for her assurance that God must have a purpose in it somewhere—but she stayed silent for a long moment, only her hand on his back and the soft sound of her breathing assuring him that she hadn't walked away. And when her words finally came, they weren't at all the ones he'd expected.

"Car, would you take us home for a bit?"

"Calling it quits for the day?" Car asked, and although her tone stayed even, Brady couldn't help flinching a little.

"Not yet. You're still on the clock. But it's almost lunchtime anyway, and I want to get an ice pack on his cheek before it bruises too badly. Then we'll figure out what happens next."

CHAPTER TEN

"Aww, come on, I haven't been out of it that long." The harsh rasp in Dash's voice bit deeper than usual, and Brady pried his heavy eyes open to see Harper helping him position his wheelchair near the table, next to where Brady sat in the recliner usually reserved for Rachelle. The fact that she was helping at all was telling, but Dash didn't attempt to take over, just sat and surveyed him with narrowed eyes. "You look like you've hit tomorrow already, and it's barely past noon."

"Yeah, right." Brady managed a halfhearted snort. "I guarantee if it was tomorrow, you wouldn't find me out here, or sitting up even this much."

"That's something,. I guess." The corner of Dash's mouth twitched in a weak approximation of his usual smirk. "City chew you up and spit you out, or just Car?"

In Brady's estimation, admitting he'd been done in by an angry mother with a wicked slap ranked somewhere in the vicinity of taking a hard poke at the tender spot on his cheek. He kept his mouth shut and lowered the ice pack, only to pause at Harper's disapproving huff.

"Rachelle told you to keep that on until the timer went off."

"Pretty sure if Rachelle knew how much worse it aches with it on, she'd forgive me."

"You're not—" Harper started, but Dash waved her off with an abrupt jerk of his hand.

"Oh, let him go. I want to see this."

Brady rolled his eyes, and they nearly closed again. This was ridiculous. He'd just barely finished the unplanned nap Rachelle had insisted on, and the slap had woken up every nerve in his body. There was no reason he should be wanting to sleep again at this point, but a bone-deep weariness weighted down every limb. Was it discouragement masquerading as fatigue? The thought was somehow more galling than the idea of his body giving up on him. If the trouble was mental, he ought to be able to push through it, especially on a day when his usual physical issues had been swept aside.

"Hmm, well, if you're taking on Rachelle, can you add one for me?" Harper turned one of the chairs away from the table and slumped onto it with one cheek resting on her fist. "I still can't believe she made me take out my earpiece right before you hit the good stuff."

"You've got a weird definition of 'good stuff,'" Brady mumbled, and Dash nearly choked on a snort.

"Not even trying to argue with that."

"You're no help." Harper jabbed an elbow at Dash, shooting him an exaggerated scowl. "I meant excitement. Action. Anything more interesting than listening to you listen in on boring office talk. I miss all the best accidents."

"Yeah, well, forgive me for learning how not to break my neck before you got here," Dash shot back. "And you didn't miss your own best accident; you just weren't exactly lucid for it."

"Ugh." Harper rubbed her forehead with a shudder, then grimaced in Brady's direction. "If you ever find yourself invisible, look out for doors that swing *toward* you. Because news flash—if people can't see you, they *will* hit you. I still don't know how Car got me out of there without anyone noticing, but then they couldn't even run normal concussion checks. So all day, it was 'Harper, stay awake,' 'Harper, who's the president?' 'Harper, how many fingers am I holding up?' until Mattox finally got a chance to sneak me in to a scanner. Also, EM flare on top of a mild concussion? Ten of ten don't recommend."

"Yeah…I'll take your word." Brady winced as Rachelle entered the room again, carrying the thermos mug he'd been given that morning and some kind of small plastic container.

"Drink up, and then DeAndre says you can have this."

"What, is it supposed to help bruises?" Brady eyed the container hesitantly, and Rachelle sighed.

"No, the ice pack's supposed to do that, if you keep it on like you're supposed to." She fixed him with a longsuffering look, and Brady managed a slight shake of his head.

"I left it as long as I could. It's about to give me a headache, and that defeats the point of today."

"I forgot the cold gets to you." Rachelle worried her lip with her teeth for a second, then shrugged one shoulder with a little pop. "Never mind. Do what you can. I've got some arnica you can try if you want it. But DeAndre says you have to finish the drink before you can touch the other."

Brady swallowed a grimace before lifting the mug, but just as the blueberry slush hit his tongue, Harper's barely whispered "No. Way." sent his attention skidding back to her.

"Pay up." Dash reached in her direction, crossing his quivering right hand across his body instead of even trying to move his left, and Harper groaned and pushed out of her seat to grab a little vase filled with marbles from the shelf above the microwave.

"Please don't break the crown. Please don't break the crown. Please don't break the crown." Her pleading tone made her sound no older than five, although he'd never heard Grace beg quite so pitifully.

"Come on. Gold." Dash continued to hold his hand out, despite the fact that it was shaking harder, and Harper moaned as she cast a wistful look at the circle of gold marbles she'd arranged along the top of the vase before reluctantly fishing one out.

"Fine. Where do you want it?"

"In the bag with the others. Fitting, isn't it?"

"Yeah, yeah, rub it in." Harper made a face but returned her vase to the shelf and slipped the captured marble into the drawer nearby where Dash's bag was stored.

"What was this one for?" Rachelle gave a little sigh as she took a seat on the floor and leaned her back against the side of the recliner.

Brady still had a hard time believing that two full-grown adults somehow carried on an entire betting rivalry with nothing but marbles, but somehow Harper's childish enthusiasm and Dash's ultra-competitive streak made it work. Exactly how it had started, he still wasn't sure, but from a few comments they'd made, he guessed Rachelle had played a large part in steering the habit away from money and toward something more innocuous.

"Just the proposition that your golden boy would get away with something today that you'd never let fly with the two of us." Dash's smirk was definitely back, but a wave of pain suddenly washed his face, twisting it into a grimace, and Brady could hear his quickly caught breath before his shoulders finally relaxed again.

"Oh, for Pete's sake!" Rachelle slouched backward, thumping her head against the recliner. "He's not the golden boy, or getting away with anything. I don't know where you guys get this stuff."

"*I* never get to give up on a cold pack before the timer goes off." Harper attempted to pout, but the grin in her voice betrayed her, and Brady could almost hear the roll of Rachelle's eyes as she shifted to face her.

"And I've never made *you* soak your hands in cold water, even though it sounds like it should help. Why? Because it's not good for you, no matter what it sounds like. That's fair, isn't it?"

"Does that mean I get my marble back?" Harper brightened as she glanced back at Dash, and he snorted.

"On her say-so? No way. Bet still stands, and we both agreed I won it."

"Fine." Harper sighed. "But you've got to tell Brady about your best wipeout. It's way cooler than mine."

"Stumbled across a knife fight." Dash's tone stayed even, but his mouth twitched a little. "And when I say stumbled, I mean I was aiming to knock the knife out of the guy's hand when they went down in front of me. Extremely good thing I learned how to fall playing football, but momentum like that doesn't just stop when you want it to. Rolled all the way across the lot and into a fence. Still got scars from it."

"Ouch." Brady winced, but Dash's body suddenly went rigid, and he clutched the arms of his chair with a white-knuckled grip. Rachelle scooted forward without a word and started carefully massaging the muscles of his lower leg, which Brady now saw was twisting at a painful angle.

"Breathe," she commanded in a whisper, and Dash forced out a puff of air before sucking in another.

Brady glanced away to give him some space and lifted the mug to his lips again, only to find it empty. How on earth had that happened? Somehow their banter had managed to distract him even from the barely tolerated taste of blueberries. He glanced at Harper, who was staring fixedly at not-Dash in the corner and lifted the unopened container.

"Want to help me figure out what this is?"

Harper's eyes lit up, but Rachelle's voice cut in softly.

"Look, but don't eat, Harper. Nuts involved."

Brady felt a pang of guilt—he'd forgotten that Harper had more food allergies than any of the rest of them—but her face was still eager as she leaned toward him. Brady pulled the container open to find a thick slice of what looked like some kind of nut bread, studded with granola and covered with a layer of decadent cream-cheese frosting.

"Oh, my word, you have to tell me if that tastes as good as it smells!" Harper flopped forward with her chin in her hands, and Brady took a careful bite and closed his eyes as the taste filled his mouth. "Well?" Harper demanded after a moment, and Brady swallowed and let out a long breath.

"Better. Way better. As in 'can I have this every day, or are you saving it for my birthday' better. That is—possibly the most amazing thing I've ever tasted."

"Someone tell DeAndre he has to find a way to make it without nuts, because I've got to try this." Harper sighed, eyeing the dessert with rapture, and Brady didn't have the heart to tell her that the nut flavor was half of what made it so good.

Dash finally slumped against the back of his chair, limp and trying hard not to pant for breath, and Rachelle ran a hand gently down his leg and sat back.

"Want to move to the couch?"

"Give me a minute." Dash's voice was rough even through its rasp, and Brady's heart clenched. If this was his normal on the day after an injection, it was no wonder he often stayed in his room. It must have taken a lot of guts to let them see him like this. Guts and…maybe worry?

"Afraid I don't have an epic battle story for you yet." Brady swallowed hard as he let the admission fall. "Just a playground scuffle gone wrong."

He kept his eyes trained on his hands as he related the incident, keeping to the bare bones and sugarcoating nothing. When he finished, no one spoke for a moment, then Harper drew a shaky breath.

"That's a perfect battle story, Brady." Her usually playful voice held tears, and when he looked up, they shimmered in her eyes. "You stepping in—it meant everything to that kid. Their moms might never know it, but kids like that need somebody to stand up for them, even if they get in trouble for it."

The conviction in her voice said she had either known that kid or been that kid, and somehow it ignited a spark in Brady that he hadn't felt since that first moment of purpose at the park. He took another bite of the nut bread and chewed it slowly, waiting until he'd finished before turning back to Rachelle.

"Is Car still around here somewhere? I think I'm ready to try again."

Chapter Eleven

"How's it going out there?" Harper's voice through the earpiece was unusually subdued, and Brady took a deep breath and mustered as much of a smile as he could before answering.

"Streets are cleaner by several broken bottles and a bunch of assorted junk, so that's something."

A door slammed from somewhere down the street, and angry voices flared on the edge of his consciousness. Brady tensed and waited, but the noise blended into the atmosphere, and he let out a shaky sigh.

"You doing okay?"

When had her tone taken on the quiet concern he usually associated with Rachelle? Brady swallowed hard.

"Fine."

"Come on, Brady. I flinch walking by some of those places, and that's only hearing what legitimately carries. How are you actually?"

Honesty. They were a team. He wasn't in this alone. They'd already seen him vulnerable today, and he'd want them to shoot straight if he was in their shoes.

"It's rough." The admission was a whisper. "I think I've heard more name calling the last two hours than my whole life up to this point. I know it's a lot of desperation and history and people's skewed sense of what's normal and right. I know I'm just getting a snapshot and not the whole story. I know I couldn't fix it all even if I knew everything. I just—it kind of breaks my heart."

"Rachelle says it's supposed to. Like—you have to see the bad *is* bad before you can even think about helping it. If all the junk on the street's just normal, then nobody thinks to pick it up."

"Right." A hint of a smile tugged at Brady's lips. It did sound like something Rachelle would say—maybe especially something she'd say to Harper, whose painful past growing up in foster care he'd only heard about in the broadest hints. "Just because you might not have the tools to fix it doesn't mean you go blind to it."

"Somebody has to notice and care."

Brady nodded as he straightened and stretched his back, then glanced around. He'd walked farther than he'd realized on the tree-lined street—far enough that he could only barely make out the traffic noises from the busier cross street they'd come on, and that the car where he'd left Rachelle when he'd caught her subtly massaging her knee wouldn't have been visible to a normal person. He brushed an elbow against the synthetic fabric of the dark blue vest they'd insisted was his best protection in the rougher neighborhoods, trying to let those assurances—and the fact that both Rachelle and Car had slipped their own on as a matter of course—calm the fears that threatened to swallow him at the thought of being totally alone in this run-down section of the city.

It was terribly ironic; the old homes and spacious lawns reminded him of nothing so much as the neighborhoods he and Eden used to fantasize about living in when they were kids, never mind that Mom's meager salary and a smattering of government benefits put them as far away as the moon. But in contrast to the well-kept downtown area, too many of these once beautiful houses were boarded up, or worse, stood with their doors hanging open, while the lawns were choked with weeds and the streets pocked with everything from lone candy wrappers to piles of discarded furniture.

Brady reached to snag a fast food cup from the edge of the curb, immensely grateful for the gloves and trash-picker that Car apparently kept stocked in her trunk. It wasn't the kind of cover he'd ever have imagined for a superhero—or whatever he was supposed to be—but at least it was useful in a small way, and no one's voice had held a hint of joking when they'd described the DAWN volunteer organization stenciled on the back of the vest as their only chance at wandering the city in safety.

"How's your energy holding, Trash Boy?" Car's voice broke the silence that had fallen again. "Need a pick-up?"

Brady glanced at the intersection he was nearing, then beyond it to the next one. His legs weren't dragging too badly yet, and as they'd hoped, his senses seemed to be acclimating to the atmosphere of the neighborhood. It might be a good place to stop for the day, but something seemed to tug him just a little farther.

"I'm going to try for one more block. I'll let you know."

"You're the boss, Super Snoop."

Brady snorted, but Harper's voice suddenly broke in, brighter than before.

"I almost forgot you still need a code name! We've got to get on that."

"Right…" Brady rolled his eyes, but Car's voice interrupted any longer answer he might have given.

"She's not wrong, Spy Guy. Whatever you end up seeing out there, you've got to get the cops to listen. It'll be hit or miss for a while, but if you can give them a name and prove it's credible, you'll have a better shot. I know you're not looking for trouble right now, but there's nothing wrong with being prepared."

"Exactly!" Harper's tone had regained all its usual pep and then some. "What do you think of Temper-Mental? Get it, because your abilities are—"

"Harper." Brady didn't even try to hold back his groan. "I get it, but please no."

"Sounds too much like a villain name." Rachelle's quiet words brought a wave of relief, and Brady silently pledged to find a way to pay back the favor. "We want the police to listen, not try to track down what sounds like a ticking time-bomb."

"Got to agree with Midge on this one," Car put in, and Harper sighed.

"Fine. Dash doesn't like it either. I thought it was pretty good."

"Keep trying." Rachelle's smile shone through the earpiece. "Maybe come at it from a different angle."

"Something with 'spy' in it? Car, help us out here."

"Doesn't that still sound kind of nefarious?" Brady wrinkled his nose, and Car chuckled.

"I mean, I'd use it, but you *might* not want to stress invasion of privacy to the cops."

"Hmm…" Harper broke off with a questioning grunt, then came back sounding puzzled. "Dash says it needs to include peaches. I don't get it."

"Over *his* dead body." Brady raised his eyes to heaven and shook his head. "I'm not going to be a Georgia peach for anyone. Go back to your ideas, Harper. They were at least relevant."

"Telescope? That's just your eyes, though. Oooh, what about some kind of bug? Like a listening device. Or a camera lens. Or maybe like a real bug that can squeeze through the tiniest cracks." She giggled. "Maybe you're a termite. What else goes through walls?"

"Windows," Brady supplied dryly, but he was met by contemplative silence. "Harper, really?"

"I'm *thinking*, and you're the one who said it. What about like radar or something? Does that go through walls or just bounce off them? Isn't there some kind of radiation—" She broke off abruptly, then came back a second later. "Hold on. Dash thinks he's got something, but we have to look it up."

"Not sure if that sounds hopeful or ominous." Brady sighed as he snagged a plastic bag from the gutter and stopped to check before crossing the street.

"There's no telling." Rachelle's voice was still smiling. "Just remember, you've got veto power. You don't have to settle unless you want to."

"Oh, we have *so* got it!" Harper squealed with sudden delight. "Gamma Ray. They go through metal and everything. Dash says it's perfect for you."

"Dash…would." Brady made sure he was safely on the other side before closing his eyes, trying to decide if the clear jab at his middle name was worth pushing back on or not. It was clever for sure, and subtle enough that even Harper probably hadn't picked up on it. And it was certainly a better code name than any of their previous suggestions. But Dash could find ways to make it sting when he wanted to, and it was his choice whether to leave that door open.

"I like it!" Car's voice brightened. "It's got that kind of mysterious quality you want with a super spy, but it packs a punch too. What's your vote, Midge?"

"I'm reserving judgment." Rachelle's voice stayed light, but the slight hesitation said she'd find a reason to back him up if he turned it down.

"I'll…keep it in mind." Brady shook his head slowly, letting the name roll around in his thoughts. "Any other options?"

"You don't like it?" Harper's voice lost its enthusiasm in an instant, and Brady winced as though he'd accidentally kicked a puppy.

"I don't—know yet. Let me try to get used to it." A pitiful sniffle filtered past the earpiece, and Brady sighed. "Harper, please don't cry."

"I'm not!" Real confusion swam in Harper's tone, but Rachelle's voice cut in quickly.

"There's no crying on the line, Brady. Are you hearing something else?"

Was he? The louder noises of traffic, TVs, and arguments had faded to nothing more than a background tapestry, so how could he possibly have picked out a softer noise unless it was right in his ear? Something that sounded like a stifled sob whispered through the tumult, and Brady latched onto it just as Harper spoke.

"What do you think—"

"Quiet. Please stay quiet!"

Harper's voice died instantly, and Brady tried to catch the sound again, but for a long moment, there was only silence. Then again, a short, whimpering breath came from his left, and Brady turned and studied the dilapidated building beside him. Almost without conscious thought, his eyes cut through the walls, searching, attempting to zero in on the source of the sound. On the second floor, he finally found it: a girl or woman—it was hard to tell—curled up on a rickety cot, shoulders shaking.

Lord, what do I do with this? If Rachelle's right and this is You—How do I help when I don't even know what's wrong? It's not like—

Brady's jumbled prayer cut off as the girl shifted restlessly on the cot, turning to reveal two details he hadn't seen before. One was the pair of handcuffs clamped around her slender wrists. The other was a face he'd studied just that morning.

"Rachelle." The word came out choked. "Call the police. Now."

"What's wrong? Where are you?" Her voice was suddenly strained, but he couldn't take time to reassure her. Not with this staring him in the face.

"It's Jayde. Jayde Morgan, the girl from the missing posters. She's beat up and handcuffed right in front of me. I mean, in the house in front of me. Get the police here now."

"Should we use..." Harper's voice was tentative, and Brady shook his head desperately.

"Use any name. Use Gamma Ray. I don't care. Just get them here! Fast!"

CHAPTER TWELVE

"Brady."

Brady shifted his position against the rickety fence, careful to keep his eyes locked on the room where Jayde was held captive. At Rachelle and Car's insistence, he'd moved to the yard of a deserted house one street over, but no persuasion was going to tempt him to lose sight of the girl until she was safe.

A warm hand touched his arm, and Brady jumped, his focus shattering and re-forming in his immediate environment to find Rachelle kneeling next to him. He gulped air, attempting to slow the frantic beating of his heart that had expected—what? Kidnappers? The police? Some tough guy who didn't appreciate a stranger staking out the random tree he'd been staring through?

"Sorry." Rachelle winced and waited a moment for him to recover. "You weren't answering."

Brady finally managed a deep breath and rubbed his aching eyes before turning them back to the house he'd been watching for hours. His pulse started to race again as he searched for the spot, an irrational fear insisting that in the seconds he'd taken his eyes off the girl, she'd somehow been whisked to another hiding place where he'd never find her. But she was there, exactly as he'd left her, and he breathed a ragged sigh of relief.

"Brady." Rachelle's hand hovered carefully for a second, giving him ample warning before she again attempted to touch him. "You can't stay out here all night."

"I'm staying till the police come."

"You *have* to eat." Her voice was gently insistent, as though talking to a stubborn child. "Remember what DeAndre said?"

"Fine. You and Car go get something and bring it back."

"Car is not leaving this neighborhood while you're in it, and that's not negotiable."

"Then I can wait. I'm just sitting anyway."

"Sitting and watching three houses away and getting hungrier and colder by the minute. You didn't even bring a jacket."

He hadn't really noticed the chill of his skin until she'd begun rubbing his arm. Brady managed what he hoped was a careless shrug.

"It's almost summer anyway."

"Almost summer in Michigan, not Georgia. The last thing you need is to run your body down today on top of what's coming tomorrow. You know that."

"I can't, Rachelle." As hard as he tried, Brady couldn't stop his voice from shaking a little. "I can't just walk away. I can't leave her here. I have to see the end of this. I have to."

"Brady…" He felt more than heard Rachelle's sigh as she sat on the grass and leaned her shoulder against his. "What are you going to do if they don't follow up tonight?"

Brady's eyes nearly closed, but he kept them focused with an effort and forced a breath through tight lungs.

"They can't. Please tell me they won't."

"I can't lie to you. It's one basically anonymous report from a burner phone among who knows how many thousands of tips. They might not find it credible. They might not be able to get a warrant. They might not have the manpower to check it for days."

"Then we have to do something. Get her out. We can't leave her."

"I want her free as much as you do, Brady." Rachelle's words dripped with pain. "But you said the door's padlocked, the shutters are bolted, and there are two guys with guns downstairs. What can we do?"

"There's got to be a way."

"If it was Harper's day, she might get past the guards, but invisibility doesn't bust locks. Dash would have a chance—an extremely dangerous chance—but we don't know how strong those locks are, and he's out of the running for two weeks. I could get through the door or the window, but super strength doesn't stop a bullet even if I had it today. You're not the only one who's helpless here."

The tears overflowed, and Brady buried his head in his knees, shaking with uncontrollable emotion. Rachelle rubbed his back gently, but the soothing gesture only intensified the ache in his heart. Jayde had no one to offer the smallest morsel of comfort or strength, and now he might be forced to abandon her as though he'd never seen her, without her knowing that anyone had ever cared or even tried to help.

"I can't do this." His voice broke on the words, and he couldn't swallow a sob. "If I have to watch—all this—and I can't even help with the worst—what's next? Witness robberies? More kidnappings? Murders? And the cops won't listen to any of it? Live with all of that burned in my brain, and never be able to help? I can't do it, Rachelle. I'm not a hero. Not that kind. I'm not nearly strong enough for that."

Rachelle didn't answer for a long moment as she continued with her careful stroking. When the words finally came, they were pitched low and almost haunting in their softness.

"I don't have the answers for you. For anyone. I wish I did. I wish I had them for me. There's so many things I want to help and can't, even though I don't see nearly as much as you do. I don't know why it's so temporary. So limited. So unpredictable. I don't understand why we were given these abilities in the first place, when most other treatments just plain don't touch us. I still don't believe it's an accident—any of it. You hearing those sniffs that probably even her captors couldn't, in the middle of a conversation over the earpiece? I can't think there wasn't a purpose for it. Is there something that's somehow better for her than immediate rescue? Are the cops going to come another day, when they'll get more proof, or catch more people, or find more victims? I don't know. I can't know. Only God sees enough of the picture to fully understand why."

It was all true, and he knew it. But the distant maybes did nothing for the dull, heavy ache that threatened to consume him.

"I'm sorry." Rachelle's voice held an uncharacteristic quiver that almost made him lift his head. "I should have prepared you for this. I should have made sure you were ready. I should have remembered—"

"Rachelle." The word came out choked and hoarse, but he couldn't let her open that door. "Please stop. It's not your fault. You wanted me to go slow. You said it would take time. You couldn't know we'd run into—this."

To his faint relief, she didn't argue, and after a few seconds, she leaned her head against his shoulder and just sat silently while he attempted to wrestle his heart into submission. God had a purpose for everything. Of course he believed that. But how long could he go with no tangible result before the questions destroyed him? What would it be like to suffer through the next day or two of his migraine with the added agony of knowing that Jayde was out there and his best efforts hadn't been enough to help her?

God, I can't do this. I'm not strong enough. Please.

The breeze was picking up, and Brady felt goosebumps prickle along his arms. His head was clouded, his limbs were heavy, and a hollow feeling was beginning to gnaw at his stomach. What good was he doing sitting here? Rachelle was right that he'd have to leave sometime, and it wasn't like his keeping watch would get the police there any faster. But even through the clinging fog of discouragement and fatigue, something fierce and hot seared his heart at the thought of giving up his post while he still had a choice.

He had no idea how long they'd sat there when Rachelle shifted and opened her mouth, but before she could voice a word, a hiss cut through his earpiece.

"Heads up, Gamma Ray. You seeing any movement?"

Brady wrenched his focus back to the house, which looked just like it had when he'd left it, and shook his head, forgetting for a moment that Car couldn't see him.

"He doesn't think so. Why?" Rachelle's voice was the barest whisper, and Brady instinctively held his breath.

"On my way to a new parking spot, and I just passed a cop car with its lights off. Could be a coincidence, but…"

Before she had finished, Brady was pulling his sight back, out of Jayde's room, out of the house, and down the darkened street. His hearing followed, catching the soft scuff of shoes, the muted crackle of a radio, a tense murmur of voices mapping out points of entry.

"I hear them." The words nearly caught in his clogged throat.

"Don't make any sudden moves or noises." Rachelle's words were barely audible. "Car, can you get around behind us without drawing attention?"

"Heading away now. I'll circle back farther down. Buckle in, newbie. You're about to get some real action."

In spite of Car's prediction, the minutes seemed to crawl by as the officers' preparation continued. Brady started to shiver, but Rachelle didn't try to convince him to leave again, just continued to lean against his shoulder and rub his arm as his attention shifted restlessly from the police outside to the kidnappers in the house. After a while, his eyes began to close in spite of himself, and he rested his head on his knees for a few seconds, until an explosion of bangs and shouts jerked him upright again to find the door breached, the suspects surrounded, and a team sweeping the rest of the house before approaching the upstairs room where Jayde had curled into a quivering ball next to the cot.

Brady drew a shuddering breath and closed his eyes as a wave of relief crashed over him, then looked up into Rachelle's anxious eyes.

"They're in. No one's hurt." Full, wrenching sobs reached his ears, and Brady returned his focus to the house in time to see Jayde being helped from the room by an officer, who she clung to like a lifeline. "And they have her."

"Does that mean you're clear?" Harper's voice was muted and nearly breathless. Had she managed to keep quiet that whole time? He'd assumed she'd probably taken out the earpiece.

"Not quite. Let's get out of here while they're busy." Rachelle helped Brady to his feet and kept an arm around him when his legs started to wobble. "Car, we're on our way. Tell us where to meet you."

"Right around the corner. Start walking, and I'll be there in a sec." An unmistakable smile tinted Car's words. "Quite a cleanup job for your first day on the force, Ray Boy. I'd stick with it if I were you."

"There's plenty of time to talk about that later." Rachelle didn't even leave a second for him to answer. "Harper, whatever's for dinner, make sure it's ready, okay? And a couple blankets. We're coming home."

CHAPTER THIRTEEN

The return to the den was a blur in Brady's mind, made all the more surreal by the way his exhausted senses faded in and out, but somehow Rachelle managed to get him through the halls, down to the lab level, and settled on a couch in the common without any significant accidents. He remembered thinking her insistence on a hoodie in addition to the waiting blankets was a bit of overkill, but he doubted he'd argued. The mug of hot cider helped as much as anything, followed by a thick shake, thankfully minus the blueberries, when Rachelle was sure he wasn't in danger of dropping it. Only then did she disappear, presumably to wherever Harper and Grace had gone—Brady was sure it'd been mentioned, but he couldn't remember for the life of him—leaving him to rest and Dash to call if either of them needed anything.

Brady wasn't sure how long he'd been lying there, hovering on the edge of sleep but thankfully minus the dreamlike stupor, when a soft current of air brushed his cheek. A hint of ham and cheese clung tenaciously beneath the strong scent of strawberry toothpaste and tropical shampoo, and two little divots formed on the cushion next to his head. After a quick calculation, Brady adjusted the angle of his chin and opened his eyes to meet Grace's with a smile.

"Hey, Gracie-girl." Thankfully his voice was a little stronger. "How was school?"

Grace shrugged a shoulder and tipped her head, and Brady raised his eyebrows, attempting to match Eden's 'you'd better not lie to me' expression.

"I got in trouble for not listening." The little girl's eyes fell, and Brady shook his head as he scooted into a sitting position and motioned her to join him. She scrambled up and curled into his side readily enough to leave no doubt that she'd only been waiting for the invitation.

"You have to listen to your teachers. They're in charge at school, right?" Brady glanced around the room, hoping he wasn't taking over territory that should be Rachelle's, but she was smiling at them from where she perched on the edge of her recliner, and he turned his attention back to Grace as she sighed.

"I know, but I heard a scary noise outside and thought it might be a bad guy, and then I thought you might hear it from super far away and come and knock the bad guy out of the window when he tried to get us, and then—"

"And then you got distracted thinking about superhero stuff and didn't pay attention to your teacher and your lessons, huh?" It was hard work to keep his face straight, but Brady gave it his best try. Man, did she have a good imagination! But it wouldn't help her to encourage phantom fears or excuses for ignoring her schoolwork.

Grace nodded, and Brady rubbed her arm gently with his thumb as he considered what to say. Rachelle and her teachers had likely already handled the obedience and attention issues, but there was more to be concerned about in her story, and some of it was probably his responsibility.

"Gracie-girl, you know—you know if you were ever in trouble, I'd try to protect you as much as I could. But I can't be everywhere or see everything, and I can't always help. Our superpowers can't stop all the bad stuff from happening, and we can't have them all the time. God's the One you have to trust to take care of you, okay? If He lets me help, I'd love that, but He's still in charge, even if I'm not there."

"Okay," Grace whispered, and Brady rested his cheek against her damp curls as they sat in silence for a moment. He hadn't realized he'd closed his eyes until Harper cleared her throat and he looked up to find her holding out a plate with a slice of DeAndre's nut bread.

"I was planning on holding this hostage for details, but I guess you've earned it." Her grin was only half teasing, and Brady was almost sure he could read sympathy in her eyes. He took the dish from her with a nod of thanks, and Grace surveyed it curiously.

"What is it? Can I try?"

"Better ask Rachelle that." Brady motioned toward her sister and waited for the answer before touching the food.

"Can I?" Grace turned her most melting look on Rachelle, who sighed.

"How much sugar are we talking?" She worried her lip as she shifted her gaze to Brady, and he chuckled.

"Not much. No frosting this time. I guess DeAndre doesn't want me up all night any more than Grace."

"Then you can have a very little bit—if Brady wants to share."

Grace whipped her head back to him fast enough that her wet braid smacked his arm, and Brady broke off a corner and slipped it into her mouth before beginning on the rest of the slice. Grace gave a little hum of satisfaction, and Rachelle couldn't help a smile.

"Bedtime when you finish, okay, baby?"

"Can Brady tell me a story?" Grace mumbled through her mouthful, and Brady winced.

"I'm not—that great at stories yet, Grace." Not to mention he had no idea how much of what had happened today was safe for her ears. "Can I listen to Rachelle do your story tonight? Maybe then I can learn how to tell them better."

Grace sighed, but she nodded and slid down from the couch, tugging on Brady's hand to bring him along. He somehow got himself untangled from the blankets without falling on his face and followed her to her room, swallowing the lump that rose to his throat as he watched Rachelle tuck her in and give her a highly abridged and slightly exaggerated version of Jayde's rescue in a soft voice that somehow had Grace's eyes blinking sleepily by the end.

"I knew Brady was gonna be a hero." The words were mumbled so low that he wondered if she'd forgotten he was in the room at all, but then she turned on her pillow and smiled over at him, and Brady's heart threatened to overflow. He kissed his finger and touched it to her nose, and she gave a tiny giggle, then squeezed her battered bear tighter against her chin and closed her eyes.

Rachelle stood and followed him into the hall, and Brady glanced toward his room, then paused and looked back.

"Anything else I need to do tonight? Or should I be trying to get as much sleep as I can?"

"Depends." Rachelle brushed a knuckle thoughtfully along her jaw as she leaned against the handrail, and Brady's forehead furrowed.

"On what?"

"On whether you meant what you told Grace, mostly."

"What I—" Brady closed his eyes, searching his memory for anything he'd said that might have concerned her.

"About needing to trust God, not people or their superpowers." A smile hovered around her mouth when he opened his eyes, but a hint of concern edged her tone. "The same goes for us, Brady. Maybe double for us. We can't start trusting ourselves to fix everything, or we'll wind up in a world of hurt. If He's the One that put us here, then any help we can give is still in His hands, not ours."

"I wouldn't—" The words broke off as the horror of the idea washed over him. Had she seen something to make her think he was in danger of taking God's glory for any bit of good these injections let him do? He shivered at the thought, and Rachelle shook her head.

"For the times it went well, you wouldn't. I don't doubt that. It's the other times, Brady. The times you can't help, or the law won't listen, or you have to leave things unfinished because your day's up. Can you leave those days in God's hands too? Can you accept that your job is to do your best and no more, and trust that He's still in control when all your abilities fail?"

Brady dropped his head as his agonized words when he'd thought help wasn't coming played over in his memory. Rachelle was silent for a moment before she spoke again.

"Today was beautiful, Brady. I have no doubt it was a gift. But I can't promise you'll see the resolution every time. Can you live with that, knowing that it's in God's hands? Or is it going to destroy you?"

It was a fair question—more than fair, considering the way he'd nearly fallen apart while waiting for someone to come for Jayde. He'd meant everything he'd said to Grace, but could he believe it himself? Could he trust God's sovereignty if the police didn't listen, or if their response was delayed? Could he survive never knowing the end of what he'd seen, but depending on God's ultimate plan to be right? What was his other choice? To go back to Georgia—to Eden and Josh, who should be working to get to Africa? To lose the friendships he'd begun to forge with Rachelle and Grace, Harper and Dash? To leave the place he knew God had led him and anyone he might be able to help just because he couldn't stand not being in control? What control had he ever had in the first place?

I do trust You, Lord. I'm sorry for ever starting to make this about me.

Brady blinked back the mist that clouded his eyes and lifted his head.

"I did mean it. And I do. I can't save the world. I can't save anyone." A weight seemed to fall off his shoulders with the admission, and he managed a wobbly smile. "All I can do is my part. Bloom where I'm planted. And let God handle the rest."

"I'm proud of you, Brady." Rachelle's smile was soft, but her eyes were bright. "Now go to bed. You've got a rough couple of days in front of you, and any stories Dash and Harper want will wait. You did excellent work today."

"*I* didn't." Brady grimaced, but Rachelle shook her head.

"You let God work through you. That's enough and everything. And I know that girl's family is thankful that you did."

Brady thought of Jayde's tear-streaked face and nodded.

"I couldn't have done it without you, Rachelle."

"I'm glad I was here." Rachelle nodded down the hallway. "Get some rest. I'll see you in the morning, but don't try to see me, okay?"

"I'll do my best." Brady offered a wry grin. "Tell Harper you can tell the stories better than I can. If she wants a rundown of the police raid, I'll do my best in a few days."

"It'll wait. And we have time. Welcome to the team, Gamma Ray."

"I'm stuck with that now, aren't I?" Brady tried to look disgusted, but he couldn't hold it, and Rachelle chuckled.

"Entirely. Congratulations, Brady. Sounds like you're a full-fledged superhero."

The Chronic Warrior Chronicles

Episode 3

Team Up

Angie Thompson

Quiet Waters Press
Lynchburg, Virginia

To anyone who's buried their heart from fear of being hurt again

You are needed, and you are loved!

Thanks to everyone who's followed along with the story, and especially Skylar, Nate, and Joshua for becoming such a big part of my fan club!

TABLE OF CONTENTS

CHAPTER ONE

"So, how are you and Josh doing?" Brady adjusted his head against the arm of the couch as he watched his sister's face on his tablet, thankful beyond measure for a good enough evening when she was also free.

"Should you still be looking at a screen? What time is it there?" Eden's eyebrows pinched together, and her lips disappeared between her teeth in the worried look he knew all too well.

"Same time it is for you, Eden." Brady allowed himself a very small eye roll. "Still Eastern. And even if it was Central, I'd be an hour *earlier*, not later. Besides, I'm doing okay at the moment."

"And I want you to keep doing okay as long as possible. Pretend it's an audio call for a while, so your eyes don't get too tired?"

"Fine." Brady sighed. "You want a view of the ceiling or the back of the couch?"

"I'm not picky." The smile came through in Eden's voice even after he'd laid the tablet next to him. "I'm just glad to talk to you."

"Yeah. So why are you avoiding my question?" Brady attempted to put as much raised eyebrow as possible into his own voice, wondering if it would work better at a distance than it usually did in person.

"I'm not avoiding anything, goofball." Eden's tone stayed light—too light—and putting the question aside with a laugh was one of her favorite deflection tactics. Brady's jaw tensed reflexively, and he forced it to relax before the strain could spread.

"So why haven't you told me how you're actually doing, Edie? And I mean *how*, not *what*. You wouldn't let me get away with it for a second, and you know it. And why have you shut down every mention of Josh? Don't tell me y'all are fighting."

"We're not fighting." Her voice trembled just the tiniest bit, and Brady kept his mouth shut, knowing the crack had started and silence would finish the rest. It took a moment, but his instinct was confirmed when Eden took a shaky breath. "He…he asked me to marry him."

"Wait, today?" Brady scrambled to get the tablet back into his line of vision, and Eden sniffed.

"A week ago Sunday."

"Edie—" He had to stop and swallow a lump in his throat before any more words would come. "I know I'm not—always the easiest to reach, but—you couldn't shoot me a text to say you're engaged?"

"I haven't answered him yet, Brady." The words wavered, but when he finally got the tablet in place again, she had turned her head so only her ear and a corner of her hair was visible.

"Eden…" Brady paused for a moment and closed his eyes, praying for the words to say. The last thing he wanted to do was pressure her to live out a fantasy he'd created, but if he'd imagined the chemistry between them, Harper might have unexpected competition in the romance business. Obviously his instincts couldn't have been *that* far off, if Josh had gotten as far as a proposal, but there was only one person he could think of that Eden might care enough to hesitate for, and the thought jerked a cold knot in his stomach. He drew a deep breath and let it out slowly, trying to keep his voice as neutral as possible. "So…that list you wrote when you were twelve—loves God; loves me; wants kids; makes me laugh; lets me get pie instead of ice cream for dessert—"

"Brady Ray Owen, Momma told you to bury that list so deep in your brain you'd never find it again!" Eden was facing the camera again, her expression the perfect mix of shock and embarrassment with a touch of fury that he'd elicited too many times growing up.

"Blame it on how many times my brain's been scrambled?" Brady let one corner of his lips turn up, then sobered again when Eden looked away. "That's it, isn't it? It's me you're worried about. What happens if you get married and go off—somewhere—to build yourself a life"—he'd come way too close to referencing the missions conversation she still didn't know he'd overheard—"and I end up needing help again. That's what you're afraid of."

Eden dropped her head, but the sound of her uneven breathing told him he'd hit the nail pretty close.

"Momma left you to me, little brother. I can't just fold that up and dump it in the Goodwill bin. You said these treatments are only giving you a day's relief every couple weeks. What if that quits? What if the funding dries up? What if you need a place to come back to…" She sucked in a shaky breath and finished in a whisper. "…and I'm not here?"

"Edie—" Brady's voice cracked despite his best efforts, and he sent up another silent, desperate prayer. Telling her he'd come all the way out here specifically to give her this chance wouldn't help; if anything, it'd probably make her feel worse. Even displaying how much it hurt him to see her life ticking by without anything to show for it would probably do more harm than good. But there was so much more at stake here than just the two of them, or even the three of them. A measure of peace crept back into his heart at the thought, and he cleared his throat and focused on Eden again. "Have you prayed about it?"

Eden's eyes flicked up to him, then away, and he could hear her hard swallow through the tablet.

"Not…yet."

"Scared?" He waited a second to let the word sink in before continuing. "What are you more afraid of, Edie? That God'll tell you not to marry the guy that's stuck by us when most people gave up? Or that He'll tell you this is His open door and you need to trust Him to take care of me while you walk where He's leading you?"

Eden's head went down on her hand, and Brady gave her a minute before speaking again.

"Hang up with me and go talk with God, huh? And trust His answer, okay? Then talk to Josh and let me know how it goes. Can we pray together first though?"

Eden sniffed and nodded, and Brady closed his eyes, wishing he could reach out and hold her hand.

"Lord, you know Eden's hurting and scared right now. She's done so much for me my whole life, and I know it's hard for her to let go of that, even though she knows You're in control. Please, would You help her see what You want from her right now? And help Josh see too. Lead them both—lead us all—in Your way. Amen."

"Amen." Eden's whisper was choked, and Brady had to blink back moisture in his own eyes.

"Love you, big sis."

"Love you too." Eden gave up on her attempts to wipe her cheeks and offered him a wobbly, broken smile before the picture cut off, and Brady laid his head back and let his own emotions come.

He'd always hated the way his migraines affected his family, as much as he appreciated their care. But the thought that Eden would consider sacrificing her future with Josh and even her calling from God just to protect him shook him to his core. And leaving her stuck in the past while he kept moving in the direction God seemed to be calling him to—the idea was like a gut punch. Okay, so maybe he did understand her perspective a little. Brady threw an arm over his eyes and sent up another fervent prayer that God would help both of them to be faithful.

"Hey." Rachelle's voice was slightly strained and quieter than her usual soft tone. "You okay?"

Brady twisted his head around to see her pain-clouded eyes watching him from her fully reclined position in her chair.

"Sorry, did I wake you up?" He pushed up on an elbow, wincing as his head protested the change.

"No, you're fine." She attempted a smile, but Brady could tell her latest flare hadn't lessened at all. "Is Eden okay?"

"I hope so." Brady groaned and sat up, leaning against the back of the couch with his hands on his head. "She's scared. Not that I blame her. I just pray she can let go and trust God."

"It's hard." Rachelle gave a tiny, painful nod. "I'll pray for her too."

"Thanks." Brady let out a long breath and glanced down at Harper, who had apparently either paused her stretching exercises or just remained lying on the floor after finishing them. "You comfortable?"

"Enough." Harper shrugged. "Just not hugely motivated to move yet. So your sister's *not* engaged?"

"It's—complicated." Brady sighed. "I think she will be soon. She just hasn't figured out how to turn off big sister mode yet."

"You and Rachelle make it sound so nice." Harper gave a little discontented huff as she stretched her arms behind her head. "The only siblings I ever knew used to fight and scream like anything. I was pretty glad I didn't have any to drag around from place to place. But then I listen to you guys and kind of feel like I missed out, you know?"

"I mean, I won't pretend we haven't had our moments." Brady pressed his lips together, trying not to wince at how badly her experience had warped her perspective. "But I don't know anybody else who'd have stuck with me through the last few years the way she did."

Something hit the wall with a smack, and Brady jumped as sudden pain shot through his head. He jerked his eyes up to find Dash glaring at the wall—or possibly just toward it at nothing in particular—while the ball he'd been intermittently rubbing, squeezing, and passing back and forth between his hands bounced and rolled across the floor toward Harper.

"You good?" Harper reached languidly up to stop the ball, and Dash answered with a grunt that was more of a growl.

"Not helping anything anyway." He jerked his chair around and headed for the door without sparing any of them another glance. "One of you take point for Mini-Midge. I'm resting up for tomorrow."

Rachelle lifted her head a little and parted her lips as if she wanted to say something, but then both her lips and her eyes pressed shut as she lay back again and tried to hold in a moan.

"You okay?" Brady watched her worriedly, unconvinced by her soft hum of assent. "Want me to drag him back here?"

"No." Rachelle took a deep breath, then rolled her head a little to meet his eyes. "Give him space. What time is it?"

"Close enough." Brady glanced down at Harper, who somehow managed to roll onto her side and pillow her head on her fist without appearing any more ready to move than when she'd been lying on her back.

"You want me to go?"

Brady couldn't tell if the tired-child look was a physical reality or a practiced facade, but he knew better than to pass judgment on conditions he couldn't see. Steeling himself against the muted stabs telling him he had just as much right to stay put as Harper, he shoved himself off the couch.

"Nope, I'll get her. Can you just try to find where you put the graduation cow after we signed it?"

"Tell Shavonne thank you again for being willing…" Rachelle's voice trailed off as though at a loss for more ways to express her gratitude. He knew it had killed her to miss Grace's kindergarten graduation, even if she'd buried her own disappointment to pour all her limited energy into making other arrangements.

"I will. You rest and prepare for the tidal wave." Brady paused long enough to lean over and gently brush her hand before heading for the elevator.

CHAPTER TWO

Please, not today. Please, not today.

The words pounded an endless rhythm in Brady's head, the same one they'd repeated since he'd woken up just after two with a burning ache snaking into the back of his skull and a storm that was only half dread churning his stomach.

Please, God.

He'd known it was a losing battle from that first awful moment, but the sliver of his mind that wasn't consumed by pain still held stubbornly to the husk of an empty hope. Or maybe it was faith? Yeah, who did he think he was kidding? The words were a prayer, without question, but they were born entirely of desperation, not trust.

He couldn't be sick—at least, this sick. Not today. He couldn't. Rachelle was still barely moving, and now Grace was home for the summer. He'd hoped to take care of her today, even if it meant keeping an eye on her across the room when his migraine inevitably kicked up. Yesterday had been too good; he'd known it wouldn't last, but he hadn't thought reality would hit so hard or so fast.

Was it his own fault somehow? He'd tried to be careful, but had he stared at a screen too long talking with Eden? Stayed up too late listening to Grace's meandering account of her evening? Misjudged not needing his sunglasses in the bit of twilight left when he'd picked her up?

It was a fruitless exercise, and he knew it. He'd never been able to connect more than a third of his migraines to any definite cause. And even following every restriction perfectly never guaranteed a good day, even if breaking them could guarantee a bad one.

Lord, I'll take not great. I'll even take pretty bad. Can't the really bad hold off for just one more day?

Bile and guilt surged in his throat, and Brady swallowed desperately as the real reason for his struggle pressed in. Of course he wanted to help Rachelle, but she'd managed without him for going on two years, so she'd find a way to cope. And it was always difficult to have a day's plans slashed without warning, but he had missed more important events than this and had always been able to deal. But Dash had scheduled today nearly a week in advance, and Brady was not ready to face what his reaction would be if the team's acknowledged rookie attempted to horn in on his day in the sun.

As if just the thought was too much to stand, the stabbing pain in his head throbbed sharper and hotter, driving everything but the physical agony from his mind, and his prayer changed to the only one he could manage.

God, help. Please help. Please.

How long the wave of misery lasted he couldn't have told—long enough to leave him empty, drained, and shivering, covered in cold sweat, and robbed of every crumb of hope that this siege would somehow settle on its own. There were only two options left—let it take its usual course and resign himself to being out of commission for at least three days straight, or take the treatment he was there for and trust God that the timing wouldn't prove too much for whatever tenuous friendship he and Dash had managed to form.

Father...

The ache that had dulled a little began to sharpen again, and Brady reached a trembling hand for the button on the nightstand.

Okay, Lord. I surrender. And please...don't let Rachelle answer this.

Who else the signal would go to, he had no idea, but if Rachelle even thought about dragging herself down the hall to check on him, he'd be tempted to lock her in her room. At least, he might if he could force himself out of his own bed. And since the chances of that were slim to none right now, he could only wait and breathe, and try to trust that she had some sort of sensible backup in place.

"Brady?"

When the whisper finally came, it grated in his ears—too high, too breathy, and accompanied by a jaw-popping yawn that ripped through his head like gunshots. Harper. Brady wasn't sure if the tears that stung his eyes were more from pain, relief, or a loneliness that made no sense when he absolutely *hadn't* wanted Rachelle to come. He managed a choked hum in response, and Harper shuffled forward.

"You need something?"

Okay, this was not going to be easy. It wasn't Harper's fault that she hadn't been blessed with Rachelle's intuition, but that didn't make communication any easier for him. Brady wracked his aching brain for the fewest words possible that would get his point across.

"Doc—" The last half of the title caught in his throat, and he swallowed desperately, willing his voice not to quit on him. "Mattox."

"What should I—" Harper's questioning tone trailed off, and he could almost hear the realization dawning on her face. "Oh. Ohhh. Gotcha."

The surprise must have knocked any precautions out of her mind, and a moan that was much too close to a whimper escaped Brady's throat as her volume and pitch rose to normal speaking levels.

"You okay?"

Aside from the fact that he obviously wasn't? Brady fought the urge to cry or scream—neither of which would have done him a scrap of good—and tried to steady his breathing. Harper was trying to help, and she understood the depths of the pain, even if she'd forgotten its source. If only he could communicate that without putting himself through more torture.

"Loud." He managed to force the word through gritted teeth, and Harper sucked in a breath that scraped like nails on a chalkboard.

"Oh no, I forgot! Rachelle's going to kill me. I'm sorry!"

She was trying. She *was*. She'd even lowered her voice back to a whisper, though the pitch was still a nightmare. But his stomach was in his throat again, and there was no way he could answer her, only wait for her to realize it and leave to get the doctor. There was silence for a moment, and he would have thought she had left except for the fact that her breathing continued to scrape in his ears. Then she gave a sigh that was blessedly softer than it might have been.

"I'm not helping, am I?" Her fingers brushed his back in a gentle apology, although she still couldn't seem to stop talking. "Sorry. Mattox just got through with Dash. I'll go get her."

He couldn't thank her, or even offer a nod of appreciation, only hope she would understand what he couldn't express. The slap of her flip-flops moved away, replaced after a few minutes by Dr. Mattox's quieter, quicker tread, then her firm hands on his arm, the sting of the needle, and finally blessed darkness.

When he woke again, it was to a familiar soft voice in his ear, but not talking to him, as usual.

"He can't help it, Dash, and you know that. You don't have to work together. You can stay in separate parts of the city. But you don't have to take it out on him."

Lovely. Less than two days after her own injection, and she was back to running interference for him. Whatever Dash's response on the earpiece might've been didn't filter through to his room, which was probably just as well, but that didn't mean he should leave Rachelle to shoulder whatever it was.

Brady ran a hand through his sweaty hair and sat up, then almost fell backward off the bed as a red truck roared past on the street. Slamming his eyes shut again, he curled his hands around the edge of the mattress and forced deep breaths, attempting to wrestle his heart back into his chest.

Right. Adjustment. Calibrate things before jumping straight in. At least Dash hadn't been around for that demonstration of just how inexperienced he still was.

Not like he blamed the guy for objecting to a tag-along with one all but accidental success under his belt. Or maybe he just didn't like the idea of partners in general; Brady had no idea how common it was for two of them to be powered up at once. Either way, his involvement would be totally out of Dash's control, which had to be rough for a guy who didn't have much control even on ordinary days.

Brady cautiously opened his eyes and adjusted his focus until the bare walls of his room settled into place again. Now that he thought about it, though, maybe there was another option. Was there any rule that he *had* to go out on the streets when he had an injection? Why couldn't he just stick around the den—helping Rachelle, watching Grace, and letting Dash have the day he'd planned for? The more he thought of it, the better the plan sounded, and Brady scrambled out of bed with a surge of hope that slowly succumbed to a gnawing doubt as he readied himself for the day.

Was this really the surrender he had promised? Ignoring the work God had put in front of him to do exactly what he'd chosen for himself instead? Of course if Rachelle asked for help, that would be a different thing—a real need he could fill, not a convenient excuse to hide from bad timing and uncertain consequences. And if God was in control as always, then was the timing truly bad? Suppose God had picked this day because of something going on in the city that he could help and Dash couldn't? Was he willing to turn his back on that for the sake of Dash's ego and his own comfort?

Sorry, Lord. Brady swallowed hard and closed his eyes, feeling a small measure of peace return as he once again surrendered. *You're in control. Just please—don't let this wreck what You want from me here.*

He finished brushing his teeth and carefully straightened his shoulders before opening the door and making his way to the den. Rachelle still lay in her recliner—he'd be willing to bet one of Dash and Harper's marbles she hadn't gone to bed at all—but she offered a smile when he appeared in the doorway.

"Hey, Brady. Car's just getting up, so you've got a little time. DeAndre left one of your shakes in the freezer; it should be thawed in about ten. You doing okay?"

"Not bad for now." Brady shrugged. "Sure you're up to quarter-backing two of us today?"

Rachelle's face went serious, and she pulled her earpiece out and hid it in her hand before answering.

"We can handle it. But listen. Don't let Dash rattle you."

Apparently she either shared his concerns about the match or thought his game face needed serious work. Brady wasn't sure which idea was more concerning. Just what had Dash been saying anyway?

"You've got as much right and as much to offer out there as he does. Take it slow, get your bearings, and don't push yourself. You work things your way and don't worry about him, okay?"

"That's assuming I actually know what I'm doing in the first place." Brady grimaced, and Rachelle shook her head.

"You've got this, Brady. Harper and I are listening, Car's got your back, and Dash is just blowing off steam. You let God lead you and trust Him for the rest."

"Midge, do you copy?" Dash's voice reached his ears through her still clenched hand, and Brady motioned Rachelle to replace the earpiece. "Those carjackers are mine, and your boy better stay out of the way if he doesn't want to get hurt."

Rachelle closed her eyes and took a deep breath, then mouthed, "God's got this," maybe to herself as much as him, before turning her attention back to Dash.

Chapter Three

Thankfully Brady remembered just in time to brace himself before exiting the elevator on the main floor, and after only a couple of deep breaths, the wave of new sensations melded into a not-quite suffocating fog.

"Take it slow," Rachelle's voice murmured in his ear, and Brady managed a slight smile.

"I'm okay. Thanks. Just readjusting. You said Car's out front?"

"Didn't even have to remind her."

"Always great to make an impression." Brady gave his head a wry shake as he made his way to the lobby and stepped out into the dark of not yet morning.

"Somebody call for a sidekick?" Car's voice reached him before his eyes had even finished adjusting, and he blinked them clear to see her grinning at him through the rolled-down passenger window.

"Something like that." Brady reached for the back door, but Car unlatched the front one instead.

"You're not relegated to the back, you know. Regular passengers, yes—not super ones. Unless you don't *want* my company."

Brady rolled his eyes, but he couldn't help grinning as he took the offered front seat.

"So, you up for your first solo flight, Gamma Ray?" Car wiggled her eyebrows mischievously as she put the car in gear and nudged it onto the road.

"Sure hope so." Brady leaned his elbow against the door with a sigh and tried to calibrate his vision with the accelerating scenery.

"Hey, you didn't do so bad last time, did you?"

"You mean with the one mission I basically stumbled on at the last minute? I guess not."

"Don't sell yourself short. You're over the first day. It's all easier from here."

"Can you *please* keep the chatter off the line?" Dash's voice cut harshly through the single beat of companionable silence. "You're not the only ones out here, and I'm trying to concentrate."

Car opened her mouth as she glanced down at her phone, but she closed it again with surprising restraint and kept it shut until she'd pulled into a parking lot and muted her phone.

"Who put the pepper in his coffee?"

Brady sighed as he pulled out his earpiece and hid it in his hand the way Rachelle had done.

"Me, unfortunately. It was supposed to be his day, and I guess I didn't call it soon enough. Pretty sure he doesn't want a partner in any case, let alone a rookie."

"Let alone a package deal." Car offered a sympathetic smirk, then sobered a little. "So how do you want to handle this? It's not like we have a second channel to switch to. And I can't exactly use sign language while I'm driving. I get it if you don't want to step on his toes, but you've got to be able to function, and unless you sprout wings or something, you're kind of stuck with me."

"I know." Brady closed his eyes and drew a deep breath, trying to steady himself on the invisible tightrope. "What do you think of turning your phone off speaker while I'm in the car? I mean, unless we need to talk to Rachelle or someone. I'll turn my earpiece up and keep it in my pocket until I need to get out. At least we can say we tried."

"You're the boss, Spy Guy." Car pressed her phone speaker back on with a little more emphasis than it needed. "Listen up. We're going to try to go dusk over here—turn off mics in the car and trust Gamma Ray's hearing to catch directions. Any time he's streetside, we're fully online again—no ifs, ands, or buts. And if any of this threatens safety, we're taking it back to normal. Clear?"

"It's a start." Dash huffed, and Brady clenched his teeth and tried hard to relax his fist so he didn't accidentally break the earpiece.

"Dash, would it seriously kill you to lighten up a bit?" The voice through the speaker was not the one he'd expected, and Brady shot a look at Car's phone where her thumb still hovered, paused in the act of muting the speaker. "You deal with Midge and me making random small talk all the time. You know they'll clear the line if you need it, same way you would. Your choice and a cat's eye says the two of you manage to make it through the day with no major disasters."

"If I choose the cat's eye too, you've got a deal."

"Fine. Same on my side. And no intentional sabotage, or you forfeit."

"Oh, sure, start adding extra conditions." Dash was clearly trying to keep up the pretense of a growl, but his heart wasn't in it nearly as much as before. Who would have thought that Harper could talk him down so fast?

Car pressed the button and glanced over at Brady, shaking her head.

"Do me a favor and hit my speaker again if anything more like that goes down? Feels like I'm missing the best part of the day."

"You mean…the back and forth in general? Or Harper specifically?"

"Nah, anything. But you have to admit she's an underrated rockstar."

He had to admit the thought had never crossed his mind. Sure, Harper was fun to be around, and she did seem to have a knack for lightening tense situations. But any fleeting thought he'd given it had chalked the effect up to her childlike attitude and naive enthusiasm that none of the rest of them wanted to tarnish. Could Car be right in thinking there was something more behind it?

"Earth to Gamma Ray." Car snapped a finger in front of his face, and Brady jerked his attention back to her. "You got any special plans for the day other than a deep dive into Shadow's psychology? Get sucked into that and you might not come back for a while."

Brady gave himself a little shake to refocus and set the question of Harper aside for later review.

"Nothing special that I know of. Back to trash picking and keeping a lookout, I guess, unless you have other ideas."

"Any street in particular?"

"That's definitely your job. I couldn't name ten streets in this city yet, let alone tell you which one I should be on."

"It's early yet to hit the neighborhoods, at least without more protection than you've got. And probably dead downtown. I say we head to Eight Mile and see what shakes out, then regroup in an hour or two."

"Whatever you think." Brady nodded, and Car's grin stretched wider as she pulled out of the parking lot and onto the road again.

"Dangerous words, rookie. By the way, you eaten anything yet? Or do we need to stop somewhere?"

"Pretty sure DeAndre would pitch a fit if I left without breakfast. As little as he tweaks the recipe, there's got to be something important in it."

"Probably blueberries," Car muttered, and Brady barked a laugh.

"Unfortunately, yes. Do I want to know what else he tries to squeeze them into?"

"Doubt it. I don't have anything against them in principle, but would it kill him to trade out a strawberry every once in a while? I didn't think he was in yet is all. Thought you might have escaped."

"He wasn't. Left something just in case, I guess."

"Sounds about right." Car chuckled under her breath. "Well, if you need to top off, just let me know. Nothing against DeAndre's cooking, but sometimes you just need a change. Or so I've heard. If your diet's anything like Shadow's, I can tell you all the safest dishes."

"Thanks." Brady attempted a smile, but it twisted into a grimace in spite of him. "I don't have it as bad most of the time. Probably need to take it easy while I'm on the shot, though."

"That's not one I've heard before." Car's brow furrowed a little, and she threw a curious look in his direction before returning her gaze to the road. "You get some sort of side effect, or what?"

"Not exactly." Brady bit his lip as he considered his answer. Most people weren't actually interested in the details of his migraines, and he could probably count on one hand the number of normal people—excluding family, medical staff, and others with similar health issues—who hadn't backed off to some extent after witnessing their severity. It would be so easy to turn the conversation—to take past experience as precedent—to say he'd rather not discuss it and leave it at that. But if they were ever going to go beyond a surface-level friendship, he would have to learn to trust her, or at least to know how far that trust could go. "So…if you knew you were getting a stomach bug tomorrow, would it change what you ate today?"

"That bad, huh?" Car shook her head slowly. "You got a point. How do you know it's coming tomorrow? You get some sort of warning?"

"Worse. And no. The only guarantee I've got is that a bad one's at least two days straight. And since it started today, I know to plan for tomorrow."

"Gotta be honest." Car paused for a moment, and Brady held his breath as he waited for the rest. "I want to say I'd kill for powers like yours. But if they only came with the rest of the stuff you all deal with, I don't think I'd have the guts." She winced, shooting him an apologetic look. "Awful pun not intended."

"Pretty sure if the rest of us had the choice of a normal life, you'd be out of a job like that." An unexpected smile tugged at the corner of Brady's mouth as he snapped his fingers. Maybe it wasn't full understanding, but just the fact that she didn't shrug off their issues as overblown or easy to handle put her further along the path than most. "So if it *didn't* have to come with all our issues, which superpower would you pick?"

"Flying. Not even close. Always been my favorite."

Brady couldn't help a snort of laughter.

"Look! Up in the sky! It's a bird! It's a plane! It's a…Car?"

Car let out a full-throated chuckle and reached over to lightly slap his arm.

"Okay, Spider Sense, just you wait. There'll come a day when you'll wish we didn't have to stick to the roads. Hey, listen, though, it's early, and you'll probably need a refill before lunch. Just give me a heads-up before you pass out, all right? I've got trail mix in the glove compartment, and I know a bakery that does awesome nut muffins if they wouldn't bother you."

"That…actually sounds kind of amazing." Brady closed his eyes and tried not to breathe too deeply as he imagined the smell. But the flicker of warmth in his heart wasn't imaginary; it was the gift of a friend willing to listen and suggest a creative substitute for the offer he'd had to turn down, without offense and without pressure. "Thanks, Car."

She couldn't have any idea of half of what he meant by that, but she smiled anyway.

"Don't thank me yet, Eagle Eyes. After a couple hours on the street, I'm guessing you'll need it."

Chapter Four

"Anything happening out there yet?" Harper gave a yawn that should have cracked her jaw, and Brady fought to keep from following her example.

"Not much. I mean, a few more cars on the street. Some places getting ready to open up. Nothing that jumps out, though."

"Hmm." Harper gave a little, discontented huff. "How about you, Dash? You're pretty radio silent today."

"Don't see why you need my play-by-play when you're getting a running countdown of every intersection of Eight Mile west of Gratiot."

The sarcasm in the words ran deep, and Brady forced a slow breath, fighting the creeping tension. He hadn't come anywhere close to monopolizing the line, and the regular check-ins were necessary to keep Car close to his position without drawing attention to herself by circling the same block over and over.

"You call that a running commentary? I'd call it a brisk walk at best." Harper tried to sound serious, but she couldn't fully keep the smile out of her voice. "Now if *you* were naming the streets…"

"Ha! I'd have to slow down just to say the names, let alone read them off."

"I'm sure." Harper's tone held laughter, but not in a mocking way. "Catch any clues yet? Or are you going too fast to see them?"

"Very funny." Dash huffed. "Nothing's stirring yet, but you know they're out there. If I don't run them down today, it'll be because they turned chicken, not because I quit."

"Speaking of quitting, I told Midge I'd remind you to take a break after two hours, and it's been at least that."

Brady's wandering attention focused in sharply again, and a crease formed in his forehead as he opened his mouth, but Dash was there ahead of him.

"She not talking to me now or what?" His tone attempted indifference, but Brady caught the thread of concern running through it.

"Very funny." Harper snorted. "She barely slept last night, and who knows how early Grace'll be up, so I took her earpiece and made her close her eyes for a while. I told her I could handle it, so don't prove me wrong."

"She actually sleeping?"

"Out cold. Probably should've sent her to bed, but I didn't want to press my luck."

"Thanks, Harper." Brady let out a relieved breath. If he'd learned anything about Rachelle in the few weeks he'd known her, it was that she only ever slept during the day when her body was entirely worn down from fighting a flare. And as early as it still was, she never would have given in with a team member out on the street if she'd had an ounce of strength to fight it.

"All part of my master plan to take over the superhero alliance and control the world." Harper attempted an evil laugh, but it quickly morphed into a completely non-threatening giggling fit.

"Can we get back to the point?" And just like that, the edge had returned to Dash's voice. Brady closed his eyes, giving himself a mental thump to the back of the head for interrupting. He wasn't sure what exactly he'd said wrong, but he'd never seen Harper's silliness draw Dash's ire without some deeper underlying cause.

"Which point is that?" Somehow Harper still managed to sound unruffled. "Were we going somewhere? Other than you taking a break for a minute, which I can tell you're doing already. How about you, Gamma Ray? Need a stop to refuel?"

"Guess it might not hurt." Brady leaned against the facade of a deserted building and pulled a package of trail mix from his pocket. He cast a look down the street, noting a small group of men lounging in the shadows a few buildings down. Something about them made the hair prickle on the back of his neck, but they were too far away to be any kind of imminent threat. Still, it was best not to be caught off guard, so Brady retreated into the recessed doorway and left his hearing on alert as he turned the rest of his attention to the nuts.

"Right, because he's covered how many blocks in the last hour?"

Yep, the scorn was thick today. Brady attempted to let out his breath silently, not wanting to hand over any more ammunition with an audible sigh.

"Different skill set, different game plan, Dash. What's with you today? You'd never talk to Midge like that, and you know it." For the first time, Harper's voice held a touch of frustration, but after a few seconds of silence, it regained its usual tone. "Besides, you better not be telling me you're *not* using your hydration pack, or she's never going to sleep again."

Dash scoffed, and Harper waited a few seconds before pressing further.

"So, is that a yes?"

"*Yes*, I'm staying hydrated. *Yes*, I'm taking a break. *Yes*, you can lock Midge in her room if you have to."

"Noted."

A sudden terrified squeak, like a stifled scream, cut off anything else Harper might have meant to say, and Brady's head jerked up, instinctively searching for the source even as he waited for Harper to pop back on with a simple explanation. But the sight that met his eyes lit his blood on fire.

"No. Lord, no!"

The three men he'd noticed just a moment ago had cornered a young woman and backed her up against the side of the building, hidden from the view of the mostly deserted street. Brady could see the terror in her eyes as clearly as if he was the one leaning over her, and he broke into a run without conscious thought.

"Brady?"

"Gamma Ray, talk!"

His pulse roaring in his ears muffled the sound of the girls' voices, and he grudged even the breath to form words as the young woman whimpered and struggled.

"No time."

"Back off! Call it in. Do not engage!" Car's words cut sharply through the fog, but it was too late. He was already committed, and if the goons were after anything worse than her money, the police would never make it in time. As it was, he was already jealous of Dash's abilities as the sidewalk seemed to slip into slow motion.

"Hey!" He finally hit the corner of the next building and careened into the intervening parking strip. He'd hoped the word would come out forceful, but his heaving lungs shrank it into a squeak that could only be described as pathetic. And almost falling over when his vision suddenly snapped back to normal certainly didn't help the impression.

Still, it served its purpose, to a point. The guys' focus slipped to him for a second, and the woman wrenched free and bolted. One of the men grabbed at her but missed, then apparently gave up, turning his attention in the same direction his friends had already fixed on—directly at the source of the interruption.

"You got a lot of nerve, boy." The tallest of the group—the one who'd held their victim against the wall—took a menacing step forward, and Brady tried to move back but ran smack into what felt like a solid block of sandpaper. Or…a literal brick wall, as he realized when the needles in his skin faded to something resembling normal sensation. Unfortunately, by that time, his escape route was completely blocked, and he found himself as surrounded as the woman had been moments before.

"Gamma Ray, where are you?" Harper's voice in his ear was almost desperate and much, much too loud. How much worse trouble would he be in if these guys noticed his earpiece?

"You—uh—really want to do this here? Where anyone could notice?" He prayed desperately that the rest of the team would take the hint. Who knew how badly he'd need to communicate with them after these guys finished whatever beating they were certainly going to give?

"Who you think's gonna notice?" The biggest thug sneered in his face, and Brady swallowed hard, but at least Harper seemed to have gotten the message. "See anyone out here sticking their nose in someone else's business? Just you? Yeah, I thought so."

An answer was not going to help. Brady clenched his teeth together, hoping to protect his tongue at least, and tried not to imagine the pain from the slap at the park multiplied by the size of the guy's muscled arm.

"You do-gooders think throwing on a vest gives you the keys to the city? Let's see how it works when they have to scrape you off the pavement." He raised his fist, and Brady closed his eyes as the other guys grabbed his arms.

A rush of air whizzed past his face, and Brady braced himself hard until a thump and a grunt told him the punch had somehow missed its target. The other two goons let go of his arms, and Brady pried his eyes open to see the right one stumble back as the left one howled and clutched his ankle. He got one glimpse of the head thug sprawled out on the ground before a blur of motion hit his midsection with the force of a freight train, scooping him up in something resembling a fireman's carry and hurtling him along at a breakneck pace before finally slamming him to a stop against a building that even on a jarring first impression was obviously wood and not brick.

It took a moment for his breath to return and his senses to align, but when his surroundings came into focus again, Brady found himself pinned up against the side of a house, somehow still uninjured, and facing a pair of the angriest gray eyes he'd ever seen in his life.

He'd somehow been rescued. By Dash. After putting himself in an impossible situation with no skills, no backup, and no game plan.

He might have been better off left to the criminals.

CHAPTER FIVE

"Talk." Dash's deep voice lacked the gravel it carried on normal days, but the word could only be described as a growl. "Or I'll start—and believe me, you do *not* want me to start."

"Brady, are you clear?" Harper's tone was strained, and Brady realized with a jolt that neither of the girls had any idea what had happened.

"Clear. Dash…" He trailed off, unsure what exactly Dash had done, and not wanting to attempt an explanation with those furious eyes less than a foot from his face.

"You got him?" The worry in her voice dissolved into a puddle of relief, and Dash's chin lifted a bit.

"Yeah. Keep off the line a minute. Haven't made up my mind whether *I* kill him after a stunt like that."

Brady half hoped that Harper would say something light or goofy to notch down the tension, but for once, she went silent, and the two of them were left alone again. Brady swallowed hard.

"I didn't—plan that. Three guys grab a woman and shove her up against a wall right in front of me—what do you want me to do?"

"How about use whatever puny speck of a brain might still be rattling around in your empty head? But no, instead you're going to jump three guys, by yourself, with not a single *useful* skill to speak of. How'd you think that was supposed to go down? Stare them to death? Freak them out by listing what they ate for breakfast three days ago? Give me one scenario that doesn't end with you laid out on the pavement."

Was that the barest hint of concern seeping out through the simmering anger? If so, it dissolved the second Brady opened his mouth.

"There wasn't an escape plan. I just—had to stop it. And that part worked. She got away."

"Oh, so that's our job now? Be the city's punching bag, so the thugs can take it out on us and let the normies go? If that's all the use you're going to make of your powers, then maybe you shouldn't have any. At least the rest of us can play defense if we have to—or just plain not get caught. You're a sitting duck that just held up a target!"

Brady understood the concern. Even the anger. He *did*. And maybe there was a better way he could have handled it, if he'd had a minute to think. But these abilities had to have a purpose, and it wasn't for him to sit in some ivory tower and watch the suffering of those around him without lifting a finger to stop it.

"I can't do nothing. You can't expect me to just walk by, superpowers or not. If that was my sister out there, you better believe I'd let them beat me to a bloody pulp before they laid a hand on her."

He'd hoped for even a flicker of understanding, but instead Dash's face darkened with rage. He lifted a fist, and Brady barely had time to close his eyes before a loud crack exploded in his ears. But when the ringing stopped and he opened his eyes again, he found that the blow hadn't connected with his skull, instead splitting the plywood nailed to the window next to him from top to bottom.

"Road Hog, come pick up your boy. Lappin and Blackmoor. And you better make sure I don't have to clean up any more of his messes today, or next time you might be cleaning *him* up."

"On my way." Car's tone was crisp and professional, and Brady winced. Having Dash on his case was bad enough, but being forced to share a vehicle with an icy driver the rest of the day might be worse.

Dash stalked off and disappeared, and Brady let out a slow breath and buried his head in his hands.

"You are *so* lucky Midge was asleep for that." Harper's words were anything but reassuring, but at least she wasn't outright scolding him—yet.

"You planning on telling her?"

"Nope. But don't get your hopes up. She's got, like, super secret-finding powers, and it's not even from the injection."

"Great." The last thing he wanted to do was increase Rachelle's worry on a day that she was already stressed and hurting. Okay, so they had a point. He'd been reckless. He hadn't thought things through. He'd put himself in danger, set everyone on edge, and pulled Dash away from whatever else he'd been working on. But when he thought back to the woman's terrified eyes, he still couldn't imagine what he could have done differently.

What was my other choice, Lord? I'm not seeing it here. I know I can't fix everything, but—is it really so bad to sacrifice myself if that's my only option?

Brady slid down against the building and rested his cheek on his arms. There was silence on the line for a long moment, and then Harper's voice came back hesitantly.

"You know, if you look at it a different way, though, that was—maybe kind of heroic?"

"Shadow." If anything, Dash's bark was harsher than before. "Do. Not. Start."

"Game plan. Always. No exceptions." Harper sighed. "I know, Dash."

"You'd better. And he'd better, if he wants to roll with this team. Because I'm not going to be there to pull him out next time."

Silence fell again, and stretched long enough that sounds from farther away began to fill the void. Birds chirping in a cascading chorus. Kids' lighthearted shouts and squeals. A puppy's excited yips. The perfect idyllic morning, if he could have entered into it. But how was he supposed to get past the turmoil in his heart, knowing they were right but still not believing he'd been wrong?

"All right, Gamma Ray, you can show yourself. Your ride's here."

Brady winced as he pushed to his feet and brushed himself off, then made his way to the street and the familiar sedan. Car's tone wasn't scolding—which might be an ominous sign in itself—but he couldn't help wishing she'd pulled out one of her ridiculous nicknames, just so he'd know they were good.

They drove in silence for a few minutes, then Car abruptly turned into a random parking lot and muted her phone before turning to look at him.

"That was an insane call, and you know it. You put yourself in a bad situation, and if it hadn't been for Dash, you'd probably be in a hospital right now. You really want a doctor other than Mattox poking and prodding and finding who knows what?"

Brady blinked hard and looked away. He hadn't meant to put the team at risk. He hadn't given any thought to consequences beyond himself and the woman. He'd told Rachelle he could trust God with the situations he couldn't help, but did that mean letting horrific attacks play out in front of him like they were a blip on the evening news? How long until protecting their secret meant never helping anyone?

"That said." Car heaved a sigh, and Brady flicked his eyes back to her. "I won't pretend I don't know why you did it. Or that I wouldn't have done the same. Or that any of the others would've held back in your place."

"Seriously?" Brady instinctively lowered his voice to a whisper, then remembered to remove his earpiece.

"There's still a difference, Crash and Burn. Like the man said, they've all got ways to protect themselves. And I might be a normie, but at least I've learned some self-defense moves. Guessing if you could say that, it would've come up by now."

"I mean, I was thirteen when my body quit on me, so no." Brady closed his eyes and rubbed his forehead, not quite sure if the action was a reflex or if an actual headache was building in spite of the injection.

"Then we've got to come up with some better options." Car drummed her fingers on the center console for a moment, then suddenly turned back around and put the car in gear.

"Where are we going?" Brady glanced over at her, and a little smile quirked the corner of her mouth.

"Sporting goods store."

"Wait, why? You want me to walk around the city with a baseball bat?"

"Now that's an idea." Car let out a short chuckle, and Brady's shoulders released a tension he hadn't realized he was still holding. "They sell other things there, Slugger. Self-defense supplies, for one thing. Not an actual weapon—you don't want that traced if you had to use it. But a whistle, pepper spray, *something* to get you out of a situation, or better yet, keep you out of it in the first place. If you can scare the thugs off without having to come up on them..." She paused for a moment working her jaw thoughtfully. "Anyway, we're going to improvise, strategize, and then...accessorize."

"Seriously?" Brady shot her a longsuffering look, and she broke into a full grin.

"My granddaddy was a down-home Baptist preacher, Georgia Boy. Never underestimate my ability to alliterate."

"Pretty sure—that's not alliteration."

"And don't you sass me, or I'll give you a taste of my grandmama!" Car raised a threatening eyebrow, but her grin stayed firmly in place, and Brady lifted his hands in surrender and leaned back in his seat, drawing a deep breath for what seemed like the first time in hours.

Maybe there was stuff he still had to work through. Maybe he needed a better game plan. Maybe he owed Dash an apology at some point—and the thanks he'd somehow forgotten. But thank God, he wasn't in this alone. And just maybe, with the team's help, he'd manage to find his way.

CHAPTER SIX

"So what did I miss?"

Somehow even in the barely less than overwhelming buzz of yet another sporting goods store, Rachelle's soft voice still reached him from deep in his pocket. Brady glanced over at Car, who was hunting through racks of random camping gear, then took a deep breath and replaced his earpiece.

"Hey. How'd your rest go?"

"Okay. Not hurting quite as much at the moment."

"Good. You needed that."

"Mmhmm." He could almost hear the little shake of her head that meant her focus was elsewhere. "So how come Harper's wearing her innocent face, Dash is radio silent, and you and Car are off the clock? Come on, Brady, this isn't even hard."

So much for trying to figure out the best time and way to tell her. Brady sighed and gave Car a quick nod to signal that he was heading outside.

"Give me a second to get somewhere quiet."

Rachelle apparently understood what he meant and didn't speak again until he had made his way out of the store and over to the side of the building.

"My fault. I'll own it. Stumbled on a situation and didn't see a way around it except for stepping in myself."

"Are you hurt?"

"No. Dash saved it. Saved…me, I guess. Took down the thugs and got me out of there."

"Got it." Rachelle was quiet for a minute, and Brady could almost hear the scenario playing out in her head as her breathing slowed and deepened. "Sure you're all right?"

"I'm fine. You can confirm with Car when she gets out of the store."

"What's she buying?"

"Not sure. Self-defense options, or—something to scare off the bad guys, I guess? Trying to find a better way if there's no time for backup."

"Good plan." Silence stretched between them for a moment before Rachelle's voice came back, a little softer and a little brighter. "Do you have a minute? Someone wants to say hi."

"Sure, go ahead." A smile tugged at the corner of Brady's mouth as he waited for the thumps and static to settle. "Hey, Gracie-girl."

"Hi." From the shy sound of her whisper, he guessed she wasn't overly familiar with the use of the earpiece, or maybe with talking to them on patrol at all.

"What are you doing right now?"

"Um…eating breakfast?"

"Ew, you're eating breakfast while you're talking to me? You'll get crumbs in my ears!"

Grace was quiet for a few seconds as Harper tried and mostly failed to muffle her giggles, but when her voice came back, it held a confidence that was almost indignation.

"No, I *won't*!"

"I know, Gracie-girl." Brady barely held back a chuckle. "I'm just teasing. What are you having for breakfast?"

"Guess."

"Cinnamon toast?"

"Nope."

"Cereal?"

"Nope."

"Apples and nut butter?"

"Nope."

"I give up."

"Pancakes, 'cause I finished kindergarten!"

"Wow, that's pretty special, huh? Pancakes, and it's not even Saturday?"

"Uh huh." Grace went quiet again—possibly back to her pancakes—and Brady was debating whether asking her to hand the earpiece back to Rachelle would be a wise idea or a sticky mess when she spoke again. "Did you catch any bad guys yet?"

"Not quite." Brady winced, knowing Dash could probably hear every word and not wanting to throw lighter fluid on the fire. "Dash did, though."

"Why were they bad guys?"

"Um..." Brady winced as he quickly ran through how much he could tell her. "They were being mean to a lady, and they didn't like it when I told them to stop."

"But Dash got them?"

"Yep. I don't know what he did, though. It was so fast I didn't even see. Maybe he'll tell you later."

Grace's giggle was cut off by a shout, and Brady's head shot up to see a man burst through the door of the shop with a large duffle bag on his shoulder. He whipped his head back toward the entrance, and the wall dissolved to show a security guard struggling up from a rack of clothing where he'd apparently been pushed, then swiveled his attention back to the man, who was throwing the bag into the back of a pickup truck.

"Grace, I have to go. Give it back to Rachelle quick, please!" Brady took a few quick steps into the parking lot but paused and ducked behind a van as the guy jumped in his truck and took off.

"What's up, Gamma Ray?" Harper's voice was sharp and focused, and Brady swallowed hard.

"What's procedure for a robbery?"

"Where are you?"

"Um—a big shopping center. There's a Macy's...and a couple sports stores?" He cast his gaze around the parking lot, desperately searching for something distinctive to hone in on. "The sign's at a weird angle; I can't read it. There's no street signs, just—a highway."

"Can you give me a city? Direction? Anything?"

"I have literally *no* idea, Harper. Somewhere I've never been before."

"How'd you get there?"

"My senses are amped up, not my memory!" The truck was getting smaller and smaller in his line of vision, powerful as it was. At this rate, he'd need Dash's super speed to keep it in sight.

"Brady, breathe." Rachelle's calm, firm tone came back on the line, and Brady instinctively sucked in a breath. "Car's on her way. Can you still see where it's headed?"

"Not for much longer."

"Keep eyes on it and get where she can see you."

Brady jogged to the end of the row, doing his best to keep the truck in view and hoping against hope that Car would somehow grow wings.

"We're in Troy. West Fourteen Mile. Someone call it in. Stay where you are, Bloodhound; I'm coming to you."

"We're on it." Even Rachelle's voice held a note of relief, though not nearly the flood that rushed through Brady's veins. "I'm on the scanner; Harper's got the number. Give us a direction when you can."

"Coming up now. Jump in and show me where."

Brady heard the motor come to a stop behind him, and he slid into the car and swiveled his head to find the truck again.

"That way. Dark blue pickup." He pointed, and Car swung her own vehicle through a set of empty parking spaces and set off in pursuit.

"He's on John R, headed for Fourteen Mile. Probably aiming for 75. Following him up now."

"Got a license plate?" Harper asked, and Brady groaned.

"Of all the things I could have actually gotten…"

"Relax, Rookie. We'll be behind him in a minute. You can get it then. He's not flooring it—smart for him and good for us."

"On Chicago headed for 75." Dash's words were clipped, but at least he seemed to be paying attention. Brady wasn't sure if that was a good or a bad thing.

"What did we see when I get the Troy cops on the line?" Harper asked, and Brady sucked in a deep breath and let it out fast.

"Standing outside the store when I heard someone yell. Looked over and saw a guy running out of the store with a duffel bag. Red ball cap, black shirt, blue jeans. Threw the bag in the back of a dark blue pickup and took off—whatever way Car said. License plate—" He leaned forward and strained his eyes, trying to narrow his focus through the traffic ahead and the uneven motion. "MOL-7667."

"Yes!" Car's tone could have been a fist pump, and Brady's attention jumped to find the blue truck curving along the exit ahead while a red sports car sped past it on the left. "He's turned right on 75, staying in Troy. Get them on the phone, Shadow!"

"She's on it. Scanner has officers en route to the shopping center. Keep eyes on him as long as you can."

"Absolutely. You got him, Fly's Eye? Or you want me to get closer?"

"I've got him." Brady rested his arms on his knees and kept his eyes fixed on the truck.

"All right. Hanging back a little. Tell me when he turns."

Brady's fists were covered in a fine layer of sweat by the time the blue pickup veered to the right again.

"He's turning up here."

"Right on Big Beaver," Car reported, and Dash's voice came back, slightly breathless.

"Follow him on, tell me where he turns, then pass him."

"Seriously, Limber Legs? Is this still about me not seeing your face?"

"This is all about how much you like your wheels, Hot Rod. Stay on his tail and face the consequences. Pull off on the next road and get your spy involved. You'll see."

Car scowled but followed orders, waiting until the next left after the truck turned on Talbot.

"Okay, now what?"

"Oh, I'm done." Dash's smug smile bled through his voice without any attempt at concealment. "Take notes, *Ray*. That's what *actual* superhero work looks like."

Brady tried to focus past the houses as Car slowed to a crawl.

"What's he— Did you—"

"Hey, Midge, you want to call in a tip to the Troy police? Tell them some lunatic's just spilled a bunch of athletic gear out of his blue pickup all over Talbot. Plate number MOL-7667."

Chapter Seven

"So." Car fished out one of the last few french fries, which even his amplified taste buds had to admit were just as amazing as she'd promised, and leaned back on her hands. "Halfway through your first day out of training. How's it going so far?"

Brady considered for a minute as he took a long sip of the second shake DeAndre had insisted they stop for.

"Could be worse, I guess. Just—trying to figure out how all this is supposed to work when we don't have—" He weighed word choices for a second, then motioned toward the earpiece in his pocket instead.

"You thinking along the lines of 'reliable backup,' or 'a crabby teammate who does half the work and takes all the credit'?"

Brady couldn't help a snort, but it turned into a groan as he flopped back onto the picnic blanket.

"You've *got* to stop doing that."

"Doing what? You saying I'm wrong?"

"I'm saying if Dash came up behind us right now, I'm the one that'd take the heat for it."

"So what I'm hearing is, 'Car, stop being so accurate.'"

"You're not helping." Brady glanced behind him as though expecting Dash to appear out of thin air, and Car rolled her eyes.

"What's got you so jumpy, anyway? Stealth isn't really his thing—that's more Shadow's department. And you ought to at least hear him coming before he's right on top of you. Besides, if he didn't beat you up for almost getting yourself killed, what's the worst he'll do to you for admitting he's a credit hog?"

"You're not the one who has to live with him." Brady closed his eyes with a sigh. "But the question was what I'm supposed to do when he's *not* around, not how to put up with him when he is."

"Don't stress over it. You'll be fine. So he wrapped the guy up with a nice bow for the cops. You're the one that tracked him and got the license plate. They'd have found him eventually without Dash, and Dash wouldn't have nailed him without you."

"You don't know that for sure."

"Don't I? Say Midge *had* happened to have the Troy PD on the scanner the second the call went out. What would he have done about it? Robbery suspect escaping in an unknown vehicle with an unknown license plate, heading who knows where? There's no way he even tries to jump on that without the details you handed him. Your powers actually work really well together—if he were a bit more…chill."

"Kind of like saying 'if the sun was a bit more dark.'" Brady squinted up at her, and Car pointed an accusing finger.

"Ohh, you said it that time, Gamma Ray—not me!" She shook her head, and her smirk softened. "Look, you'll do fine without him. Anonymous tips aren't worthless, you know. You'll have plenty of details the cops can corroborate, and our credibility's pretty good for—what—less than two years? Probable cause is the best anyone's got to give—unless you go out and join the force yourself."

"I wish." Brady sighed, and Car cocked her head curiously.

"That what you'd actually choose if you could hold down a job?"

Brady hesitated a moment, turning the idea over before tossing out an answer.

"Honestly, I don't know. I hadn't really gotten that far before—" He motioned vaguely in the direction of his head. "And considering pro ballplayer, dolphin trainer, and cross-country skier were never realistic goals to begin with…"

"Cross-country in Georgia?" Car's eyebrows shot up, and Brady tried hard to keep his face straight as he nodded.

"Oh, yeah. Absolutely. In fact, I was voted most likely to get frostbite from all the Olympics I watched that year."

Car snorted and aimed a fake swat next to his head, then pushed to her feet and glanced around.

"All right, Superstar, let's see what you're really made of."

"Come again?"

"You need at least some basic self-defense moves. Pepper spray's all well and good, but you *are* going to feel it if you have to use it. Probably more than most. That's a last resort, okay? And look, I'm no martial artist, but I can at least teach you a little bit about breaking a hold. Come on."

"Do I have to?" Brady grimaced, and Car put a hand on her hip.

"Depends. You one hundred percent committed to never stepping in again yourself, no matter what the bad guy's got going on?"

Brady groaned and pushed himself to a sitting position.

"Come on, up! Just a couple moves and then I'll let you rest."

"Who died and made you the boss?" Brady fought a yawn as he climbed to his feet.

"And I quote: 'whatever you think.' Told you you'd regret those words, rookie."

"Can I take them back?"

"Nope. Now, baseline understanding, you're not here to fight anyone. You're not looking to win. You're looking to get away—that's all. If you can do it without fighting, you do it. Any of these moves are just to get you to the point you can run away. Are we clear?"

"I'm not a fighter, Car. I think this morning made it pretty obvious." Brady sighed at Car's raised eyebrow. "Fine. Yes. We're clear."

"Good. Don't want you getting delusions of grandeur, Frostbite."

"Are we doing this or what?"

"Nice deflection. Now come at me."

"Do what?"

"Come *at* me, so I can show you the moves to get away."

"This is such a bad idea." Brady scrunched his eyes closed for a second, and Car sighed.

"You want me to find an actual instructor that works on your schedule? And that won't suspect when something kicks your senses up unexpectedly? Didn't think so. Move, recruit!"

"I'm—supposed to do what again?"

"Grab me. Swing at me. *Act* like you're trying to hurt me."

"I—" Brady raised his hands slowly, then dropped them back to his sides. "I can't."

"You're not going to actually hurt me. I'm not going to let you."

"I still…can't."

"Seriously?" Car threw her hands in the air. "What's the issue? Spit it out. What can't you do?"

"Just—" Honesty was not going to be his friend here, and Brady winced as the words left his mouth. "Lay hands on a girl. Even playing around—training—whatever. I can't."

"Of course I draw the knight in shining armor." Her groan was thick with frustration. "You're going to get your helmet bashed in for real next time, Sir Chivalrous. That worth it to you to make sure you don't—in training, accidentally, pretend to—take a swing at a girl for once in your life?"

"Sorry." Brady swallowed hard and turned away. Car's disgusted huff followed him, and he ducked out of the way as a slap barely missed the back of his head.

"Whoa, wait, hold up!" It wasn't anything like the tone he'd expected, and he looked back to find her staring at him with her mouth slightly ajar.

"What?"

"That wasn't—supposed to miss you. I wasn't aiming to miss. I was trying to knock some sense into your stubborn head, and you weren't even looking. How on earth did you duck it?"

"I just…" Brady trailed off, trying to put a name to the half-recognized instinct that had prompted his move. "I kind of—heard it? Felt it coming—I guess?"

"Think you could do it again?"

"You really want to smack me that bad?"

"I want to—" Her hand shot out toward his cheek, and he jerked back from her just in time. "—see if you can repeat it. That's—actually really impressive."

"What, that I don't particularly care for getting hit?"

"No, that you can react like that with no warning. That's definitely something we need to test out. Are your reflexes like that naturally, or is this a weird sense side effect?"

"I don't—think I'm always that fast. But it's not like I get people trying to hit me that often."

"Except your last time out."

"Don't remind me." Brady groaned and rubbed his cheek, remembering the sting from the slap he certainly hadn't ducked.

"So what's the difference today?"

"I'm not totally sure." He closed his eyes and tried to play the sensations back in his mind. "I wonder if—it could be *because* of that. I think I—recognize that rush of air from a slap now."

"So you're saying it might not work for other things you haven't experienced."

"No idea. But I'd really rather not become your punching bag to find out."

"I guess that's fair." Car's face broke out in a grin again, and she threw him a wink. "You should definitely practice with it, though. That's a good skill to have. And if you can't spar with a girl, you should find another way to learn just some basic defense moves. It's important for anyone who's planning to be out on the streets, not just you."

"I get it." Brady sighed. "I'll do my best, okay?"

"You know, you could always ask Dash to help. I'm sure he'd be more than willing to throw a couple of holds on you."

"Yeah, I'm pretty sure he would." A chuckle slipped out in spite of him, and Car punched him lightly on the arm.

"So what's next? Ready to hit the road again? Or you need to chill a bit?"

Brady considered for a second, trying to decide whether he actually needed the rest he wanted to ask for, or if the time spent driving out to wherever they were headed next would be enough. But before he could make up his mind, a scream cut through the air, and Brady's head snapped around until his eyes hit the sleek apartment building nearby.

"What?"

He couldn't answer for a second with all his concentration focused on the high-rise and nerves strained trying to pinpoint what was wrong inside it. But finally his senses synced and latched on to the spectacle of an angry man pounding on a bathroom door while the woman inside huddled against it.

"Come on!" Brady took off running toward the building, digging his earpiece out of his pocket. "Might have a situation. Looks like domestic violence. I have to get closer; Car can tell you where."

Chapter Eight

"Hey! White Knight!" Car's voice melded into the rush of background noise, but a piercing whistle directly in his ear brought Brady to a stop with his hands clasped to his head. When his vision and hearing refocused in the park, she was in front of him, her expression half a frown and half a wince. "Sorry. Only way I knew to stop you. One: what are you going in for? And it better not involve any variant of knocking on that door."

"I'm not." Brady shook his head hard, trying to bring his scattered thoughts back in order. Running toward the danger had been more of an impulse than a conscious plan, but— "I have to get closer. It's blurry—too small—too far. I can't hear if he's threatening—see if he's got—"

"You do know all these buildings are carded, right?" Car raised an eyebrow. "And the angle from right outside's just going to make it harder."

Brady groaned and pressed at his aching eyes, then trained them upward, searching for the spot again.

"Here." Car sighed, and Brady pulled his gaze back to find her holding out her phone, complete with its purple-flowered case.

"What?"

"I'm a delivery driver, Country Boy. The people want their food. The people want their groceries. The people don't want to walk to the gate in the pouring rain. I get privileges. Do *not* mess that up." She clapped the phone into his hand but held on when he tried to take it. "You know this means you're cutting our line too. I'll be in the car and ready for you, but you're on your own getting back to me. I've got to be able to trust that you're listening to the rest of the team. And *not* putting yourself in danger. Or I keep you on a much shorter leash next time, no matter what the situation is."

"I got it. Honest." Brady glanced back up at the building, where the pounding seemed to have switched to yelling, and Car let the phone go and moved out of his way.

"So are we holding off calling it in until you get closer?" Harper seemed to have a knack for dropping off until he'd almost forgotten she was listening. Brady slowed to a jog as he reached the fence, attempting not to look suspicious to the neighbors, and gulped a couple of deep breaths before he answered her.

"Yeah. Hold off for now. I don't know for sure—if there's more than banging and yelling yet."

"Got it. Watch yourself with people around."

"I know. Going quiet." Brady held his breath a little as he touched Car's phone to the scanner, and the gate swung open. He hurried across to the building, where he swiped the phone again and stepped into the elegant lobby.

The concentrated sensations of the building washed over him, and he stood still for a moment and closed his eyes as the sounds and smells rushed in. But finally the man's angry voice bled through the tapestry, and Brady took the few steps to the elevator and attempted to keep the thread of it as the metal doors closed around him.

Lord, please don't let me miss it.

He hadn't realized just how much an elevator shaft would shield things until he was consciously trying to listen from inside one. It took almost his entire concentration to hold onto the voice, let alone try to judge where it was coming from. With the fraying corner he had left, he tried to match the rising sensation beneath his feet with the height he'd been looking at from outside.

The garbled words grew slightly louder, then started to fade again, and Brady quickly pressed the button for the next floor, then stepped out into a buzz of sound that hit his straining ears like a tidal wave and made him grab hold of the wall for a moment.

When the angry voice sharpened again, Brady took a few cautious steps, trying to pinpoint the source. Lower. Definitely lower. And coming from the right. He trained his vision on the floor as he headed in that direction, intensely grateful that no one in the apartments directly beneath him appeared to be at home. The stairwell at the end of the hall was a huge relief, and Brady ducked into it and followed the sound down two flights to where he could clearly see the woman still huddled in the bathroom while the man paced back and forth through the apartment, alternately yelling and muttering. If his mother had ever caught him talking to a woman that way—no, talking to *anyone* that way—Brady was pretty sure he'd have gotten more than a drop of tabasco on his tongue.

"Okay, I'm on the…ninth floor. It's apartment—" He shot his gaze to the door, then back to the room. "930. Guy's been yelling loud enough for the neighbors to hear, so it has to be reasonable to call. She's not saying anything now, but there was definitely a scream. She hasn't taken her hand off her cheek, and the skin's pretty red."

"Can't exactly tell the cops that, but it'll help if they can see it." Harper was definitely in her focused mode. "Any more details you actually *could* have heard? Besides indistinct yelling?"

"Rather not repeat most of it." Brady winced. "But it's—definitely threatening. Telling her he's not putting up with her nonsense—get out of the bathroom or she'll get worse—she's making him mad and she'll regret it."

"That should be enough. Calling now." Harper clicked off, and after a moment, Rachelle's voice came on again.

"You somewhere safe?" Her words were low and tight with pain again.

"In the stairwell."

"Stay there, okay?"

"Not going anywhere." Pounding echoed through the enclosed space, and Brady rubbed his head, which was starting to ache even with the injection. "If Harper's still on, tell her he's banging on the door again. Pretty sure I'd pick it up even without my hearing. If I was a neighbor, I'd definitely be worried."

Rachelle relayed the message, and after a few minutes, Harper's voice came back on.

"I put the call in. Don't know if they're coming or not. But that's the best we can do. You going to leave, or try to stick it out for a while?"

Realistically, what more was there for him to do here? Sit around and wait until the police showed up—or didn't? How seriously would they take Harper's call amid all the rest of the crime going on in the city? And it wasn't like he'd be any help once they got there; if anything, he'd be busy trying to keep out of sight. But the thought of leaving someone in danger, even if he couldn't help, cut hard across the grain.

"I—" He hadn't decided where that sentence was going when the latch of the stair door creaked on the landing below him, and Brady instinctively backed into the shadows.

The beep of a phone dialing sounded as close as if it had been in his own hand, followed by a timid, whispering voice. It only took a few seconds for him to realize that one of the downstairs neighbors shared his own concerns, and had finally gathered the courage to act on them.

"You were saying?"

Harper's voice in his ear was much too loud in the echoing stairwell. Brady shushed her in as soft a hiss as he could manage, wincing as the whispers below him paused. He held his breath until the cautious words resumed, then crept up the stairs as quietly as he could, waiting until he'd ascended two landings before daring to take a deep breath.

"Everything okay?"

The words were barely a breath in his ear; he wasn't sure he'd ever heard Harper's voice so soft. But he didn't dare disturb the fearful whisperer three flights below. He reached up and tapped the earpiece twice, in a signal he'd heard the others use for "all clear, can't talk," then sank down on the landing and rested his head against the next flight up. The quiet words of the neighbor faded in and out of his ears, substantiating Harper's report and giving a witness that the police could actually find and question. The pounding seemed to have stopped, and he shot a quick look at the apartment three floors down to see the man sitting on the bed with his head in his hands. Relieved at the lull in tension, Brady let his eyes slide closed as he waited for the way to clear.

"You have got to be kidding me!"

The sharp words reverberated through the stairwell, and Brady's head snapped up as his eyes popped open. His senses scattered as if he'd just been woken from sleep, and when they focused again, he rubbed at his eyes, not sure if he was awake or dreaming.

"Dash?" Rachelle's tone was soft and worried, but Brady's clouded brain couldn't quite reach the reason.

"Yeah." The sarcastic word vibrated through his head in stereo, perfectly matching the glare on the face in front of him. "Why don't you ask Sleeping Beauty here why he freaked you out by going no contact for an hour? Cause he's got one doozy of an explanation."

"I—what?" Brady blinked hard, and Rachelle gave a little gasp in his ear.

"Brady?"

"Yeah, I—wait—" He stared up at Dash's scowling face as clarity began to dawn. "You said—an hour?"

"Brady, are you all right?" Rachelle's words trembled. "You went dark and then—didn't answer. We didn't know what—"

"Oh no." Brady buried his head in his hands as understanding flooded him.

"Come on, someone, details!" Harper pleaded, and Dash gave a disgusted huff.

"Your boy was dead asleep in the eleventh floor stairwell. Not a mark on him that I can see. And no reason for silence either."

"I didn't—I wasn't—" The realization was getting worse by the second. "A lady came out below me—really scared and quiet. Reporting the noise and yelling. I went dark so I wouldn't spook her. Figured she was a better witness for the police. I just—closed my eyes for a second. I didn't mean to—"

"You've been through a lot this morning. No wonder you needed rest." Understanding bled through the relief in Rachelle's tone, but Dash slapped the railing hard enough to send shock waves through Brady's body.

"Midge, I told you, he is *not* ready for prime time! And I'm done babysitting. Next scrape he gets in, he's on his own. Am I clear?"

"Go back to looking for your carjackers, Dash. We'll take it from here." Somehow Rachelle's words managed even more gentleness than they'd held before. "Brady, get back to Car and get some protein. If you need more of a nap, take it. Just—with some warning, and maybe not in a stairwell, okay?"

"I'm so sorry." Brady closed his eyes for a second, but when he glanced up, Dash was already gone.

"Shh. We'll debrief later. Figure out what to do better next time. Car's been no-contact longer than we have. Go let her know you're okay."

Chapter Nine

Car didn't say a word when he crawled back into the passenger seat, or through the whole embarrassed explanation, or until she'd driven enough blocks to make him wonder if she meant to speak to him ever again. But then a low percussion began to build between her chest and her throat, and she pulled over quickly and put her head down on the steering wheel. For a panicked instant, Brady was afraid she was choking, but the next second the noise took on an undeniable note of laughter before building to outright guffaws.

It took a moment for her to bring them back under control, and when she finally rested her head back against her seat and glanced over at Brady through streaming eyes, her breath continued to hitch as though she might be seized with a new fit at the slightest provocation.

"You just can't—win for losing today, can you?" Another chuckle bubbled up, and she swallowed it back with an effort. "This morning you—jump in to save the day, and get—smacked down hard. Then you're sitting still—trying not to get involved—and you fall asleep. You got a medium-range setting somewhere in there, Squid Sense, or just the extremes?"

"This is beyond embarrassing." Brady covered his eyes, and Car gave another laughing snort.

"Can't really help you there, rookie. But I very much doubt Midge is going to stick you in the doghouse over this, no matter how much you scared her. She knows how bad this stuff can wipe you out. And I can't see Shadow holding that kind of grudge. Can you?"

"You're conveniently leaving someone out of that analysis."

"You know…even that might not be as bad as you think. He *has* come after you twice now, and nobody forced him to do it."

"Not sure that really counts for anything. *I* wouldn't want to face Rachelle if I'd left someone hanging out here, whatever I thought about them myself."

"I think you're selling yourself short. If you heard *he* was in trouble, Rachelle wouldn't be a blip in your mind. Would she?"

"I guess not." Brady started to bite his lip, then let it go quickly as the unusually sharp pain registered.

"And I don't know Dash as well as the rest of you, but he works too hard on that 'don't care' persona for it to be entirely natural. I know he talks a good game, but I have a feeling if you got in trouble again, he'd find himself somewhere close, no matter what he says. *Not* that I'm suggesting you test that theory." She raised a finger in warning, but the corner of her mouth curved in a smirk, and Brady huffed.

"Oh, believe me, I'm not trying to! Not sure how that helps when I didn't mean to the other times."

"Well, let's give it another shot. Third time's the charm? Or do you need to rest some more before you go back out there?"

Brady considered a moment before shaking his head.

"No, just let me get some trail mix, and I think I'll be good. Got any ideas for where I might be less likely to get into trouble—or run into Dash?"

"Well, he's not exactly prone to staying in one place, so I can't guarantee the avoidance. Unless you know a specific area he's patrolling today."

"Not really." Brady shrugged a shoulder apologetically. "Trying to chase down some carjackers."

"Then he could be literally anywhere. There's no pattern to those thefts; they've been all over the city. I still think the neighborhoods are a good default, unless you've got something special in view. I'd try sending you to go strip down an abandoned house like Midge does when she's out of ideas, but knowing you, you'd probably pass out from the fumes and strike out completely."

"Yeah, let's maybe *not* do that." Brady shook his head wearily as he rested it against the seat, and Car knocked lightly on the glove box before putting the sedan in gear and turning her attention to the road.

"Trail mix. Knock yourself out. Not literally, please." She shot him a wink. "We'll go back to trash cleanup for now. Not the most glamorous job, but at least it's useful. Makes the place look like somebody cares, you know?"

"You're saying we…don't actually?"

"That's the spirit, DAWN Kid. You're right, some people do care; it's why our cover exists in the first place. And the people are grateful; that's why the protection sticks. It's easy to get discouraged when the blight's all you see everyday. But you think just a little more when you go to drop a cup on a clean sidewalk than when there's already trash blowing everywhere. So it's not just a cover story; it's a real need you're meeting, even just in a tiny way."

Somehow the words reminded Brady of the time they'd had to move into a rundown trailer park after the land they'd been renting got sold. "We keep our part of the world as nice as we can" had been Mom's mantra, but he'd definitely felt the temptation to leave his toys in the yard or stomp waves of muddy water against the lattice just because no one else seemed to care.

"So how does this DAWN thing work exactly? People just volunteer wherever?"

"Some of the time. They do more organized events, but those are hit or miss with your schedules. There's a vetting process for volunteers—don't want drug dealers going around in vests, giving the program a bad name—but Dr. Mattox has connections on the board, so she gets privileges to oversee things for her patients. That's why you get to skip most of the red tape. And the people here respect DAWN's work enough that we've never had an incident, even on our own."

"Until this morning." Brady winced, and Car sighed.

"Yeah…that could've been bad for more than just you. We're not here to get in the criminals' faces. I mean, DAWN's not really a crimefighting organization at all; it's just a good cover. Which is why we have to be careful with it."

"Loud and clear. Does that name stand for something? Or is it just, like, a new day?"

"Oh, now that's a can of worms." Car chuckled. "Nobody seems to know for sure. I mean, it stands for *something*, but some people say it's Detroit Association Working in the Neighborhoods, and others insist it's Detroit Alliance to Win the Neighborhoods. Official records just say DAWN. So—Detroit something something Neighborhoods. You fill in the blanks, I guess. Speaking of which, there's a job worthy of a DAWN patrol. What do you think?"

Brady glanced out her window to find a playground overgrown with weeds and littered with trash.

"Guessing you don't have a lawnmower in your trunk."

"Afraid not. But if you can get the trash, I can get someone to come back and cut it later."

"Okay then." Brady straightened his shoulders and grabbed his gloves. "Can you guarantee I'm not going to stumble over a nest of rattlesnakes or something?"

"I mean—we do *have* rattlesnakes, so—not entirely? But I've never seen one in the city."

"That was supposed to be a rhetorical question." Brady groaned, and Car laughed.

"You want complete safety, go home and go to bed. If His Speediness chews you out for daring to clean up a playground, I'll throw him in the lake. Unless you make a bonehead move like finding someone's drug stash and sticking it in your pocket—then you're never allowed in my car again."

"I really hope you're kidding. If you think my common sense is that far underwater, maybe I *should* go back to bed."

"I'm saying you're fine, Overload. Or you will be when you let the nerves settle—and I'm not talking the ones in your skin. Yes, you've messed up. But so has everyone else. Shadow ever tell you about the time she climbed up a fireman's ladder to get a closer look, and then almost didn't make it back down in front of him?"

"She didn't!" Brady groaned, and Car nodded knowingly.

"Life with her is an adventure, believe me. At least you had solid reasons behind the stuff that went wrong, even if the execution could've been better. And I'd like to see Dash out here with Shadow for a day and not lose his mind. At least he can *see* what's going on with you."

"You're going to give me nightmares." Brady shivered at the thought of Harper hurt and invisible somewhere, and Car nudged his arm.

"Get out of here. Clean the park. Clear your head. Chill for a bit. Whatever hits next, going in stressed is just going to up the chances of something more going wrong. Right now, you're out fixing up the community. Concentrate on that. We'll take the rest of it as it comes."

"I'll try." Brady sighed, and Car raised an eyebrow.

"Do it. Go. Now!" She made a move as if to shove him out the door, and Brady found a small smile twitching at his lips as he ducked out of the way and headed for the playground.

Car was right; the work did help to ground him, although picking up broken bottles from what should have been a safe space for children didn't lead to the most peaceful reflections. But it did feel good to make the world a little better, and he tried to imagine what the lot would look like with cut grass and a fresh coat of paint. Whether it would get it—whether anyone would ever finish the job—whether it would be covered in new trash in another month, he couldn't know. But for today, at least he was doing his part.

He was nearly finished with the last corner when Rachelle's voice reached him from the earpiece in his pocket.

"Anybody anywhere close to Oakland? North End radio patrol just called in a green sedan circling the neighborhood suspiciously. Don't know what's up, but it might be good to have eyes in the area."

Brady waited for Car to report in with their location, but Dash beat her to the punch.

"Coming in from Northville. Be just a minute."

Keeping an ear tuned for updates, Brady lifted the trash bag and glanced around to make sure he hadn't missed anything. But a sudden whistle from behind spun him around to see Car motioning urgently for him to join her.

"What's up?" He started to jog toward her, but she shook her head and motioned at the full trash bag.

"Toss that, and get in! We're only a couple blocks from that area; might as well go see what's up."

"I thought Dash was on it." Brady hesitated, and Car rolled her eyes.

"Just get *in*! It never hurts to have backup, just in case, and we're closer than he is, if we hurry."

Brady stuffed the trash bag into a nearby bin and raced for the door that Car already had open.

"We're right down the street. Be there before he is."

Brady was still fitting his earpiece as Car put the call in and swung into the street, but he still heard the abrupt change in Dash's motion and what sounded like the frighteningly close rush of a car engine.

"Back off! This one's mine, and I do *not* need an extra liability."

"Dash, please, no talking on the interstate." Rachelle's voice was tight with strain, and Brady was sure this was not the time to continue the argument. Car raised an eyebrow in the direction of her phone but didn't say anything more, just continued driving as though she'd never been told to stop. Brady silently read the street signs until she confirmed his suspicions by turning on Oakland—the one street they'd just been ordered away from.

Chapter Ten

"You're going to get me in so much trouble." Brady all but mouthed the words, covering his earpiece in an awkward attempt to muffle the sound. Not that he minded sticking Car with the blame when she totally deserved it, but he certainly didn't want to distract Dash at such a dangerous juncture, or add more than his own pride to today's casualty list.

Car pointed fingers to her own eyes, then aimed them out the window, and Brady sighed and trained his vision past her, through the crawling thicknesses of houses, fences, and trees, until they landed on a green sedan idling at an intersection.

He tapped Car's shoulder and pointed, and she pulled over to the curb and let him out. After making sure that the house in front of him was abandoned, Brady slipped through a sagging gate and crouched in an intact corner of the fence where he could see the green car clearly.

"What part of 'back off' do you not understand?" Dash's harsh whisper in his ear made him jump, but when Brady glanced up, at least he wasn't towering over him again—for now.

"Take it out on me, Sunshine," Car cut in firmly before he could respond. "We were literally just down the street. And we got here before you did."

"Oh, wow, you beat the guy literally running in from the suburbs by what—thirty seconds? Real fancy wheel work there, Hot Rod. Won't be hard for you to leave again either, will it?"

"Cool your jets, Rocket Man. What's your plan for watching them? Yard next door, where they can watch you the same way? Or blow past them every few seconds, rattling their windows and totally spooking them?"

"She does…have a point, Dash." Rachelle's voice was soft and apologetic. "You're hands-down the best at hunting fugitives, but you're not built for stealth any more than I am. This is solidly in Brady's wheelhouse."

"Seriously?" Brady could almost have sworn a note of hurt had crept into Dash's tone. "After everything that's happened today, you're giving this one to him?"

"This isn't about favoritism, or whose turn it is, or who's had more success today." Somehow Rachelle's words had grown even more gentle, as though she was holding something very delicate and precious. "And I'm not giving it to anyone. You have a perfect right to be there if you want. I'm just…trying to find the best use for all our available resources. And I think you're a lot more valuable out on the street than you would be sitting still and spying."

"I kind of see Midge's point." Harper's voice held an unusual thoughtfulness. "I mean, it's not that you *can't*, and I know you called it, but there's way more important things out there that you can do, if you don't jump on all the little stuff."

Well, that was far from the most encouraging comment he'd heard today. Brady was half tempted to respond in kind, if just to remind them that he was still there. But some intuition held his tongue in check even as Dash scoffed.

"Oh, sure. Watch this end up an assassination attempt or the drug bust of the decade, just when I give in and get tied up somewhere outside city limits."

Brady wasn't sure if his objection was rooted more in safety grounds or the potential loss of credit, but it did give him a new thought, and he tunneled his gaze as far into the car as it would go, searching for anything that might give them a clue what the man was up to.

"Doubt it's either of those. I don't see anything that looks like drugs in the car, or any gun at all."

"Yeah, and what if you're wrong?" Dash's words edged sharp again, and Brady grimaced. When would he learn to leave well enough alone and quit trying to help? Obviously, Dash had no interest in accepting him as a partner, and just as obviously, the girls had much better instincts on how to talk him down.

"If I'm wrong, I'll say something as soon as I spot it. And stay out of the way, like I currently am. What else would *you* do?"

Nope, nope, nope—wrong question. He could feel the soaring tension on the line before anyone said a word, and Dash's answer sounded mad enough to spit nails.

"*I* wouldn't have snagged someone else's call in the first place, Preacher Boy, so you can come off your high horse."

That was a bridge much too far, and the apology Brady had been ready to give died on his lips as his own temper flared.

"Seriously? You want to go there? Because I don't recall asking you to butt in on the situation in Troy this morning, which was mine by *any* definition."

"Oh, and you would've done what? Played cat and mouse through town until he stopped somewhere, and then waited around until the cops took your tip seriously enough to follow up? Assuming you didn't fall asleep in the middle of it."

"And tell me how that's worse than whatever you're planning on doing here." Brady gritted his teeth, trying to ignore the cheap shot that he still couldn't call entirely unfair.

"I've done just fine on my own for over a year now, and I sure didn't ask for your 'help' today!"

"You know what, forgive me for not being able to schedule the days I can't even crawl out of bed. Because I wouldn't have touched one of 'your days' with a stick if I'd had a fraction of a choice!"

There was a long second of silence, and Brady closed his eyes and leaned his head against the rickety fence, already feeling the subtle slide of his heart into what was always a roller-coaster drop when he'd given in and let anger and frustration take over.

"Yeah, well, forgive me for not having any days that qualify as 'better,' so I can take my pick of the 'worse' that never lets up."

And there it was. The quiet tone edged in a touch of defeat that was so much worse than any yelling. Brady buried his head in his hands, embracing the stinging pull of his hair against his scalp as an incomplete punishment for the hurt he'd probably caused.

Yes, the guy could be a pain. Yes, he'd made some valid arguments. Yes, he'd had it up to his eyeballs with being subtly—or not so subtly—ridiculed for things that were only marginally his fault. But none of that justified him snapping back. Even less when he knew that caustic attitude masked an ocean of grief and heartache he'd only barely brushed the surface of. Never when he was supposed to represent Jesus to those who needed Him most.

"Not even worth it." Dash's words were rough, but Brady's throat was too clogged to say anything. "One from five says it turns out to be nothing but overly suspicious neighbors."

"Deal," Harper answered quietly—probably more for Dash's sake than from any real intuition about what the driver of the green car might be up to.

"You win. Made for the job? Knock yourself out."

Protests, defenses, and apologies warred in Brady's heart, but every time he tried to force one to his lips, the words wouldn't come. Some deeply rooted instinct warned that talking about it now would only make things worse, no matter which way he approached it, and the complete silence of the girls seemed to signal agreement.

Lord, how could I have messed this up so badly? And how am I ever supposed to fix it?

He wanted nothing more than to find a quiet room somewhere, where he could unpack the whole situation, settle his heart before God, and work out what his next steps needed to be, away from the scrutiny of listening ears. He was going to cry at some point—guilt never failed to do it to him—but he certainly didn't intend to do it in Dash's presence, and for more than the sake of his own pride. Brady could only imagine what kind of attention-seeking stunt that would come off as in this moment, and he wasn't aiming to draw any more notice than absolutely necessary for the rest of the day—maybe for the rest of his life.

But he couldn't just pull his earpiece and go down on his knees at the moment. Not only would Car have the right to collar him for going dark in a dangerous neighborhood, but he had a responsibility to those he was here to protect, whether he'd come by it honorably or not. Brady leaned his head back against the fence and tried to blink away the sting in his eyes as he watched the driver's head bob to the beat of a rap song.

From what he could see of the car and its occupant, he was growing more and more doubtful that anything actually illegal was going on. How much worse would it feel if he had blown up their team and whatever scrap of friendship had existed between him and Dash for the sake of absolutely nothing?

Rachelle would forgive him; he didn't have any doubt of that. She'd understand the annoyances that had pushed him there and probably give him more grace than he deserved, even though the rift would hurt her more than anyone. Harper would let it go, but who knew what kind of permanent mark it would make on the cynical streak left behind by her rough childhood? Thank goodness Grace hadn't been a witness to the whole mess, but she couldn't help but feel the increase in tension, and the thought of her little wet thumb pressed into her mouth sent a pang through his heart. And all of that was only the collateral damage, not the massive bomb crater that now separated him from Dash.

The green sedan started moving again and pulled just around the corner, and Brady watched numbly as a young man exited one of the houses, threw two suitcases in the trunk, and slid into the passenger seat with a greeting to the driver.

"Beautiful." Brady closed his eyes and pinched hard against the bridge of his nose. "Sorry about your marble, Harper. False alarm. Just a guy early and probably lost on the way to pick up a friend."

There was silence on the line for a few seconds, and Brady could imagine the others contemplating the bleak fact that they'd come away from a potentially team-destroying argument with not even a good tip to show for it.

"We couldn't have known that." Rachelle's voice was as gentle as ever. He almost wished she'd lecture him; it'd be easier to deal with than the quiet caution in her tone. "It might have been something, and we're better safe than sorry."

Neither Dash nor Harper said anything, and Brady didn't blame them. He didn't dare reply further.

"Come on back, Gamma Ray." Even Car's words sounded subdued—maybe apologetic. "We're going off the grid for a while. Find some place to eat dinner. We'll let you guys know when we're back on."

"Okay. Take care of yourselves."

He didn't want to eat. He didn't want to talk. He didn't want to do anything but curl up in a corner and forget everything that had happened. But that wasn't going to be an option. He'd have to just put on the bravest face he could manage until he got home where he could bury his face in his pillow and stay there for days.

"Come on, Gamma Ray," Car repeated, and Brady swallowed hard, pulled himself up, and headed slowly back to her.

Chapter Eleven

"Forgiven me yet?"

Brady hadn't been sure they were going to revisit the subject at all, but apparently Car had only planned to lull him into a false sense of security by waiting until they were almost through with dinner before bringing it up. Or maybe she'd figured he had his hands full enough acclimating to the dizzying sounds and smells of a busy restaurant without shoving more emotional turmoil in his face. Either way, it seemed the reprieve was over.

"More my fault than yours." He kept his gaze trained on the remnants of his macaroni, not ready to meet her eyes yet.

"You can find a way to put absolutely everything on yourself, can't you?" Car made a sound somewhere between a sigh and a huff. "Tell me how on earth it's your fault that *I* jumped on the call he'd already claimed, or that *he* wouldn't back off when everyone else saw the logic in it."

"My fault for snapping back."

"Are we pretending he *wasn't* being unreasonable?"

"Doesn't matter what he was doing. My reaction's on me. Not him. Not you. I should've kept my mouth shut."

"So how does it help anything to just give him his way, whether he's right or not? I don't do that with any of you, and I'm just the driver/sidekick/support personnel."

"I'm not saying—" Brady broke off with a sigh, and Car waited a moment before nudging his arm with the tray.

"Go on. Finish that, whatever it was. Because I want to know what it is you are saying and what it is you're not saying. And if you haven't figured it out yet, you need to."

Brady let out a frustrated breath as he rested his head in his hand. Why couldn't she let it go with the parts that were black and white instead of making him sort through all the grayish edges?

"I'm not saying he gets to make every call." The words came slowly, but Car didn't interrupt. "Or that I wasn't a better fit for the job—if it had actually been one. But there's stuff going on there that I don't know about, and losing my temper is never the right choice, no matter what."

"Okay, so you didn't handle it like an angel. Did he?"

"Irrelevant."

"So you're not admitting you had quite a bit of provocation?"

"Whether I did or not doesn't matter. I can't control what he does. I can control what I do. Or at least I'm supposed to be able to."

"Fine. Take responsibility for the yelling or whatever. You know what your own line is and if you crossed it. But what you're not going to do is tie the whole mess on your back with that one flimsy string. Right or wrong, I'm the one that put you there and got him riled up in the first place, so that part's on me. And if you're on the hook for your reactions, then so is he. That leaves what—less than a third of the situation that's in any way your fault?"

"You're not helping."

"Helping you wallow in a bigger puddle of guilt than you could've possibly earned? You better believe I'm not. And I'm not taking you home early either. Give him whatever apology you think you need to, but that doesn't change the fact that you've got a job to do out here, and I'm not letting him or you sideline the sharpest pair of eyes in the city because of an argument he started."

"Have you been talking to Rachelle?" Brady sighed as he flicked a glance up at her face, but Car just grinned.

"Don't have to. I've known her longer than any of you. Is it working?"

Brady shook his head, but his eyes lifted toward the ceiling instead of falling to his lap. He sent up a quiet prayer for help and wisdom before glancing back at Car.

"Is there a way we can do something and stay completely off the line? I really don't want to antagonize Dash any more before I get a chance to apologize—and I'm not interrupting him again to make that happen."

"I'm not the one who set up your earpiece, so I don't know how to switch it to a different call, or whatever." Car gestured toward her phone with a shrug. "Besides, you don't think Mama Midge would kill you for being out on the street with no line of contact? If it was me, I'd be way more scared of her than Dash."

Brady bit back a groan of frustration. He was sure Rachelle would understand, but he didn't want to saddle her with more reasons to worry. Besides, it was one thing to chicken out silently and another to announce it to everyone by asking for instructions on how to make it happen. But what was he supposed to do? Act like nothing had happened? He was sure Harper would play along, but if Rachelle had the same instincts as Car, things could get sticky. And he had no idea whether just ignoring the situation would play any better with Dash than actually trying to address it.

"Look, you can't just—"

"Dash, this is it." The tension in Rachelle's voice reached him all the way from the earpiece in his pocket, and he cut Car off with a sharp wave. "Carjackers. Just took off from West Baltimore, headed south on Cass."

"Be on Woodward in two seconds. Shadow, give me a turn for Cass. What kind of car, Midge?"

"Milwaukee, just after Grand. Sharp left after the turn; it's your first cross."

"Red Chevy Malibu. Plate hasn't gone out."

"On it."

In moments like these, the three of them operated like a well-oiled machine. Brady all but held his breath as he fitted the earpiece, not wanting to miss a word but hoping no stray sound would draw attention to his presence on the line. When he glanced up, Car had her phone to her ear. Her eyes darted toward the door, then back to Brady with her eyebrows lifted.

"That's literally the next street over." She almost mouthed the words, muffling the phone with her hand as she jerked her head toward the corner.

Brady's gaze followed the motion without thought, cutting effortlessly through several walls and a bank of large windows into what he thought for an instant was the street before realizing it was too narrow to be more than an alley. He pushed past the guys hovering on its edges, but the next building held strong. Car seemed to understand his head shake and hand signal indicating that there were too many walls in the way, and her lips pursed in disappointment, but she kept her phone glued to her ear even as she signaled for their server.

Brady returned his attention to the corner, and his vision bled through into the alley again without any conscious effort on his part. If Car had the slightest intention of butting in on this situation, he wasn't going to have any part of it, but it probably didn't hurt to be prepared to move, just in case they needed to get out fast.

"Got them in sight. Cass just crossing under 94."

"Police are a couple minutes out." How Rachelle kept her voice calm and working with the strain she was under, Brady had no idea.

"Turning right on Palmer. I'm on their tail."

"Jumping ship somewhere on campus, you think? That's a bold move," Harper murmured, but Dash didn't answer until he had something new to report.

"Not jumping yet. Left on Warren." Another stretch of silence, broken only by his breathing, then, "And we're back. Right on Cass again."

"So are the cops," Harper reported. "You should at least get sirens soon."

"Weird," Car muttered, and Brady flicked his gaze back to see her frowning down at her phone. "Why turn off before they're in sight and get right back on again? Unless you're trying to get caught."

With as little as he knew of the geography of the city, he couldn't even offer an educated guess. Brady found his eyes drawn back toward the alley like a magnet as Dash ticked off the cross streets, until Car touched his arm and nodded toward the door.

"Come on. Let's at least get mobile."

Brady opened his mouth to protest, and she lifted her hands in surrender.

"Not saying we touch it with a ten-foot pole. But they're coming right at us, and I want to be able to *move* if we have to. Let alone if we're needed for something."

He nodded and followed her out of the restaurant, turning right on the sidewalk automatically before her soft whistle pulled him up short.

"Hey. We're parked this way." She nodded to the left, and Brady turned to follow her, but some kind of subconscious alarm bell sounded in his brain, and he stopped in his tracks. "Earth to Gamma Ray." Car squinted at him curiously, then her eyes widened. "You sensing something?"

"I—" Whatever unclear explanation he might have come up with died on his lips at the memory of the earpiece and the importance of not distracting Dash in a crisis. Even he wasn't sure what he was reacting to, but everything in his body was pulling him in the opposite direction. He took a few steps back toward the corner he'd first started for, letting his vision and his ears search through the dark interior of the next building and out the long banks of covered windows to the alley.

Something was up here—the young men he'd barely been conscious of before were tense, alert, pacing in tight lines, their hands hovering over pockets or waistbands. Brady's heart skipped a beat; he put a hand over his earpiece and turned to Car with the softest hiss he could manage.

"Something's going down in that alley. Five guys with guns. Not sure what they're waiting around for, but it can't be good."

"Want me to call?" Car fingered her phone hesitantly, then held it back to her ear as Dash's voice came back with another street name. "Man, they're almost on top of us!"

Brady could hear the sirens now, even though his ears were still straining for any clue from the alley. Tires screeched somewhere in the vicinity, and Dash's voice echoed in the distance, "Left on Selden!" A red car skidded to the left and barrelled into the alleyway, and one of the guys ran out behind it, dragging something long and studded with sharp points behind him.

All at once, the picture sharpened into perfect focus. A carjacking. A longer, looping route back to the road where they could expect pursuit. Guys waiting in the shadows with guns. And a wicked spike strip spread across the alley.

Brady barely had time to jerk his head to the side before a blur of motion almost too fast to catch flashed on the road.

"Dash, hard right! Now!"

CHAPTER TWELVE

"What—in—"

Dash's voice was rising to a dangerous level, but a tidal wave of relief crashed over Brady as the speeding blur skidded to a stop at the far opposite end of the alley. But there wasn't even a second to dwell on it if he wanted to keep Dash from rushing back into danger.

"Ambush! It's an ambush. Guys with guns—and a spike strip—right behind you."

"How—" Dash's head swiveled toward his shoulder, and Brady saw him freeze for a fraction of a second. The wail of sirens rose to a deafening pitch as a squad car roared up the road he'd just vacated, and Brady's heart stuttered.

"Dash, the cops!" Of course that was their target; they couldn't have known they'd be chased by a super-speedster who could outrun a car on foot.

"On it." Dash's voice took on a note of grim determination, and he disappeared in a blur. Brady's breath died in his lungs as the second stretched in slow motion in front of him—the police car screeching into the alley, the hiss of air as its tires connected with the spike strip, the pop and crack of a bullet smacking into the windshield.

Then suddenly a whirlwind hit the two guys standing along one wall, sending them crashing into each other and the ground. Their companions' attention was pulled away from the car, and bullets smacked wildly into the building opposite. One of the officers was on the radio calling for backup while the other cracked open his door to return fire. Another thug dropped to the ground with a howl of pain, and Brady clenched his fists so hard his short nails bit into his palms. Was Dash out of danger, or was he still in play somewhere? And if he was, how long could he outrun random gunshots?

One of the downed criminals scrambled to a crouch and tried to bolt for the other end of the alley, but another squad car screamed into view from that direction, cutting him off before he could reach the neighboring parking lot. A third car followed them in, and the rest of the guys still standing dropped their guns and put their hands up.

"Come on, come on!" Brady whispered under his breath as he surveyed the chaotic scene, the trembling in his hands creeping up into his shoulders. "Dash, where are you?"

An agonizing second of silence crept by before a sound he couldn't identify surged toward him and a sudden gust of wind nearly knocked him off his feet. Brady snapped his head around to see a tall figure slide to a stop a block past them, just as a familiar voice came over the earpiece.

"You don't look at all suspicious just standing there on the sidewalk, watching a dark building, *Ray*. I'd suggest you get back to your wheels before the cops tape the whole block off and start rounding up stragglers."

"Oh, thank God!" Brady's knees went weak, and he clutched at the building for support as the savage tension released in a rush, leaving him suddenly dizzy and faint.

"Whoa!" Car caught his arm and lowered him to the ground, and he could feel the nervous energy radiating from her fingers even as she tried to keep her voice calm. "Breathe. Put your head down and breathe. He's right; we've got to beat it."

"Is everyone okay?" Rachelle's voice shook a little, and even through the fog, Brady felt a dim pang at the thought of what those chaotic seconds must have meant for her, unable to even see what was happening the way he had.

"I'm fine," Car informed her quickly. "Just—if this all went down where I think it did, I really need to get back to the garage before the cops block it off. Gamma Ray's—probably past the danger point of actually passing out? Not sure if I should—"

"Oh, for the love…" Dash huffed an exasperated sigh. "Grab your car and get out of here. I'll make sure he's not roadkill."

Car seemed to accept that assurance and hurried back in the direction they'd come, and Brady pried his eyes open as a fierce rush of wind from the road materialized into Dash.

"You—all right?" Brady hadn't expected his voice to come out quite so rough, and he swallowed hard, trying to force some moisture back into his throat.

"Please." Dash snorted. "You're the one sitting on the ground, looking like you're about to keel over."

"Dash. That was—" He motioned toward the alley, then broke off with a shudder as the coppery tang of blood reached his nose.

"Watched the whole thing, huh?" A note of something like understanding began to creep into Dash's voice. "How squeamish are you?"

"It's not—" Brady closed his eyes and swallowed hard. "You were in there, and—I couldn't see where—when you got out. I thought—"

"Yeah, well, I'm out. And fine—pretty much."

Brady's head shot up, and his eyes immediately zeroed in on the dark splotches on Dash's athletic pants, the way his right hand stayed clenched around the hem of his shirt.

"That's…your blood. Isn't it?"

"Seriously?" Dash shot him a poison look. "Don't start, Midge. Cut my hand up a little, that's all. And expecting a couple nasty bruises. Could've been—" His voice lowered suddenly. "—a lot worse."

The picture of one of those wicked spikes penetrating Dash's foot seared Brady's mind like a red-hot iron, and he tried to force down the bile that rose in his throat and just concentrate on the fact that he was actually here—and safe.

"Can we define 'a little'?" Harper spoke for the first time since things had spun sideways. "Are we talking a paper cut or a slice from palm to elbow? You know your medical definitions are suspect."

"We're talking the door on a cop car not being nice and soft when you hit it at max speed, so—somewhere in between. It'll probably scar, but I'm not bleeding out; how's that?"

"*That* is getting you back here to get it looked at. Right away." Rachelle's tone allowed no argument. "You're both done for the night. I'll give you one chance to bring yourself in, and if you don't, I *will* come after you."

"You wouldn't." Dash cocked his head defiantly, but Rachelle's voice stayed steady.

"I would, and *you* know it better than anyone."

Dash made a face, but it morphed into a wince.

"Fine. Got done what I wanted to anyway. I'll head back once your wheel man's in play again."

There was no argument from the other end of the line, which probably meant they agreed that, even injured, he was more capable of handling himself alone on the street than Brady was. Was today determined to strip away every trace of what little ego he had? Brady put a hand on the wall to pull himself up, but Dash brushed his shoulder.

"Hey. You're not going to black out if you stand up, are you?"

"No. And aren't you the one who said we have to get out of here?" Brady managed to get to his feet and steadied himself against the building until his head cleared.

"Yeah, about that—how'd you end up here in the first place?" A hint of suspicion appeared in Dash's eyes, and Brady held up his hands.

"We didn't jump it. I swear. We'd just finished dinner—you can check—headed back to the car so we didn't get caught in something when I saw the guys in the alley. I had no idea they were connected until the car turned in—and you called out."

"That's...a pretty big coincidence."

"Maybe. Or maybe I was—meant to be there. Either way, I'm glad I was."

Dash studied him for a moment, as though trying to read his deepest thoughts.

"Why'd you even try? It's not like I was primed to listen to you after—everything."

"Speaking of which." Brady swallowed hard. "I'm sorry. I was out of line—shouldn't have gone off on you."

"That's your version of going off?" Dash scoffed a little. "Needs work; that's all I can say."

"I don't—really have any plans of getting better at it. And I didn't know you'd listen. I just—had to try. Why *did* you? Listen, I mean."

"No clue. Adrenaline and autopilot, probably." He shrugged a shoulder, but his eyes narrowed as he studied Brady. "And you didn't *have* to—you know that, right? No one even knew where you were; you could've hung me out to dry, and you'd never have caught any flak for it."

"Dash…" A deep shiver worked its way up through Brady's core. "Please don't kid about stuff like that."

Dash's gaze dropped, and his hands balled into fists, but then he hissed and pressed his palm against his shirt.

"And please go get that looked at. I'll stay out of trouble until Car comes back. Or I'll owe you a whole bag of marbles. I know I haven't proved myself very well today, but I can take it from here. I promise."

Dash eyed him for a long second before tilting his chin and cocking an eyebrow in warning.

"You break that, and I'll lock you in the den next time you've got an injection. Hear me?"

Should he mention that the punishment was exactly what he'd have picked for himself that morning? Although, looking back, would he still? There'd been setbacks for sure—plenty of them—but how could they possibly stack up against the reward of Dash's life?

"Got it. And I'm going."

"Don't go far, Gamma Ray. I'm leaving the garage, on my way to your position."

"And I'm out." Dash crouched for an instant, as if to gather his strength, then disappeared in a blur.

"Not sticking around for me to catch him, is he?" Car asked, and Brady let his lips relax into a tremulous smile.

"You'll have to try harder than that, I'm afraid." He saw the tan sedan pull around the corner and headed for it as fast as his still shaky legs would allow. "And Rachelle's ordered us home, unless you want to pick another fight today."

"Think I'll stop while I'm ahead." Car pulled up next to the curb and leaned over to unlatch his door. "Nice job, Hero. Let's get you back."

Chapter Thirteen

Brady woke slowly in the quiet dark of his room and lay without moving as his senses crept sluggishly in. The hazy fog and cottony fullness that had finally crowded out the searing pain in his head. The bone-dry ache in his throat that warned he couldn't ignore his body's need for water any longer, whether he wanted to or not. The breathing that definitely wasn't Rachelle's, coming from the chair next to his bed.

He pried his heavy eyes open and tried to blink back the watery sheen that coated them, and the figure swam into cloudy focus.

"Dash?" The word came out way rougher than he'd expected, and he lifted a trembling hand to the nightstand and felt for his water bottle. He raised his head just enough to take a tiny sip, then dropped it back onto his rumpled pillowcase, more drained from that weak effort than anyone had a right to be.

"You alive?" The gravel was back in Dash's voice, but Brady was too tired to tell whether the familiar bite had returned with it.

"Little bit." It had been a rough one—two whole days of a full-blown migraine, not counting the time he'd been allowed to skip thanks to the injection. And if he didn't give his body the rest it demanded today, he was likely to throw himself straight into another one, which would be way too soon for Dr. Mattox to even try to touch.

Rachelle had experienced these recovery days, and he had a vague memory of Harper's puzzled expression over some answer that had come out particularly garbled, but he was pretty sure Dash hadn't. There was no getting around it now, though; even if he was willing to chance the consequences, his best on a day like this was something in the range of a quarter normal speed—and that was being generous. Besides, it wasn't like Dash hadn't seen him vulnerable, especially after the day they'd somehow survived. The hazy thought attached itself to a disconnected memory, and Brady licked his lips as he tried to call up the relevant words.

"You win—much good—for disasters?"

Dash's eyebrow gave the barest twitch, and he crossed his arms.

"Am I supposed to make heads or tails out of that? Or did Midge forget to mention to watch you for a stroke?"

Brady groaned and closed his eyes, not fully sure how badly he'd mangled the question, but grasping for any words he could find to explain.

"Normal. Brain's just—tired. Can't talk."

"You think?" There was the sarcastic edge he'd waited for, but the scoff that followed came out softer than he expected. "Better not try. Don't want to send it back into a tailspin."

Brady curled his fingers in a weak approximation of a thumbs-up, but the gesture brought other pictures flickering back, and he sucked in a breath that might have been a gasp if he'd had the energy for it and pried his eyes open again.

"You—okay?"

"Oh, of all the…" Dash huffed and fixed him with probably the best approximation of a glare he could muster on a day when he didn't have full control of even the smallest muscle groups. "I'm *fine*, and you're as bad as Midge. Six stitches and a mild lecture. That's all."

Brady breathed a silent prayer of gratitude, thankful that God could read his heart without the need for words, before his scattered thoughts refocused on what he'd missed ever since he woke up.

"She—all right?"

"Midge? Yeah, she's fine. Doing relatively okay today, and one of the ankle-biters called a playdate. She wanted to be here when you woke up, but she didn't think you'd want Grace to miss. Harper hadn't gotten up yet last I checked."

"Good." Hopefully Dash wouldn't have trouble figuring out which part he was referring to. Brady closed his eyes and let himself drift for a moment before coming slowly back to his surroundings. "You can—don't have to—stay. I'm—fine."

"Could've fooled me." Dash gave a little snort and shrugged a shoulder. "Not like I've got much better to do. You kicking me out?"

Brady considered shaking his head, but it was still much too heavy.

"No. Just—not probably—best company."

"Then quit talking." Dash crossed his arms, and his glare returned. "Less you remember of this, the better anyway. I owe you one. Don't abuse the privilege."

Brady was pretty sure the score was more even than that, but he wasn't exactly capable of arguing the point at the moment. Leave it to Dash to drop his thanks when his listener could barely get a coherent word out. At least he'd already managed his own apology; he certainly hadn't planned how to handle whatever kind of heart-to-heart this was meant to be when he was stuck in recovery mode.

"You too." It was the best he could manage, and he could only hope there hadn't been something included in there that Dash would take as an insult. The corner of Dash's mouth twitched up for just a second before he caught it and narrowed his eyes again.

"Do you seriously not know how to keep your mouth shut?"

"Rude." Brady couldn't hold back a yawn, and when it ended, his eyes were too heavy to open again. He reached for his water bottle and took another sip, then let his head sink deeper into the pillow. There was silence in the room for a long moment, but just as he was beginning to slip back into sleep, Dash's voice reached him again, deeper and rougher than he'd ever heard it.

"Your sister called yesterday."

It took a few seconds for the words to sink in, and longer for Brady to untangle his mind from the clinging tendrils of fog and fatigue enough to answer.

"Eden?" As a question, it was nonsense; even his exhausted brain recognized that. He could only hope that Dash would somehow understand at least one of the concerns wrapped up in that word and not assume his muddled state had warped his memory of just how many sisters he had.

"Talked to Rachelle for a while. Guess she'd sent you a picture the day before. Figured you were sick when you didn't answer. Wanted to be sure someone knew. Message is something like call her when you feel up to it. Not before. And tell her what you think of the ring."

The tension in Brady's shoulders relaxed, and a smile tugged lazily at the corners of his mouth. Thank God, she hadn't let her fear hold her back from her calling. It might not be a smooth ride, for either of them, but if his dreaded day out with Dash was any example, God would make everything worth it in the end.

"You have no idea how good you have it." Dash's voice might almost have been a snarl if it wasn't so badly choked. Brady's heart stuttered, and he lay still, roused into fuller consciousness, but not daring to attempt an answer that would almost certainly not come out the way he meant it. "You know some families could care less how you're actually doing here, right? Let alone even think of taking you back."

He'd never pried into the details of Dash's past beyond a few vague hints he or Rachelle had let slip. She and Grace were orphans, and Harper was a foster kid; somehow he'd never thought to question whether Dash might have close family still living. And they'd what—cut contact? Abandoned him here? Left him against his will? A hot lump formed in Brady's throat, and his eyes stung like they might threaten tears if there was any moisture left in his body.

Sure, he'd lost relationships to his illness over the years. Schoolmates, friends, even more distant relatives who couldn't cope with the migraines or didn't know how to try. But family—family was different. As much as he'd hated watching them sacrifice, hearing the disappointment in Eden's voice when another plan was canceled, seeing the worry lines deepen in Mom's face as the years dragged by, he'd never feared that they'd give up on him. Family stuck together, no matter what. Or at least, he'd thought they did. Maybe his meager upbringing had been blessed in ways he'd never imagined.

No wonder Dash hid himself behind a mask of cynicism and ridicule. No wonder he worked so hard to keep everyone at arm's length. No wonder he'd expected to be backstabbed at the first opportunity. What did you say to a guy whose experience proved even the words "we're family" meaningless?

The wheel on Dash's chair squeaked and Brady pried his eyes open just enough to see him turning toward the door. Whether he was embarrassed by what he'd just shared or had taken the silence to mean Brady had fallen asleep again, there was no way they could leave things on that note.

"Dash." The word was weak and hoarse, but Dash paused in his reach for the door handle and let his shaking fingers fall back into his lap before cutting his eyes warily in Brady's direction.

And suddenly, a new realization struck. Dash didn't have to be here, in his room, attempting an intelligent conversation with a semi-coherent bowl of mush. No one had forced him to come to the rescue while they were out on the streets. Rachelle was a convenient excuse, but even she only worked if the person valued her opinion in some measure. Dash might have been burned, might hate that he still cared, might deny the fact to everyone including himself—but the truth was he *did* care, as much as he tried to fight it.

"Thanks for—having my back."

"Yeah, well." Dash looked away and stared into the corner for a moment, then returned his eyes to Brady with his usual scowl in place. "Don't get used to it. You start jumping my days any more than once in a blue moon, we're going to have words. Got it? So you'd better figure something out, because you won't have a bodyguard next time."

And there it was. The hint of concern bleeding through the thick layers of sarcasm and feigned contempt. Brady let his eyes fall closed again, and a hint of a smile curved his lips.

"On it."

"I doubt that." Dash huffed softly. "Oh, and you seriously owe me. Harper says our bet didn't count disasters that *almost* happened, so I'm down a marble on the day. You better prove your neck was worth it. Up to eating anything?"

"Not yet. I'll try—later. Light."

"I'll tell DeAndre. Rest up." The door clicked open, and this time Brady didn't call him back. If they were even the smallest bit alike, Dash probably needed time to process all the emotions this conversation had stirred, or at least to tamp them down so they weren't so dangerously close to the surface.

"Thanks."

Dash could take that for as much or as little as he wanted, but Brady let it encompass everything as he gave way to his exhausted body and finally sank into sleep.

The Chronic Warrior Chronicles

Episode 4

Car Alarm

Angie Thompson

Quiet Waters Press
Lynchburg, Virginia

To anyone who's been cast aside for a reason you couldn't help

It's not okay, and it's not your fault!

Thanks to everyone who's continued to support me through this journey, and to affirm the bits of truth I can offer through my one small voice.

TABLE OF CONTENTS

CHAPTER ONE

Terse, indecipherable muttering pulled Brady's attention away from the throbbing in his temples as he reached the end of the quiet hallway and stopped in the door of the den. Rachelle stood in the corner, looking away from him, back ramrod straight and hands fisted on her hips, and Brady edged a step closer.

"You all right?"

Rachelle whirled to face him, then dropped her eyes to her feet like she'd been caught stomping puddles in her church clothes—or whatever behavior little girls caught lectures for instead.

"Sorry. I just—" She shook her head and lifted a hand but stopped before running it through her hair. "Sorry. Please tell me I didn't wake you up."

"You didn't. One of those mornings I can either lay in bed and think about the headache or get up and try to take my mind off it. So I'm up."

"I understand." Rachelle hid a yawn against her shoulder and sighed. "Anything I can do?"

"Tell me if there's a way I can help?"

"Help what?" Rachelle's forehead puckered in a frown, and Brady tipped his head to the side.

"Whatever had you so upset just a second ago. I didn't catch what you were saying, but it didn't sound too happy."

Rachelle closed her eyes, and her shoulders sagged.

"I didn't mean anyone to hear that. Good lesson for me. It could've been Grace, and she sure doesn't need to pick it up."

"What exactly *were* you saying?" Brady raised an eyebrow, trying to reconcile the idea of Rachelle using words she wouldn't want Grace to repeat, and she shook her head.

"Nothing specific. Generic grumbling in Spanish. Which is a habit I picked up from my dad and still haven't fully broken, apparently."

"Your dad was Hispanic?" Okay, so maybe that wasn't the part of her confession he should have been focusing on, but the corner of her mouth quirked up in a hesitant smile.

"With a name like Rivera, you couldn't tell?"

"With a name like Rachelle, I wasn't sure." Brady shrugged a shoulder, and Rachelle gave a little nod of concession.

"Fair. Rachelle was my mom's pick."

"And Grace?"

"I'm not—totally sure." She caught her lip between her teeth for just an instant, then quickly let it go. "Speaking of which, how is your head actually?"

Brady wasn't sure if the connection was entirely in her brain or if his just couldn't grasp it, but since she seemed to be driving at something specific, he let it go and weighed his answer carefully.

"Somewhere between the bad side of normal and the functional side of bad?"

"That's…both oddly specific and frustratingly vague." Rachelle's mouth quirked thoughtfully to the side, and Brady couldn't help a slight grin.

"Can I eat breakfast? Definitely. Read a book? Maybe. Jog around the block? Not on your life. Probably be simpler if you named whatever it is you've got in mind rather than waiting on me to come up with it."

Rachelle sighed, but the corners of her mouth curved up.

"What I've got in mind is, I don't expect Harper to be much use today, so are you okay by yourself if Grace wakes up early, or should I wait to head out till Dash is up?"

"Head..." Light finally dawned in his brain, and Brady crossed his arms. "Seriously, Rachelle? If you're not going to warn people, you should have a costume change or something. At least with Dash and Harper no one has to guess when they're powered up."

"Well, if you're playing fashion critic, I'll have you know this *is* a costume change." Rachelle's eyes twinkled just a little as she ran a hand down her plain, forest-green skirt. "It's about the strongest material you can get—almost as tough as I am on the days I need it. I got tired very fast of ripping a seam when I stretched the wrong way. And if it doesn't scream 'superhero' like a bright pink bodysuit, isn't that kind of the point? If you could tell at a glance, then so could the world, and what kind of mess would that be?"

"So were you planning on letting me know at some point? Or just slipping away when you were sure Grace was covered? Which, by the way, I can definitely handle."

"I would have told you." She might have been more believable if she'd managed to hold his gaze instead of trying to stare down the table. "I just didn't—don't want you to try to do more than you should—just to cover for me."

"You are...so not one to talk." A vague stirring of hurt tightened his chest, but as he studied Rachelle's bent shoulders, the sensation faded into sympathy. "Rachelle, come on. We're a team. That means we have just as much right to take care of you as you do us—even if it means pushing ourselves a little sometimes. At least give me a chance to be honest with you before you decide not to trust me."

"It's not—" Rachelle looked up quickly, and Brady could read the pain in her eyes. "I do trust you, Brady. I just—I have to ask so much more, with Grace, and I don't want to—make other people take on my responsibility."

"You're not pawning off your responsibility on anyone." Man, he'd known her conscientious streak and motherly instinct were strong, but he'd never guessed they ran quite this deep. "We're all in this thing together—and that includes you and Grace. Just because you're a package deal doesn't mean you owe us more for helping out." Brady paused as a sudden thought struck him. "Have they ever…" He turned to look back toward the hallway, but Rachelle shook her head emphatically.

"No, they haven't. It's not any of you. I just—worry." She pressed her lips tightly shut, and Brady moved closer and rested a hand on her shoulder.

"You should really stop that. The Lord's orders."

"I know." Rachelle drew a long breath that shook a little. "I'll keep trying. Thanks for the reminder."

"Welcome." He studied her downcast expression for a moment. "Want a hug?"

He'd been prepared for her to refuse, but not for her to jump back like he'd touched her with a live wire.

"No! Not yet." A flush of color tinged her cheeks, and she swallowed hard. "I mean—thanks, but—I'm not fully with it yet today. Ruined a cup already this morning, and you don't need a broken back on top of everything."

"You ruined—what?" The fear in her eyes was too sincere for a made-up excuse, but Brady couldn't quite follow her reasoning.

"That." Rachelle jerked her head toward the counter, and Brady noticed for the first time the object sitting on it, which would have resembled the metal thermos mug that rarely left her side if it hadn't been bent and crushed like a used soda can. He blinked at it for a second, but then comprehension began to dawn, and his voice softened a little as he turned back to Rachelle.

"Grabbed it too hard?"

"Yep."

"And that's what prompted the muttering in Spanish?"

"I should know better than to have favorites." She started to turn away, swiping her eyes against her sleeve, and Brady caught her and turned her back toward him.

"Hey. So stuff is fragile. That doesn't mean you can't enjoy it—or be sad when it breaks."

"I know." Her answer was choked, but she didn't pull away from his hand.

"Yeah…I'm not sure you do." Brady studied her for a second longer before stepping closer and wrapping his arms around her shoulders. Rachelle went rigid, and he could almost feel the rock-hard muscles that could have easily knocked him through the wall, but he tried to ignore the thought as he rested his chin on her hair. "Don't hug me if you don't feel safe, but that doesn't mean I can't hug you."

Rachelle made one soft noise that might have been either a stifled sob or a grunt of protest, but then she relaxed against him as the tension slowly drained from her body. They stood that way for a long moment before Rachelle drew a deep, fortifying breath and Brady let her go and stepped back.

"Thank you." Her eyes shone with the remnants of tears as she looked up at him. "I didn't know how much I needed that."

"Glad to help." Brady smiled down at her, trying not to wince as his head reasserted itself with a painful throb. "You called Car yet?"

"I told her I'd need her, but I wasn't sure when."

"Well, call again and tell her you're ready any time. We've got your back and we've got Grace, so go protect the city, Mighty Midge."

Rachelle groaned a little—probably over his use of her code name—but her lips curved up in a smile.

"I couldn't do it on my own. I wouldn't even try. Thanks, Brady."

"More than welcome." He moved to stretch out on his usual couch, then turned a warning look back toward Rachelle. "And I'm not falling asleep. Just saving my energy. You try to stall and I'll shove you out the door."

"Not if I don't let you, you won't." Rachelle laughed outright for the first time that morning, and Brady grinned.

"Go finish getting ready. I'll hold down the fort till reinforcements arrive."

"All right." Rachelle slid one of the earpieces into her ear and held a second out to Brady. "Just be careful today. Don't stretch yourself too far."

"Same goes for you." Brady reached to take the earpiece but held onto her hand for a second. "Be safe out there."

"I will. Tell Grace I'll have new stories for her tonight." Rachelle slipped from the room with a smile, and Brady closed his eyes and leaned back against the cushions to wait.

Chapter Two

The patter of bare feet on the vinyl floor blended seamlessly into the distant pounding of Rachelle's hammer, and Brady didn't realize he'd been joined in the den until something fuzzy tickled his cheek. He opened his eyes to see Grace's face leaned over and staring down into his, while her hair fell in a curtain of messy curls around them. Barely resisting the instinct to sit straight up, which wouldn't have done either of their heads a scrap of good, Brady carefully scooted back, then propped himself up on his elbow with a weak grin.

"Hey, Gracie-girl."

"Where's Ellie?" Grace's thumb was inching toward her mouth, and Brady shook his head as he pulled the earpiece and held it out.

"Where do you think?"

"Ohhh…" The little girl's eyes widened and sparkled, and she scrambled up on the couch next to him without a word of warning. Brady managed to extricate his face from the tangle of hair that now stuck out like a ragged bush all around her head and sat up a little straighter, leaning his head against the back of the couch and letting his arm fall around her shoulders. "Does she got her powers?"

"Yep, she does. And *you've* got super bedhead today, looks like."

Grace giggled as she snuggled deeper into his side.

"Seriously, though." Brady winced a little as he pulled back to survey the mess. "We really need to do something about that. Can you brush it by yourself, or does Rachelle have to help?"

"She helps, but not when she gots powers. 'Cause she might make me bald!" Grace scrunched her face up, and Brady couldn't help a chuckle.

"Okay, so how do you fix it on the days she has powers?"

"Harper can."

"Uh…yeah, pretty sure Harper can't today. Remember yesterday? Rachelle said she's still going to hurt a lot, and her hands are really bad."

"Oh." Grace looked down and picked at a tiny lint ball on her pajamas, and Brady nudged her shoulder.

"So what did you do before Harper came? Ask Dr. Mattox?"

The little girl's eyes went wide, and she shook her head emphatically as her thumb pressed hard into her cheek. Okay, he probably should have known better. The doctor's intense, focused personality wouldn't endear her to most children, and Rachelle would be especially reluctant to beg such a personal favor from their reserved host.

"Never mind, Gracie-girl. I won't do that. Just trying to figure out what we do instead. I don't—really have much practice. Do you know anyone else who does?"

"Mrs. Kelly." Grace moved her thumb enough to mumble the word around it, but the wary look in her eyes didn't fade.

"Okay. Who's Mrs. Kelly?"

"She's—um—something at school." She gave a little shrug, but her thumb edged out of her mouth again. "When Ellie gots powers, or her hands hurt bad, I wear a hat, and Mrs. Kelly fixes it."

Brady swallowed hard, imagining how difficult it must have been for Rachelle to confess her limitations to the school staff and ask for help, especially with something as necessary and intimate as brushing her sister's hair.

"And what would you do if her hands hurt bad, but it wasn't a school day?"

"We stay in messy hair and pajamas and watch TV." Grace's lips turned up for a few seconds, but then she dropped her gaze again, and her next words came in a whisper. "But then when she's better, it hurts, and I cry."

Well, that settled it. Brady closed his eyes and let out a long breath as he steeled himself for the task ahead.

"Okay, then, do you think you'd cry if I tried to brush it for you? I might not do it right. I've never tried to brush long hair before."

"Do you pull?" Grace's face scrunched up into a suspicious frown, and Brady offered her a tentative smile.

"Can't promise I won't by accident, but I'll sure try not to."

"Do you get mad if it takes long?" She chewed the end of her thumb, clearly wary of his answer, and Brady shook his head emphatically.

"Never. I promise." He weighed his words for a moment before questioning further. "Does someone else get mad at you for that?"

Grace swung her head slowly in a roughly negative motion, but after a few seconds of silence, she murmured something that his ears couldn't catch.

"What was that, Gracie-girl? I can't hear you."

She stayed still long enough that he'd begun to suspect she wouldn't respond at all, but then the answer came again, pitched just a fraction louder.

"Papá sometimes."

"Your papá...sometimes thought your hair took too long?" Brady kept his voice quiet, trying to match her mood even as his brain scrambled for an appropriate response.

"Mhm." Grace gave a tiny nod against his shoulder and offered a hum of what might have been agreement. "When it was late, and I messed it up, and Mommy had to fix it. Mommy put her hands up like this and said, 'She gots your hair, Javy. What can I do?'" She was quiet for a little while again before looking up at him. "But I didn't take Papá's hair."

"I know you didn't." Brady couldn't entirely hold back his chuckle. "That's something grownups say sometimes. I think she meant your hair was a lot like your papá's. That's all."

"Oh." Grace relapsed into silence again, and Brady gently squeezed her arm.

"And no, Gracie-girl, it's not your fault that you have really pretty, thick, curly hair that takes a long time to brush. I won't be as fast or as good as Rachelle or your mommy, but I won't get mad at you. Okay?"

"Okay!" Grace scrambled off the couch and disappeared down the hall, and an instant later, a startled gasp and a muffled exclamation of "look out, whirlwind, you'll break somebody!" heralded Harper's disheveled appearance in the door of the den.

"You look—" Brady caught the words on the tip of his tongue, not sure how well "rough" or "tired" would go over, before finishing with the mostly true "—better than yesterday."

"Yeah, right. Thanks for trying." Harper limped painfully to the nearest couch and fell on top of it, not even bothering to cross to her usual spot along the back wall. "You haven't—seen Rachelle yet, have you?"

"For a couple minutes. Flare day. She's out on patrol."

"Oh." Harper let out a short, careful breath, swallowing hard in an obvious attempt to cover her disappointment. "Never mind, then."

"Anything I can get you?"

"Pretty sure all my cold packs are warm and in my bed, so I doubt it." Harper blinked hard and fast, but Brady felt pretty sure she was more underselling than purposely playing up her misery.

He pushed himself off the couch, holding onto the wall for a few seconds when his head gave a sharp protest, then crossed to scan the refrigerator. A first glance seemed to confirm her suspicions, but a closer examination showed one of the small gel packs caught between the shelf and the wall.

"Ohh, where *were* you last night?" Harper breathed a long sigh as she twisted her arms to sandwich the relief between the backs of her hands and scooted a little to prop her feet on the back of the couch. "Wherever it was, hide it in the same place. I need this so much more right now than I thought I did then."

Brady bit his lip as a smattering of the inane phrases he'd always wished people would quit using threatened to roll off his tongue. For all his years of living *with* an illness, since coming to the den, he'd developed a much better appreciation of just how difficult it could be to watch someone else in pain and know you were useless to help. But before he could find the better way to express sympathy that he'd always just assumed existed, Grace appeared in front of him, nearly jabbing a prickly hairbrush into his eye as he bent down.

"Before we start, Gracie-girl, can you help me with something?"

Grace nodded, and Brady took the brush from her and motioned toward the hallway.

"Can you go find Harper's cold packs in her room so we can get them cold again?"

"Okay!" Grace raced for the hallway, and Harper offered something between a weak smile and a quizzical look as her eyes moved from him to the brush.

"You actually—going to try to tame that mop?"

"I'm the best option she's got today, so yep." Brady lifted his chin and tried to look confident, but the knowing half-smirk on Harper's still-too-red face brought him back to reality with a sigh. "Okay, yeah, I have no idea what I'm doing. Any tips?"

"Water. Rachelle's got a spray bottle around here somewhere. Use it more than you think you should. The wetter her hair, the easier it works. And don't try to go from the top down. Brush out the ends first and move up, or you're liable to make a bigger mess."

"Thanks." Brady sent her a grateful smile, and a hint of a spark lit Harper's tired eyes.

"And just one more thing."

"What's that?"

"Do it where I can see. I need a good distraction, and this is gearing up to be fun."

CHAPTER THREE

"Hey, Brady?"

"Mmm-hmm." Brady didn't dare lift his eyes from the remnant of the tangle he was attempting to separate, afraid that if he let it out of his sight, he wouldn't be able to find it again.

"Rachelle wants to talk to you."

"Seriously?" He barely stopped his eyes from falling closed as he tapped the brush experimentally against the very end of the knot. "You just do *not* know how to keep a secret, do you?"

"That's unfair." The pout came through in Harper's voice even without seeing her face. "You've been sitting right there, and I haven't said a thing."

"No, you've just been randomly giggling like a—" Brady paused as Grace's laughter again infected Harper. "—like a six-year-old. Oh, and your 'nothing' is completely unconvincing. I'd suggest you scrap any plans of becoming an actress. Or a conman."

"Aww, how can you say that?" Harper was clearly trying to hold onto her frown, but it was definitely slipping. "I'll have you know I've been told I'm an excellent spy."

"Uh huh." Brady worked the snarl free and allowed himself an unamused glance at Harper's couch. "If you mean when you're invisible and not talking, I believe it. If not, someone was clearly a better liar than you are."

"He says he wants me to get better at lying," Harper reported into the earpiece, and Brady yelped and nearly dropped the section of Grace's hair that he'd separated with so much difficulty.

"I did not! I never said lie to her, just—"

"Hmm?" Harper hummed innocently, and Brady groaned.

"Just tell her I'm a little busy right now and don't have a hand free to put in the earpiece. Which is *entirely* the truth."

"Ellie uses hair clips," Grace reported helpfully, and Brady barely resisted the urge to knock his head against hers.

"Maybe next time we can remember that *before* we start, huh? I can't exactly get up to find them right now, and you're going to leave puddles if you try."

Grace giggled again, and Brady set himself back to the task of separating the next section of her hair, trying not to worry about Rachelle's reaction or to wonder if she was picturing things better or worse than they were.

"What in—" The rasping exclamation cut off abruptly, and Brady worked to keep his shoulders relaxed and not let the threatening tension bleed through into his fingers. Without wishing Dash any worse of a day than usual, he'd really hoped the guy would lean toward the later end of the spectrum today instead of almost half an hour before his usual time. "You want to explain what's going on here?"

"What's it look like?" Brady set his jaw and darted a defiant glance upward before returning his attention to the mass of curls in front of him, and Dash snorted.

"Not sure if you're playing beauty salon or water park, but looks like you're losing either way."

"Thaaanks." Brady drawled the word out with all the sarcasm he could muster, and Grace giggled as she drew her wet-pajama-clad knees up to her chin.

"We're brushing my hair!"

"Yeah, no kidding. Midge sign off on this?"

"She's out today. So I'm in. You got something to say about it? Let's see you try."

"Ha." Dash gave something between a huff and a snort. "I'm not calling it an upside, but getting roped into doing girls' hair ranks somewhere between 'nope' and 'never' on the list of stuff I wish I could still do."

"Yeah, well…" Brady generously applied the spray bottle to the next section of Grace's hair, prompting a further giggling fit as the water seeped into her already more than half-soaked pajamas. "Harper, you are so not helping. If I'm doing it wrong, will you just say so?"

"But this is so much more fun." If she was trying for another pout, she was failing spectacularly. "Ugh, Dash, grab an earpiece, would you? I'm apparently failing on all sides."

"And how much of this mess am I supposed to try to hide?"

"I just don't want to worry her. Or distract her. That's seriously all." Brady sighed, and Dash raised an unusually expressive eyebrow.

"So we're doing the 'yeah, honey, everything's fine' bit where you're scraping the burned scraps of dinner off the walls? No way she falls for that, even with a better actor than Harper."

"You know what, just don't get me in serious trouble while I'm unable to defend myself, okay? Is that too much to ask?"

"I charge double for PR work. Triple for hopeless cases."

Brady started to roll his eyes, but the motion made him dizzy, and he turned his blurred vision back to Grace's hair.

"I think my fingers are going to be permanent prunes after this, Gracie-girl. But I'm pretty sure we're getting there. More than halfway, I think. Next time we have to do this, I might just put you in a bathing suit."

"Or put a towel on my neck," Grace suggested obligingly, and Brady groaned.

"You have some seriously good ideas, and they keep coming seriously late. Why didn't you think of that before we started?"

Grace only shrugged, and Brady carefully lengthened a frustrated sigh into a calming breath.

"Well, it's too late now. You're already very wet, so we'd better finish the job and make you very, very wet."

That brought the giggles back, and Brady let his lips curve a little as he tackled the next dripping knot.

"You tell someone you were heading out today, Midget?" Dash's words were gruff and clipped in the way Brady was learning to associate with his protective instinct, especially toward the girls. He knew Rachelle had nothing to fear on that score, but when he glanced up at Dash again, the other guy's narrowed gaze pinned him sharply. "Yeah, and how's that supposed to work when he's not even connected? You have to keep a line open, even if you're just stripping houses. You act like it's nothing, but there's plenty that can still go wrong."

"I was on with her until—" Brady bit his tongue as Dash swiped a hand to cut him off, his eyes squinting into tinier slits as he listened to Rachelle's answer.

"Okay, well, you'd better both be telling the truth. You know your line with Car isn't enough. You need a connection back here if anything happened." He was quiet for another few seconds, then gave a snort that suggested laughter. "You know what? Fair. She wants to know if the connection works both ways, or if we're allowed to keep secrets from her just because she's on the wrong end of the line."

"I'm not—!" Brady broke off with a frustrated groan. "Look, the one and only reason I'm not talking to her right now is because I literally do not have a hand free to put the earpiece in. Okay? If it feels suspicious, it's entirely y'all's fault for not making a completely true story sound even halfway convincing."

"Nothing, just excuses," Dash reported into his earpiece, and a growl built in Brady's throat as he shot a glare across the room.

"Will you *stop*?"

"You don't like it, get on and defend yourself." Dash raised an eyebrow, and Brady's scowl deepened as he surveyed the puzzle in front of him.

"Gracie-girl, hold this for just a second." He stuck the handle of the brush in his mouth, wrapped the two separated sections of hair around his other hand, then reached the brush over for Grace to take. He felt around the couch cushion for his earbud and pushed it in, then had to adjust the sound when a loud thump sent a wave of pain through his head. "Rachelle?"

"What exactly *is* going on there, Brady?" Thankfully, her voice sounded more curious and amused than tense or worried, and he breathed a silent sigh of relief.

"It's seriously nothing. My hands have been full. That's the only reason I haven't been on."

"Mmhmm. And why are your hands full?"

"I'm—practicing for beauty school, apparently."

"Oh, Brady, seriously?" He could almost hear her lip start to wobble. "Did she ask you for that?"

"Nope. I volunteered." He switched the hair to his other hand again and reached down to take the brush back from Grace. "She—kind of looked like she needed it."

"I can imagine." He couldn't tell if the sound she made was more of a laugh or a groan. "The fog's awful today, and her hair frizzes worse than mine. How long have you been at it?"

"Uh…a while?"

"At least you have her laughing and not crying. You probably don't know how impressive that is."

"I've gotten a few tips. Not all of them—when they would have been useful, but…" He trailed off, hoping maybe they could leave it there, but the returning suspicion in Rachelle's tone killed that plan.

"What exactly did they forget to tell you?"

"Mostly—little things like hair clips."

"And…?"

"You're not going to turn around and come back here are you?"

"If you don't tell me, I might."

"Fine." Brady's shoulders slumped as Harper's giggle rippled through his ear. "So, they *didn't* forget about the water, but they *might* have forgotten how to keep it to just her hair."

"Ohh…" He could almost hear her eyes widening and then closing. "How bad is it?"

"Ask me when we finish."

"Looks like they couldn't decide between a pajama party and a pool party, so they went for both at once." Dash's voice was about as dry as Grace was wet, but Brady was almost sure he heard a chuckle in Rachelle's next words.

"I'm sure Grace could think of worse combinations. Do you *need* help? Because I'm not doing anything that can't wait, if you do."

"No, we're fine. Making an awful mess, but honestly fine. Don't worry about us, okay, Rachelle? We've got things here. Maybe not the way you would, but we're figuring it out. Trust us, and concentrate on what God gave you today, okay?"

"Thanks, Brady." Rachelle's voice was soft, and he was pretty sure he could hear her swallow.

"Welcome. Go save the city, Mighty Midge."

Chapter Four

"Are you almost done yet?" Grace squirmed a little under his hand, and Brady blew out a long breath as he tried to keep his eyes focused.

"Almost there. Give me—" The effort of calculation was too much for his building headache, and Brady let it go as he eased what might be the last tangle free and surveyed the heavy curtain of dripping curls. Parts of it still looked a little tangled, but was that how curly hair always looked? He could have sworn he'd been over those sections more than once, and he certainly couldn't remember ever seeing Grace with every hair perfectly in place, like some sort of fashion model.

"Okay, Gracie-girl, we're done. And you're about wet enough to fill the creek. Go get out of those pajamas and into some dry clothes, okay?"

"Okay!" Grace bounced up and ran for her room, raining droplets all the way. Brady glanced at the wet towel and the trail of tiny puddles, then closed his eyes and laid back against the cushions as his headache kicked up the way it'd been threatening all morning.

"Watch the floor. Get it in a minute." The words came out more of a mumble than he'd meant, and he rested an arm across his eyes and pulled the earpiece before the sounds of Rachelle's latest construction or demolition project could take over his brain.

"Yeah, he's still with us," Harper reported softly after a few seconds. "Just…in preventive hibernation."

"Tell her—" Brady swallowed hard and took a deep breath but finally forced the words out. "Not awful. Just bad. Might lighten up."

Harper relayed the message, and Brady focused all his attention on his breathing, relaxing every tight muscle he could find in his neck and shoulders, praying the threatening storm would move on without too much damage.

Lord, I'm not asking for a good day. Just a functional one. Please?

The worst of the throbbing was fading toward a dull ache when a hot little sigh puffed against his hair, and Brady moved his arm just enough to offer Grace a weak smile before covering his eyes again.

"Did fixing my hair hurt your head?" The words were barely audible, even with his nerves kicked up to eleven, and Brady swallowed hard as a pit of dread that had nothing to do with the migraine swirled in his gut.

"Nope. Been hurting already. Just—played nice and—let me finish your hair first." He took a few seconds to breathe again, then reached his free hand out toward her.

Grace made an inquisitive little sound, then carefully touched her palm to his, and Brady nearly shook his head but caught himself in time.

"Other hand. Thumb out, Gracie-girl. Come on."

After a few silent seconds, a wet thumb slid cautiously into his hand, and the corners of his lips turned up as he squeezed it.

"Thanks. Not your fault, okay? I'm going to rest a while. Can you and Dash get breakfast?"

"Okay."

"Thanks a lot." Dash huffed, but the lack of force behind it sounded more for show than anything.

"Nag Harper—if she'll move. Want me today—better not push it."

"Fine. You picking a cereal, munchkin, or going to pester DeAndre?"

Grace didn't say anything, but after a moment, cereal rattled into a bowl and onto the table, and Brady turned on his side and let himself drift as the clawing grip on his head tightened and then slowly relaxed. After a little while, something soft and damp brushed his hand, and he squinted his eyes open to see Grace seated on the floor with her tablet, cuddled up against the front of his couch.

"Want to come share, Gracie-girl?" He kept his voice to a whisper, and Grace's eager eyes answered the question without words. Brady curled up just enough to move the pillow about a foot from the arm of the couch, and Grace wedged herself into the gap, remembering almost right away to turn the screen away from him. Brady offered her his best smile before his eyes closed again, and Dash groaned loudly.

"Aww, come on, what is this? Some cutesy photoshoot? Cameraman comes in here and starts filming a cheesy Christmas movie, and I'm dumping you off that couch myself."

"Oh, come on, it's absolutely adorable!" Harper's words melted together in the way they always did when she started gushing over a book or a movie scene, and Brady did his best to ignore them both, as well as the heat that was starting to rise in his cheeks.

"If by 'adorable' you mean 'about to rot my teeth,' I'd say you're right on the money."

Either Rachelle or Car must have demanded an explanation, because Harper launched into a ridiculously detailed description. Brady hid his face in the pillow, but Grace's soft giggles kept his protests locked behind his lips.

"I'd send you a picture, but my phone's buried and probably dead and definitely too far away. You'll have to sweet talk Dash into getting it if you want it."

"Yeah, not happening." Dash scoffed. "And he'll probably thank me for it someday."

"Okay, okay." Harper sighed. "How's the project coming?"

Brady relaxed again as the conversation turned back to the details of the house Rachelle was working on, and he let the words flow around him as he floated in and out, then finally drifted to sleep.

When he woke up some undetermined length of time later, not much had changed in the room—Grace was still curled up in the corner next to his head; Harper was lying on the couch with a gel pack pressed against her cheek; Dash was sitting at the table, rolling a ball back and forth between his hands.

Brady gave his neck a tentative stretch and was relieved to find that the ache had contracted back to its morning levels, or maybe even a little less. He debated for a few seconds which direction to experiment in before reaching under his pillow and cautiously fitting the earpiece. The background thumps through the speakers didn't spike the pain again, and he gave a sigh of relief before speaking quietly.

"What you working on now?"

"You're back." Rachelle's soft voice lowered even more, as though trying to protect his ears. "How are you feeling?"

"Better than—" Brady paused. "How long was I out?"

"Little more than an hour."

"Better than I was then. Not going to push myself; don't worry. How's your job going?"

"Got the stair rails, flooring, and cabinets done. Getting ready to make a run for the dump and then see if we can pick up the new appliances."

"Still can't believe you got that whole house gutted and put back together in a couple hours."

"Not the whole house." Rachelle laughed a little. "The roof was still solid."

"For a wonder," Car muttered.

"And there's plenty of work left to do on painting and wallpaper. Maybe we'll put Dash on that next week."

"Very funny, Midge. There's about a dozen things I'd rather get done than speed-painting a shell of a house. Pretty sure the normies can handle that much. Besides, what do you want me to do? Run across town with rollers and paint cans? That wouldn't stick out at all."

"I could always drop them off for you." Car's voice sparkled with mischief, and Dash rolled his eyes.

"Nice try, Lead Foot. Your subtlety gauge could use work, you know."

"Who says I'm trying to be subtle, Quick Draw? That's not my schtick. Never has been."

"Right. My mistake." Dash huffed, but the corner of his mouth turned up.

A door slammed somewhere, and Rachelle's voice came back on the line, a little breathless.

"Well, we shouldn't have to worry about a crowd at the dump site in this rain."

"Getting bad out there?" Brady's brow creased, and he glanced up at the ceiling as though he could pierce through it to the sky above like he might have with his powers.

"It's coming down pretty good. Might be indoor jobs most of the day, looks like. Is there a blanket or a towel in here? I can carry a lot in one load, but not a whole trailer full of junk."

"Don't worry; I've got you covered. Or the seats covered, at least." Car's grin was as plain as if she'd been sitting in the room. "Take a breather. My job now."

"Fill me in on the details? I missed most of it." Brady propped himself up on his elbow, and Rachelle complied, describing the house she'd been working on, the improvements she'd made, and what she imagined it could be in the future. Her enthusiasm was catching, and Brady felt himself being swept along in the current of her vision. She'd be great—and probably dangerous—as a real estate agent, or a used car salesman, or a telemarketer—just as long as she believed in whatever she was trying to pitch.

"So where are you going after this?"

"Next house on the list, if they've got the supplies ready."

"You really like this work, don't you?"

"I mean, I didn't plan on being a contractor when I grew up." Rachelle chuckled a little. "But yes, I like it. I like making the neighborhoods a little bit better. I like turning this power into putting things right, not just knocking them down. And it's a lot less risk than being out on the streets."

"You know you're going to give the rest of the volunteer crews a bad name," Brady teased. "It's going to take twice as long for someone to get out and paint it as it did for you to do everything else."

"For all they know, I've got a full work crew out with me. We're just the most efficient crew in town. In fact—Car!"

The last word was a scream, and Brady jerked bolt upright as the sickening sound of crunching metal and breaking glass ripped through his ear, then cut to deafening silence.

Chapter Five

"Rachelle!" The word burst from three sets of lips at once, but only silence echoed back for a heart-stoppingly long moment.

Harper lay frozen on the couch, mouth hanging slack, face somehow white beneath its unnatural flush. Dash leaned forward in his chair, hands clasping the metal bars as though about to snap them in half, looking ready to launch himself into an impossible run. Grace sat jammed into the corner of the couch, eyes bouncing between the three of them, thumb pushed so far into her mouth it was a wonder she hadn't choked on it. But before he could make a move toward her, or even decide what it should be, a little moan came over the earpiece, and Brady's breath caught.

"Talk to us, Midget." Dash's voice took on a note of command, but the lack of the usual bite in his tone made it somehow soft at the same time.

"We…the truck…" The words sounded dazed, but a sudden gasp seemed to signal renewed alertness.

"What happened?"

"Oh no. Father, no, please!" Rachelle's voice caught on a sob, and Brady's fists clenched as his entire body tensed with the need to do something—to be there—just to know what exactly they were up against. A warning throb of pain snaked up the back of his skull, and he concentrated every bit of strength he could scrape together into forcing his muscles to relax. If he let the stress send his body into a spiral, he'd be no good to anyone, least of all her.

"Where are you? What do you need?"

"Car!" Rachelle's tone rose sharply. "Carmel Esmee Manigault! You stay with me, do you hear?" Metal groaned and ripped, and her breaths came short and fast. "Dash, are you there?"

Did that mean she hadn't heard him that whole time, or just that it hadn't fully registered? Brady forced a deep breath, but Dash's voice stayed unbelievably calm.

"I'm here. Ready to help. Give me details."

"Bad accident. West on 96, coming from Chicago. Get us an ambulance—fast!"

"Harper—"

"On it." The words were out of Harper's mouth before her name had left Dash's, and in the next instant, she had the phone to her ear.

"Car, come on!" Hinges groaned in the distance, and something heavy scraped and crashed in a terrifying cacophony. "Car!"

"Lord Jesus." Brady breathed the words, unable to even grasp the full weight of the prayer, struggling against the terrifying pictures flooding his mind.

"Give us something, Midge. What are you looking at?"

"She's…I don't know…" Rachelle sucked in a ragged gasp. "So much blood. She—I can't tell if—" A couple of seconds crawled by, filled only with Rachelle's labored breathing, before her voice came back. "That's not good. We might be dripping fluid. I've got to move her."

"Do what you have to." Dash's voice was grim, but the words carried complete confidence, and Brady could only hope some of that strength was flowing across the line to Rachelle.

Glass crunched beneath her feet, simultaneously too close and much too far away, and Brady held his breath until her voice came back.

"Okay. We're away. Far enough, I hope."

"Start your first aid." How Dash could continue to speak so calmly at a time like this, Brady had no idea. "Talk me through it."

"She's breathing. Not conscious. I'm shaking. Might break a bone if I tried for a pulse."

"Never mind the pulse. She's breathing, she's got one. What else?"

"Her arm." Rachelle caught back a sob. "So bloody. Truck lost control—clipped the barrier and spun out—right into us."

"Find the bleeding. Where's it coming from?"

"Shoulder mostly. It's bad, Dash."

"You have to find a way to put pressure."

"I can't." Her voice was raw with a terror Brady had never heard. "I don't have control. I'll crush it."

"Rachelle! Breathe."

She sucked in a ragged, choking gasp, and Brady closed his eyes and finally found his voice.

"Father God, help Rachelle right now." The words flooded from him like a spring-fed creek, as though fueled by some source beyond himself. "Help her hands to be gentle. Help her mind to be clear. Keep Car alive. Get the ambulance there quickly. Protect them both. Please, Father."

"Amen," Rachelle whispered brokenly, but her next breath was deeper and not quite as shaky.

"Test your strength against something, Midget." Dash's tight control couldn't entirely mask the strain in his tone, but Brady was not going to regret that prayer, no matter what deeper issues it might have stirred for anyone else. "Get back in your zone. You can do this. She needs you."

Rachelle's hard swallow carried all the way through the earpiece, but after a few deep breaths, her voice came back.

"I'm—applying pressure. Not sure if it's helping, but—I haven't cracked a bone yet."

"Keep it up. Stay out of your head. Do your best. Don't overthink. Harper, where are we on an ambulance?"

"On its way. I don't know where from."

"Midge, I don't know what they'll allow, but try to send them back here. Tell them you're a patient, Car's got family, whatever. Let us know where you're going as soon as you can."

"Dash…" Her words cut off with a little sob, and Brady's heart sped up a beat as the question he'd almost forgotten in his worry for Car resurfaced.

"Rachelle, are you okay?" She hadn't been asking for him, but he needed to know. "Physically? Do you need—"

"No. Yes. I mean—yes, I'm okay." The words should have been reassuring, but the note of fear rising in her voice was anything but. "It's just—they'll make me—if they find—" The disjointed words cut off on another sobbing breath, but before Brady could begin to make sense of them, her tense voice came back on the line. "I hear the sirens. I've got to lose the earpiece. Get someone—please!"

"On it." Dash's face set in hard lines, and he shot a challenging look at Brady. "You tracking Mattox down, or am I?"

"I—what?" Brady hated how clueless he sounded, but his spinning brain was trying to assemble a jigsaw puzzle in a hurricane, and he couldn't keep up.

"Wake up, greenhorn! What's a doctor or a paramedic going to find if they start poking at her today? You want to find out? Or you think they'll just let her walk away after a crash like that?"

A choking, terrified cry—part wail, part scream—erupted from the corner where Brady had somehow tuned out the fact that Grace was still watching. Without giving anyone time to react, the little girl shot from the couch and bolted down the hall, and Brady gritted his teeth against the exclamation of dismay that would only have upset Rachelle more if she learned its source.

The sirens were wailing in his ear now, throwing his world off balance, and he could barely make out male voices and the squawk of radios, and Rachelle's shaky words, too far away to understand. It was agony to pull the earpiece, but he couldn't help anything if his stubborn clinging to that one line of connection sent him down for the count.

"That settles it." Dash gave his wheelchair a push that sent him halfway to the door. "You handle the kid. I'm going after Mattox. Harper, stay put and keep an ear out in case she needs something."

"I will." Harper's voice was shaky, and tears stained the fiery red of her cheeks.

"Hey." Dash paused at the door on his way into the hall. "Chin up. We'll get her back. Car too. Okay?"

Harper nodded slowly, and Dash waited until she met his eyes.

"And you're not sidelined. You're our only line of communication right now. You're vital. Got it? Stick to that earpiece like glue."

"I will," Harper murmured again, and Dash threw a look back at Brady.

"If you want to tell Midge you left her mini-me alone in her room with all this, it's your funeral. I'll leave you to it."

"I'm going." *Pray for me* was on his lips, but he caught it in time, sending up his own wordless plea instead. Dash gave a terse nod and disappeared.

"Brady?" Harper's choked voice stopped him on the way out the door. "Don't forget—what happened to her parents."

Oh, Lord... Brady's eyes closed as the memory slammed into his heart. What must Grace be feeling right now? What must Rachelle be feeling? *God, be with her, please. And be with me. Give me the words. Please.*

"I'll remember." He swallowed hard and looked back at Harper. "Take care of her, okay?"

"I will." Harper's whisper followed him as he headed out the door and down the hall to look for Grace.

Chapter Six

"Gracie-girl?" Brady threw a worried look around her room, trying to find any places he might have missed that a barely-six-year-old could hide. The room wasn't that big to begin with, and it didn't have many hiding spots, let alone ones he hadn't checked yet. But where else would she have gone? He'd definitely heard a door click when she'd run from the common. Had she gone through the emergency door? Into Dr. Mattox's lab? Out into the main part of the medical center?

Lord, please… Brady's heartbeat picked up, and his head began to pound harder as he stepped back into the hall, but before he had time for more than a panicked glance around, the sight of the opposite door stopped him, and he softly poked his head inside and felt his heart crack at the sight of the blanket-covered lump curled up at the foot of Rachelle's bed.

"Hey." He whispered the word as he slid onto the edge of the bed and placed a careful hand on the curve of the lump that formed her back. It shook under his hand, and his heart cracked further. "It's okay, Gracie-girl. Rachelle's okay. She's strong today, remember? Those cars can't hurt her." He so hoped that was true. "She's not hurt. She's helping people. And Dash just went to find Dr. Mattox so she can help us get her back here."

Grace drew a couple shuddering breaths but didn't answer—at least not that he could hear.

"Can you come out, please, Gracie-girl? I know you're scared. But I can't hear you if your head's all covered up." Brady waited for a minute, but the lump didn't stir. "Come on, please? I can't talk to a blanket." Again, no reply, except that she seemed to curl up even smaller. "Grace, I need to be able to tell Rachelle you're okay, and I can't do that if I can't see you."

That brought a mumbled response of some kind, but between the blanket still covering her head and the thumb that he had no doubt was planted deep in her mouth, he couldn't even come close to deciphering it.

"Gracie-girl, I don't have my super hearing today. I can't understand you. I really need you to come out, please. I don't care if you keep the rest of you wrapped up, but I need to see your face free."

There was another long second of silence, then the lump slowly started to uncoil itself until one dark brown eye and a tear-streaked cheek finally peeked through a crack in the blanket.

"Can I see your whole face, please?"

Grace hesitated, and Brady wondered for a heart-dropping second whether he'd pushed too hard, but finally she wriggled the crack far enough open to display her other eye.

"Good girl." Brady kept his voice as gentle as he knew how, praying he didn't say the wrong thing and scare her back into her cocoon. "Now what were you trying to say?"

Grace's reply was mumbled around her thumb and just as indecipherable as before, if not quite as muffled, and Brady's heart cracked further.

"I still can't hear you, sweet girl. I want to help, but you're going to have to lose the thumb—I mean, take it out of your mouth." Brady swallowed hard, and a shiver rippled through him at the unintentional picture.

Grace scooted a little closer, moving the blanket roughly to her hairline, but she chewed thoughtfully on her thumb for a long few moments before cautiously inching it to her lips. Brady leaned down just in time to catch the whispered words that he'd nearly had to have her repeat for a third time.

"Did Ellie…say check on me?" The thumb sucked back into her mouth like a stopper in a drain, and Brady weighed his answer carefully, trying to gauge what part of the truth he could tell her without stumbling into a trap that would hurt her more.

"She didn't have to, Gracie-girl. She knew we'd take care of you." At least, he hoped she could trust them for that. "She didn't get much time to talk because the ambulance came and she had to hide the earpiece." Grace ducked her head, and Brady quickly laid a hand on it before she could retreat back under the blanket. "But I know it's the first thing she's going to ask when they get her back here. She doesn't want you to be scared. She loves you so much."

"What if she's hurted?" The words came in a trembling whisper, and Brady slid the blanket just enough to let him carefully stroke the top of her still damp hair.

"She's not. And if she was, we'd take care of her. Just like always. That's what Dr. Mattox and the nurses are here for, right? There's plenty of people here to make her okay again if she wasn't."

Grace's reply was incomprehensible, and Brady sighed. He glanced around the room, searching for some sort of inspiration, and his gaze snagged on the old-fashioned rocking chair squeezed into the space between the end of Rachelle's bed and the bathroom wall.

"Tell you what. Can we try this?" Brady slid into the rocker and held his arms out to Grace. "Then you can be right next to my ear, so maybe I can hear better."

Surprisingly, this time Grace's hesitation only lasted for a few seconds before she scrambled off the bed and curled up on his lap, still half-mummified in the blanket and looking like it might take an escape artist to pry her loose. Not that he was planning to try at the moment. Instead, he wrapped an arm around her, tangled blanket and all, rested back against the chair as comfortably as he could, and settled her head against his shoulder.

"Okay, tell me again, Gracie-girl? She's not hurt, but even if she was, she's coming back here. That means the doctors can take care of her, right?"

"They didn't make Ellie's mommy better…when she was in the hospital." Grace's breath hiccuped like the threat of tears was imminent.

Rachelle's mom? He'd never heard Grace refer to her that way before. Or had he just assumed they were full siblings? A stepmom would definitely explain the difference in their ages. But then when had her birth mom died? Hadn't Rachelle referred to her in more recent contexts? Or had she switched to calling Grace's mom by that name?

Brady gave himself a mental shake to refocus. He could sort those details out later. Right now, his priority was a little girl who was scared to death—drowning in layers of trauma from the car accident that had taken her parents, and maybe something else that had happened to Rachelle's mom, and the fear she probably lived with on a daily basis from having most of the adults in her life sick to some degree more days than not.

"You're right; the doctors can't fix everything. And just because you're in a hospital doesn't mean bad things can't happen." His heart clenched at the thought of Car, and he sent up a whispered prayer on a steadying breath. "But Rachelle's okay. And we're all here to help her if she needs us. We'll take care of her, okay? And you. I promise."

Grace lifted searching eyes to his face, and Brady tried to meet her gaze with all the honesty he could.

"If…" She trailed off and dropped her gaze, and Brady stroked her cheek and tried to lift her chin.

"It's okay, Gracie-girl. You can ask me."

"If…something…happened to…Ellie…could I stay with you?"

"Oh, Grace." Brady felt like someone had punched him in the gut. No six-year-old should be worrying about her sister dying, let alone the question of who would get custody if it happened. "I—I don't know, sweet girl." The admission broke his heart even more than the question. "If anything happened to Rachelle, I would do my very best to take care of you. We all would. But—it wouldn't be my choice. The judge would have to decide that. And I don't know if they'd let me keep you or not. They might—not like that I don't have a job to take care of you. Or—" *Think the medical center is a bad place to raise you. Not believe someone with my issues could take care of you the way you need. Not see what kind of future I could give you.* All the worries Rachelle carried with her every day, sister or not. "—or think I haven't known you long enough for you to stay with me."

"But Ellie didn't." The words were barely decipherable around her tight grip on her thumb, and Brady's brow furrowed as he tried to make sense of them.

"She didn't what?"

"She didn't know me a long time. Just after Mommy and Daddy died."

"You…" Brady closed his eyes, trying to put his tottering thoughts in order. "You didn't know…Rachelle…before your parents died?"

He was sure he must have heard her wrong, but Grace nodded emphatically against his chest.

"Uh huh. When she came to see me after her mommy died. And said now we both lost our mommies and daddy, but we could be sisters if I wanted to."

"Were you…not sisters…before?" How did that even work? He was positive Rachelle's whole basis for custody had been the family relation—or had he totally misheard everything she'd told him?

"Uh huh. 'Cause our daddy was the same. We just didn't know, but now we did."

Didn't know. How did you just *not know* you had a sibling? A handful of scenarios popped to mind—none of them good. Just how much of their life as he'd painted it in his mind was completely made up? Had Rachelle lied about their past? Or had he totally missed the gaping holes that were now staring him in the face?

"I don't know, Grace." The words came on a whisper, feeling truer than ever before. "I—I promise if anything happened to Rachelle, I'd do my very best to take care of you. Even if I don't totally know what that would be. Okay?"

Grace's nod was slower this time, but she didn't pull away from his grip.

"Are you sure Ellie's okay?"

"I'm sure. Trust me. She's already being a hero again."

"She is?" Grace looked up hopefully, and Brady swallowed hard, afraid to go into too much detail about Car's injuries and searching his brain for a less traumatizing example.

"Yep. I think I heard her rip a whole door off so Car could get out of the wreck."

"You did?" Grace's voice squeaked up with interest, and Brady grimaced a little.

"I think so. I can't tell you for sure. I couldn't see it. We'll have to ask her about it when she comes back, okay?"

Grace nodded and settled back against his chest, and Brady closed his eyes and tried to ignore the swirling questions clamoring in his mind. Rachelle would have to bring clarity to a lot of things when they finally got her back.

CHAPTER SEVEN

Brady waited until Grace's death grip on her blanket had relaxed a few degrees before broaching the suggestion that they go back to the den and see if Harper had any updates. Grace chewed her thumb for a moment, but finally nodded, and Brady somehow managed to get her up and not drop her when the unaccustomed pressure on his shoulder and neck sent a wave of dizziness rushing through him.

Please, Lord. He closed his eyes, forced a deep breath, and shifted her against his shoulder a little, and the warning bells quieted enough to let him carry her out to the den. Dr. Mattox and Dash were there when he arrived, the former at the counter, typing furiously on a pad, and the latter next to Harper's couch, arms crossed and face set in stern, focused lines.

Shoving away the questions that hammered in his heart, Brady set Grace on his own couch—at least, the one he most often claimed—and collected her tablet and headphones from the set of bins along the wall before returning to her side.

"Put these on, Gracie-girl, and don't take them off until someone tells you. I'll come let you know as soon as I find out what's happening, okay?"

Grace's fist trembled against her mouth, but she didn't protest when Brady slipped the headphones on her and started whichever show was automatically queued up before striding over to join Dash and Harper.

"You brought her out here?" Dash scowled at him, but Brady didn't even flinch.

"What'd you want me to do? Leave her? What've you heard?"

"Ambulance is on its way here." Harper swallowed hard. "Well, here to the ER, not *here* here. She's ducked the paramedics so far, but I'm not sure that's totally a good thing."

"Means Car's sucking up all their attention."

"Sounds like her arm." Harper nodded with a shaky breath, and Brady winced.

"Mattox is going to check—and claim treating physician privilege for Rachelle—or she says she is." Dash's scowl deepened. "Not sure what we're still waiting on."

"An orderly and a wheelchair to keep up appearances." Brady jumped as Dr. Mattox's voice sounded directly behind him. "But they seem to be in short supply at the moment. I'm working on it as fast as I can."

Harper put a hand to her earpiece and motioned for silence, then shook her head urgently.

"They're almost at the ER."

"Oh, of all the—" Dash gave his chair a heated shove across to the other end of Grace's couch and glared at the doctor. "Get me out of this thing, and take it and him. She doesn't have time."

It wasn't until Dash started scooting and pushing himself toward the couch that Brady's clouded brain latched onto the realization that "this thing" was his chair, and only after Dr. Mattox had helped him—not altogether gently—into the corner, then shot a raised eyebrow back over her shoulder, did the idea dawn on Brady that *he* was supposed to be the "him" in question.

"You—want me to do what?"

"Go with her and push the wheelchair. *If* you can handle that." Dash's fists were still clenched, and his breaths came hard, probably in reaction to that awkward and incredibly fast transfer, but beneath the obvious current of tension, Brady thought he traced a thread of a different concern—possibly a recognition that he really might not be up to it.

His throat tightened at the sight of the empty chair—an occurrence he'd never experienced outside of stumbling on a gut-wrenching therapy session—and shot a glance back at Harper. But that was no better—the wet clumps of lashes on her closed eyelids shredded his heart, even without the glistening trails on her burning cheeks that she hadn't even attempted to wipe away.

Okay, so it was asking a lot on a day when his head was already teetering on the edge. But more than a cover story, Rachelle surely needed a friend, and if he didn't step up now, how much longer would she have to wait? Just knowing she was safe—having some definite word on Car's condition—giving what he could, just like they already had—it was worth the price of a bad day or three, if that's what it cost in the end.

"I'll go. Let me grab my glasses. Dash, tell Grace—" He nearly choked and had to swallow hard before he could finish. "Tell her I'm going to bring Rachelle home."

Dash's terse nod was the only confirmation he got—and all the assurance he needed—before Dr. Mattox strode out the door, leaving him to run to catch up.

The enigmatic doctor didn't say a word as he followed her through the lab level and only stopped long enough to toss him an extra lab coat, which Brady managed to throw on in the elevator, hoping that it would hide his lack of scrubs well enough to pass. He doubted he actually looked much like a hospital employee, even with the wheelchair, especially with the sunglasses that he thankfully remembered to pull down before they reached the door. Never mind—explaining his presence was the doctor's job, if it came to that. He could only hope her silence meant she was formulating what she had to say to get them where they needed to go.

At least she seemed to be taking this seriously. Of course, she didn't want them exposed any more than they did—hopefully just for publicity and funding reasons, not because she was breaking some major ethical code in creating a team of half-baked superheroes and keeping them in her basement. But as focused and aloof as she tended to be, her passion for her research—and the patients who might be helped by it—was undeniable, and her willingness to leave her lab on such short notice today to see Rachelle to safety spoke volumes for her commitment.

As he followed the doctor down paths, around corners, and past buildings, Brady couldn't help but be struck at the sheer size of the medical complex. He'd known their center was one small cog in a much larger machine, but somehow walking through the middle of it made the scope much more real than he had ever noticed before. Or maybe it was his own urgency to get to Rachelle that made the walk stretch so long. At least the rain had tapered off, although the moisture still hung heavy in the air.

After what felt like an eternity, Dr. Mattox finally swiped her badge at the back door of one of the buildings and let him into a set of bustling corridors that definitely gave off an air of "emergency." The tension and distress were palpable in the air, and Brady couldn't help hoping he'd never have to come here with his senses enhanced, even as he offered a silent prayer for the strangers filling the rooms around him and the medical staff trying to help them.

Dr. Mattox veered off toward a nurses' station so fast that Brady almost missed it and had to find a way to turn the chair in the next hallway and make a U-turn back to her. He wasn't sure if she saw him coming or just expected him to follow, but by the time he reached the spot where she'd stopped, she was on the move again. Brady forced a deep breath, trying to push back the harder pounding in his head that all the tension certainly wasn't helping, and thanked God that his longer legs let him keep the petite woman in sight as she turned at another corner.

He rounded the bend just in time to see the doctor march across a busy open area, scattering the nurses in her path, and throw open a curtained divider without breaking stride. Brady caught just a glimpse of Rachelle's too white face before the path closed again, then had to navigate around nurses and equipment to reach the spot the doctor had bulldozed her way to.

"I specifically put orders in her file that she wasn't to be treated until I got here." The doctor's tone bit like a thin crust of ice, and for all his worry over Rachelle, Brady couldn't help pitying the unsuspecting nurse on the other end of it.

"No one's started treatment, and I've never had a consulting doctor object to basic vital signs." The nurse sounded more annoyed than apologetic, and she turned her back and began inflating the blood pressure cuff on Rachelle's arm. In an instant, Dr. Mattox reached over and yanked it free, then faced the speechless nurse with fire in her eyes.

"Do you have any idea just how fragile her joints and muscles are, or how much damage 'basic vital signs' could cause? No? Then I suggest you follow my orders to the letter and not assume standard protocol applies when you've been explicitly told it doesn't."

"She's sitting up after a car crash, and a blood pressure cuff is going to kill her?" The disbelief in the nurse's voice was rising, but Dr. Mattox ignored her and motioned Rachelle toward the half-open curtain.

"Miss Rivera, there's a wheelchair waiting just outside. Do you need help, or can you walk?"

Rachelle nodded mutely and lifted herself off the bed with hesitant movements that Brady could only hope were an attempt not to break anything rather than a signal of some injury that had crept through her defenses. She didn't look up as she approached, but when she reached the curtain and caught sight of the wheelchair, her hand flew to her mouth, knocking her head backward a little as the motion hit harder than she'd meant it to.

The reaction brought her eyes up to meet Brady's, and her lips parted, but Brady shook his head and nodded toward the chair, not wanting to raise the nurse's suspicions any further, as the sight of a supposed hospital staff member wrapping the doctor's very fragile patient in a tight hug certainly would. Rachelle blinked hard, but she settled herself in the chair without argument as Dr. Mattox exited the room, followed by a scowling nurse. The doctor motioned Brady forward, and he obeyed, trying to ignore the way his neck and shoulders tensed at even Rachelle's slight weight—or did the injection make her actually physically heavier? Never mind—no way was he going to ask that.

"Wait, please." They had turned the corner and were presumably out of sight of the annoyed nurse when Rachelle jerked her hand up to signal a stop. "Car. We can't— I don't know— Please." Her words choked off as the doctor shook her head.

"I'll find out. But our first priority is getting you out of here. That was much too close. You know your blood pressure is through the roof right now."

Rachelle closed her eyes, but not before Brady had seen the tears pooling in them, and he spoke without thinking.

"Can you just get us out of the building? Then come back and check? I'll take care of her. I promise."

"Keep moving." Dr. Mattox's voice stayed low, but there was a warning edge to it, and Brady winced as he remembered their position. Of course they couldn't talk freely—not in a crowded emergency room where anyone could overhear. But as he continued pushing the wheelchair along the path the doctor indicated, his resolve hardened all the more.

Somehow, they were going to take care of Car. She was one of their own, almost as much as Rachelle was. Maybe she was where she needed to be for now, but that didn't mean they were cutting her loose. They'd get the truth—find a way to help her—be there for her in every way they could be, just like she'd always done for them.

But he couldn't put any of that into words in this setting, so he settled for squeezing Rachelle's shoulder tightly as they paused at a corner for a passing gurney.

Chapter Eight

No one spoke until they were once again outside the walls of the emergency building, but then Dr. Mattox turned and stopped so fast that Brady nearly rammed the wheelchair into her.

"Can you find your way back to the lab from here? If so, I'll try to get some information on your driver. If not, I'm afraid it'll have to wait."

"I—" Brady's automatic agreement stuck in his throat as he eyed the matching buildings all around him and tried to reconstruct the path they'd come by.

"I can direct." Rachelle's voice was too small, too thin, too shaky. Was it just the emotion and adrenaline working out of her system, or was there something more beneath the surface? Maybe it wasn't the best idea to send the doctor away before she'd actually been examined.

"Very well. Then you stay planted in that chair—or your bed or recliner, I suppose—until I have a chance to check your current levels against your baseline. We're only guessing how your body holds up to a shock like this, and I don't want any nasty surprises."

Rachelle nodded silently, and Dr. Mattox sidestepped them and hurried back in the direction of the building they'd just left. Brady hesitated an instant, then crouched down next to the chair and put an arm gently around Rachelle's shoulders. He could feel the tremor that coursed through her, but she shook her head and didn't relax against his touch.

"You shouldn't even be out here. How's your head?"

"Doesn't matter. Getting you and Car safe is the important thing. How're you holding up?"

"Brady…" She attempted her usual gently scolding tone, but the slight tremor in her voice betrayed her. "I'll talk. I promise. But—don't stay outside. Please just get us home."

"I can do that." Brady stood and began pushing again. "You still have your earpiece? I didn't have time to grab mine."

Rachelle put a hand to her pocket, but instead of making any serious effort to find it, she tipped her head up to study his face.

"How bad *are* you right now, Brady? And why are you here if—"

"One—I'm not that bad. It's…" He had to pause a second to search for a word. "Manageable. I took the earpiece out to talk to Grace. That's all. Two—if you think I can't—"

A moan from Rachelle interrupted him, and he returned his attention to her to find her eyes closed and one hand pressed to her throat.

"Grace. Oh, Father." Her breath started to speed up, and her eyes blinked rapidly. "Was she—did she—"

"She didn't hear everything. She was sitting in the common with us when—everything went down. Our reactions scared her pretty bad, but—I think she's better now. I told her you're okay. She just needs to see you to prove it."

Rachelle was silent for a long moment, and from the hitch in her breathing, Brady was sure she was fighting tears.

"She used to—have nightmares. I'd die in a wreck—or in the hospital—and she'd be all alone. We'd be up all night sometimes. I prayed nothing would ever—" She broke off with a stifled sob, and Brady stopped at an intersection in the path and squeezed her shoulder harder than he would have dared if she hadn't been on the injection.

"Rachelle, breathe. This didn't take God off guard, and He can get Grace through it as much as He can you. Okay? Tell me where we're going from here, and then put that earpiece in and tell Harper we're coming. That'll help Grace more than anything."

Rachelle sucked in a shaky breath and motioned toward the correct path, then straightened her shoulders, lifted her chin, and forced a couple of normal breaths before fumbling in her pocket for the earpiece.

"Harper?" How she could swallow the tremor in her voice that quickly was a marvel. Brady almost regretted forcing her to do it, but he was pretty sure she'd rather keep up the brave front as long as she had to than try to pull herself back together after she'd let herself actually give in. "I'm all right. They made it in time. Is Dash there with you?" She waited a few seconds, probably for Harper to relay the news, then spoke again. "Yes, I promise. Brady and I are on our way back. Dr. Mattox is checking on Car. Do you know if anyone's told DeAndre?"

If someone had, it certainly hadn't been one of them. Brady wasn't sure how she managed to keep track of details like that in the middle of such an overwhelming crisis, but Rachelle's next words told him he wasn't the only one feeling guilty over it.

"No, no, no. Not your fault, Harper. Don't even try to get up. I just—want to make sure—she has someone when…" The thought trailed off, and she swallowed hard. "Maybe we'll stop there before we come down. Is Grace—"

He couldn't hear Harper's answer, but by the fraction of tension that bled from Rachelle's shoulders, he guessed it wasn't awful.

"Just tell her I'm okay and I'm coming, please. Oh, and—" She paused and bit her lips together before continuing. "I'm in a wheelchair. Just as a precaution, but I promised I'd stick to it. Can one of you—find a way to explain?" There was a shorter pause, and her voice shook a little when she replied. "Thanks, Harper. Take care of yourselves. We'll be there soon, all right?"

Brady gave her time for a couple of breaths before leaning over to put himself back into her line of sight.

"You want to go to the kitchen first?"

"I—I think I have to. Grace…isn't alone…right now, but—"

But Car is hung unspoken in the air between them, and Brady nodded.

"I hear you. Just show me how to get there."

The rest of the walk back to their own building was mostly silent, and from the way Rachelle's fingers worked the fabric of her skirt, he guessed she was composing what she planned to say, but whether to DeAndre, Grace, or both, he wasn't sure. Or maybe she was just praying and trying to collect herself. His heart ached, and he wanted to find some way to help her, but at the moment, the best he could do was just take her where she needed to go. When they stepped back into the familiar hallways, Brady breathed a sigh of relief, but Rachelle's shoulders stiffened as they neared the kitchen.

"You want me to do this?" Maybe *he* should have been the one preparing what he needed to say, but he hadn't consciously thought about it until that moment. Rachelle bit her lips together, then shook her head.

"No. She was— I was— I need to do this."

Brady nodded and pushed her up to the window, where he could see DeAndre at work on the other side of the room. It took a moment, but he finally noticed them and came to slide the window open, his curious look fading to concern as he took in Rachelle's position.

"All right now, what happened to you?"

"I—it—" Rachelle choked a little and had to swallow before she could go on. "It's not me; it's—Car."

Brady could see the shift in the nutritionist's face, the animated look of worry shifting to a grave mask, as though he was preparing himself for a blow. He shut the window without a word and disappeared back into the kitchen, but almost before Brady could think, he was next to them, having apparently appeared through some door Brady had never had reason to know about.

"What happened, sweetheart?" He bent next to Rachelle and laid a hand on her arm, and something—probably the kindness underlying the tension in his tone—sent tears rolling down her cheeks.

"She— There was an accident. She's in the—ER. I don't know, but—her arm. It's bad."

"They bring her here?"

"Yes. Dr. Mattox is—trying to check, but—"

"And you're okay?" DeAndre lifted her chin, and Rachelle nodded as her tears fell faster.

"All right. I'll find out. Make sure there's family with her. You go downstairs and take care of yourself and the little one. And let people take care of *you*, hear?" He looked down for a second, then met her gaze and narrowed his eyes. "Car would've been out on the street today with or without you. Got that? Accidents happen. She knows the risks. There's no part of this that's your fault. Do I need to park myself here till you believe that?"

It took a moment for Rachelle to respond, and Brady couldn't help but admire DeAndre's instincts. She couldn't fight against his logic without keeping him away from Car even longer—the exact thing she most wanted to avoid.

"No. I know." Her voice was small and shaky, the words the barest possible agreement, but something in them signaled that she recognized the truth.

"All right." DeAndre stood up and met Brady's eyes over her head with an assessing look. "You got her?"

"We all do." Brady gave him the firmest nod he could muster, and it must have been enough, because DeAndre returned the gesture and disappeared down the hall again. "He's right, you know." He leaned over and ran a thumb across the tears on her cheek, and Rachelle drew an unsteady breath.

"I know. Can we—go home now?"

Home. It wasn't what most people in the world would call a home, but he couldn't think of another place that better fit what Rachelle—what all of them—needed at the moment. He whispered a silent prayer of thanks that God had brought them together as he headed them out of the back hallways and toward the elevator that would take them to the den.

Chapter Nine

Knowing from personal experience that the click of the door at the end of the hall could be heard from the common, Brady was slightly surprised when their entrance didn't trigger some kind of instant commotion. But in the next second, he shook his head at his own foolishness. What was he expecting—Dash to come running out like he was on the injection? Harper to forget her own flare and jump up from the couch she hadn't left all day? The only one he could realistically have expected to see was Grace, and she might easily still be wearing her headphones as instructed, or else be cowering in the corner, unsure what she'd find if she ventured out of it. Brady picked up the pace as much as he could and finally brought Rachelle's wheelchair to a stop just inside the common.

There was silence for a heartbeat, then Dash let out a deep breath and Harper rolled her head into her pillow to muffle a sob. Grace sucked in a wet gasp around her thumb, and Rachelle's hands trembled as she instinctively reached out, then pulled them back into her lap.

"It's okay. I'm okay—I promise. Don't—just—I'm so sorry."

"You'd apologize for the apocalypse, wouldn't you?" Dash attempted an exasperated growl, but he couldn't erase the relief in his tone. "Forget that. Just tell us how you actually are."

"I'm fine." Rachelle's voice broke a little. "Just shaken. More—more mental than physical, I think."

"You sure?"

"As I can be. Dr. Mattox'll check me out when she gets back. Nothing hurts. I promise."

"Good." Dash jerked his head in a stiff nod, and Rachelle reached over to lightly touch Harper's shoulder. She peeked a watery eye out from the pillow and offered a wobbly smile.

"I'm okay. Just—kind of need to get the tears out."

"I know. You're fine. I don't want you to aggravate your skin, that's all. Maybe at least take your face out of the pillow? Nobody's judging you for crying."

Harper gave a weak nod and shifted her head a little more so most of her face was visible, and Rachelle offered an attempt at a smile before glancing over at Grace, whose head was bent fixedly over her tablet again. Brady took a step toward the couch, then paused and glanced down at Rachelle.

"You staying in this? Or moving to your chair?"

"Moving." Rachelle automatically started to stand, but Brady's hand on her shoulder stopped her, and she sat back with a grimace. "Sorry. Can you—"

"I've got it." Brady rolled the wheelchair as close to her recliner as he could get it, then held out his hand to help her, but Rachelle waved it away and pushed herself up and into her usual place. She glanced over at Grace again, then looked from the wheelchair to Dash and back up to Brady. He nodded, understanding her unspoken concern, and moved the chair back to the corner of the couch where Dash slouched. Dash reached a hesitant hand out to grip it, and Brady bit his lip. "Need help?"

"No." Dash jerked his head to the side, but Brady couldn't quite tell if it was a shake or a signal. "I've got it. Just set the brake." His voice dropped to a hiss. "And for the love of Mike, talk to your girl. She won't listen to anyone but you right now, and I don't think any of us want to find out if that extends to Midge."

Brady swallowed hard and closed his eyes as a new strain of headache began to pulse above the bridge of his nose. He'd never meant to make Grace trust him and only him; he'd just happened to be the one who was in a position to go after her. He could only hope whatever stubbornness she'd displayed in his absence was based in some sort of misguided obedience and not a sign that she'd somehow transferred her full trust to him over anyone else—especially not Rachelle.

"Hey, Gracie-girl." He slid between her and Dash on the couch and reached over to touch her headphones. Grace immediately clapped her hands over top of them and jerked her wide, wet eyes up, but when she caught sight of his face, she immediately let go and allowed him to slip the speakers off her ears. "It's okay, sweet girl. Rachelle's okay. The doctor wants her to sit still for a little while until she has time to check, but she's not in the hospital anymore. She's right here, and she's safe. Want to come see?"

"Can I?" Grace's lips trembled around her thumb, and Brady turned her shoulders to face Rachelle.

"Go ahead. You can't hurt her."

Grace immediately flung herself off the couch and onto Rachelle's recliner, hugging her tighter than would probably have been safe on any normal day. Rachelle gave a little sob and buried her face in her sister's hair, though her hands remained tightly fisted at her sides.

"Oh, baby." Her words were thick with tears, and Brady blinked hard as he laid his head back and tried to let the tension drain away. "I want to hug you so hard right now, but if I tried it, I'd break you."

Grace murmured something into her shirt that Brady couldn't hear, but Rachelle's response indicated that she had managed to translate it.

"No, don't stop, baby. Please, hug me hard. I need it so much."

The break was back in Rachelle's voice, and Brady had to wipe the moisture out of his own eyes as his heart cracked anew. Whatever their mysterious past or the family secrets they might hold, there was no denying the love that existed between them now. A wave of dizziness and pain washed over him, and he laid his head back and tried to concentrate on breathing, praying that the sensations would fade again as he simultaneously thanked God that they had held off until everyone was safe and together.

The room was quiet for a few minutes, although Brady was sure everyone was busy with their own thoughts and emotions and hopefully not paying any attention to him. When his head began to subside again, he pried his eyes open and took a cautious survey. Dash had gotten himself back in his chair and parked it near the door, though whether to watch for the doctor, guard against more trouble, or keep an eye on all the girls at once, Brady wasn't sure. Harper still lay on the couch where she'd been most of the day, arms stretched over her head and feet elevated like they were still hurting her, but with a more peaceful look on her face than he'd seen in hours. Grace was sitting in Rachelle's lap, curled up against her chest, and Rachelle seemed to have overcome her fear of her own powers enough to begin carefully rubbing her sister's back.

"How you feeling?" Brady murmured, trying to gauge her posture for any sign of hidden pain, and Rachelle blinked her eyes open and looked over at his couch.

"I'm okay. How are you? I know the glare still bothers you on overcast days, even without the pressure changes, and you've had tons of stress, on top of pushing me all the way back here."

"Really?" Brady sighed. "I told you, you're worth it. And I wasn't the only one who sacrificed to get you back."

Rachelle's gaze drifted over to Dash with a grateful look, and he glared at Brady.

"Thanks a lot."

"Just sharing the love." Brady offered a weak smirk, and Rachelle pressed her lips together, possibly to hide a smile.

"I don't know what I'd have done without any of you. Harper, just knowing someone was there was a lifeline. I'm not sure I've ever—" She swallowed hard and hesitated for a moment before continuing. "—ever been that scared."

Grace murmured something that sounded like "heroes can still get scared," and Rachelle pulled her a little closer.

"You're right, baby. They can. There was a lot to be scared of today, and I don't know that I was much of a hero, but—"

"Says who?"

"Quit that!"

"You're kidding, right?"

The answers came from every direction at once, and Brady chuckled as Rachelle was left speechless under the barrage.

"What do you know? It's unanimous," Harper mumbled, and Dash cocked an unusually expressive eyebrow in Rachelle's direction.

"You want to give me one way you could've done more out there? Other than jump out and grab the truck that hit you before it made contact? Which would probably have needed my power on top of yours to make it work at all—if you could somehow break out the wrong side without making Car lose control in the first place."

"I just wish I could've done more." Rachelle shook her head slowly, and Brady scooted closer to her end of the couch.

"You got her out of that car—how bad was the door smashed in?—and kept her from bleeding out until the ambulance got there. How much more could've gone wrong if you *hadn't* been there? Have you thought of that?"

"I've been trying not to." The words were a whisper, and Brady winced.

"Okay, don't think about it. But don't make yourself nuts thinking about the impossible things you didn't do either. Fair?"

"All right." Rachelle swallowed hard, but before she could say anything more, the door clicked, and purposeful footsteps sounded in the hall. Everyone in the room stiffened, and in the hush that followed, you could have heard a pin drop. After what seemed an eternity but could only have been seconds, Dr. Mattox appeared in the doorway and surveyed them with sober eyes.

"I assume you're all waiting a report on Miss Manigault?"

"Can you—even give us one?" Rachelle's voice caught, and Brady's heart sank. He hadn't even thought about the privacy issues the doctor might have to violate in talking to them, as closely connected to Car as they were. But Dr. Mattox's mouth quirked just the tiniest bit at the corner as she cocked her head to the side.

"Under normal circumstances, no, but with her family's permission, I can."

Rachelle closed her eyes, and Brady silently thanked DeAndre for understanding how much she especially needed to know.

"She's in surgery right now. They're not afraid for her life, but her arm is a different story. There's no final word on the damage yet."

The silence hung like a heavy blanket, and it was Dash who finally broke it.

"Worst case?"

"Worst case is she loses it entirely. Anything between that and no lasting effects is possible. They'll have a better prognosis once she's in recovery. Rachelle, stay where you are. I still want a full exam."

Rachelle nodded, still with her eyes closed, and Grace snuggled a little closer. Brady reached out and laid a hand on her shoulder, then beckoned her toward himself.

"Come on, Gracie-girl. Sit with me a minute while the doctor looks at Rachelle, okay?"

Grace nodded slowly and clambered onto his lap, and Brady offered another silent prayer as he wrapped his arms around her.

Chapter Ten

"Rachelle?"

Dr. Mattox's sober voice woke Brady from the uneasy half-doze he'd fallen into, and he sat bolt upright on the couch, biting back a wince at the spike of pain that accompanied the sudden motion. The doctor had given Rachelle a clean bill of health—or as clean a one as she could until the injection wore off—and he hadn't expected to see her back until dinnertime, if that. Brady's eyes met Harper's, then Dash's, and he was sure the same thought burned in each of their minds, but it was Rachelle who put voice to it.

"Car?"

"No. No word yet. But reception says the police are upstairs asking to talk to you."

Rachelle's face lost a bit of its color, and she gripped the arms of the recliner so hard they creaked, then caught herself and immediately let go. Grace wrapped her arms around her sister like a little octopus, and Rachelle forced a calming breath.

"It's okay, baby. I'm not in trouble. They just want to know about the accident. That's all."

Grace's hold relaxed just the slightest bit, and Dr. Mattox cocked her head.

"Should I tell them you're not available?"

Rachelle swallowed hard, then shook her head, but Brady could tell it cost her an effort.

"No. That'll just make it look like I—like we—have something to hide. Or like I was hurt, and then they'll want all the records I can't show. I'll—I'll be careful, but—I think I have to go."

"Do you want me to come along and steer things?"

"As my doctor? That'll look even more like I'm hurt or hiding something." Rachelle tugged nervously at her skirt as she scooted carefully out from Grace's arms and stood, looking uncharacteristically irresolute. Brady took just a second to gauge his strength, then sat forward.

"What about just moral support?"

Rachelle couldn't hide the hope that leapt in her eyes, even as her head tilted into a slow shake.

"Brady, you've done enough today. You don't have to—"

"Thought we'd agreed to leave the 'have to' out of it. Do you want me there? Because if you do, I'm up to it."

Rachelle opened her lips, closed them again, lowered her eyes, then finally raised them to Brady's face.

"Are you sure?"

"Totally." Brady managed to get to his feet without triggering a spike in his head and motioned for Rachelle to lead the way. She straightened her shoulders and started for the door, balling her fists at her sides as if to steel her nerves.

Brady waited until they were partway down the hall, but when she didn't relax, he reached around and gently rubbed her arm. Rachelle didn't react at first, but finally she let out a long, controlled sigh.

"What are you most afraid of?" Brady kept his voice low, and Rachelle shook her head slowly.

"I can't talk about it now. I'll fall apart. Just stick with me, please—if you can."

"What else am I going to do? Send Dash? I thought we're trying to stay *off* the cops' radar."

A tiny snort escaped her, and Brady's lips twitched at the thought of Dash trying to stare down an equally intense policeman.

"If you see me start to grip a chair—or anything—please stop me. The last thing I need is to break something in half in front of them. I'm going to have enough explaining to do as it is."

"What are you going to tell them?"

"As much of the truth as I can. If they caught me in a lie, they'd really start digging."

Brady nodded, and neither of them spoke again until they reached the reception area where two police officers stood. Rachelle swallowed hard, lifted her chin, and came forward, and Brady tried not to read too much into their curious expressions.

"You're Rachelle Rivera?"

"Yes, sir." Her voice trembled slightly, and Brady stepped just a little closer.

"And who is this?"

"Brady. He wasn't involved in the crash. He just—"

"I'm a friend," Brady interjected. "She was kind of shaken up by everything, and I didn't want her to be alone."

"You're in pretty good shape for crawling out of that wreck." The shorter officer cocked his head—thoughtfully or suspiciously? Brady couldn't tell, but Rachelle nodded.

"I was on the passenger side. Bumped around a little, but the doctor says no real damage."

"You were in the car that got hit?" The taller officer took up the questioning. "Can you tell us what happened from your perspective?"

"The truck was a little ahead of us." Rachelle closed her eyes as though trying to picture the scene. "I don't know how fast it was going—maybe a little faster than we were—I feel like I might have seen it pass us? And then—it all happened in a second—it lost control—swung left and clipped the barrier—then spun into us. I think Car—Carmel—she was driving—I think she might have swung right trying to miss him, but—" She broke off with a shiver, and the policeman took out a notebook and began writing.

"Was there anything you could see that made the truck lose control? Anything on the road, or another driver acting up?"

"No, nothing. Not that I saw. It was raining, and the road was slick, but…" She trailed off, shrugging helplessly. "I don't know."

"And where were you on the way to?"

"We were helping with a house renovation in Barton McFarland, taking a load of stuff to the dump."

"Was anyone else with you?"

"In the car? No, sir." Rachelle started to bite her lip, then quickly let it go, and Brady held his breath, hoping the next question wouldn't be how two girls were planning to unload that trailer at the dump without help.

"And who was in charge of this renovation?"

"It's a DAWN project. We just showed up."

Thankfully, the officer just nodded and continued to take notes, apparently not seeming to notice that she hadn't fully answered his question. After getting the address and asking a few more questions about the type of work "they" had been doing—all of which he'd be able to verify with DAWN—he returned to the time of the wreck and had Rachelle answer most of the same questions she already had. Brady tried hard to remember that it was an investigator's job to test people's stories and that the repeated questions didn't necessarily speak to any concrete suspicion, but it didn't help. Of course, Rachelle had nothing to hide in that part of the story—she really had been just a passenger and not doing anything particularly outlandish when they took the hit—so her account stayed consistent, as he should have known it would.

"So you said the truck drifted left, clipped the barrier, and then spun which direction?"

"Right. Into our lane."

"And it hit where on your car?"

"The driver's door mostly—I think. I mean, I wasn't really assessing the whole thing for damage, but that's what it seemed like."

"Did it rip the door off?"

Brady's heart skipped a beat, but Rachelle's answer didn't even hesitate.

"No. Caved it in. It kind of pinned Car's—Carmel's arm up against the seat."

"The paramedics said she was on the ground when they got there."

"She—she was." Rachelle's pale face blanched a little more, and her breathing started to pick up. "I—she—she was—bleeding badly, and—I didn't know when help would get there. And something was leaking somewhere—I could smell the gas. I couldn't—I had to—"

She cut off with a desperate shake of her head, and Brady put an arm around her shoulders and squeezed as hard as he could. Would that admission be too much? But what else could she say? None of their other witnesses were going to admit to getting Car out of that wreck, and the officers wouldn't be satisfied with a missing piece that large.

"*You* got the door off and pulled her out?" The officer's eyebrows rose as he eyed Rachelle's petite form, and Brady could only hope that no one had given them her diagnosis as well.

"I—I had to." Rachelle blinked hard against the moisture in her eyes, and the officer shook his head slowly.

"Hysterical strength's an incredible thing, isn't it? What about the other driver? You notice what happened to him?"

"No." Rachelle's tears were flowing freely now, and her hand trembled as she lifted a sleeve to brush very gently at her cheeks. "I was trying to do first aid—waiting on the ambulance—Car was the only one I saw."

"You haven't heard how she is, have you?" Brady interjected, and the officer glanced over at him.

"Afraid not. Just that it'll be a while before she can interview. You're sure there's no other injuries you want us to report?" He turned his scrutiny back to Rachelle, who offered what was probably meant to be a head shake as she continued to wipe at her tears. "Well, just call us if anything pops up. Doctors can miss stuff on the first pass, you know."

"All right."

Brady knew she wouldn't be calling even if something appeared once the injection went away; there was no way she was making her medical records part of a lawsuit, even if they could somehow redact the results of the experiments. Any attorney worth their salt couldn't help but question how a girl with such fragile joints and muscles could walk away from a wreck like that, and the last thing any of them needed was someone snooping around into what her "good" days actually entailed.

"Is there anything else you need from her?" Brady pulled Rachelle a little closer, and she turned and buried her face in his shirt. The officer considered a moment, then closed his notebook.

"No, I think that's all. If there's anything else you think of that might help, give us a call." He handed Brady a card, nodded to his shorter partner, and the two of them left the building.

Brady and Rachelle stood still for a long moment after they had gone, Rachelle trying to gulp back the tears that definitely hadn't been for show.

"Hey," he whispered finally. "You're okay. It's over. Hysterical strength, huh?"

"Hysterical something," Rachelle choked on a mixture of a laugh and a sob, and Brady huffed as he squeezed her shoulders.

"Hysterical nothing. They just don't have a clue how strong you really are—on any level."

Chapter Eleven

"Come here." Brady drew Rachelle over to a quiet little seating area as she continued trying to dry her eyes. "Just breathe for a minute. Cry if you have to. That was rough, and having to relive it—" He shook his head sympathetically as Rachelle buried her face in her hands.

"I'm sorry—I just—remembering Car—"

"I know." Brady rubbed gentle circles on her back, keeping his voice as low and soothing as he knew how. "I know, and I wasn't even there. You did everything you could. Don't lose sight of that."

"I just wish we could hear something. Brady, if she loses her arm…"

"It's not going to come to that." Brady swallowed the lump that rose in his throat and put all the confidence he could muster into the words. "And if it does, God'll get her through. But whatever happens, it's not your fault. You know that, right?"

Rachelle gave a little choking groan, and Brady felt his heart plummet.

"Rachelle, don't do that to yourself. You heard what DeAndre said. She'd have been out on the road with or without you. Maybe on that same stretch of highway, only without you to pull her out of the wreck. You can't blame yourself. That's totally unfair."

"It's not that." Rachelle's whisper was barely audible, and Brady leaned close to listen better. "It's—Brady, how do I know if I did the right thing? If ripping the car door off caused more damage? If

I put too much pressure on her arm? You don't even know how strong my grip can get, and neither do the doctors—except Dr. Mattox, and she's not a trauma surgeon. How do any of us know Car wouldn't be better off if I *hadn't* been there?"

"You can't think like that." Brady tightened his grip on her shoulder, and she shifted just a little closer. "What are you always telling me? God has a reason for these days, and we've got to do our best and leave the results to Him. That goes just as much for you. She needed help, and you did everything you could. She was already bleeding bad and had a door smashed in around her—I really don't see how extra-hard pressure on the wound could make it noticeably worse. God had you there with her for a reason, and it wasn't just to tell the cops where you'd been and where you were going. Okay?"

Rachelle forced a long, deep breath, then nodded slowly.

"Speaking of—of being where you're needed—thanks for taking care of Grace."

"Everybody did their part. I'm glad I could help her." He paused, trying to decide whether the returning questions would be better saved for later, but Rachelle turned a questioning look on him, and he sighed. "You don't have to answer this, but—I was just curious. Grace said something about…your mom…and her mom?"

Brady could see the realization wash over her face, and her shoulders drooped as though a heavy weight had settled on them. He immediately regretted the question, but it was too late to take it back.

"You don't have to talk about it now. Or ever. I just wondered—"

"No." Rachelle shook her head slowly but emphatically. "We need to talk about it. I should have told you a long time ago. I just…" She took a deep breath and covered her eyes for a few seconds, then dropped her hand back to her lap but didn't look up at him again. "I didn't have these issues when I was little. Or—not to know it. Now that I look back, I probably shouldn't ever have been able to stretch the way I could, but all we thought at the time was that it made me great at gymnastics."

Brady didn't quite see the relevance of her medical history to the topic at hand, but he kept quiet, and Rachelle continued softly.

"I was eleven when I had a bad fall. Hurt my knee and my shoulder, and then it was like my body exploded. The pain never stopped. It spread everywhere. I missed school—weeks at a time. It took years to get a diagnosis. My mom was a nurse—and a bulldog. She worked harder than any of the doctors. Rearranged her whole life to take care of me. I don't know what I'd have done without her."

A lump formed in Brady's throat at the thought of his own mom and Eden, but Rachelle knotted her hands in her lap so tightly that her knuckles turned white, though she still didn't lift her eyes.

"My…my dad couldn't take it. Me being sick—not having answers—Mom being so focused. He was home less and less, and then…one night…about two years in…we'd been to a youth event at church—first one I'd gone to in months. When we got home…all his things were gone, and…there were divorce papers on the counter."

Brady's breath froze in his lungs for three full beats before a soft sniff from Rachelle brought him back to life with a rush of white-hot fury.

"He left you?" His voice was dangerously low, and Rachelle kept her head down as she nodded.

"Mom saw him a couple times after that…in court. He paid support but…didn't want visitation. I never—never saw him again." She choked and tried to stifle a sob, and Brady wrapped his arm around her shoulder and held on as hard as he could.

"Cry, Rachelle. I can't half grasp how much that hurts, but you don't have to hold it in. I don't know how he—how anyone could be that heartless—like any of it was your fault, or your mom's! That's not—" He broke off, unable to find words for the enormity of the pain and anger that filled him. Rachelle's hitching breaths beneath his hand ripped his heart in two, and his voice burst free again in a broken flow of prayer. "Father God, help Rachelle. I can't believe—I never knew she was carrying all this. How her dad could do that—why this world is so messed up—why I've somehow been so sheltered from all the worst parts—I don't understand any of it.

But You're not blind to it. You've been with her all along. Please heal her heart. Help her know You love her more than any father ever could."

Rachelle drew a shaky breath and lifted her head enough to lay it against his shoulder.

"I'm sorry."

"Don't!" Brady almost snapped the word, but Rachelle shook her head.

"I'm sorry I…didn't tell you before. The others know because…it mattered to them. I told myself you didn't need to. Truly, I just…hate telling people. I didn't want you to know…how broken I was."

"Rachelle—" Brady's voice cracked, and he had to clear his throat before he could continue. "I always thought my life had been rough. You know my dad died when I was little—we always just scraped by—and that was before I got sick. I never knew half how blessed I was just to have family that cared enough to stick by me, no matter what. But I hate that you think I'd see you differently just because someone else treated you like dirt."

"It's not…not you, Brady." Rachelle sucked in a ragged breath. "Don't ever feel bad that you haven't walked in our shoes. You—just hearing you talk about Eden…knowing how much she's still on your side…it gives us hope. Reminds us of how things are meant to be. Sometimes that's painful, but…it's the kind of pain we need. The kind that proves we're not numb. It's good for all of us—me, Dash, even Harper. My dad taught me that I was a burden, but…all of you help me fight those thoughts."

"You keep things on yourself that you'd never let us get away with, don't you?" Brady rubbed her shoulder gently, and she pulled back a little and offered him a wobbly smile.

"Guilty. But I didn't finish answering your question. Just after my twenty-first birthday, my mom had a bad bout of the flu. It progressed to pneumonia before we realized…they took her to the hospital…had to intubate. I was there…sitting in her room…when I got the call that my dad and…and his new wife—Grace's mom—had been in a wreck. Killed instantly. Somehow they tracked me down…as next of kin. That's when I…" Her voice gave out, and Brady forced a shallow breath.

"That's when you first met Grace?"

"First learned about her existence." Rachelle wiped futilely at the fresh tears streaming down her face. "I met her the next day. My mom had died…late that night. She never even knew…" She choked on her words again, and Brady just held her in silence as the enormity of the sacrifice washed over him.

He'd been in awe of how hard she worked to give Grace as close to a normal life as she could manage—and that was believing Grace was a full sister who'd grown up with her from birth. But the daughter of a father who'd abandoned her and a stepmother she'd never met, who'd come into her life in the wake of a devastating double tragedy—and in spite of all that, she'd never shown the slightest indication that the little girl was anything less than the light of her life.

"How?" He could barely force the word through the tightness in his throat. "I can't even—"

"Brady, you've met her. How could I not? She's my sister…whether we knew each other or not. What my dad did wasn't her fault. And—" She broke off and looked away, but Brady waited her out, and after a few seconds, she shook her head. "It's silly. My mom picked my name. There's no reason to believe hers didn't. But sometimes I look at her and hope…maybe he found it too."

Grace. Brady put a hand over his eyes, unable to process the flood of conflicting emotions that churned in his mind. But finally a single strain rose to the top, and he reached over and tugged on Rachelle's chin until she allowed him to lift it.

"Rachelle, you're incredible. Whatever inspiration or strength you get from me—from any of the rest of us—we get ten times as much from you. The way you take care of Grace—of everyone—I honestly don't know how you do it."

"I wish I could do more." Rachelle brushed her sleeve across her eyes. "Especially for Grace. You're all used to it, but she went from a normal family to—what's really only a couple steps from a medical ward, and a sister who might or might not be there for her on a moment's notice."

"That's not true!" The words came out a little too forceful, and Rachelle jumped. "Sorry. I didn't mean—it's just that you're *always* there for her. Maybe that looks different some days than others. Maybe you can't give her everything that a healthy sister would. But a healthy sister couldn't give her everything you can either. God gave her to you, not someone else, and you've given her everything you have. She loves you, Rachelle. More than anything. Does she even know…"

"No." Rachelle shook her head hard. "She knows when we met, of course. That we had different moms. It might—have to come out someday, but—I still hope she never has to understand why."

"Because you're afraid it'll tarnish how she sees her dad?" Brady leaned down to look her straight in the eyes. "Or are you afraid it'll change how she sees you?"

Rachelle's eyes flicked away, and Brady's heart broke a little more.

"I'm not saying you should tell her. That's your call to make, and I don't know why she'd need to know. But there's something I think *you* need to know." He waited until Rachelle turned her full attention on him again before he continued. "When she ran out of the room after the accident, do you know where I found her? Not in her room. Not in any of the rest of ours. She was on *your* bed, cuddled up under a blanket, and all she wanted to know was that you were okay. She thinks the world of you, Rachelle. And she's got good reason to. Don't let your dad's lies take that from you too."

Rachelle didn't answer for a moment, but finally she gave a slow nod, and Brady felt a little of the tension start to drain away.

"You ready to go back downstairs? I've got a feeling someone's been watching for you."

CHAPTER TWELVE

"Pretty far past her bedtime, isn't it?" Brady kept his voice low as he shifted his head for a better look at Grace, whose eyes were blinking sleepily behind her tablet.

"Isn't it getting past yours too?" Rachelle whispered back, settling her sister's head a little closer against her shoulder.

She was right, of course, and he was probably playing with fire next to dynamite trying to stretch it much longer after the day he'd had. But while he didn't try to argue, he didn't make any move to get up, and Rachelle didn't press the point, just like she didn't nudge Grace to go to bed. Brady couldn't blame her, any more than he could blame Dash, who was visibly drooping in the corner, or Harper, who was fidgeting with her cold packs and whimpering intermittently on the couch. They all needed sleep—there was no denying it—but they all seemed to feel the same reluctance to leave the little circle of the closest thing to home and family that most of them had.

He was vaguely wondering whether any of them would end up actually going to bed—and what it would mean for them in the morning if they didn't—when a step sounded in the hall, and he turned lazily to face it, half expecting Dr. Mattox to be surveying them with a raised eyebrow. But it wasn't the doctor's petite form that filled the doorway, and Brady's breath caught in his throat as he recognized the powerful build of the nutritionist.

Everything in the room seemed to freeze in the same instant, except for Dash, who was still working to raise his head and took an extra second to go rigid in his new position. The silence stretched long and deafening, and no matter how hard Brady tried to loose his tongue, he couldn't force the question out.

"How—" The word that escaped Rachelle's throat was barely more than a croak, but it managed to shatter the ice, and DeAndre closed the distance to her chair in two quick strides.

"She's going to be all right."

"Oh, thank God!" Brady's body went limp against the couch as the entire room seemed to release its collectively held breath. Rachelle clapped a hand to her eyes, Harper rolled over and buried her face in the pillow, and Dash slumped back in his chair hard enough to move it a little.

"She's seriously okay?" Harper's question was almost a sob and muffled in the couch pillow, but DeAndre didn't appear to have trouble understanding it.

"Out of surgery, out of recovery. She's talking some, but still pretty drugged up. I'm sure she'll want to show you in person as soon as she can, but it won't be tonight. She's got enough family camped out in the waiting room to keep things humming for days. I barely got in to see her myself."

"But you did see her?" Dash's tone was sharp in spite of its deeper than usual rasp, proclaiming forcefully that he wasn't going to be placated by anything less than eyewitness testimony.

"Saw her. She's alive and mostly awake. Banged up, but she'll heal. She asked about you, Rachelle."

"I hope you told her not to worry." Rachelle brushed at her eyes before meeting DeAndre's gaze. "If not, the next time you talk to her, tell her I'm fine. Have they said—is her arm—" She broke off with a hard swallow, and DeAndre shook his head.

"Looks like they saved it. Won't know the whole result till there's been some time and therapy, but if I know Car, she's not going to let anything stop her from getting back behind the wheel."

"She's stubborn like that." A hint of a smile played around Rachelle's mouth for an instant before her face became serious again. "They're sure it's going to be okay? It didn't—I didn't—"

"Well, given that nobody up there knows exactly what you *did* do, I can't tell you for sure. But I did hear that if she'd gotten in much later, they might not have been able to save it, so whatever you did, we're all grateful for it. Even if most of them don't know who to thank."

"I don't need thanks. I'm just glad she's okay." Rachelle's shoulders trembled a little as she sat back in her chair, and DeAndre's eyes narrowed.

"Speaking of okay, what'd you have for dinner tonight?"

"The usual." Rachelle offered a half shrug, and DeAndre huffed.

"The usual for a normal day, or one where you're powered up?"

"You know those portion sizes don't make sense to anyone but you." Rachelle's wince and apologetic tone only deepened the frown on the nutritionist's face. "It's not important; I'm almost done anyway."

"And the last thing you need tomorrow is to have absolutely no reserves to draw on because you ran on fumes today." DeAndre turned on his heel and strode out the door before she could make any more protests, and Brady propped himself up on his elbow and offered Rachelle a troubled look.

"Seriously? I thought you were just staying still because you felt like it. Were you even planning on telling us?"

"What were you going to do about it? Scrounge scraps from the dumpster?" She offered a wry smile that faded into a sigh. "It wasn't on purpose, Brady. I barely thought about it until he asked. I'd probably have been sitting here just the same either way. My mind's about as tired as my body right now."

"Okay, then." Brady pushed himself up and waited for his head to clear before crossing over to the other side of her recliner. "If it didn't have anything to do with *your* strength or energy, would you want her put to bed?" He nodded at Grace, now fully asleep and curled up against her side. "Or would you want to keep her here with you?"

Rachelle bit her lip as she glanced down at her sister, but when her eyes met Brady's again, she let it go and offered a genuine smile.

"I appreciate the offer. And I'd honestly take you up on it. But after today—if she wakes up with a nightmare, I want to have her close. And unless it's early, I might not be able to get to her."

"I'm not trying to talk you out of it. You going to stick here, or you want her in your room?"

"I think we'll be good right here, thanks. Maybe…just bring us a couple blankets?"

"I can do that. You going to need anything else? Want someone to stay out here with you?"

"Absolutely not. We'll be fine. All of you go to bed. I mean it."

"Not the worst idea I've heard tonight." Harper sniffed hard and pulled her head out of the pillow, wiping at her wet cheeks, but not attempting to tame the tangled mop of blue hair that hid most of her face from view. "Pretty sure I left the fan on when I came out here this morning, so my sheets should be good and freezing by now."

"Don't get too cold, Harper." If Rachelle's mumbled words were any indication, the fatigue was starting to hit her hard, but her concern was still centered on everyone around her. "Use a blanket if you have to."

"Okay, Mama Midge." A weak smile peeked out behind the blue curtain as she turned to limp to the refrigerator to trade out her cold pack. "Hopefully tonight'll end the worst."

"Touch the button if you need it. I'll redirect to the nurses' station, so don't put me in the equation."

"Got it. I'll be okay." Harper shuffled painfully toward the door, but a quiet word from Rachelle made her pause.

"And Harper?" Rachelle waited until the other girl turned back toward her. "I don't know what I'd have done without you today. I know it was rough for you, but—thanks for sticking with me."

"Glad you're okay. You and Car both." Harper rubbed at her eyes again. "I'm leaving now before I start bawling again."

"Go. Sleep well."

Harper nodded and disappeared, and Rachelle closed her eyes and drew a few slow breaths. Brady took a step toward the hallway, then glanced back and changed course for where Dash still sat slumped in his wheelchair.

"You going to take help, or does she have to watch you struggle all the way to your room?" He kept his voice to an undertone, and Dash's eyes narrowed just slightly. If he'd had a little more control, it would probably have been an intimidating glare, but Brady just held his gaze and raised an eyebrow, not wanting to draw Rachelle's attention with any more argument.

Dash huffed and shifted his eyes from Brady to Rachelle and back, gripping the wheels of his chair with hands that he couldn't stop from shaking. But finally his shoulders slumped, and he offered something between a sigh and a grunt.

"My door. No farther."

"Deal." Brady kept his face carefully neutral as he gripped the back of the wheelchair, savoring the slight offering of trust but not wanting to give any outright sign that might mar it.

Rachelle turned toward them, and Brady could see the surprise register on her face, though she tamped it down immediately and cleared what might be gathering tears with a couple of fast blinks.

"Dash. Thanks for keeping my head straight today. And for everything you gave…to get me back here—"

"Leave it, Midge. Not like you haven't talked me through tight spots before. I'm calling it quits for the night. You get some sleep, hear?"

"I will. You rest, okay? Don't worry about me."

"Make it mutual, and I'll consider it."

"It's a deal." Rachelle offered a tired smile, and Dash jerked his head roughly in Brady's direction. Taking that as a signal, Brady guided the wheelchair out into the hall and up to Dash's door, then dared to push the envelope just a little by holding the door open until he finished working himself inside.

"Night, Dash."

"Yeah, sure," Dash mumbled, and a grin tugged at the corner of Brady's mouth as he closed the door and went to Rachelle's room to retrieve the blankets Grace had curled herself up in just that morning. He spread them over the dozing pair in the recliner as gently as he could, but Rachelle's eyes blinked open, and her mouth was following suit when DeAndre appeared behind them with a heavy tray. Brady stepped back to give him room, but then a hint of mischief overtook him, and he made his silent retreat to the hall while Rachelle was still distracted by the food.

"Night, Rachelle!" He held the call until he was halfway to his room, and her reply sounded half-scolding and half-laughing.

"Brady—"

"Tell me tomorrow. Like you said, it's getting late."

"Good night, Brady." He wasn't quite sure whether he actually heard her answering sigh, or whether he'd just learned her patterns well enough to imagine it. "Sleep well. Call if you need anything."

"And you let the world slide off your shoulders for a while and get some rest, okay?" He moved over to Harper's side of the wall for a moment, where he could see her chair from a distance. "God's still got this. We'll be all right."

Chapter Thirteen

"It's so good to hear your voice." The relief in Rachelle's tone was palpable, and Brady had to agree. Even with daily updates from DeAndre and official confirmation from Dr. Mattox, there was nothing quite like Car's familiar—if still slightly weak—voice in his earpiece to prove that things were truly moving back to normal.

Not that "normal" usually involved all four of them in the den and Car in a hospital bed, but at least it was a start.

"How much trouble have you all been getting in without me?" Car's raised eyebrow came through clearly in her voice, and Harper giggled.

"We've been good. Promise. Nobody's gone out on the town alone."

"Well, you better not let me hear any different. I'm planning on crushing therapy and being out on the street again before you know it."

"So we're just not allowed to get sick until you're better?" Dash snorted. "Why don't you tell us when you figure that out, huh?"

"Not sure what you're complaining about, Roadrunner. You don't need me in the first place. Being the only hero on the block for a couple months too much for you? Or are you scared they'll start asking to ride piggyback?"

"As if!" Dash scoffed, and Brady chuckled.

"How are *you* doing, Gamma Ray?" Car's tone took on a more sober note. "You were kind of rough before I got knocked out, and I can't see the rest of the day helping."

"I'm fine." Brady's lips twitched, and he shook his head slightly, even though he knew she couldn't see him. "The day after was rough, but not one of my worst. Wouldn't have called you even if you weren't laid up for repairs."

"Fine. I see how it is." Her pretended pout worked just as well from a distance as it would have in person, and Brady's grin widened into a full-on smirk.

"Yeah, well—"

"Ugh, hold on a sec. My auntie's calling. Can you stay on for another minute? I'll be right back."

"Go ahead." Rachelle shook her head with a soft smile and waited until Car's line went dead before turning to Brady. "I notice you didn't tell her just how close you were to the point where you'd have been calling her."

"She didn't ask." Brady grinned, and Harper laughed.

"I'm glad it wasn't any worse." Rachelle sighed. "You did way too much, especially with your head as bad as it already was."

"We've been over that." Brady rolled onto his stomach and propped himself on his elbows to better meet her eyes. "Nobody made me do anything, and you'd have done the exact same thing in my place. So drop it, okay? 'Thanks' is more than enough, and you've said it at least twenty times already."

"Dash and I have the over/under at thirty, so she's still got a way to go." Harper stretched with a yawn, and Rachelle huffed.

"Seriously? Since when did being thankful qualify as the subject of a bet?"

"It qualifies because your *excess* of gratitude for what wasn't a big deal is entirely predictable."

"And it doesn't matter anyway, because Harper just ruined it when *she* had the under." Dash glared at Harper, who gave him a too innocent grin. "I should get half as a penalty, now that you've poisoned the well."

"Fine. But she wasn't going to make it anyway." Harper shrugged, and Rachelle rolled her eyes.

"You're both ridiculous. You know that, right?"

"But you love us for it." Harper blinked rapidly as she rested her chin on her hands, and Rachelle couldn't help laughing.

"Okay, I'm back. What did I miss?" Car's voice came on the line again, and Brady grinned.

"Nothing important. Harper thinks she's funny, and Rachelle can't let go of the unnecessary gratitude. That's about it."

"So what else is new?" Car chuckled, but then her voice softened. "Speaking of gratitude, though…I'm pretty sure I owe some that's completely necessary."

"Car, don't." Rachelle sighed, and a collective snort echoed around her in stereo.

"Seriously, Midge? Whatever little piece *we* did deserves thanks, and you don't?" Dash crossed his arms and pinned her with a scowl, and Harper shook her head.

"Should've bet on that one. I definitely could've called it."

"Rachell, quit, and let someone else give you your due for once." Brady wasn't sure if his raised eyebrow was what finally tipped the scale, but Rachelle bit her lips together and settled back in her chair.

"Didn't even open my mouth. Love it." Car's grin came clearly over the line. "Let me tell you, whatever you think you did or didn't do, I know I'd have been in serious trouble without you. On that note, though, can somebody fill me in on what exactly did happen? Details are a little hazy on this end."

"I'm—kind of glad of that, actually." Rachelle attempted a light laugh, but it wasn't quite natural.

"Yeah, I'll bet you are." Car's voice softened a little. "But you can tell me, right? It's not like I don't know you could rip my car in half with your bare hands."

"It wasn't quite that drastic." Rachelle's smile relaxed, but then her face grew serious. "Do you remember anything?"

"I remember a red blur rocketing toward me at something like Mach 7, then nothing till I woke up here. Apparently I was a hoot in recovery, but since I can neither confirm nor deny—and I'm pretty sure at least half of what I supposedly said is my brothers being…my brothers—I'm choosing to disbelieve anything that doesn't have video evidence *with* verifiable metadata."

Harper was dissolving into uncontrollable giggles, and Dash's head began shaking slowly.

"Definitely missed her calling. Should've been a lawyer."

"Aww, that almost sounded like a compliment, Rat Race. Don't tell me this is the near-death bonding experience that makes you soft and sappy all of a sudden."

"You wish!" Dash jerked his head back with a snort, and Car's full-throated laugh filled their ears.

"Glad you two are back to normal." This time there was nothing unnatural in Rachelle's smile, and Brady settled his head back against the couch with a silent sigh of contentment.

"So, details?" Car pressed after a moment. "Somebody's liable to walk in here any minute, and I'm dying for a good story."

"It's not that good of a story." Rachelle cut her eyes to the corner where Grace was busy on her tablet, then shrugged a shoulder. "The only thing I really did was yank the door off to get you free. Sorry about that, but I don't think it was salvageable."

"Could've guessed that. So *all* you did was yank the door off, huh? Faster than the fire department would've, right?"

"Probably. I was too scared to think about being careful."

"You say that like it's a bad thing." Car chuckled affectionately. "But you had to do more than that if I was as close to bleeding out as they say."

"That wasn't exactly because of my super strength. I was scared to death I'd take your arm off. I got you out of the wreck and put pressure on it the best I could. That's seriously the whole story."

"'Got you out of the wreck' is doing some heavy lifting there. I know thanks isn't enough, but…it's the best I've got."

"It's the best any of us have. And it's more than enough. I'm just glad you're okay. And I owe you thanks too, by the way."

"Oh, this ought to be good." Car's eyebrow was definitely raised again, and Brady stifled a chuckle.

"Well, I do. If you hadn't kept the EMTs occupied, I couldn't have slipped under the radar long enough for Dr. Mattox to spring me without an exam. And you know how *that* would've ended."

"So what I'm hearing is, if I'm going to get hurt, it better be life-threatening. That about sum it up?"

"That's not—"

"It's pretty much the only thing you're thanking me for." Car's tone was teasing, but then her voice went soft. "Kidding, Chelle. Glad you weren't caught—even if I had to be knocked out to make it happen. Your cover gets blown, I'm back to full-time regular delivery runs, and how boring would that be?"

"You know—"

"Ugh, hold on." Car's voice cut in with a frustrated sigh. "Dom, can you hold off just a couple minutes? I'm on the phone."

An indistinct voice came through in the background, and Car's voice deepened into a growl.

"No, you won't. Because it's *private*. Get out."

More background muttering followed, cut off by Car's groan.

"It is not a boy! But it's gonna be Momma yanking you out of here by the collar if you don't let me finish up with my friends in peace. Go!"

There was a pause, and then Car's voice came back with a huff.

"Sorry. My brother Dominic's here. It's kind of a miracle I had this much time to talk—hard to get any kind of alone time with the wacky family I've got."

"Don't complain too hard. You're really blessed to have them." Rachelle's tone was soft, but there was a hint of a tremble to it, and Car's turned serious right away.

"No, I am. I know that. Even if they do annoy my socks off sometimes. I wouldn't actually trade them, as much as I like to pretend. Wouldn't trade any of you either, even when you work my last nerve."

"Oh, now who's getting sappy?" Dash interrupted, and Harper snickered.

"Yeah, well, don't get used to it. I'm signing off now, just because my brothers are like a pack of dogs with a bone when they think they smell a mystery, and they'd have your secret identities out faster than the cops ever could. You take care of yourselves while I'm not there to keep you in line, hear?"

"You wish!" Dash shot back.

"Bets for how fast she crushes therapy?" Harper's grin widened, and Rachelle sighed.

"Take care of yourself, Car. And let your family take care of you. We'll be okay."

"Can confirm. We'll look out for each other. Going dark now, so we don't blow our cover." Brady's mouth tipped into a smirk as he pulled his earpiece, but not quickly enough to miss Car's laugh.

"Sap. Total sap. And if anybody asks, I'm denying everything." Dash crossed his arms, and Car must have come back with an equally snarky comeback, judging from Harper's giggle.

"You can't deny one thing, Dash." Rachelle pulled her earpiece and offered a soft smile to the room in general. "She's stuck with us, just like we're stuck with each other. And I can't think of a team I'd rather have watching my back."

The Chronic Warrior Chronicles

Episode 5

Savior Complex

Angie Thompson

Quiet Waters Press
Lynchburg, Virginia

To anyone who hides their pain behind a mask of smiles and laughter

You deserve to be seen and known fully, even in the dark and lonely places.

Thanks again to all the readers who have come with me this far. Your excitement and God's grace are the only things that got this episode out on time. And thanks for putting up with all the cliff-hangers!

Table of Contents

CHAPTER ONE

"You know, Dash, you should really find a way to do your job without putting so much strain on judicial resources." Harper flipped a lock of blue hair out of her eyes and let it hang over the arm of the couch but didn't lift her gaze from whatever she was watching on her phone. Dash turned his head slowly and regarded her with a partially raised eyebrow for a moment before he sighed.

"You planning to let me in on exactly how I'm wasting judicial resources? If I didn't catch so many crooks, they'd be able to get through them faster—is that it?"

Harper gave a slightly distracted giggle, but after a few seconds, she laid down her phone and scooted up to look at him better.

"No, it's just you've got another one referred for a competency eval because he won't stop blabbering about this freaky wind that blasted him out of nowhere and wouldn't let him turn around. Ran him right into a cop car, apparently."

Dash snorted, and Brady huffed a laugh from where he sat on the couch next to Harper's.

"Judge doesn't believe it? I can't imagine why."

"He's not alone. It was the public defender that requested the evaluation." Harper stretched her arms behind her head and sat up a little farther. "Guy's going to spend longer trying to prove he's not nuts than he would've out on bond before it's over."

"Yeah, well, the guy was shooting off a gun next to a park, so forgive me if I file that complaint somewhere between 'I don't care' and 'serves him right.'" Dash's eyes lifted in the way that meant he'd attempted to roll them, and Brady shook his head slowly.

"Clandestine superheroes meet criminal justice. Next time, we'll learn about evidentiary issues with contraband seen through a wall."

"Only if you slip up, we will." Dash turned his raised eyebrow on Brady, who wrinkled his nose but resisted sticking out his tongue.

"I don't know. According to Madame Court Reporter, they're working really hard to throw out that drug warehouse bust since the police can't produce their tipster. If that gang walks because I can't come forward—"

"Hey." Harper sat forward and locked her eyes on Brady. "You coming forward wouldn't help. Might even make it worse. There's precedent for anonymous tips, but through a wall? Goldmine for the defense. Not to mention every thug on the street'd be gunning for you—and I don't mean metaphorically."

"Yeah, I know." Brady let out a long breath as he laid his head back to look at the ceiling. "I just don't know if you following up the cases is a net positive or negative. It's good to see they get justice, but—"

"Only *if* they get justice." Dash's voice was deepening toward a growl, and Brady gave a little grunt of agreement.

"You want me to stop telling you then?" The slightly wistful note creeping into Harper's voice brought him back to reality with a jolt. Tracking their cases through the courts was something she enjoyed, something that distracted her from the pain, and—maybe most importantly—something she could share with them. He couldn't connect with her over her sappy romance novels, but he could over this, unless he did something completely dense like tell her to quit talking about it because sometimes the system let things slip.

"Since when is he the discussion police?" Dash snapped, and Brady raised his hands in surrender.

"I'm not! Don't quit telling us, Harper. It's good to know how things go down—even just to see which warehouses we should start checking again because somebody got off."

"Oh, good point!" Harper's eyes lit with their usual sparkle, and Brady breathed a silent sigh of relief, not missing the glare Dash was pinning him with but turning his focus toward Rachelle so he didn't have to acknowledge it. "You're awfully quiet over there."

Rachelle didn't look up from the laptop perched on top of her in the recliner, and Brady refrained from further comment, not wanting to interrupt anything she might be working on, but Dash turned slowly to face her, his eyes squinting in what might have been concern.

"Midge! Your ears out of joint today or what?"

"What?" Rachelle blinked and looked up, pulling off one of the headphones that Brady knew didn't entirely block out conversation, and Dash huffed.

"Missed that whole topic, didn't you? Not like you not to have an opinion, no matter how stubbornly middle-of-the-road it is. What's got you so focused?"

"No, he's right, Mama Midge." Harper's brow furrowed a little as she leaned forward. "What are you working on?"

"Nothing. I'm through for the day. Just—scrolling through the news." She moved as if to shut her laptop, but Brady reached over and held it open as he scanned her face.

"Hey. Don't shut us out. What's up? It can't have been a good story."

Rachelle bit her lips together and hesitated a second before shaking her head.

"Nothing new. An interview with Donovan King's mom."

The mood of the room shifted subtly, but enough to be felt, and the last lingering sparks of humor vanished.

"They still haven't found him?" Brady kept his voice low, and Rachelle shook her head. "Have they made any progress with—"

"No." Rachelle swallowed hard. "Demolition's going ahead tomorrow. They swear they've searched the building and he's not there, and his mom still swears she'd find him if they'd let her in.

But the owner's not taking that kind of responsibility, and there's no proof he's actually in there, so..." She drew a deep breath and let it out in a quiet sigh.

No one said anything for a minute, and Brady closed his eyes and sent up another prayer for the little boy and his family. He couldn't imagine how hard it would be to have a child lost—let alone a young deaf boy who couldn't even hear the voices calling him—let alone suspecting that he might have wandered into a condemned building scheduled for demolition. The family had tried to rally the community, and the protests had been enough to pause the work for a day, but apparently time had run out.

"Of all the rotten days for us all to be healthy." The words would almost have been comical if not for the threatening choke in Harper's voice. "Why is it we get flares when the streets are all but dead, but when there's something out there we could actually help with? Nope, have a good day for once. Bye!"

The silence stretched long again before Rachelle broke it, her soft words tinged with pain.

"We've always known we don't get to choose. If our flares don't follow a pattern, our powers won't either. We can't pick our missions, no matter how much we want to. We have to trust that we're getting the ones we're meant to. There's nothing else we can do."

Harper looked away, but her frown didn't soften, and Brady's heart hurt for her. It was hard enough for him to deal with those questions knowing that God was controlling everything; how much harder would it be for Harper, who had to put her trust in some abstract universe or pure chance to make things work out in the end?

"*Most* of you don't get to choose." Dash's tone was defiant, but the words came slowly, and Rachelle whipped her head around to pierce him with a fierce glare.

"Three days, Dash! That's nowhere close to enough. Your movement time is still off, even for you. There's no way you're going out there again, so you can save your breath. Got it?"

"Wow, who died and made you the doctor?" Dash mumbled, but he didn't argue any further, likely proof that he agreed with her assessment, even if he didn't want to admit it.

"I mean, it's not like I couldn't give y'all a list of surefire ways to knock me out in a couple hours." Brady offered a half-apologetic shrug but didn't dare look at Rachelle as he made the suggestion.

"Brady, no. Seriously, we are *not* going there. I feel as bad about Donovan as anybody. Worse, when I think about Grace. But we can't trigger flares to help where we want to. That's a can of worms we can't open. We know the injection works and doesn't make us worse on our regular schedules. But if we start messing with it—trying to get it more often—trying to fit it to our timetable—there could be side effects. It could make us worse. Or it could stop working altogether, and then we're back where we started and not helping anyone. None of us are going down that road. Understood?"

"Understood." Brady sighed, but when he glanced over at Harper, his heart clenched at the sight of her curled up around her pillow with her face hidden against the back of the couch.

"Harper?" Rachelle asked gently, but the younger girl waited several breaths before answering her.

"Yes. I heard you." Her voice was muffled, and Brady couldn't tell whether it held more frustration or hurt.

Rachelle opened her lips, then closed them again, pressing them together hard. Brady followed her cue and held his tongue, sending up a silent prayer for Harper, for little Donovan and his family, for God to send someone to help if they couldn't. They all sat in silence for a few minutes, Rachelle watching Harper's back with sympathy in her eyes, Brady letting his gaze roam the room so she wouldn't catch them all staring, Dash glaring at the wall as though he'd like to drive his fist through it. Finally, Harper flopped over with a groan that was half playful and half desperate.

"Oh, for the love of Mike, will somebody please talk? Nothing we can do. I get it. But this place is like a tomb, and it's *not* helping!" She flung her pillow at Brady in what he hoped was mock frustration, and he managed to duck before it hit his head.

"Hey, I thought Rachelle said we're not trying to trigger anything!" He smiled a little as he tossed it back to her, and her eyebrows lifted.

"Pillow fights trigger you?"

"I mean, anything smacking my head, yeah. It doesn't happen enough to be sure on the probabilities, but it's definitely bad. If you want surefire, though, try loud speakers or strong smells. Spicy foods especially."

"Mmm, yeah. I can see that," Harper murmured, and Rachelle sighed.

"Let's take triggers off the table for the moment, huh? Give me ideas of what I can do to celebrate back to school week for Grace."

"Well, if you want triggers off the table, I suggest something other than Thai food." Dash's voice was dry, but Harper giggled a little, and Brady drew a relieved breath at the sound.

"Thanks—I wasn't really considering it." Rachelle sent him a raised eyebrow that rivaled one of his own, and the hint of a smirk twitched at the corner of Dash's mouth.

"What about something we can all do? T-shirts to decorate or something," Brady suggested, and Dash groaned.

"Seriously? If this involves any kind of pink or sparkles, I'm out. Got it?"

"Noted." Rachelle laughed, and the tension in the room relaxed, but Brady couldn't completely tune out the wistful look that lingered in Harper's eyes.

CHAPTER TWO

Brady woke gradually and lay still, trying to put words to the dull feeling of alarm vaguely pulsing in his brain. It took a few moments and turning tentatively onto his side for the faint scent creeping beneath the door to register, and he sat up straight and had to hold onto the bed to balance himself as the pieces snapped into place in his cloudy mind.

When he was sure he was steady, he got to his feet and opened the door, glancing down the hall before moving silently to the empty room across from his. The light was off, but the door was partially open, and when he pushed it the rest of the way, Harper looked up with wide, guilty eyes from where she sat on the bed.

"Was there a part of 'we're not triggering ourselves' that you didn't understand?" Brady kept his voice to a whisper as he sank down next to her, his sinuses filling with the spicy kick of the take-out container that sat on her lap.

"I said I heard her." Harper dropped her eyes to her feet and tried to sound defiant, but Brady didn't miss the slight wobble in her voice. "I didn't say I agreed."

"And you had to push it all the way, didn't you? Mexican wouldn't work; you had to go for Thai?"

"If I'm doing a thing, I might as well do it right." Harper forked up a piece of chicken and took a tiny bite, whimpering a little as she reached for the large mug sitting on the nightstand. She sucked in a couple deep gulps and several gasping breaths before reaching for the fork again.

"Harper." Brady reached over and stilled her hand, waiting until she turned her blinking, watering eyes on him. He studied her face for a few seconds, then sighed. "Do you even like Thai food?"

"This…isn't about me." Her voice still sounded strained, and she winced as she swallowed.

"And how much of that do you have to eat?"

"I don't know. Till I'm sure it's working?"

Protests warred in Brady's head, but as happy-go-lucky as Harper usually was, she had a stubborn streak a mile wide when she once set her mind to something, and if Rachelle's airtight reasoning hadn't convinced her, it was unlikely anything he said would make a difference.

"If you're going through with this, you need better than water to wash it down." Brady slid from the bed and slipped out the door and down to the common, where he filled another cup with some of Grace's milk from the refrigerator before bringing it back to the room and setting it next to her.

"Really? Milk?" Harper whispered, and Brady paused with a sudden rush of worry.

"Wait—is dairy one of your—"

"No, it's fine." Harper waved a hand. "Just sounds weird."

"Look it up if you don't believe me. But milk's way better than water." He nudged the cup closer, and Harper lifted it and took a tentative sip, then let out a little breath of relief.

"Okay, yeah. I see that. Thanks."

Brady sat down on the bed next to her again, and Harper fiddled with the chicken on her fork before glancing up at him.

"Shouldn't you get out of here?"

"Yeah, right." Brady gave a soft snort. "Headache's already starting. And there's no way I'm going to spend tomorrow in bed, waiting for a half-bad one to fade or get worse. Not when you're out there."

"Sorry." Harper swallowed hard and looked away, and the corner of Brady's mouth tipped into a weak approximation of a smile.

"Are you really, though?"

"I—" Harper's wide eyes jerked back to him before she caught herself and trained them on the floor again.

"Harper, you didn't even close the door." Brady sighed softly. "Maybe you weren't *trying* to trigger me, but you weren't going to complain much if it happened. You can't argue with that."

Harper pressed her lips together hard, and Brady rested a gentle hand on her shoulder.

"You scared?" His voice was barely a whisper, and Harper swallowed hard and didn't answer for several seconds.

"Maybe a little?" she managed finally, and Brady's tension relaxed just a fraction.

"About the mission? Or everything Rachelle was saying?" He paused, then added, "Or…what she's *going* to say?"

Harper gave a little snort and took another bite of her chicken, and Brady closed his eyes, trying to push the steadily growing pain in his head to the back of his consciousness. After a few more sips of milk and some deep gulps of air, Harper turned toward him again, and he looked back down at her.

"Maybe all of the above? I mean, I know Midge'll forgive me—eventually. And I know I can slip in. I just…if…"

"If something goes wrong, you'd rather not be on your own?"

"Yeah." The admission whispered out on a wavering breath, and Brady nodded his understanding. "And we're pretty much the power team for this one, right? You scan the building, and I slip in?"

"Right." Brady offered her a half-smile, and Harper sucked in a deeper breath and fanned her face for a second before picking up another bit of chicken. "Feeling it yet?"

"Little bit. It'll take some time to hit for real. You?"

"Oh, yeah. Probably take a couple hours of trying to sleep before it sets all the way, but I'll have to head back to bed in a few minutes if I don't want to keel over on the way."

"I really am sorry." Harper swallowed hard as she trained her eyes on her lap.

"Yeah, I know." Brady eased her chin up and waited until she met his gaze, then nodded his understanding. "We're in this together. Half the blame, half the credit?"

"I don't care. You can even give me all the blame and take all the credit. I'm just glad you'll be there."

"This one means a lot to you, doesn't it?" Her face was wavering in and out of focus, and Brady blinked hard until her bitten bottom lip solidified in front of him.

"Yeah. It does." Harper's voice stayed low, but after a minute, her eyes flicked up again, and a hint of a frown creased the dim sheen of sweat on her forehead. "If you're going back to bed, you'd better get. You already look rough."

"Feel it too." Brady forced himself off the bed and managed to steady himself before he ran into the wall. "See you in—a couple hours?"

"Sounds good."

Harper offered a weak smile, and Brady dragged himself back to his bed and threw his arm over his eyes, trying to let sleep take him back as the overload of spices clawed deeper and deeper into his brain. He wasn't sure if he actually managed to drop off or just lost track of time, but when he came back to something close to full awareness, the fallout of his choices hit him squarely in the head and stomach. Brady rolled on his side with a groan and fumbled for the button on his nightstand, squeezing his eyes hard shut against the faint light from the hallway.

It was only a few minutes later when a heated step sounded in the hall, and Brady could feel the tension radiating off Rachelle from the moment she hit his doorway.

"You too?" Hurt and anger mingled in her voice, and Brady's stomach dropped dangerously. He'd thought he'd prepared himself for her reaction, but the reality cut much deeper than the worst he'd imagined.

"Wasn't—" Brady swallowed hard and drew a shallow breath, trying to calm the rolling in his gut. "—much choice."

"Don't you start, please!" The words quivered with emotion, and Brady shut his mouth hard. "Harper's not even talking to me, and now you're ducking responsibility? I thought you of all people would back me up." Her voice was too close to breaking, and Brady gritted his teeth and reached for the words that swam just out of reach in the fog of pain.

"I was…already…sick. Only thing was…how sick."

"You—" Rachelle paused, closed her eyes, and forced a few deep breaths before she continued in a slightly softer tone. "Where was she?"

"Across." Brady jerked a hand in the general direction of the other room, closing his eyes as Rachelle's blurry face tightened again. "She…was going. Want her…alone?"

"Brady." Rachelle's voice cracked, and he could feel the shudder in her long exhale as she sat down on the edge of the bed. "I'm terrified. We have no precedent for this. What if something goes horribly wrong? This isn't what we were meant for."

"Chelle." He hadn't meant to shorten her name; his lips just didn't manage to fully form it. "Please. For…for Harper."

Rachelle waited for long seconds that dragged like minutes before she spoke again, her voice soft and sad.

"I don't like any part of this. But I guess I can agree it's better to have you both together. I don't know—" She broke off with a groan. "This is still a problem. If we're a team, we're supposed to act like one. Dash is going to be mad enough to spit nails, and I don't blame him. Everyone making their own calls is not sustainable. We're going to have to have a long talk when the two of you get back."

Brady was trying hard to listen, to understand, to agree, but the pounding in his head was reaching a crescendo, and he couldn't hold back a moan. Rachelle laid a hand on his and squeezed it gently.

"I'm sorry. It's not the time. I'll have Dr. Mattox come here once she's done in Harper's room." She stood and went to the door again, then paused and stepped back. "Take care of her, okay?"

"Yeah." The word was barely a breath, and Rachelle brushed his arm lightly before moving away again and closing the door behind her, leaving him to wait for the doctor.

Chapter Three

The total stillness nagged at the shadowy edges of Brady's returning consciousness, and he found himself reaching out for…he wasn't entirely sure what. Some voice—movement—proof that he wasn't entirely alone in the world he was slowly coming back to. Noises started to filter in from a distance—monitors beeping, a hushed conversation, someone moaning in their sleep—but somehow the searching part of him wasn't satisfied.

Blinking his eyes open, Brady attempted to rein his wandering senses back within the walls of his room, at the same time trying to sort out the unsettling impression of something missing…or lost. But it wasn't until he'd reoriented himself and was heading for the bathroom to brush his teeth that the truth slammed into him like a brick.

The world itself wasn't too quiet; all the noise and activity he could ask for swirled outside the walls and on the upper floors. But the den was eerily silent—a phenomenon he'd never experienced coming back to with all his senses on alert. Of course, it was incredibly early, or late, depending on how you counted it. But no matter the hour, he'd always woken to the sound of Rachelle's voice, or a whisper of movement in the common, or *something* to remind him that at least one of the team they'd built here had his back no matter what, and the intangible pang sharpened into a deep ache in his heart as the weight of the choice settled on his shoulders.

Not that he blamed Rachelle for being angry—it had been a very clear violation of a more than reasonable rule. And as badly as he felt for the little boy and his family, he'd never have chosen to take this step if not for Harper. But as soon as his foggy brain had connected her with the spicy scent, he'd known that his course was set. He couldn't let her go through with this alone, no matter how much trouble it put him in. And even with the sting of Rachelle's hurt and disappointment, he still didn't see how he could've made a different choice.

Was I wrong, Lord? I don't want to try to play God here. But the thought of her out on her own scares me cold. If I've messed it all up, I'm sorry. I know it's not the best plan, but it's the best I could think to do. Just please bring us through this safely. Please?

The silence hadn't lifted by the time he'd finished readying himself for the day—or maybe he'd just gotten unexpectedly better at controlling his enhancements early in the morning. He could only hope that they weren't actually working any differently than usual; it would be a cruel irony if intentionally triggering their abilities somehow weakened them too much to work for the task they'd been so desperate to accomplish.

Drawing a deep breath, Brady steeled his nerves and entered the hallway, but he'd only taken a few steps when something brushed against his arm. Brady yelped and pivoted toward the touch, then blew out an exasperated breath.

"Seriously, you've got to stop doing that!"

"Because a voice from out of nowhere is going to startle you less?" The words were lighthearted enough, but Harper's tone was a little subdued in comparison to her normal manner.

"Did Rachelle give you what for already?"

"Nope." Her expression might have been invisible, but he could hear her hard swallow as if it was right in his ear. "But her sad and disappointed look is almost worse sometimes."

"You're telling me." Brady sighed and leaned back against the wall, focusing on the area where he'd last heard Harper's voice.

"I told you to give me the blame." There was a soft sound like her teeth scraping her lip, but still no movement that he could catch.

"Doesn't work like that, and you know it. If I'd left the door closed and stuffed a towel in the crack and still ended up bad, then maybe. Joining you was my choice, and I know it as well as Rachelle does. I'll take my lumps. I just hope they're not as bad as she's afraid of."

"You notice any changes yet? Still functioning at full power?"

"Not sure if I am, but pretty sure you are. I've wondered for months which of our powers would beat, but I've got to give. I can see all the way into and out of your room, but you might as well not be there at all from what I can tell."

"Not a single trace?" A bit of the mischievous spark had returned to Harper's voice, and Brady's heart warmed a little at the sound.

"Not really. Every once in a while, I think I catch just a flash of something—like a hint of a sparkle off glitter—but I can't even be sure it's there before it disappears."

"That's the costume." Harper giggled a little. "Sounds like it, at least."

"And what…is your costume made of again?"

"Dr. Mattox knows a guy in materials science. This stuff was a semi-failed experiment—works great if what's behind it is also invisible, but if there's color there, it refracts it all over the place and becomes a sort of glitter-rainbow-kaliedoscope. Not quite what they were looking for, but it works great for us."

"And Dr. Mattox just—knows a guy who's got the exact kind of experimental fabric that you need?"

"They went to school together, I guess. Maybe they both practically lived in the labs? Who knows. But she does seem to have a guy for just about everything. Or at least one with the connections to get it."

"She doesn't happen to have a guy in the medical field, does she?"

"Are you kidding? She *is* the guy in the medical field."

"Of course she is." Brady sighed as he glanced toward the common again. "You ready to stop stalling and face this?"

"Guess we'd better. Donovan's counting on us." He could almost hear her chin lift and her shoulders straighten. "You want to go first, or should I?"

"Like anyone'll be able to tell. Including me." Brady pulled in a deep breath and pushed himself off the wall. "Let's get it over with."

"I'm coming." Harper's footsteps kept pace with him as they walked down the hall, but it wasn't until she stopped short on reaching the common that he realized she was in front of him.

"Ow! Seriously? We've got to work on that." Brady rubbed at his shoulder, then belatedly took in the scene in front of him and fought to swallow the lump that rose in his throat.

No one had abandoned them to their fate. Rachelle occupied her usual recliner, although the way she sat with her knees curled up to her chest somehow turned his mind to the image of Grace with her thumb in her mouth. But perhaps even more poignant was the sight of Dash on the couch next to her, lying rigid beneath a blanket, his face nearly expressionless except for a twitch at the corner of his eye. The other guy rarely showed himself outside of his room in this much of an "off" state, and Rachelle would never have broken his sleep in the middle of the night if she hadn't deemed it truly important. Brady's stomach clenched at the renewed realization of just how far beyond the two of them the consequences of their choice might reach.

"Breakfast's on the table." Rachelle spoke softly, obviously trying to keep her voice natural, although Brady could still trace the thread of hurt.

There was a second of silence before a chair scraped to the side, and one of the cantaloupe slices sitting on Harper's plate rose into the air.

"Thanks." Brady moved over to join her and picked up the cup with his shake, glad for the excuse to avert his eyes for a brief moment.

Everyone was silent as they ate, and Brady searched his mind for something to say that wouldn't come off entirely awkward and lame. Rachelle understood his reasoning, even if she didn't fully agree with it, and whether Dash did or not, attempting an explanation wouldn't move the needle at all. He'd aligned himself with Harper for this mission, so there was no benefit in trying to backpedal, but he didn't want to just ignore the tension and dig the knife in deeper for anyone else. Unfortunately, none of the ideas that occurred to him managed to walk that line, and he hadn't found a way to break the stillness when Rachelle took it out of his hands.

"Do the two of you have a plan for today?"

"Gamma Ray scans from outside, I sneak in."

Brady hadn't realized Harper had left the table until he heard her voice from behind him. He instinctively spun around, then rolled his eyes as the futility of the move hit him.

"Okay, but how are you getting there with Car still in therapy?"

Harper was quiet for a moment, and Brady wondered why the question hadn't occurred to them before. Ever since Car's accident, they'd kept their missions confined to the immediate area of the medical center, except for Dash, who'd never been dependent on her help. She was hoping to be cleared to drive again within a few more weeks, but that did nothing for them today. Had Harper even considered the very stationary location of the building before going ahead with her plan?

"The bus." Whether she had or not, Harper's delayed reply held nothing but confidence. "I can't get it myself, but together we'll be fine. It'll get us close enough."

Brady found himself almost hoping that Rachelle would have an argument to counter the plan, but instead she nodded slowly.

"Brace yourself before you get on there, Brady. That's a lot of smells and residues in a small space. When are you heading out?"

"ASAP. No idea how early they're starting the demo. Plus the sooner we get out there, the sooner we get back. Want to bet on how long it takes us?" Her voice took on an almost wistful note, and Brady could only imagine the pleading look she was sending to Dash.

"You…in so much…trouble." Dash's words were barely audible, painfully hoarse, and mumbled through lips that hardly moved. The sound wrenched Brady's heart, and he was glad for once that he couldn't see Harper's expression. He was turning away to give Dash what dignity he could when another labored word broke the silence. "Three…hours."

"Three marbles if we get it done in three hours—minus one for every half-hour after?" There was a slight choke in Harper's voice, in spite of the genuine enthusiasm that threaded it. "Rachelle, can you—would you—keep time?"

"All right." Rachelle closed her eyes for a second, then reached for her tablet, and Brady pinched his nose and surreptitiously rubbed at the threatening moisture in his own eyes.

"Deal." Dash's answer came back too late, but his chin jerked just the tiniest fraction. "Get moving and…get back."

"Will do." Harper's invisible smile was genuine this time, and Brady only jumped a little when her hand touched his arm. "Ready, Gamma Ray? Let's go save a kid."

Chapter Four

"You sure we're safe out here at this time of night?" Brady glanced warily over his shoulder, trying not to peer too deeply into the ominous shadows. He'd never realized just how much he felt the safety his usual DAWN vest afforded, but its absence seemed to weigh on him almost as heavily as the backpack of suspicious-looking tools that Harper had packed, but of course couldn't carry. It stood to reason that they couldn't risk attaching the volunteer organization's name to a mission like this, which was probably more illegal than he liked to think about, but the idea of being caught with a burglar kit instead was even worse. And of course he hadn't thought that through before signing up to accompany Harper through the streets in the dead of night on the way to her little breaking and entering mission.

"You're fine." Even though he knew she was right beside him, the voice coming from the eerily empty street still raised goose-bumps on his arms. "If anybody tries to come up on us, I can blind-side them long enough for you to get away."

"I would've felt a whole lot better if you'd said that wouldn't happen in the first place." Brady flexed his fingers against his leg, trying to concentrate on the texture of his jeans instead of the noises skittering behind the inky darkness.

"Okay! Nope, we're perfectly safe. Nothing bad ever goes down in Detroit after midnight. See how dead everything is? Not even a cop car in sight. Doesn't that mean everybody's home sleeping like they should be?"

"Not helping, Harper. And we've already established you're a horrible liar. Is the bus even running this early—or late?"

"Come on, I'm not *that* scatterbrained." Without facial expressions, it was hard to judge whether the wounded tone in her voice was real or put on. "It's running. I checked."

"Did you check on how I'm supposed to pay for two of us when I look like I'm boarding alone?"

"Ugh, can we please not go there?" Harper let out a pained groan. "You can't, obviously, but with Car on the shelf, I'm out of options. It's not like I'm purposely trying to jump the fare—or would do it if I had another choice. Is it worse than sneaking into a place on Car's pass, or spying on people through their walls? There's only so much I can do and still function at all."

"Hey." Brady instinctively reached out a hand before realizing he had no clue where she actually was. "Sorry. I wasn't trying to criticize. You've thought it through. I hadn't. That's all."

Harper drew in a long breath, then let it out slowly.

"Never mind. Sorry. Too sensitive."

"We've all had to navigate those questions." Rachelle's sober voice came quietly over the earpiece. "We're doing our best to do what's right. That's not always easy—on either end."

Brady couldn't escape the feeling that they were treading ground they'd probably covered long before he'd gotten there, and edging dangerously close to a much more relevant conflict at the same time. They'd have to have the conversation out at some point, but it would probably be better for everyone to wait until the mission was finished.

"So have you ridden the bus here before? With or without a fare."

"Once or twice when I was following somebody. Car kind of spoils us. I used to ride the bus all the time before I came here."

"That was in…" Brady paused and weighed his memories carefully before attempting what was still half a guess. "LA?"

"You almost said San Francisco, didn't you?" Harper's grin shone through her voice again, and the corner of Brady's mouth turned up at the sound. "You do know there's more than one city in California, right?"

"Come on, Harper, I'm a rural kid. It's not just California. I couldn't tell Boston from New York from Tampa if I woke up in one of them."

"You need a massive dose of culture." The sidewalk scuffed oddly behind him, and when he turned to look back, something hard connected with his ribs.

"Seriously?" The word came out too loud, even for a still apparently deserted street, and Brady dropped his voice to a whisper again. "Just because I don't know one maze of metal and brick from another, you—what even was that?"

"Sorry." Her tone somehow held both apology and suppressed laughter. "I was doing my best ballerina impression. You were supposed to keep walking, not stop in the way of my knee."

"Ballerina impression?" Harper was still largely an unsolved puzzle in his mind, but if that kind of thing happened spontaneously even when she was invisible, he could at least assume that some part of it was natural and not put on for attention. "Did I get a mission with you or Grace? Should I tie a balloon to your wrist so I can keep track of you?"

"Oh, come on, I'm not the one with crayon drawings tacked up in my room." An invisible elbow jabbed him in the side before he could feel it coming.

"Okay, that's totally different, and you know it." Brady attempted to elbow her back, but she easily evaded his blind jab. "So, Miss Culture, what's the biggest difference between Detroit and LA?"

"Ha!" Harper's incredulous laugh rang out in defiance of all caution. "Ask me what's the same; you'll get a shorter list. This is way more spread out than LA would even think of being. And not nearly enough skyscrapers. I mean, who ever heard of a city with lawns this size before you make it to the suburbs? It's totally weird."

"Hey, that's my hometown you're talking about." Rachelle's voice was still quiet, but Brady thought he could finally detect a smile hovering around its edges.

"I didn't say bad; I just said weird. I mean, you all know your city's not normal, right?"

"Yes, well, I prefer 'unique.'" The smile was obvious in Rachelle's voice now, and a weight lifted from Brady's chest at the sound.

"Besides, weren't you just giving me a hard time for thinking all cities were the same?" He shot a grin in the general direction of where Harper had last been, and she snorted from a little farther ahead.

"Let's just say you could do a lot more crime fighting on foot in any other city in the country. You've seen what it's like without Car around. This place was built for vehicles, not foot traffic. LA is totally different."

"Except for the buses?"

"Okay, the buses I'll give it. Not that helpful for superhero work, though. Not if Car's available anyway. Too much waiting. And way more risk of getting stepped on. Or found out. Plus, you have to hope there's someone else waiting, or they won't even open the door."

"So what I'm hearing is it's *invisible* superhero work that buses aren't that great for."

"Oh, 'cause your senses just *love* confined spaces, right? Especially when they trap all the dirt and smells of hundreds of sweaty people crammed together like—"

"Okay, okay, I give!" Brady shuddered a little as he raised his hands in surrender. "Point taken. I'd die. Bus is a last resort. Are we almost there?"

"Just a couple more blocks. We're seriously lucky there's an all-night route so close. Most of them take at least a few hours off after midnight. Not sure what our play would be then."

"Wait till they opened back up?"

"Yeah, but the whole point is to get in and out before the work crew shows up, and who knows how early that is? And how long's it going to take even your super sight to search a building that size?"

"That's…a really good question, actually. Especially in the dark." Brady stopped in his tracks and tunneled his gaze into the empty office building they were passing. "Wow. Yeah. I can still see about as far, but it's way harder to make out details. I've never really tried it at night if the building wasn't lit—I didn't even think."

"Still better than anything else we've got." Harper's voice was suddenly tight, and her footsteps sped up a little, as though afraid someone was going to yank her back to the den the moment a slight crack formed in her carefully crafted plan.

"Not saying I won't try. If I can catch any movement, it should help. How many floors is the building?"

"Nine or ten." It was Rachelle's voice that answered. "No idea how much clutter you'll have to sort through. Or what kind of tiny hole he might be hiding in. His deafness might work to your advantage, though. Even if he's trying to hide, he won't know how much noise he's making."

"Did they say he'd played in that building before?"

"Yeah. It's scary to think about. His mom said he was really upset when the equipment came in. That might be why he went back."

"Why was he allowed in there in the first place? Was anyone even paying attention? Who lets their—" Brady broke the sentiment off, not wanting to stick his nose into what was none of his business, but he couldn't imagine his own mother—or any mother—knowing their child liked to wander into dangerous places and not doing anything to prevent it.

"I know." Rachelle sounded just as conflicted as he felt. "With as much press as they've gotten, someone'll be looking at it. That's not our job right now. We just need to keep him from ending up under a pile of rubble."

"We?" Harper's hard swallow came clearly over the earpiece, at least to Brady's ear. "Does that mean you're with us?"

"I was never against you, Harper." Sadness shadowed Rachelle's tone again. "I want this to work as much as you do. I'm not happy with the way you got there, but I know your heart's in the right place. I'm going to do everything I can to help you complete this mission and get all of you safely home. Okay?"

"Thanks, Midge." There were definite tears in Harper's voice now, and Brady would have reached out to her if he'd had any idea where exactly she was.

"Of course." Rachelle's response was a little choked, but her next words held a smile. "That doesn't mean I might not ground you when you get back. Fair?"

"Fair." Harper laughed as she gave a wet sniffle. "Come on, Gamma Ray, pick up the pace. We don't want to miss our ride."

CHAPTER FIVE

"You doing okay?" Rachelle's soft whisper brushed his ear, and Brady let out a tightly controlled breath before he answered.

"Harper's right. This is an awful solution. I've got to look like the worst kind of germophobe, but—" He sucked in another breath and tried not to choke on the lingering odors.

"Is it the smell or the touch?"

"Touch. By far. My hand barely brushed the seat, and it hasn't come clean yet." Brady glanced nervously around the bus, not wanting to sound judgmental, but the rest of the scattered passengers seemed to be busy with their phones, or at least not paying him any kind of attention. Thankfully the ridiculously early route wasn't heavily frequented; he wasn't sure how he'd have explained the apparently empty seat by the window to a packed crowd.

"You're going to rub a hole through those jeans."

A warm hand brushed his arm from literally nowhere, and Brady jerked involuntarily, then gulped air as he tried to steady his racing heart. This was ridiculous. He *knew* Harper was right there. The fact hadn't even left his mind. But somehow it didn't lessen the shock of being brushed against or spoken to without any of the visual cues that usually buffered his startle reflex.

"You are really…not helping me stay under the radar." Brady kept his voice as low as he could manage, hoping that any reply Harper might make would pass for the a sound from his earpiece. Harper apparently had something of the same thought, because she waited until the older lady riding a little way behind them had looked down at her book again.

"Yeah, well, you're not going to help your cause by hyperventilating and passing out from some microbes on a bus seat."

"Did you have to put it that way?" Brady tried to swallow a groan, and a soft huff sounded from their earpieces.

"Accurate." Dash's voice still carried more than its normal gravel, but at least he was alert enough to engage in the conversation.

"You know what, neither of you are helping." Brady tried to suppress a shudder as he reflexively rubbed his hand across his jeans again, and an invisible arm linked itself around his and tugged it away. Brady barely bit back a yelp of surprise as he quickly leaned over so his hand rested in a more natural position and glared toward the window and the space where Harper's face had to be. "Seriously? What was that for? I thought our goal was *not* to draw attention."

"Secondary goal was to pull you out of that spiral, which I absolutely accomplished." Her voice somehow managed to convey both smugness and humor while still staying below the level of normal conversation. "Besides, you saved it pretty well. I'm impressed."

"Context, Harper? You know we can't see *either* of you right now." How Rachelle kept that patient tone with the questions that had to be running through her head after their scattered conversation, Brady had no idea.

Harper gave a somewhat exaggerated account of the scene, punctuated by soft giggles that thankfully didn't seem to draw attention, and Brady drew a deep breath and shook his head as the tangle he'd gotten himself into took on a new aspect. Harper was unpredictable enough when he could see every move she made, let alone when he couldn't even be positive exactly where she was in space. He'd been compelled to come along out of a vague desire to protect her—or at least to watch out for her—but how was he supposed to do that when he couldn't even begin to guess what her next move would be in a given situation?

"Watch...yourself." The strain in Dash's terse words was a little too pronounced to be fully rooted in medical reasons, though the fact that it wasn't followed up with more probably was. At least, Brady had no doubt there was more he wanted to say, but it was Rachelle that voiced it instead.

"He's right, Harper. You have to be careful. I appreciate you looking out for Brady, but don't do it in a way that's going to get you caught, all right? Especially with the way his senses are amplified right now, a touch or a noise without warning could startle him way worse than you'd expect."

"I know, I know." Harper sighed. "Although honestly, as long as they figure he's on the phone, nobody pays attention."

"Mmhmm, because people talking on the phone just randomly jerk their own arms around sometimes," Brady deadpanned, then tried to hold his ground and not flinch as her elbow connected with his ribs. Okay, so maybe *that* move had been entirely predictable.

"What I'm saying is, you're not used to a partner, so please be careful." The resignation in Rachelle's tone said the result had probably been just as easy to anticipate at a distance.

"Fine, Mama Midge. I'll watch myself. And the bus stops—ours is the next one." The bell sounded, and Brady glanced over in time to see the portion of cord just opposite their seats rise to sit parallel with the rest of it. "Start slow and let me out first so I don't get the door closed in my face, okay?"

"You know I could have done that, right?" Brady raised an eyebrow at the empty seat, and Harper huffed.

"Sure, and hit me in the face trying, which would be perfect for not drawing attention. Nobody can see the whole bus, so they'll all assume someone else pulled it. I *am* actually capable of thinking things through, you know. And I've been doing this for a year and haven't been caught yet."

"Sorry, Harper." Brady's shoulders slumped a little as he gave himself a mental slap. She was right; she might be reckless, impulsive, and downright silly at times, but it wasn't fair to treat her like a child, especially not when she could still claim significantly more street experience.

"Nah, you're good." And her voice somehow bounced back to perky with the same speed it had fallen to hurt. Brady was sure on a normal day, his head would have throbbed just from trying to process the shift. "This is us. Hop up."

The bus pulled to a stop in front of an entirely dark bank of buildings, though whether they were abandoned or just closed for the night, Brady didn't bother to check as he paused next to the seat for a few seconds, patting his pockets as though checking for his phone as he waited for Harper to squeeze out. Something bumped the front of his shoe, and he started forward, not hurrying as fast as he otherwise might have for fear of running into her. But thankfully, no mishaps occurred, and with a quick word of thanks to the driver, he was out on the pavement and watching the bus roll away, leaving him standing on a deserted street corner, entirely alone as far as anyone could tell.

"Very nice stalling tactic." Harper's voice from over his shoulder reassured him that she hadn't left him to figure out the way on his own, and he let out a relieved breath before turning to face in the direction of the sound.

"Thanks for the bump. I wasn't sure how long to stand there otherwise."

"No problem." Harper's smile was fully back; he could hear it in her tone even if its physical presence was as hidden as the rest of her. "You up for more walking? We've still got a few blocks left to go."

"What we're here for, isn't it? Which way?"

"Hey, hold on, let's try something!" The excitement in Harper's voice doubled, and Brady braced himself for either a good idea or a very bad one. "I'll lead the way, and you see if you can track me."

Brady gave her a full five seconds, but when the silence continued to stretch, it was obvious she wouldn't notice the glaring flaw in her plan without help.

"Harper…you're invisible."

"Yep." The word carried nothing but profound unconcern and cheerful acknowledgement, and Brady rubbed at the bridge of his nose, hoping that the building tension wouldn't start to form an actual headache.

"So how am I supposed to track you if I can't even see you?"

"That's entirely the point. You're way too dependent on your eyes. Probably everyone is, I guess. But you've got other things going for you; you're just not thinking to use them. Come on, close your x-ray eyes and concentrate. Where am I, and where am I going?"

"Harper—" The word started to lengthen into a groan, but Harper's coaxing cut it off.

"Come on, just try it? It's a good exercise, honest! You don't have to walk with your eyes closed, just stand still and figure out what you're hearing. I'll make sure you don't get creamed."

Taking a deep breath, Brady closed his eyes and focused his hearing in, close but sensitive, in a way he'd never consciously tried before. He was used to listening at a distance, or else trying to keep it as tightly reined as possible, and picking up on the tiny sounds around him had only ever been instinctual, not a skill he'd sought to develop. Was that barely there noise the scuff of a shoe or just an empty fast food container sliding on the sidewalk? No, blowing trash would move more erratically, and those squeaks, quiet and halting as they were, were evenly spaced. And when he focused in that direction, he could just hear a measured flow of air, softer and more stationary than the light breeze, which had to be Harper's breathing.

"You're…off to the left." Brady opened his eyes and studied the pavement in that direction, trying to tune both his hearing and his sight to catch any small anomaly. "You're moving toward the corner, and…you just stepped past the lamppost."

"Whoa." The cautious footfalls stopped dead in their tracks, and the corner of Brady's mouth turned up as he imagined her eyes flying wide. "I figured you could get the general area, but how…"

"Your footsteps moved a little to the right, and that's the only thing you could have been avoiding. Plus, there was a leaf blowing right there that crunched under your foot."

"That's incredible!" Rachelle breathed, and Harper snorted a little.

"Okay, that's it, Gamma Ray. No more easy mode. I'm heading toward the hotel. You follow, and try not to lose me."

Her footsteps started off at a rapid pace, but at least she wasn't trying to hide them anymore. Brady hurried to catch up as he followed the sound around the corner and toward their ultimate objective.

Chapter Six

"How much farther?" Brady quickly scanned the street ahead of him before turning his attention back to Harper's footsteps a few paces ahead and to the right. The one disadvantage to paying such careful, close attention was that his ability to scan for distant threats was limited, but thankfully this portion of the city appeared entirely dead at this time of night…or morning.

"Just across the street and around the corner." With no one around to hear, Harper didn't attempt to muffle her voice, but it was the words, not the volume, that stopped Brady in his tracks.

"Wait, seriously?"

"Yeah, why?"

"Hold on." Brady held up a hand and listened again, this time more intently. Somewhere ahead of him, a tree rustled in the light breeze, and a few solitary cars passed on distant streets. A door swung closed in the building to his left, and footsteps began to jog casually down the stairs. He could hear sighs and snoring, shuffling feet and the rustle of blowing trash, but nothing like…

A soft whistle from the guy on the stairs broke his train of thought with the reminder that he and Harper were the only ones out of place in this scenario, and any number of bad consequences could result from even a random commuter spotting them where they didn't belong.

"Look out, someone's coming." He reached a hand out instinctively before remembering that the last thing Harper needed to worry about was being *seen* anywhere. But of course, he couldn't say the same for himself.

Brady broke into a fast jog, casting his eyes around for some place of concealment until they landed on a portico just around the corner. Ducking into its shadow, he stayed as still as possible and tried to steady his breathing just in case the early riser came his way. Long seconds ticked silently by as the footsteps retreated in the opposite direction and a car roared to life. When the echo of its motor retreated up the street they'd just been walking on, the tension in his muscles finally relaxed, and Brady pulled himself up with a sigh.

"You still here?" He really hoped Harper wasn't going to make him find her through hearing alone again, especially when his heart was still pounding a little too fast from the near miss. Okay, so maybe it hadn't been *that* near, but just the thought of what might happen if someone caught him sneaking around out here made goosebumps prickle on his overly alert skin.

"Right on top of you. Thanks for the warning."

"Like you needed it." Brady snorted a little, and Harper hummed thoughtfully.

"You have no idea how easy it is to get knocked over or run into if people have no clue you're there. Helps to know when to move to the grass, if nothing else. You ready for this?"

"Yeah. Which way?" Brady turned in the direction her voice seemed to be coming from—why, he wasn't sure, except that somehow it still felt polite to face her, even if he couldn't actually see her. But the instinctive motion, or maybe his realization of how ultimately pointless it was, made him just self-conscious enough for his cheeks to warm a little at her giggle.

"Turn around, Gamma Ray."

Brady faced back toward the street, probably a little too fast, and somehow only then did the sight on the other side of it register. Covered chain-link construction fencing staking out the perimeter. Heavy equipment looming idle but ready for use at a moment's notice. And behind it all, the silhouette of the abandoned hotel that had become all too familiar from the news reports over the last few days.

"This is it?"

"In the flesh. Or—brick, I guess. Let's go."

"Whoa, hold it!" Brady threw out an arm again, not sure if it would actually block her but hoping she would at least notice and take the hint. "What are you planning to do? Just waltz in without even scanning the place first?"

"Always does," Dash growled, and Harper huffed softly.

"It's not like I'm used to having options. Takes too long to look around by myself, and they're not going to catch me anyway."

"Yeah, well, I'm here this time, so we're playing it careful." If he'd known exactly where she was, he'd have nudged her shoulder, but since he didn't have that option, he turned his attention back across the street. "Just one guard on patrol, and he's on the other side. Let's get across the street and under the tree line. Unlike you, some of us still need camouflage."

"Why do I still put up with you?" Harper heaved a dramatic sigh and, having the advantage of sight, bumped him lightly on the shoulder. "Fine, we'll do it your way, but hurry it up. The sky's not quite as dark already, and who knows how early they'll get here."

The unsettling sense of something vaguely not right gnawed at Brady's instincts again, but he forced it to the back of his consciousness as he hurried across the street and found a space behind some low-hanging branches that kept him reasonably covered while still allowing him a decent angle on the condemned hotel.

"How good are your eyes in this light?" Harper unzipped the backpack and started rifling through it. "Can you tell what I'll need to get inside? I'm guessing they haven't left an unboarded ground floor window."

"No, and the front and back doors are chained with padlocks." Unease surged back hard, and Brady could feel the frown tightening on his forehead. "How's Donovan supposed to have gotten in there in the first place? It's not like he had bolt cutters, or they wouldn't be able to say nobody was there."

"Kids find ingenious places. Or maybe they put up the locks after they supposedly rechecked, to stop anybody else from trying to find him." The bolt cutters and a pair of vise grips rose out of the backpack and performed a few experimental maneuvers, but Brady's attention was jolted away from the odd sight as the source of the anxiety that had been nagging at his subconscious since they reached the corner suddenly burst into the open.

"That's what's wrong! Where on earth is everyone? They've had at least a dozen people out protesting, right? And the demo company had to put extra guards on the place to make sure nobody broke in looking for him. So why are they down to a single guard and nobody making a ruckus on the morning they're supposed to raze the place? Something is very much off here."

"Wait, there's nobody?" Rachelle's concerned tone harmonized perfectly with the worry swirling in his gut. "Last night, Ms. King was threatening to sleep in front of the gate. This doesn't sound right at all. Are you sure you're in the right place?"

"Oh, it's the right place, all right. Temporary fences, heavy equipment, and everything." The tools rose into the air, and tree branches bent out of the way as Harper stood up and pushed into the open. "Maybe they couldn't stick the night out and decided to come back in the morning. Who knows? But I've got to get in there before the crew shows up. Wish me luck!"

Her jogging footsteps retreated toward the fence, and Brady trained his eyes on the nearest section, watching as the solitary vise grips attacked the nut that held the clamp in place.

"Which is exactly why someone should be there." The faint sounds of Rachelle worrying her lip with her teeth carried clearly through the earpiece. "I don't like this one bit."

"Neither do I. But what's our other option?" Brady could feel his heartbeat picking up speed as the tool spun faster and the clamp came loose. Metal squeaked lightly as one end of the panel lifted out of its base and began to slide open. "We're already up against the clock. If we wait to try to figure out what's going on, do we even have a chance?"

"Oh, we are *not* waiting." The gap in the fence stood still, widened a few more inches, then closed most of the way with an emphatic tug. "I don't care if his mom and everybody's given up. I haven't. We're getting him out of there. That's what we came for; that's what I'm doing. You still with me, Gamma Ray?"

"I'm here. If you're near the door, don't start on the chain yet. The guard's coming your way."

Two taps sounded on the earpiece, a signal that Harper had heard and was wisely going dark, and the seconds seemed to tick by in slow motion as the guard sauntered around the rear portion of the perimeter. Just opposite the back door, he paused and leaned against the fence to light a cigarette, and Brady's breath froze in his lungs as possibilities flowed through his head. If the guard took a break—if Harper coughed or bumped something—if he noticed the gap she had left in the fence— But after a few excruciating seconds, he moved on again, not sending so much as a glance in the direction of the shifted panel, and Brady let out a shaky breath as he tried to coax his heart out of his throat.

"Okay, I think you're good." He kept his voice to a whisper, just in case, and trained his eyes on the chain in time to see it suspended and then attacked by an apparently autonomous pair of bolt cutters. Harper did her best to muffle the noise and somehow managed to keep the chain from freefalling when it came open. The slight clank when she laid it on the porch wasn't enough to call up even a tilt of the head from the guard, and the door creaked softly open and then closed again as Harper slipped into the house.

"Wow, it's dark in here!" Even in a semi-whisper, Harper's voice managed to convey both awe and excitement. "Probably should've brought a flashlight, but that'd draw attention."

"Harper, please be careful in there." Brady could tell Rachelle was trying to mask her fear, but it wasn't entirely successful. "That place is condemned for a reason—probably a hundred reasons. We don't know if the floors are rotting, if the ceiling's collapsed, if there's massive holes in the walls. This is such a bad idea. You need to keep yourself safe, or you're no good to Donovan either. Be as slow and careful as you possibly can, and then bump that up by a factor of five, okay? Brady, can you try to scan for any obvious hazards? You probably can't pick out rotten boards, but—"

"On it. Harper, when I'm through with this, which way do you want to search? Top down or bottom up? Watch out in the lobby; one of the columns looks like it could go any minute."

"Why don't I start bottom up and you start top down? That way I won't have as many stairs to climb, unless you find him right away."

"Sounds like a plan. I really hope I can spot him. It's extremely dark in there. If he's curled up asleep in the shadows…"

"Don't forget you've got more than one tool in your belt. I'll keep as quiet as I can. Maybe that'll help."

"We'll go dark over here too. Please call if you need us." Rachelle drew a long breath and let it out quickly. "And please, please be careful. Both of you."

"Thanks," Brady whispered, and Harper hummed.

"Aye aye, Mama Midge! Come on, Gamma Ray. Bet you can't clear two floors in the time it takes me to do one. But I guess—no." Her voice sobered suddenly. "Let's not race. Go as slow as you need to. We can't let Donovan down. Looks like we're all he's got left."

CHAPTER SEVEN

At first glance, the sixth-floor bedroom looked just as empty as the dozens of others he'd already searched this morning, but appearances weren't anything close to enough for a mission like this. Brady bored his eyes into every dark corner, through every peeling wall, under every pile of junk, doing his best to make sure that no child-sized hiding place was left unexplored. After satisfying himself that there was truly nothing to report, he turned his vision to the room opposite it, but the dark shapes began to blur and swim in front of him. For a few seconds, he gritted his teeth and tried to push on, but apparently pure willpower was no longer enough to counteract the strain on his body.

"Somebody mark the back bedroom, sixth window from the left, please. I have to rest my eyes a minute, and if I lose my place…"

"I've got it." Rachelle's voice somehow managed to convey worry and reassurance all at once. "Back bedroom, sixth window from the left. Close your eyes and relax. Are you staying hydrated? This kind of prolonged search isn't anything like your normal pattern. You haven't come across anything yet?"

"Nothing." Brady sighed as he pulled an electrolyte drink out of the backpack and took a long gulp, then let his aching eyes fall closed.

"And your…instinct…subconscious…whatever we're calling it when you zone in on something without even trying—that hasn't kicked in at all?"

"Not a peep. Every time I try to not focus and just see what it picks up, it keeps bringing me back to Harper. Or at least, my ears go back to her. My eyes have absolutely no reference point."

"Guess I'm impossible to resist." Harper let out an absent little chuckle. "Didn't really expect it to take this long, but I have to watch pretty much every step in here. If you don't know what people have been using this place for, you don't want to."

"Harper—"

"Please be careful. I know, Midge." Harper huffed. "I've got my gloves on, and I'm keeping my eyes open. Wish I'd brought a snack with me, but it's probably best not to touch it in here anyway."

"Do you need to come out and refuel for a minute?"

"Don't have time. I can't see the sky, but I can see the treeline a whole lot better now, and I don't like it. This is too slow as it is. We can't afford a break."

"Sorry." Brady took another sip of his drink and put the cap back on, then opened his heavy eyes and trained them on the building again.

"Don't be." Rachelle's words were almost harsh in their firmness. "You're out there to help as much as you reasonably can, not to go blind from overwork. There's nothing wrong with pacing yourself, Brady. And if I thought Harper would listen, I'd say the same to her."

He'd rarely heard her tone bleed frustration so obviously. Harper must have thought the same because she was quiet for a minute, and her voice was subdued when it came again.

"Sorry. I'm not trying to push too hard. We just have to find him. We have to!" The last words caught in her throat a little, and Brady sent up a silent prayer for calm and strength for both of them.

"Breathe, Harper. I'm almost through with the sixth. That'll put us more than three-quarters though. If he's in here, we'll find him."

"We have to," Harper whispered, and Brady swallowed hard.

"I'm going back to scanning. Talk if you need to; I think I can tune it out." He focused his eyes back on the floor he'd had to abandon earlier, but despite his confident statement, the sound of Harper's heavy breathing over the earpiece refused to fade into the background.

"It's almost 4:30. You two going to be okay if I put the news on?"

"Yeah, go ahead." It wasn't like his hearing was helping much right now anyway. "Give me my spot again first?"

"Back bedroom, sixth window from the left," Rachelle repeated, and Brady pulled back just enough to count quickly before tunneling his vision into the building again at a slightly different angle from the one he'd originally chosen.

"Thanks. I got it. Let you know if I need you again."

"All right. Take breaks if you have to. That goes for both of you."

"Got it." Brady picked up his methodical search and was just finishing the sixth floor when a sudden clatter broke his concentration and yanked his focus over and down to one of the stairwells, somewhere in the area around the third or fourth floor. He held his breath as he ran his eyes over the immediate vicinity, but literally nothing appeared to be moving. "Harper, was that you?"

"Yeah, sorry." Her voice sounded more than a little winded, but he couldn't tell how far she might have made it on the stairs. "Go back to where you were. Door opened faster than I was prepared for is all."

"Sure you're okay?"

"I'm *fine*." The irritation in her tone worried him almost as much as the breathlessness. It wasn't like Harper to lose her temper, unless some particularly painful annoyance hit during the very lowest point of one of her flares. She was much more prone to hurt than anger—and even more likely to cover negative feelings of any type with a joke and refuse to acknowledge their existence.

But there was no use trying to convince her to take a break. If Rachelle's powers of persuasion weren't enough to sway her, likely nothing would.

"Slow down, Shadow." Dash's heavy rasp somehow still managed a note of command, and Harper's next breath came a little deeper. "Try to go too fast…you'll miss something."

"Right." Harper released a shaky sigh, and Brady silently revised his mental assessment. "Sorry. Probably didn't get enough sleep."

"You think?" Dash's response was delayed, but his dry emphasis came through perfectly, and Brady bit back a chuckle that would only have made Harper think he wasn't taking this seriously.

"So when we get back…" Harper paused for a few seconds, and Brady wasn't sure at first whether she meant to finish the thought or not. "…help me talk Midge into a nap before the lecture?"

"You'll owe me."

"I know. Thanks, Dash." Harper swallowed hard, and there was silence on the line for a few seconds before Rachelle broke it hesitantly.

"You don't usually need a nap on a mission day, Harper. I know you're scared, but try to pace yourself, okay?"

"Yeah. Sorry for snapping. Did I…" Her voice trailed off on a question, and Brady hesitated slightly before prodding her.

"Did you what?"

"Miss my landing. I…lost track a little. Not sure if…" The statement faded into nothingness again, and Brady tried to calm the tension knotting in his gut as he dragged his gaze back from the stairwell to the spot he'd last left off searching.

Harper obviously needed a break even worse than he had, but even with Dash managing to talk her down a little, there was no way she'd agree to take one any time soon. And it wasn't like he didn't understand her reasoning; already a man in a hard hat had joined the guard and started to wander around the equipment. It wasn't only in her imagination that they were running out of time.

Brady increased his own speed as much as he could without entirely sacrificing thoroughness, praying that if there was a clue he'd moved on from too quickly, God would bring his attention back to it, the same way He had in other circumstances. He tried to focus his hearing within the search path, but between Harper's breathing and the soft buzz of the early news filtering through Rachelle's earpiece, he was forced to give it up as a lost cause and turn all his powers of concentration to his straining sight.

The background hum morphed into a drone of actual words as Brady checked and cleared one room after another. Weather, traffic, a report on a particularly bad shooting from the night before—they all meandered through the back of his mind like ordinary background noise. Then suddenly the words "Donovan King" snapped his hearing to the forefront, and the building faded from his consciousness as his ears took over.

"—come under fire this week from a mother who believed her missing son might be hiding in the building. But late last night, this station received a statement from the boy's aunt claiming that Donovan isn't missing at all. In fact, it appears that he's been with his father in Battle Creek the whole time. We haven't received any comment from the father yet, but according to the aunt, multiple witnesses claim to have seen Donovan going and coming from the house in the last few days."

"Really a shocking turn of events…" The female anchor's voice tapered off into a murmur again as Harper's uneven breathing and Brady's own pounding heartbeat filled his ears.

"Rachelle." He had to force the word through lips that were suddenly dry. "Please tell me they didn't just say—"

"You heard that?" Rachelle's voice was choked with a medley of emotions he couldn't even begin to identify.

"He was never even there." Brady repeated the words in a whisper, trying to process the seismic shift taking place in his brain.

"All right." Rachelle sucked in a deep breath that shuddered a little on the exhale. "Don't try to unpack it now. We'll debrief when we get you back. Let's make that happen as quickly as possible."

"What are you talking about?" Harper's voice trembled, and Brady realized for the first time that she couldn't possibly have heard the report.

"Come on out, Harper. They've found him."

"What?" The question was paper-thin and haunting in its fragility, as though she'd just discovered they were too late instead of not being needed at all.

"They found him. He's safe. That's why nobody's protesting." Rachelle's voice gentled even further, as though soothing a hurt animal. "You've done your part. Let's get you home."

Brady wasn't sure how much restraint she had used to keep from commenting on the fact that their mission had been useless from the start—that if they'd listened to her and followed the existing rules, the whole situation would have been fixed by the time they woke up this morning. Harper must have had the same thoughts, and after a hard swallow, her voice came back, smaller and weaker than before.

"Chelle?"

"We'll talk, Harper. I promise. But right now, you need to get out of there and back to Brady. Can you do that?"

"I—I don't—know." The catch in her breathing grew suddenly more pronounced, and Brady's eyes shot back to the building, searching instinctively—uselessly—through the vacant mass for an invisible figure. "I don't—feel—very well."

Chapter Eight

"Harper, find a clear place and sit down." Rachelle's voice managed a surprising level of calm, despite the urgency swelling beneath it. "Get your head between your knees. Hear me?"

Harper's answering hum was almost a whimper, but after a few seconds, her erratic breaths slowed just a fraction, and the sound became more muffled.

"Are you there?" Rachelle's question could have been directed at either her position or her ability to still hear them as far as Brady could tell, but either answer would be relevant at the moment.

"Mm-hm." The murmured answer was still much weaker than it should have been, and Brady continued the silent prayers that had been half-consciously forming in his head ever since Harper's announcement, not wanting to clutter their only lifeline at this critical moment by whispering aloud.

"Okay, just breathe. When you can, try to tell me what you're feeling. Is it the usual?"

"It—" Harper paused for a few thankfully longer breaths. "Maybe. It's—yeah, mostly lightheaded. Dizzy. My eyes went blurry for a second. But—that's never happened when—" Her words cut off as her breathing sped up again, and no one finished the thought that had to be on all of their minds.

"We'll figure it out when we get you back, okay?" Rachelle had every right to an "I told you so," but her tone held no hint of it. "Let's treat it like that for now, until we know differently."

"And what? Lie down somewhere and try to sleep the worst of it off until my next phlebotomy? I can't, Midge, and you know it."

"Not that exactly, but you need to take it as easy as you can. Keep your head down for a while. Brady, how are things outside?"

"Another operator just showed up. We can't be in real danger yet; there's no way they could run this job with three guys, but…"

"I have to get out of here." Harper's words were a moan, and Brady was sure he heard tears in her next wavering breath.

"Play it smart, Shadow." It was as close to a snap as Dash could manage at this hour of the morning, but it hit home if Harper's little sob meant anything.

"I'm—trying. What's my other option, though? Gamma Ray sneaking in for me to lean on? That's more dangerous by, like—exponentials."

"You won't help anything by trying to rush and making it worse." Rachelle's tone somehow managed to blend firmness and gentleness in equal measure. "Keep breathing. That's the best thing you can do right now. When you're a little bit steadier, we can talk about what comes next."

Harper didn't answer, and Brady hoped it was a good sign that she had stopped trying to argue.

Father God, please make her better. Please get us out of here. Get us home safe. We signed up for consequences, but—can they please hold off until someone's there to help?

No one said a word for several long moments, and Brady watched the early demolition crew members prep the equipment for the day, throwing a few glances back toward the decrepit building that even his own eyes would have sworn was entirely empty. What if someone discovered the open fence or the cut chain? Would they have to delay the demolition to search the area again? But then what if someone *did* stumble across Harper? It was probably too risky to hope for as a solution.

"Okay, I'm going to try to get up now." Harper's voice finally broke the silence, just a little bit stronger than it had been before.

"Are you sure? That's awfully fast." The worry hadn't left Rachelle's tone, and Brady held his breath a little, waiting for the response.

"It's—not as bad, honest. And it's even odds it stays the same, or gets worse. Longer I wait around in here, the less margin we have."

It was a valid point, and none of them could argue it, but Brady could sense everyone else on the line holding their collective breath as Harper's breathing sped up again, punctuated by unsteady noises.

"Take it slow. Lean on something. Hold onto the wall if you have to."

Harper murmured something that might have been "I know," and Rachelle waited a moment, possibly to let her test her steadiness, before pressing her further.

"How you holding up? Any worse standing?"

"I—I'll be—okay…" The strength was draining from her voice at an alarming rate, and Brady clenched his fists until his short nails bit into the unusually tender skin of his palms.

"Harper, you're not ready. We still have time. Sit down."

"I…can't."

"Harper!" Rachelle's voice had taken on an edge of sternness that was almost severity. "Listen to me. I don't care where you are; you need to put your head down. Do it now!"

"I—" The weak word faltered and nearly disappeared beneath Dash's fierce bark.

"Shadow. Sit. Now!"

Her faint answering whimper faded into a soft exhale and a distant thump, and Brady's heart rate doubled even as his mind fought against the reality that was all too clear.

"Harper?" Rachelle's plea was almost desperate, and Brady wondered if she was stuck in the same mire of conflicting emotions. "Harper, please answer. Even with just a tap. Can you hear me?"

"Father God, help us." Brady breathed the prayer without conscious thought, and Dash cleared his throat hard.

"Quiet! We've got to know the worst. Gamma Ray, can you—" His hard swallow came clearly across the line. "—can you still hear her?"

Hear her. Her breathing! Brady closed his eyes and tried to concentrate. He was almost sure he could hear three distinct patterns, but…

"I think so. Have to be sure. I need your earpieces out. Give me ten seconds."

Rachelle's breathing faded away instantly, and Dash's cut out with a growl a second later. His initial count hadn't been wrong; there was definitely still airflow on the other end of the line, labored and weak as it was. The seconds seemed to crawl by as he listened, wishing he had some way to summon the rest of the team back early.

"I'm coming, Harper." Brady whispered the promise into the near-silence. "I told you we're in this together and I meant it. Hold on for me. Just hold on."

"Well?" It was Dash's rasp that joined them first, and Brady waited until he was sure he could hear Rachelle again before he answered.

"She's there. Still breathing. Still no conscious response, so—game plan?"

"I'm getting Mattox," Dash bit out, and Brady could hear Rachelle's sharp inhale.

"Dash, you can't!"

"You said that before." Had he really just thrown Harper's defiance up in her face? "What else? Be there in three minutes. I won't get caught."

"And tomorrow?" Rachelle's voice was strained almost to the breaking point. "You're going to leave me alone with—we don't even know what?"

Dash made an inarticulate sound somewhere between a snarl and a groan that Brady figured spoke his feelings about as clearly as it was possible to express them.

"Besides, it's three minutes once you wake up from the shot." It was dangerous work, challenging Dash's plan that way, but there was no time to be careful of egos. "That's what—half an hour at least? That we don't have to lose. I'm going in."

Rachelle's teeth scraped hard across her lip, and Brady was sure she wanted to protest, but she apparently agreed with his assessment enough not to argue out loud.

"Yeah? How?" Dash's bark was not one to inspire confidence in the fainthearted, but Brady didn't have to guess at the layers of concern and frustration beneath it.

"Same way she did. I don't have invisibility, but I *can* make sure no one's looking when I go to sneak through. She's already opened the path; I just have to follow."

"And if she doesn't wake up? How are you going to find her?" Rachelle's tone was hesitant, but he wasn't sure if she was afraid of discouraging him or of giving him too much hope.

"Like she said, I've got other senses. If I ever needed them, it's now. I've been keyed into her all morning without even trying. Maybe now I know why. I'm not saying it's going to be easy, but who else is there?"

Somewhere to his right, a gate rattled open, and Brady turned to see two more men in hardhats entering the site.

"There's seriously no time. Guys are showing up for real. Nobody's watching the back. It's got to be now or never."

"Brady, if we—" Rachelle swallowed the rest of her thought, and Brady's forehead creased as he waited.

"Go on. Anything you need to say, get it out now."

"If you—" She was fighting against the break in her voice, but it was battling back hard. "If you get trapped in there—the both of you—"

The weight of what she couldn't put into words settled over him as the threatening sob won out, and Brady drew a deep breath that somehow held more peace than the situation deserved.

"Rachelle." He waited a few seconds as she choked back the tears. "It was the wrong call to come out here. I know that. But God didn't have to wake me up in the middle of the night to bring me with her. He hasn't lost control. I don't want you to lose us—either of us. But I'd never forgive myself if I let it be her and not me. Whatever happens, you know I'm safe."

"I know." The words still quivered a little, but her usual strength was returning. Somehow that glimpse of her vulnerability felt like a badge of honor—like she hadn't had to mask her true feelings to him, even in such a dangerous moment. "But since I'd—really rather not explain to Eden how you ended up under a pile of rubble—tell us what you need."

CHAPTER NINE

"Just stay quiet so I can concentrate." Brady gave the area a quick, comprehensive glance, confirming that none of the men were facing toward the treeline, then raced to the open section of the fence. Another hurried scan, and he slipped through and sprinted for the back door, pausing to calm his pounding heartbeat only after he reached the safety of the dark hallway.

Thankfully, he'd spent enough time with his eyes inside the building that morning to be familiar with its layout, and as soon as he could draw a deep breath, he headed for the stairs. The stench in the place was almost overpowering, and when he reached for the railing without thought, the filth that coated his hand brought him within a hair's breadth of being sick.

"Which floor?" He forced the words through gritted teeth as he did his best to shut down the senses that weren't helping.

"You tell me." Dash's voice was flat. "Missed the landing. Anyone know if she turned or kept going?"

Brady's climb ground to a halt as the memory hit him squarely in the chest. In retrospect, they should probably have paid more attention when she started seeming out of it. But at the time, he'd been focused on his own search, not on keeping tabs on Harper's every move. Had she backtracked when she realized her mistake, or kept going? And how far had she made it in either direction?

"Okay." He paused and tried to center himself without breathing too deeply. "She was heading for the fourth, right? So that would make the most likely spots four and five—three to six at a stretch. Agreed?"

"Tell me again how much easier this is for you?" Dash gritted out, but Brady was too intent on scanning the stairs in front of him to take offense, even if he'd wanted to.

"Never said it was easy. But the whole point of me going in is to make it *quick*. Which means I have to start on the floors where I'm most likely to find her. Be quiet for a minute."

Pausing on the third-floor landing, he listened carefully, but he couldn't hear any difference in the volume of Harper's breathing in his ear. He took the next set of steps as fast as he dared and listened again, but nothing seemed to have changed.

"Picking up anything?" Rachelle asked softly, and Brady tried to push back the growing sense of dread gnawing at his gut.

"Not yet. Let me try one more."

The line stayed relatively silent as he followed the stairs to the fifth floor and held his breath on the landing. But after several tense seconds, he was forced to let it out with a long exhale.

"It's not going to work this way."

"Which way?" Rachelle's question came back immediately, and Brady swallowed hard.

"The earpiece. I can hear her through it, but it's masking everything else. Direction, distance, anything that might help me find her. I'm going to have to go dark. Completely."

"Brady…" A hint of a quiver had returned to Rachelle's voice. "This is such a bad idea."

"This whole day has been a bad idea." Brady couldn't help pointing out the obvious, and Dash snorted what almost might have been a laugh. "I know you don't want to be out of touch. I totally get why. But this is a massive haystack, and I'm looking for an invisible needle. I need every scrap of concentration I can scrape together. Can you trust me?"

"It's never been you." Rachelle gave a shaky sigh. "Before you try, though—are you absolutely sure you don't feel…off?…at all?"

It was a valid question—more than valid, considering what had just happened to Harper—especially if he was about to cut his only lifeline. Brady closed his eyes and gave his body the most careful attention he could muster.

"I'm as sure as I'm going to get. Anything wrong is just—it's side effects of my senses, not the injection."

"As in?"

"As in, I want to spend as little time in this disgusting smell trap as humanly possible. And I want an hour-long shower when we get back."

"That's fair." Rachelle managed a tight chuckle, then drew a deep breath. "The minute anything feels weird—just the slightest bit—you come back online, okay?"

"Promise. And Rachelle?"

"Yes?"

"Pray for us both, please."

"I'll do that." He could hear tears clogging her voice again, and maybe just the slightest catch in Dash's rough tone as he cut in.

"Quit stalling. Do it now, or let someone else take over."

"I'll be back. Gamma Ray out." Brady pulled the earpiece and muted the volume before sticking it in his pocket. Sending up another wordless prayer, he listened intently, but no trace of Harper's faint breathing filtered through to the stairwell. If only he knew which floor to search!

Don't forget you've got more than one tool in your belt. Harper's words from earlier echoed back through his mind, and Brady frowned. She'd been encouraging him to stop being so dependent on his sight, but— Sucking in a sudden breath, he turned back the way he had come and knelt to examine the stairs. His own shoes had left slight traces in the layers of dust and grime. Was there any chance he could find how far Harper's had made it? What kind of treads did her invisible shoes have, anyway? Or had his tracks already obliterated any traces she might have left?

Trying to stick to his own shoe prints as well as he could, Brady retraced his steps to the halfway landing and studied the lower flight carefully. Harper had made it to somewhere in this vicinity at least, if she'd truly passed the fourth floor landing like she thought she had. After a minute of careful concentration, a few oddly smooth scuff marks began to appear, not really resembling a regular shoeprint, but in a size that roughly matched Harper's feet.

The prints didn't come straight up; instead they wavered back and forth across the width of the stairs, further strengthening his suspicion that they belonged to Harper. His footprints had covered some of them, but as he studied them more carefully, he thought he could tell where she'd paused and stood for a few seconds when she realized that she'd come too far. And then…

Down. She'd backtracked. Brady retraced his steps, following the faint marks until they veered off toward the fourth-floor entrance, then reached in his pocket for the earpiece.

"Found her trail. Fourth floor. I'm going in."

"Be careful," Rachelle breathed, and Brady hid the earpiece again, then opened the door and scanned the worn, matted carpet for any trace of a recent track. But although he could pick out a few impressions that might have been hers, it took longer to spot them than it had on the grimy stairs, and who knew how much ground she had covered in searching the floor before she passed out?

All right, Lord. It's back to my ears. Let this work, please.

Brady closed his eyes and rested his hand against the wall to ground himself, swallowing back the gag that rose in his throat as a new layer of dirt coated his fingers.

Harper. This is for Harper. Concentrate. Move.

He focused his hearing hard on the space around him, trying not to let sounds from outside or other floors seep through, searching for the faint, uneven breathing that was Harper's only lifeline. If only it was as simple as walking the halls until he tripped over her, but after searching from a distance for hours, he knew better than anyone how many corners there were to get lost in—and that was looking for a *visible* figure.

Allowing his eyes just enough attention to keep him from running into a door or stepping on a needle, Brady took a few hesitant steps forward, paused, listened, then repeated the cycle. The creak of the gate reached him from somewhere off in the distance, and his heart rate started to pick up speed. They were running out of time. Badly.

Lord, please. Don't let her die in here. She's not ready. Please.

A wisp of sound so faint it hardly deserved the name brushed his ear, and Brady froze, holding his own breath as he waited for it to repeat. When it did, he took a cautious step toward the other side of the hallway and was rewarded with a miniscule increase in volume.

Please, Lord!

Pressing his ear against the wall made it just the tiniest bit clearer, and Brady thrust his vision into the room on the other side just long enough to find which door it connected to before rushing over and ducking through the opening.

"Harper?" His voice automatically kept to a whisper, and he had to shake himself out of quiet mode. "Harper?"

No answering noises reached his ears as he shuffled carefully through the room, feeling next to the furniture, on top of the bed, near the floor beside the walls.

Father God, where is she? Don't let me miss her!

Closing his eyes, he concentrated on listening again for her breathing—it was still there, closer, but— Brady stood and moved carefully in the direction the sound seemed to be coming from, until his shoulder bumped something solid. He opened his eyes and found himself against the back wall, but Harper's breathing was still— Brady sucked in a breath as understanding flooded in. Taking only a second to orient himself on the floor, he rushed out of the room and into the hallway, skidding around the corner of the nearest crossing corridor just as a roar from outside shook the building.

Brady's heart leapt into his throat, and he cast a panicked glance toward the front of the old hotel. Thankfully, the equipment seemed to be just starting up and not moving in yet, but if they'd been out of time before, they were definitely dipping into the negative at this point.

He raced down the hallway opposite the one he'd originally searched and paused outside the door, desperately attempting to focus his hearing on that one faint strain of breath beneath the all-consuming roar of the heavy machinery.

Father, please!

He put his hand on the knob of the door, but some barely felt instinct made him hesitate. Holding his own breath, he moved a few shuffling steps to the side, and his foot bumped against an invisible obstacle in the apparently empty corridor. Kneeling down without any regard to what kind of grime might be coating the ancient carpet, he reached a hand out, and it brushed against something soft and warm. Two more seconds of cautious exploration, and he was gripping Harper's hand and fighting hard against the tears that wanted to overflow at the worst possible time. Offering another silent prayer, he fished quickly in his pocket and fitted the earpiece with fingers that trembled a little in spite of his best efforts.

"Rachelle, can you hear me? Dash? I've got her."

Chapter Ten

"Is she all right?" The trembling in Rachelle's voice almost matched the vibration of the ground beneath him. Brady desperately wanted to take a moment to let them all process the mixture of relief and remaining fear, but they didn't have a second to spare.

"Not sure. She's still unconscious. They're firing up the machinery. We have to get out of here now."

"How?" The desperation in Dash's tone bit deep, and Brady gritted his teeth as he quickly sorted through his options. Not that he'd call Harper heavy, exactly, but there was no way he'd be able to lift her in his arms like he might have if she was smaller.

"I don't think I can pick her up. I'll have to drag her. Maybe I can get some better leverage once I get her to the stairs."

"Are there blankets left anywhere?" Rachelle asked, and Brady nodded before remembering that he was currently as invisible to them as Harper was.

"Yeah. Roll her onto one and use it to drag her?"

"It might help, if you can do it fast."

"On it." Brady threw a glance around the hallway, then ran to the nearest room with a thin blanket still on the bed. He ripped it off and spread it close to Harper, then gripped her as well as he could and tried to roll her on top of it. It was harder work than he imagined, especially not being able to see half of what he was doing, and he was breathing hard by the time he finished.

"You all right?" He could hear the worry in Rachelle's tone as he glanced back toward the front of the building, where another machine was revving up to join the ominous chorus.

"Yeah. Just hope she doesn't roll off the blanket. I can't really tell if she's centered." He paused for an instant, then threw his remaining pride to the wind. "Count down for me?"

"Tell me how."

"Don't try to keep time; just count down in my ear—maybe from 30? Don't know why it helps, but it does. And I'm going to need all my breath."

"Absolutely. Start now?"

Brady rolled his shoulders and gripped the corners of the blanket nearest Harper's head. With a silent prayer and a deep inhale, he nodded hard.

"Now."

Rachelle immediately began counting down, almost exactly hitting the cadence he'd muttered under his breath on far too many days as he tried to push through the pain to accomplish some embarrassingly easy task. Brady focused on the blanket and the carpet in front of him, concentrating on one step at a time, letting the slowly decreasing numbers give him a midpoint to reach for.

When Rachelle reached zero, Brady allowed himself a quick pause and a deeper breath before he continued on again, and she immediately restarted the count in his ear without being prompted. He tried not to look up, just to continue putting one foot in front of the other, and finally came within an inch of ramming into the wall that signaled the end of the hallway. A tricky turn, a short corridor, and finally they were in the stairwell, where the vibrations from outside seemed to double.

Father God, please get us out of here! Please give us time!

"Okay, somebody help me. Best way to carry her when I can't just pick her up?"

"I've been looking." How Rachelle had managed that on top of keeping her voice so steady in his ear, he had no idea. "Can you get her arms over your shoulders like a backpack? I think that's your best bet."

"I can do my best." Brady positioned Harper as carefully as he could, then scooted a few steps down and reached back, feeling for her arms.

"Do. Not. Drop. Her." Dash's pauses felt intentional enough to be for emphasis, and Brady exhaled hard.

"Believe me, I'm trying! It's right up there with falling on my head under 'things to avoid at all cost.' That good enough?"

Dash grunted in response, and Brady tuned out the noise as he pulled Harper's invisible arms over his shoulders, then held on with one hand and gripped the rail tightly with the other.

Father God, please help me!

Straightening slowly, Brady attempted to balance Harper's body on his back without tipping too far in any direction. The weight on his shoulders and the sight of the stairs stretching down in front of him made his head spin, and he turned to the side and faced the railing to keep the view from overwhelming him. The trembling beneath his feet increased, and he swallowed hard, not daring to look around and try to gauge the crew's progress.

"Starting down. Please pray. This isn't going to be easy."

Rachelle's soft voice immediately complied, and Brady began making his way down, sliding one step at a time, switching which hand held the rail when the one holding Harper grew too shaky for safety.

Father God, get us through this. Give us time—a delay—something. Please don't let my strength give out.

Whether it was an answer to prayer or just a slow start to the workday, somehow the building didn't fall apart around their ears as Brady inched downward—to one landing, then the next, then the next. By the time they reached the second-floor exit, he could barely stay upright as the trembling in his arms spread through his back and legs.

"I have to take a break." He hated the catch in his voice almost as much as the weakness that forced him up against the wall, trying to support Harper as his breath came in ragged gasps.

"Breathe, Brady. You're all right." Rachelle's voice shook even through the deafening roar in his ears. "God's got you this far. Rest a second. Lord Jesus, please give him strength!"

Brady gulped air in desperate gasps, trying to force energy back into his limbs. He couldn't remember the last time he'd exerted himself at anything close to this level. Of course, on a normal day, trying anything like this would put him down for the count long before he reached this point, and he'd never done much more than walk the streets while on the injection.

Lord, please! One floor to go. Don't let me fail now!

Something began to shift outside the walls—the shaking beneath him and the thunder around him both intensified, not in the static way they'd had before, but on an ever-growing line.

"They're coming!" Any idea of staying quiet fled; no one outside was going to hear him, and he wasn't even sure Rachelle or Dash's straining ears could catch his words amid the cacophony. Throwing all his strength into the effort, he gripped Harper's arms in both hands and forced his shaking legs to take the next set of steps faster than he'd tried before. One—two—three—almost to the halfway landing—on it—only—

A deafening shockwave rocked the stairwell—sound, motion, and a million stinging particles churning the enclosed space like a ship in a storm. Brady tried to keep his feet, but the landing bucked and surged beneath him, Harper's weight on his shoulders unbalanced him, and with a guttural cry, he plummeted down the last half-flight of stairs and into the wall below.

The world blurred, swam, and rocked in front of him for an interminable moment, then suddenly Rachelle's anguished voice cut through the fog.

"Brady? Are you there? What's happening?"

"I—" Brady choked and coughed on the dust as he turned his fuzzy gaze past the somehow still intact wall in front of him and surveyed the scene beyond. "They've—hit the building. Other end. Stairwell's still—standing."

"Where are you?" Rachelle swallowed the tears clogging her voice, and Brady sat up, trying to ignore the pain screaming from every inch of his exposed skin.

"Bottom of the stairs. Fell about half a flight. I can move."

"Harper?" Dash gritted the word before he'd even finished, and Brady sucked in a shallow breath.

"On my leg. Have to get—through this door and out the hallway—before the whole place comes down. I can't lift her again."

"Drag her by her shoulders, or by her shirt. Whichever you can grab easiest. Are you sure you can do this?"

"I've got no choice." A nearby section of the building gave an ominous groan, and Brady scrambled out from under Harper, careful not to lose contact completely, then gripped her invisible form as well as he could and tugged her toward the half-open door. His arms and back screamed in protest, and he gritted his teeth and sent up a silent, desperate prayer for strength.

The building shook again, and pieces of the ceiling and the floor above rained down on them. Brady could actually see a faint outline of Harper's face in the thick layer of dust that coated it, and the sight spurred him harder toward the door at the end of the hall, even as the portion of the building just beyond them collapsed on top of itself. Brady closed his eyes and buried his face in his shoulder but continued to shove backward, moving blindly, hoping with every step that the ceiling above him wouldn't suddenly fall on them. Then without warning, his back hit something solid, and he nearly dropped Harper as he clutched for the latch and stumbled out into the somewhat fresher air. Two more tugs, and Harper's feet were clear of the doorway, and Brady knelt to gasp a breath, knowing they still hadn't reached anything like safety.

"We're—outside—the building. Still—too close. Have to—"

"Heads up, Gamma Ray!" The new voice on the line sent a shock through his exhausted body, and Brady's head jerked up of its own accord. "Reinforcements on scene. Can you get her to the fence? We can take it from there."

"Car?" The word rasped out of his dry throat as the remaining section of the building swayed dangerously.

"It's me, Search and Rescue. You got to get both of you out of there before the whole place comes down. Can you do it without being seen?"

Brady tightened his trembling fingers around Harper again, sent one comprehensive glance through the remaining walls to confirm that no one was watching the area near their improvised exit, then lurched to his feet, dragging Harper along, dimly praying and hoping that he'd run into the fence before anyone turned their direction. But instead of cold chain links, warm fingers gripped his arm, then a dark hand reached down and helped him drag his invisible burden through the gap in the fence.

"What—how are you—" Brady's legs gave out, and he sank to the ground next to Harper as the near end of the building gave way with a sickening crack and Car swung the fence closed behind them.

"Easy, there, Hero. You got a couple yards left in you? If we can get her over to the street, DeAndre's got the truck."

Chapter Eleven

Whether they accomplished it through some outright miracle or sheer grit and good timing, Brady was never sure afterward, but somehow between his protesting body and Car's one good arm, they managed to drag Harper's still unconscious form as far as the sidewalk without raising any kind of outcry from the demolition site. Then DeAndre scooped her up in his muscular arms and laid her in the back seat of the extended cab, and Car nudged Brady toward the front passenger door before sliding in on the other side and taking Harper's head in her lap.

Brady leaned back against his own seat and closed his eyes as the waves of reaction washed over him—relief, raw pain, and all the various flavors of fear he'd lived through in the last few hours. DeAndre slid into the driver's seat and handed him a baggie of some kind of granola-nut mix, and Brady took it obediently, but when he tried to open it, his hands shook so badly he didn't dare continue.

"Eat it; don't just look at it," DeAndre growled without glancing over, and Car finished wrestling her seatbelt under Harper and held out her hand.

"Give it here. D, you okay with crumbs in the seats for a good cause?"

"Crumbs I can deal with. Passed out kids are a lot harder to explain, especially when they're visible."

A weak smile tugged at Brady's lips, and he rubbed his gritty hands against his jeans.

"You got anything to clean up with first? I don't think you or anybody want this anywhere near my mouth right now."

"Sanitizer and wipes both in the glove box. Do I even want to know what's on them?"

"Doubt it. I don't even want to know most of it." Brady doused his hands several times with sanitizer before taking the open bag back from Car, trying not to let the mixture slip from his trembling fingers as he attempted to lift it out.

"Eat it; don't pick at it!" If DeAndre's voice had been a little rougher, Brady could almost have believed it was Dash snapping at him. He gave up on trying to be careful and let the crumbs pepper him as he raised his shaking hand to his mouth.

"Brady, are you all right?" How Rachelle had stayed silent during these last few minutes he had no idea, but if he had to guess, he'd say it was a tangle of emotions very much like his own that clogged her voice now.

"I—I think." It wasn't like he'd taken time to catalog every ache in his body, or planned to try before he was sure he wouldn't have to move again for a while. "Sore. Shaky. Might take an all-day nap once I finish that shower I wanted. No migraine coming on that I can tell."

"How's Harper?"

"Still out." Car answered for him, and Brady leaned his head back and tried to calm his still pounding heart as she continued. "Breathing fine, as far as I can feel. Really hard to say anything else at this point, but I haven't found any knots on her head. You got the doc waiting?"

"She's on standby. Can't call anyone else in until the visibility comes back, though, so I don't know how long it'll take for a full workup."

"You'll keep me posted when you find out, won't you?"

"Of course."

"You'd better." Car's voice gentled a little, but it turned stern again as she fixed a narrowed gaze on Brady. "Do I need to put

GPS on you two until I'm fully functional again? How on earth does one of you end up in a spot like that, in this part of town, completely on your own—let alone two of you?"

"Don't tell me you've missed the news the last week," Brady mumbled, and Car's eyebrow lifted.

"So you just decided to take things into your own hands?"

"Credit where credit's due, Whiplash. Whose do you figure the bright idea was?" Dash's tone was still a little gruffer than usual, and Car huffed out a frustrated breath.

"Shadow, obviously. But I can't take my worry out on her right now, and he's a convenient target."

Brady blinked as the conversation swam into focus in his exhausted brain. Had Dash actually just—defended him? Maybe not technically, but he *had* butted in to redirect the blame to where it mostly belonged, his usual protectiveness of Harper notwithstanding.

"Know what? I don't even care that much. Make me the target if you need one. I'm just—so glad I went with her right now." His voice cracked a little at the end, and he could hear a hard intake of breath that might have belonged to Rachelle.

"Amen. We absolutely still need to talk—all of us—but I can't help but see God's hand in it now—in you being there for her, I mean, not the both of you being there to start with."

"We did kind of fall on our faces with what we went out for." Brady managed a weak chuckle, but the next instant, a sudden cold fear swept over him. "Rachelle. They did find him, for sure? It wasn't just rumors?"

"No. Donovan's safe." Rachelle lowered her voice to a soothing murmur. "Dad's neighbors have him on a doorbell camera yesterday afternoon. There's no way he was in the building. He's safe. You're safe. Harper's safe. Rest and breathe."

Brady tried to relax the tension in his muscles just a little and took another handful of granola in answer to DeAndre's look. No one said much for the next few minutes, and finally DeAndre pulled the truck up to the dock behind the medical center.

"All right, Rachelle, where are we bringing her? Car, take this and open the door when we get there." DeAndre dropped his badge into Car's outstretched palm and paused with his hand on the door.

"Dr. Mattox has a gurney waiting inside. Lay her on top of it, but don't cover her up; it'll just look empty that way."

DeAndre gave a short nod as he climbed out and headed for Harper's door, and Car's brow furrowed as she glanced at Brady.

"How are we getting *you* out of here, Bloodhound? I haven't forgotten what this atmosphere does to you."

"I had." Brady swallowed a little harder, then shook his head. "You know what, I don't care. I'll hold my breath. I just want to get back."

"All right. Do what you have to. Just don't pass out on me. If I have to drag you with this arm, I'm sending my PT to you with his complaints. Brace."

Brady barely had time to suck in a breath before DeAndre opened the door and bent over to lift Harper out, flooding the truck with the vile scent of the dumpsters. Brady kept his lips tightly shut and tried not to inhale as he scrambled out his own door and up to the entrance with Car right behind him. She swiped DeAndre's ID, and the door opened to reveal Dr. Mattox, arms crossed and foot tapping, next to an empty gurney. In only a few seconds more, DeAndre joined them, cradling an invisible figure whose form entirely disappeared when he laid her on the thin bed.

Dr. Mattox immediately began pushing her down the corridor, heels clicking urgently, although Brady wasn't sure if her haste was born out of worry for Harper's condition or fear that some other staff member would try to commandeer the apparently empty gurney before she could get back.

"I want that finished before lunchtime. Understood?" DeAndre pinned Brady with a glare as he tapped the bag Brady hadn't even stopped to think before bringing along.

"Do my best," Brady mumbled, feeling a little of the strength he'd leaned on begin to slip away now that they were both safely back in the center.

"Because your other option is an IV." The big man didn't need any help to look intimidating, but he put his hand on his hip anyway, and Brady raised his hands in surrender, trying not to wince when his shoulders gave a sharp protest. DeAndre's stern look softened just a little, and he shook his head. "You've put your body through a lot in just a few hours. I know you're tired, but you've got to take care of yourself if you don't want medical attention of your own."

"I got it. Honest."

"All right. Can you make it down by yourself? Car, you better run if you're going to get over to therapy on time. I don't want your mama coming after me for making you late."

"Going. I'm going! You all keep me updated." Car pointed a warning finger at Brady for a second, then raced down the hall, and Brady took a deep breath and steeled his quivering muscles.

"Yeah. I can make it. Thanks for coming for us. Both of you." He glanced in the direction Car had disappeared, and the corner of DeAndre's mouth twitched up just a bit.

"She knows. Now get down there. They need to *see* you're all right, not just hear it."

Brady nodded as he pushed off the wall, but his legs wobbled a little on his first step, and DeAndre raised an eyebrow.

"I'm fine." Brady waved him back. "I've got my orders. I'm going."

DeAndre stayed still but continued to watch until Brady disappeared from regular sight around the corner, and Brady sent up a silent prayer of thanks for the small but strong network of support that God had gathered around them as he made his way slowly back to the lab level. When he reached the door of the den, Rachelle threw her arms around him without a word and just held on for a long moment, and Brady could feel the repressed emotion radiating from every muscle.

"Hey," he whispered finally. "You know you're going to need a shower as much as I do, right?"

"I can think of about a hundred things I care about less right now," Rachelle murmured, and Brady felt his smile returning just a little, even as tears pricked his eyes. But in the next moment, she stepped back and surveyed him critically, shaking her head as she took in the part of the damage that was visible. "Okay, shower first, before you get too stiff. When you're done with that, where do you want to set up camp? Common, or your bed? I'll have things ready before you're out."

"Rachelle, don't worry about me, please." A lump rose in Brady's throat as he shook his head. "Go help take care of Harper. I'll be all right."

"Harper's in the best hands she can be right now, and Dash is going to leave skid marks in the hall outside the exam room if he paces much harder. There's nothing I can do for her at the moment, and I don't want you suffering worse than you're already going to because I let something go or didn't notice it when I should have."

"Any word from the doctor? Or is it still too soon?"

"Too soon when half the imaging won't work on her body, and we can't even draw blood yet. We have theories, but there's no way to test them until she's visible. She's got monitors on now, though, and we're hoping she'll wake up soon. Dash promised to update us the second something changes. You're my priority at the moment."

"Rachelle, I—"

"You fell down half a flight of stairs, dragged and carried a not-especially-petite girl through a massive building, and almost had the whole thing come down on your head. Your part's done for today, Brady. Relax and let yourself be taken care of this time. It's our turn now."

Chapter Twelve

By the time the sensation of crawling filth had been scrubbed from the last of his skin, Brady couldn't argue any longer with Rachelle's instruction to rest. His entire body screamed with fatigue, and a number of bruises he'd barely had time to notice were beginning to make themselves felt. He eyed his bed as he ran a towel through his hair with his less-sore arm, but the idea of voluntarily lengthening his time there held enough distaste to override the small amount of extra comfort it might offer. Instead, he dragged his weary legs out into the hall and met Rachelle waiting just outside his room.

"Okay, couch, now." She didn't give him a second of space to argue, and Brady wondered idly just how much he still looked like he'd almost had a building come down around his ears. "Where do you need heat, and where do you need ice?"

"Ice on my right shoulder and left knee would probably help. Maybe my right side too. Let's deal with the rest of it later."

Rachelle bit her lips together but didn't protest, only helped him settle himself on the couch and carefully applied ice packs to the affected areas. He did his best not to react but couldn't help a sharp intake of breath as the cold touched the spreading bruises.

"Comfortable?" Rachelle raised an eyebrow from where she knelt next to him, and Brady winced as she smoothed back his hair. "Also, what am I supposed to do about the knot on your forehead? I know you can't do ice there; can I try the arnica?"

"What can it hurt?" Brady offered an attempt at a wry smile, and Rachelle closed her eyes and looked away. Ignoring his protesting muscles, Brady reached for her hand and squeezed it gently. "Sorry. Not trying to make light of it. Just—"

"I know." Rachelle swallowed hard as she squeezed back, but she didn't meet his eyes. "Is it…wrong that I feel like it's a good thing…that Harper's unconscious right now?"

Brady's forehead furrowed a little as he tried to digest the question, and he couldn't help a wince as the knot she'd pointed out gave a sharp pang.

"Depends. You afraid you'd say something you'd regret? Not wrong to recognize that. But I don't think you would. You might need time to work your emotions out, but you've been more than gentle with her all day. What's changed? Just the adrenaline drain? Or thinking about what might have happened?"

Rachelle shook her head and laid it down on her knees. Brady didn't try to push her, just waited quietly, and after a few moments, her muffled voice came again.

"It's—maybe both of those things—a little, but more just—seeing all this—knowing what tomorrow'll be like for you—"

"Rachelle…" He wasn't even sure what he intended to say, but somehow just her name made her shoulders convulse in a sob.

"I'm trying, but—I'm so angry with her right now, Brady. It's not—the ignoring advice is one thing. No one ever—made me president. We can talk all that out later. And I don't fault her—where she's at spiritually—of course it's a hard ask to trust fate—or a God you don't even believe in—to work things out. But pulling you into it—putting you in that kind of danger—making things worse when she knows how bad they are without it…"

"Chelle, don't." Brady suddenly had to fight against a lump in his own throat. "I'm not defending her choosing to go out there, but—you know she didn't see this coming. None of us did. Even when you warned us off yesterday, it was the side-effects we were all worried about, not the building coming down on our heads. And it was my choice to go in after her. She didn't mean for me to be in there at all, let alone to get hurt. And she's probably got the same number of bruises—we both fell down those stairs. I'm not blaming you for being angry and hurt, just—please don't make it because of me. It was my choices that got me here, and I wouldn't trade the result for anything. You know that, don't you?"

"I know you're the most selfless person I've ever met, and you'd have gone in after her if you knew it would kill you, just as long as you thought it might save her."

"Pot, meet kettle," Brady murmured, and Rachelle choked out a startled laugh. The corner of Brady's mouth quirked up a little at the sound before he turned serious again. "Tell me I'm wrong, though. If you'd been out there with her, what would you have done differently?"

"No, I know. I'm not criticizing anything you did. I just hate that she put you in a position where you had to."

"Do me a favor, okay?" He waited until she lifted her head and met his eyes again before continuing. "You need to talk things out with Harper; I'm not arguing that. But don't hold her responsible for this—for me. I chose it, not her. I don't want you holding a grudge for my sake. And she's got enough to work through without that guilt."

Rachelle blinked hard and laid her head down against the couch, and Brady sent up a silent prayer for God to heal her heart. As tough as the morning had been for him, he couldn't imagine the stress of listening in on it all without being able to lift a finger to help.

After a little while, Rachelle shifted enough to prop her chin on her fist, and she was just opening her mouth when Dash's disembodied voice from the earpiece Brady hadn't realized she was still wearing suddenly cut her off.

"Midge? She's waking up. Don't know if you think you're safe yet, but I figured you'd want to know."

Rachelle jumped as if about to shoot to her feet, and Brady gripped her arm just in time to prevent it.

"Hey, careful! Last thing any of us need today is for you to throw a knee out."

"Sorry. You're right." Rachelle blew out a steadying breath before climbing up much more deliberately. "Dash says Harper's waking up."

"I heard." Brady gave a weak grin and sat up, pausing with a groan as his battered body protested, and Rachelle bit her lip.

"You're sure you're up to this? Nobody's going to blame you if you stay here. I can tell Harper you're all right. And you don't have to worry about me."

"No, I need to—" Brady shook his head with a grimace. "I was going to say 'see for myself,' but I guess I can't do that yet, can I? You know what I mean, though."

Rachelle gave a small nod and didn't offer any other protests, but she stuck close to his side as they made their way at a snail's pace down the halls toward the exam room. Dash was there when they reached it, sitting next to the apparently empty bed, but Dr. Mattox was nowhere in sight.

"Harper?" Rachelle whispered, and Brady held his breath as he waited for the answer.

For a few seconds, there was no response except a long sigh, but finally the reply came, soft and wondering, like she might have been in a dream.

"Rachelle? Where am I?"

"It's all right, Harper. You're back in the lab. Just take it easy. Everything's going to be okay." How Rachelle could ever have doubted herself, Brady wasn't sure, but her voice was as gentle and soothing as if she'd never struggled with the hurt and anger she'd so recently confessed.

"Did I…pass out?"

Brady wasn't sure he'd ever heard Harper's voice so fragile, and his heart ached at the sound as Rachelle answered.

"Yeah, you did. Had us all scared for a little while."

Dash muttered something about the understatement of the year, and the corner of Brady's mouth quirked up, but Harper's reply still sounded mildly puzzled.

"But I'm…invisible? That's not…supposed to happen."

"No." Rachelle choked on what might have been half a laugh and felt gently along the bed until she could grasp Harper's hand. "It's definitely not. I have theories, but we'll have to wait until we can actually see you again to test them."

"Like what?" How Harper managed to sound so persistent and so weak at the same time was a puzzle, and Brady watched Rachelle's reaction carefully as he sank onto the stool behind him to take some weight off his throbbing knee.

"Like—" Rachelle pursed her lips in thought as she took a seat on the bed. "You were dealing with an extra severe flare today, for one thing, and from a source you're not used to. The injection went to work on that, but it probably took more than usual, and it might not have had enough left for your blood when it wasn't the main culprit. We'll find out as soon as we can draw it—or see it. Okay? Meantime, you just rest. Whatever the mechanism was, you've obviously overworked today."

"I guess." Harper's pillow crackled, and the covers bunched as she turned restlessly onto her side, but the next instant, she sucked in a sharp breath. "Wait. I was in the hotel. How did I get here? Who—"

"Harper, lie still!" Rachelle spoke firmly for the first time, gripping harder against the invisible hand she held and reaching up to put a restraining pressure on her shoulder. Harper gasped and moaned, and the bed creaked a little as she fell back against it.

"All right?" Dash's face tightened as he leaned forward, his voice taking on the protective bark that Brady was learning to recognize.

"What happened? Did I fall? Why is my back so sore?" A layer of real pain wrapped her words, and Brady couldn't help a wince.

"That's on me. Sorry. I was the only one close enough to get you out, and I probably wasn't the gentlest. How bad is it?"

"Like I—got dragged through gravel and then—dropped down stairs. How not gentle were you?"

"It wasn't his fault, Harper." Rachelle cut in before he could answer, but instead of the bite it might have held, her voice shook just a little. "You got out of there less than a minute before the whole building came down. I'm sorry you're hurt, but Brady's the only reason you're still alive right now."

"Seriously?" The word was a whisper, and Brady swallowed hard.

"It wasn't—I didn't—"

"You want to bet on what you didn't?" Dash growled, and Brady blinked and sat back, not quite swallowing a groan at the sudden movement.

"Was I…did you…really?" Harper's voice wobbled, and Brady stood to try to reach her but had to hold onto the wall as a dizzy spell washed over him and his knee gave an even sharper protest.

"Listen, let's talk about this later." All of a sudden, Rachelle's hand was on his back, steadying him against the spinning room. "We'll have plenty of time for the details when you're not both half dead on your feet. Whatever non-existent rank I don't have, I'm pulling it now, okay? You both need to rest."

Somehow with Harper awake and the last of the uncertainty gone, Brady's last bit of strength seemed to drain away, and with a final glance at her bed and Dash sitting guard next to it, he surrendered to the inevitable and let Rachelle lead him away.

Chapter Thirteen

"Are you honestly sure you're up to this?" Rachelle hovered anxiously next to his bed, and Brady held tight to the covers as he eased his legs off the side, willing himself with every bit of strength he could scrape together not to either tip over or give an audible grunt of pain.

The migraine itself had been bad enough, especially when layered with the souvenirs of his latest adventure in the form of throbbing bruises and aching muscles, and now the recovery period seemed determined to drag on, the clinging fog having lasted well into its second morning. But Brady was beyond done with staying in bed, especially with the gnawing anxiety that came from having retreated there before Harper came back to visibility and not having actually seen her in more than five days.

"I'm—not trying to claim I'm—anything close to a hundred percent." Brady managed to lift his hazy eyes and offer Rachelle a weak grin. "But I'd be worse off—stuck in here another day. Pretty sure I need the fresh air."

Rachelle shook her head resignedly but didn't protest any further, and Brady levered gingerly to his feet, letting out a breath of relief when his leg didn't immediately collapse under him.

"Be careful," Rachelle murmured, and Brady nodded as he shuffled the two steps to the door and gripped the rail that ran along the wall to keep his balance. "Going all the way to the den?"

"Depends." Brady bit his lip as he glanced down the hall, then back at Rachelle, and her smile softened.

"Harper's still in her room, if that's what you want to know."

"Am I allowed?"

"Yes, she's awake and dressed. You might want something warmer on, though; it's still an icebox in there."

Brady paused and considered for a few seconds, eyeing the path back into the room before letting his remnant of pride slip away.

"Would you mind grabbing me a hoodie? Should be one right at the top of the dresser."

"Of course." The stiff set of Rachelle's shoulders relaxed a little as she retrieved the hoodie and helped him slide it on after his clumsy fingers threatened to drop it. "Need a hand across the hall?"

"Not yours," Brady muttered, and the corner of Rachelle's mouth twisted in a grimace. "Think we don't still need you right now? Might not last much longer, but I won't be the one to throw your shoulder out."

She shrugged and nodded toward Harper's door, and Brady managed to get partway down and across the hall without his body giving out. He knocked carefully and waited for Harper's listless "come in" before slipping inside. She was lying on her side, facing the wall, her skin still tinted with a reddish glow, and several fans clustered around her, chilling the room to the approximate temperature of an igloo.

"Hey." Brady whispered the word, and Harper stiffened, then rolled swiftly to her other side, her mouth hanging open as her wide eyes met his. "How you doing?"

"How are you here? Rachelle said you were still hurting."

"Little bit, but over the worst of it." Brady pulled the waiting chair close and sank into it, resting his arms on the edge of Harper's bed. "What about you? You still look pretty miserable."

"I'm okay." Harper mumbled the words against her pillow, and Brady gave her a cautiously skeptical look, making sure his eyebrow didn't raise far enough to restart the ache in his head. "You've heard the deal. Triggered the EM worse than usual, and didn't get the normal relief for my blood. Serves me right."

"Hey." Brady reached for her arm but caught himself in time, not wanting to irritate her skin any further. "I'm not saying we made the right call. But your heart was in the right place. That counts for something."

Harper bit her lip and drew in a shaky breath, and Brady searched his brain for something that might cheer her up.

"Have you heard any more about Donovan? Not sure if Rachelle doesn't know or just hasn't told."

"Yeah. They figured it out. Dad came into town for visitation and found him wandering the streets. Took him home without saying anything. Mom just assumed he didn't show up and panicked. Not sure who gets the bigger share of blame—Dad for taking him or Mom for letting him wander. The family court'll have their hands full for a while figuring it out."

"Poor kid." Brady grimaced. So much for a happier topic.

"Yeah." Harper sucked in a wet-sounding sniffle. "I kinda—wish we could've found him—that day. I mean, I know it's good he wasn't there, I just…" Her voice trailed into silence, and Brady's forehead furrowed as he watched her.

"You just…?" He let the questioning inflection hang in the air, and Harper shook her head slowly.

"I just—I wish we could've shown him—someone really cares, you know? Like—cares about him—just him—not about proving a point—or sticking it to somebody." Her fingers worked the sheet convulsively, and Brady watched them for a while before meeting her eyes again.

"This is about more than just Donovan, isn't it?"

"It—" Harper choked on the word and swallowed hard. "I don't—know if you'd get it. You didn't—grow up living out of a backpack and a suitcase—sleeping in beds you didn't dare claim as yours—listening to grownups arguing about how your issues messed up their lives." She buried her face in her arm, and Brady's heart cracked in two.

"Harper?" He tried to keep his voice steady, but it wavered in spite of him. "You're right, I don't get it. I don't get how anybody could treat any child that way, least of all you. Health issues or not.

You didn't choose your body, and you sure didn't ask to be dumped on the state. The fact that anybody dared to take those frustrations out on you makes my blood boil. But out of that whole mixed-up mess, there's one thing I'm very grateful for, and that's that your mom—or whoever gave you over—did it right and kept you alive. Because this world would be a whole lot sadder place without you in it."

Her chest convulsed with a ragged sob, but after a few shaky breaths, she pulled her arm away and swiped hard at her cheeks, pulling tendrils of hair out of her messy braid and over her wet face like a shield. Brady watched her for a moment, something sparking in his mind at the familiar motion that he'd seen before but never paid particular attention to.

"Can I ask you a question?" he ventured finally, and Harper's forehead furrowed, but she nodded slowly. "Okay, so, the blue. Is there—a special reason for it?"

"I got…tired of sticking out…for reasons I couldn't help." Her voice was quiet, almost fragile, and Brady sucked in a tight breath.

"So you found a way to stick out that was your choice."

"Gave people something to concentrate on…besides my face."

"Okay, but—you know you don't need that here, right?" Brady's hand itched to reach out and brush the hair from her cheeks, but he held back, trying to put all the sincerity he could into his voice instead.

"Yeah." Harper swallowed. "I know. I'm mostly just—used to it now."

"All right. I'm not complaining. I'm just sorry—that anybody ever made you feel like you had to hide—or to be someone other than who you are. You're worth knowing, no additions, deletions, or corrections. And you're worth caring about. Just you. For no other reason."

"I don't see—how you can say that." Fresh tears were beginning to stain Harper's cheeks. "I *heard* you the last few days, Brady. You were beyond miserable. Way worse than normal. And it's my fault. I know it is. You were only even there because I was. And I'm the only reason you risked your life in that building. If I'd just listened to Rachelle, we'd both be fine right now. And nobody's even said 'I told you so.'"

"Harper." Brady waited until she lifted a watery eye from her pillow to look at him. "I'm not arguing that you messed up. It was a bad call, even if your reasons were good, but I know you know that. And that's not the point. The point is, you're worth it. Worth coming with. Worth going after. Worth being sick for. Not because you're perfect. Because you're valuable. Scars and flaws and all. God made you, and He doesn't make mistakes. Beyond that, He loves you. And I hope one day you'll be able to understand everything that means."

"If I was—really sure you and Rachelle had it right—your way would be the kind I'd want to follow." Harper's voice was just above a murmur, and Brady hesitated, not sure if he should press the question farther. This was the first time he hadn't heard her gloss over or totally change the subject when any type of religious topic came up, but something in his spirit warned him not to push too hard.

"I'm praying for you, Harper."

"I know." She offered a weak smile. "And I know you didn't really want to be here, but—I'm kind of glad you are."

"Got over that a long time ago. Till I get some sort of neon sign pointing me elsewhere, y'all are pretty well stuck with me."

"What, is this a sap fest all of a sudden?" Dash's voice behind him was as gruff as usual, but there was just a hint of a bite to it. Brady sat back and scooted the chair away from the bed a little, nodding his head in the direction of the wheelchair before a wave of dizziness held him still again.

"I was just…telling her if she wanted to come out of this without bumps and scrapes, she should've taken you, not me. You would've gotten her out of there way before disaster struck."

Dash grunted incredulously and cut narrowed eyes at Brady as he wheeled his chair up to Harper's side.

"Assuming I'd found her in time."

"Eh, you'd have done it. She was right in the middle of the hallway. You couldn't have helped tripping over her."

Harper giggled a little, and Dash offered a slight eye roll, but the tension in his body relaxed just the tiniest bit.

"Hush up and take the compliment, Owen. You won't get another one for a while."

"Do I need to separate the two of you?" Brady could hear the smile in Rachelle's voice even before she appeared in his peripheral vision, although he had no idea how long she'd been listening.

"Rather you didn't." He let his lips curve in reply as he glanced up at her, and Dash huffed.

"Don't start on the sap again." He shot them both a glare, but the bite had gone from his voice.

"No problem. I'll be quiet." Brady leaned back against the wall and let his heavy eyes slide closed. "I'm just glad we're all still here. Together."

"Me too." Harper's smile was a little wobbly, but it still came through clearly in her tone. "Believe me, me too."

Made in the USA
Columbia, SC
24 June 2024

37374376R00228